THE
STRANGER
YOU
KNOW

THE
STRANGER
YOU
KNOW

Jane Casey

EBURY
PRESS

1 3 5 7 9 10 8 6 4 2

Published in 2013 by Ebury Press, an imprint of Ebury Publishing
A Random House Group Company

The Random House Group Limited Reg. No. 954009

Addresses for companies within the Random House Group can be found at:
www.randomhouse.co.uk

A CIP catalogue record for this book is
available from the British Library

The Random House Group Limited supports The Forest Stewardship
Council® (FSC®), the leading international forest certification organisation.
Our books carrying the FSC label are printed on FSC® certified paper. FSC is
the only forest certification scheme supported by the leading environmental
organisations, including Greenpeace. Our paper procurement policy
can be found at: www.randomhouse.co.uk/environment

MIX
Paper from
responsible sources
FSC® C016897

Printed in the UK by Clays Ltd, St Ives PLC

Hardback ISBN 9780091948337
Trade paperback ISBN 9780091948344

To buy books by your favourite authors and register for offers visit:
www.randomhouse.co.uk

For Kerry Holland

Some flying from the thing they feared, and some
Seeking the object of another's fear . . .
. . . And others mournfully within the gloom
Of their own shadow walked, and called it death . . .

'The Triumph of Life', Percy Bysshe Shelley

1992

The garden was quiet, the air still. As still as the girl who lay under the tree.

So still.

Her eyes were closed. Her hands lay by her sides, palms up. Her hair spread across the grass like yellow silk. And the flowers under her were like the stars above her.

He put out his hand and felt the heat radiating from her skin, even now. Even in the moonlight he could see the blood on her face, and the bruises around her neck, and the way her eyelids sagged, empty. Her eyes – her forget-me-not blue eyes – were gone. Her lip was split. Her face was swollen.

She was beautiful. No one would ever be as beautiful. She was perfect.

It surprised him, but he didn't mind that she was dead. He could look at her, really look at her, without being interrupted. Without being afraid that she would say something, or do something, that might hurt him.

He could touch her. He reached out, but stopped himself. He could never touch her again.

His breath came faster. He wanted to touch himself but he couldn't do that either. Not here.

It was just because he loved her so much. More than anyone. More than anything.

Jane Casey

Forget-me-not.
'I won't forget,' he promised. 'I'll never forget.'
He almost thought she smiled.

THURSDAY

Chapter 1

I'd seen enough dead bodies to know they can look peaceful. Calm, even. At rest.

Princess Gordon was not that sort of corpse.

It wasn't her fault. Anyone would have struggled to look serene when they had been battered to death, then shoved into the boot of a Nissan Micra and left to stiffen into full rigor mortis.

'I'm going to need to get her out to give you a proper cause of death, but from a preliminary examination she was beaten with something hard but rounded, like a pole, sometime within the last twenty-four hours.' The pathologist stood back, touching the back of one gloved hand to her forehead. 'I can't narrow it down for you yet, but I'll have a look at stomach contents during the post-mortem and make an educated guess.'

'I can make an educated guess for you now. It was her husband.' The voice came from beside me, where Detective Inspector Josh Derwent was taking up more than his fair share of room in the little ring of officers and crime-scene technicians that had gathered around the back of the car. The garage door was open but it still felt claustrophobic to me to be in that small, cluttered space. The air was dusty and the lighting cast long, dark shadows. I felt as if the piled-up junk was reaching out to grab me. Derwent had his hands in his pockets, with his elbows jutting out on either side. I had already inched away twice, to get out of range, but there was nowhere left to go.

'She wasn't married,' I said.

'Partner, then. Whoever that bloke is in the house.'

'Adam Olesugwe.'

'Him.'

'What makes you say that?' The pathologist was new, earnest and heavily pregnant. I wished she would just ignore Derwent. She had no idea what she was dealing with.

'Bound to be him.'

'If you're basing that on statistical probability—'

Derwent cut her off. 'I'm not.'

One of the response officers cleared his throat. I thought he was going to raise his hand and ask for permission to speak. 'He said he came back and she was missing. He said someone must have come into the house and attacked her.'

'Yeah, he'd know. He was the one who did it.' Derwent waved a hand at the body. 'Say this wasn't a domestic. Say it was a burglary gone wrong or a random murder. Why bother putting her in the car? Why not leave her in the house?'

'To hide her,' the response officer suggested.

'Why, though? It's hard work, moving a body. And she's a big girl, too. Look at that arse.'

'Sir.' I didn't usually try to manage Derwent's stream of consciousness but I had seen the look of shock on the pathologist's face. Dr Early, who had arrived late and made a joke about it. Derwent hadn't laughed.

'What is it, Kerrigan?' He glared at me.

I didn't dare say why I'd actually interrupted. It would only provoke worse behaviour. 'Just – why would Olesugwe move the body?'

'He was planning to get rid of the body but then her sister came round.'

It was Princess's sister, Blessed, who'd found the body and called 999. Last seen in hysterics being comforted by a female officer at the kitchen table, she'd been too incoherent to interview.

4

'Why would he want to kill her?' Early asked.

'Your guess is as good as mine. She was having an affair, or he was, or she didn't do the ironing.' He looked down at the pathologist's rounded belly. 'She was four months pregnant, according to Olesugwe. Women are more likely to be victims of domestic violence when they're up the duff.'

'That's a myth.' Dr Early put a protective hand on her stomach, as if she was trying to shield her unborn child from Derwent's toxic personality. I personally felt lead-lined hazard suits should have been standard issue for anyone who came into contact with him, pregnant or not.

Derwent shook his head. 'They did a study in the States. Murder is the third most common reason of violent death for pregnant women.'

'What else kills them?' I asked.

'Car accidents and suicide. Women drivers, eh?'

'Well, this lady didn't die in a car accident and she certainly didn't beat herself to death.' Dr Early folded her arms, resting them on top of her bump.

'That's my point. He killed her,' Derwent said. 'He gets angry about something, he beats her up, it goes too far, he dumps her in the car, starts to clean up, gets interrupted by the sister and all bets are off.'

'There was a smell of bleach in the kitchen,' I remarked.

'And no sign of a break-in. Wherever she died should look like an abattoir but I didn't see a speck of blood in the house.' Derwent pushed past a couple of officers and peered into the back seat of the car. 'Bags. If you forensic boys would like to do your jobs and get them out for us, I bet we'll find blood-stained clothes in Olesugwe's size.'

Dr Early looked down at Princess's body. 'I'll need some help to get her out of the boot.'

'Nice to hear a woman admit she needs some help,' Derwent said, and walked out without waiting to hear what Dr Early had to say in response, or, indeed, offering any assistance.

The doctor's lips were pressed together and her eyes were bright. I recognised the signs of someone trying not to cry. I'd been there, many times. 'Is he always like that?' she asked me.

'Not always. Sometimes he's worse.'

'I don't know how you can stand it.'

'Neither do I,' I said.

The reason I could stand it was because in addition to his numerous personality defects, Derwent was a brilliant copper. He left the SOCOs to their work and took both Olesugwe and Blessed to the nearest police station, Great Portland Street, where Blessed confessed to the affair she'd been having with Olesugwe, and Olesugwe admitted that Princess had found out about it. The murder weapon – a metal pole that had been used as a clothes rail in the couple's wardrobe – turned up in a shed in the garden of the small house, stuffed in a bag behind a lawnmower. Olesugwe had the key to the shed's padlock on his key ring, as well as the only set of keys for the Nissan. When I pointed out that neither the padlock nor the car boot was damaged in any way, he admitted moving the body and hiding the weapon.

'But he still won't admit that he killed her,' I said to Derwent as we left the police station, heading back to the office to get the paperwork underway. I shivered as the cold hit my face. We were on foot because Derwent had flatly refused to drive through central London to Somers Town, where Princess had breathed her last, when our new offices were in Westminster and it was twice as fast to go by public transport.

'He's still looking for a way out. I bet he'll say it was Blessed who attacked her and he was just trying to help her.'

'Do you think that's what happened?'

'Nope. Doesn't matter, though. He'll still lie about it.'

'I don't think Blessed would have called the cops before they were finished tidying up if she'd been involved.'

'She might have. She might be thick. Most criminals are.'

'I've noticed,' I said. I was only a detective constable but I had seven years of experience behind me. Derwent tended to forget that.

Instead of answering me, he sighed. 'What a waste of fucking time.' It wasn't my imagination: Derwent's mood was darker than usual.

'We got a result,' I pointed out.

'Anyone could have got it. Even you.'

'We did a good job.'

'The local murder team could have handled it.'

'They were too busy.'

'Is that what the boss told you?' He shoved his hands deeper into his pockets and walked faster. I lengthened my stride to keep up.

'Why else would he send us up there?'

'Why indeed?'

I realised I wasn't going to get an answer out of Derwent. Besides, I wasn't sure I wanted one. There was a chance he was referring to the fact that I was out of favour with the boss, and I couldn't imagine that Derwent would be pleased if he knew about it. Especially if he knew why.

I'd have been sensible to keep my mouth shut and walk in silence, but there was something I wanted to know. 'You were a bit off with Dr Early. What was the problem?'

Derwent's jaw clenched. 'She shouldn't be doing that job in her condition.'

'She's more than capable of doing it.'

'If you say so. She probably won't even be able to reach the table to do the PM.'

'I'm sure she'll manage.'

'She shouldn't have to.' Derwent flipped up the collar of his coat, hunching his shoulders as a scattering of rain spat in our faces. 'It's no job for a woman anyway. But when she's got a baby on board, she shouldn't be near dead bodies.'

'You are so old-fashioned it's untrue. Are you worried her unborn child will see the corpses and be upset? Wombs don't come with much of a view.'

'It's just not right.' His voice was flat. No more arguing.

I held my tongue until we got to the tube station and discovered that two lines were closed, just in time for the evening rush hour. We forced our way onto a packed Metropolitan line train to Baker Street, switched to the Bakerloo line and suffered as far as Charing Cross. It was a positive pleasure to resurface from the super-heated, stale depths of the Underground, even though the cold autumn air made my head ring as if I'd just been slapped.

Even with the inspector as a companion it wasn't a hardship to walk through Trafalgar Square and on down Whitehall as the lights came on. It had rained properly while we were on the tube, a short but sharp cloudburst, and the pavement had a glassy sheen. Fallen leaves were scattered across the ground, flattened against it by the rain, looking as if they had been varnished to it. The going was slick and my shoes weren't designed for it. Opposite the Cenotaph I slid sideways and collided with Derwent, clutching his arm for support. He bent his arm so his biceps bulged under my fingers. I snatched my hand away.

'Steady on,' Derwent said.

'It's the leaves.'

'I know you, Kerrigan. Any excuse to cop a feel.' He crooked his arm again. 'Come on. Hang on to Uncle Josh. I'll look after you.'

'I can manage, thank you.'

'It's not a sign of weakness, if that's what you're think-ing. It's good to recognise your shortcomings. Look at Dr Early. She knew she couldn't shift that body on her own so she asked for help. You could take a lesson from that. Accept help when it's offered.'

'Is that what you do?'

He laughed. 'I don't *need* any help.'

'Of course not. The very idea.'

'Seriously, if you need to hold on to my arm, do it.'

'I would if I did, but I don't.' I would rather take off my shoes and walk barefoot than reinforce Derwent's ideas of chivalry. He would see it as proof of what he'd always thought – women need looking after. And I was junior to him, as well as being female, so he was totally comfortable with patronising me.

It made me want to scream.

We turned the corner into Parliament Square and I gazed across at the Houses of Parliament, not yet tired of staring at them even though I saw them every day on my way to work. They were a Victorian idea of medieval grandeur and there was something fantastic about them, something unreal about the delicate tracery, the honey-coloured stone, the soaring gilt-topped towers. From here, Britain had ruled the world, temporarily, and the buildings remembered. They were a physical manifestation of the superiority complex that was bred into the British, my father had said once. He had little time for the Empire and less sympathy for the country he lived in. I didn't think you could characterise a whole nation that way, but then I wasn't in the comfortable position of being foreign. Nor could I count myself as British. I was born in London of Irish parents, bred and raised as an Irish girl, despite the fact that we lived in Carshalton rather than Killybegs. I'd learned to dance the Walls of Limerick and played 'Down by the Sally Gardens' on the tin whistle and struggled into thick, sheep-smelling Aran jumpers knitted by relations and swapped the soda bread in my packed lunches for my friends' white crustless sandwiches. I'd played camogie, badly, at weekends, and played hockey equally badly at school. I was Irish by blood and English by accident and I didn't belong to either tradition, or anywhere else. I'd grown up feeling as if I'd lost something and it was only now I was starting to wonder if it mattered.

Derwent threw out an arm. 'Look at that. What a disgrace.'

'The Houses of Parliament?' I asked, surprised. I should have known Derwent was unlikely to be experiencing post-colonial guilt.

'Those fuckers. Shouldn't be allowed.' He was refer-ring to the protesters camping on the grass in the middle of Parliament Square, occupying the space where the anti-war crowd had maintained their vigil, and where the demonstrations against globalisation had raged. There were regular police operations to clear the lawn, but some-how the campaigners came back in ones and twos, and it was rare to see it empty.

I tried to read the banners but it was hard to see them in the dusk, especially since they were rain-sodden. 'Capitalism is evil?'

'Dads Matter.'

'Oh, them.' The Dads Matter group was the militant alternative to Fathers for Justice, a pressure group for men who felt they had been victimised by the family courts. Dads Matter was small but growing and prone to extravagant publicity seeking. Its leader was Philip Pace, a handsome, charismatic forty-year-old with a background in PR. He was a smooth talker, a regular interviewee on news and current affairs programmes and had made the Top Ten Most Eligible Males list in *Tatler* the previous year. I didn't see the attraction myself, but then I wasn't all that keen on zealots. As the public face of Dads Matter, he made it his business to be reasonable and moderate, but as a group they were neither. 'What's their new campaign? Twenty-Twenty?'

'Someone hasn't been paying attention to briefings,' Derwent said. 'It's Fifty-Fifty. They want the courts to split custody of children equally between parents. No exceptions.'

'Oh, that sounds reasonable. What about abusers? What about protecting children from that?'

'Dads don't harm their children. They love them.' For once, Derwent's ultra-sarcasm had a decent target.

'What bullshit.'

'You don't think fathers have rights?' Derwent's eyebrows were hovering around his hairline. 'I thought you were a liberal, Kerrigan. If I said feminism was wank, you'd report me.'

'You say that frequently, and I haven't yet. Anyway, it's not the same thing. The courts make their decisions on a case-by-case basis. Sometimes the mothers get full custody because the dads aren't fit to be involved with their families. These men are just sore losers.'

'Doesn't mean they're not dangerous. You know they've been sharing tactics with extremist anti-abortion activists in the States, don't you?'

'I didn't, actually.' I was amazed that Derwent did. He generally didn't bother with reading briefings. In fact, I wasn't aware of him having read anything properly since we'd been working together.

'Pace was over in Washington recently, trying to get a US branch up and running. He appeared on a platform with the pro-lifers at a massive rally, though he doesn't want that to get out in this country in case it puts people off. They've got a lot in common, though. It's all about the sanctity of the family, isn't it? Two-parent happy families with hundreds of smiling, cheerful children. Fucking fantasyland. If you didn't read the briefing notes you'll have missed this too: they found a Dads Matter-affiliated messageboard on the Internet with a list of names and addresses for family court judges and their staff. Everyone is very jumpy about it. They're expecting parcel bombs and anthrax and God knows what.'

'How did I miss all of this?' I felt as if I hadn't done my homework and I'd been caught by my least favourite teacher – which was basically what had happened.

'Dunno. Maybe you're too busy concentrating on what's right in front of you to get a decent idea of the big picture. That's why you're a DC. You do all right at the small stuff, but you need a bit of a flair for strategy at my level.'

Maybe if you didn't leave all the paperwork and form filling to me I'd have time to read about the big picture. 'Thanks for the advice.'

'Freely given,' he said. 'Listen and learn.'

'I do. Every day.' It was true. If I wanted to know about misogyny, right-wing conspiracy theories or competition-grade swearing, working with Derwent was roughly equivalent to a third-level education.

Our route took us close to where the protesters stood, rain-blasted and pathetic, huddled in their anoraks like penguins in nylon hoods. Most were middle-aged and a touch overweight. They didn't look dangerous.

'They can't all be evil, and they must miss their children,' I said.

'Pack of whingers. If they loved their kids so much they wouldn't have left them in the first place.' He glowered at them. 'Anyone who's got the nerve to sit under the statue of the greatest Englishman who ever lived and make it look like a gypsy camp has got no principles and no soul.'

'Winston Churchill?'

'Who else?' He looked at me as if he was waiting for me to argue, but I knew better than to try. Derwent needed a fight occasionally, to do something with the aggression he seemed to generate just by breathing. But I was not going to be his punchbag today.

I could have sworn his ears drooped.

Chapter 2

Back at the office, Derwent threw himself into his chair and waved at me imperiously.

'Go and find the boss and tell him where we are with the case.'

I felt a thud of dismay. 'Don't you want to do it?'

'I've got things to do.'

'So have I.'

'Mine are more important.'

'How do you know?'

'Because I'm senior to you so whatever I have to do is bound to be more important.' As he said it he was reaching over to pick up a copy of the *Standard* that someone had left on a nearby desk.

'Look, I'd really rather not—' I started to say.

'Not interested. Tell someone who cares.' He glanced up at me. 'Why are you still here?'

I turned on my heel and stalked across the room towards the only enclosed office, where Chief Superintendent Charles Godley was usually to be found. I rapped on the door and it opened as I did so, Godley stepping towards me so that we almost collided. I apologised at the same time as he did. My face had been flaming already because I was livid with Derwent, but embarrassment added an extra touch of heat to my cheeks. I was aware of Derwent grinning at his desk on the other side of the room, and the speculative glances from my other colleagues across the tops of their monitors. I knew, even if Godley didn't, that there was frequent, ribald speculation he had brought me on to his team because he wanted to sleep with me. I knew that Godley attracted rumours of that sort like roses attract greenflies; he was head-turningly handsome with ice-blue eyes and prematurely silver hair, and I was the first woman he had recruited in a long time, though not the last. I also knew that people had picked up on the fact that I was extremely awkward around him all of a sudden. The general theory was that we had had an affair and I had ended it, or he had ended it, or his wife had found out and *she* had ended it.

They couldn't have been more wrong.

'Did you want something, Maeve?'

'DI Derwent asked me to update you about the Somers Town murder – Princess Gordon. We've got one in custody.'

'Her husband?'

'Partner.'

'Give me the details.' Instead of inviting me into his office he stayed where he was, standing in the doorway, in plain sight of everyone on the team. Maybe he did know about the rumours after all.

Briefly, I explained what we had found out. Godley listened, his blue eyes trained on my face. He had a gift for total concentration on whatever was in front of him, and it was a large part of his charm that he made you feel as if you were the only person in the world when he was listening to you. I could have done without the rapt attention, all the same. It made me too aware of my voice, my face, my tendency to wave my hands around while I was explaining things, my suspicion that my hair had gone frizzy in the damp evening air.

Not that he cared about any of that. He cared about the fact that I had worked out, beyond any doubt, that he was utterly, totally corrupt. He was paid by one of London's biggest drug dealers, a ruthless gangster with an appalling record of violence, and I wasn't sure exactly what Godley did for him in return. I didn't want to know. I had worshipped the superintendent, blindly, and finding out that he was a fake made me more sad than angry. And for all that he was on the take, he was still a supremely gifted police officer.

I'd promised him I wouldn't give him away, because it was none of my business and I couldn't throw him to the wolves. He'd promised me it made no difference to how he did his job, and he'd also promised not to treat me any differently. But he had lied about that, and I was starting to change my mind about interfering. I still couldn't reconcile the two facts: he was a boss who inspired total loyalty in everyone who worked with him, and he gave away inside information for money. He'd said it was more complicated than I knew, and I wanted to believe him, I really did.

I just couldn't trust him.

'And the sister?' Godley asked.

'DI Derwent wants to interview her again, but he doesn't think she was involved.'

'Unless she's a fuckwit.' Derwent crossed the room, folding his stolen newspaper as he approached, and sat down at a desk that was currently unoccupied. He started casually, carelessly ransacking the desk, opening and closing drawers. 'Who sits here?'

'I don't know,' I said. I did know, in fact, but I didn't want to tell him. The desk belonged to DCI Una Burt, his superior and emphatically not a member of the very select group of colleagues that Derwent could stand. Nor was she one of the even smaller group who liked him. 'I know they don't want you to go through their things.'

'That's a nice stapler.' He clicked it a couple of times, very fast. 'That's better than the one I've got.'

'Josh. Concentrate.' Godley's tone was mild but Derwent dropped the stapler and turned around to face the boss.

'The CPS were happy for us to charge Olesugwe but they

agreed with me that we need to know more about Blessed before we decide what to do about her. I think Olesugwe will plead eventually but at the moment he's still hoping for a miracle. Which he's not going to get, because he's fucked. Did Kerrigan tell you about the keys?'

'What about them?'

'Kerrigan had a look through his personal effects before we interviewed him. She spotted that he had the key to the shed and the car, and she just happened to ask him if there was a spare set of car keys anywhere.'

'The car was fifteen years old,' I explained. 'I thought it was probably second-hand or third-hand and there was a good chance it was down to one set of keys.'

'Well done,' Godley said, without enthusiasm, and I blushed, wishing that Derwent had just said nothing.

Apparently oblivious, he grinned at me. 'You see, you look vague, but you're actually not all that stupid when you try.'

'Thanks.' *For nothing*, I added silently.

'Makes me wonder why you're being left out of the big investigation.'

'What investigation?' I looked at Godley, whose face was like stone.

'Josh. That's enough.'

'It just doesn't seem fair of you to shut out Kerrigan. She hasn't done anything wrong.'

'That's not what's going on and you know it.' Godley stepped back into his office. 'Come in here and shut the door, Josh.'

Derwent was flipping through the newspaper again. He flattened it out on a double-page spread near the centre and with a flick of his wrist sent it spinning towards me. It landed by my feet. 'Have a read of that, Kerrigan. It's as close as you're going to get.'

I picked it up. The headline screamed: SERIAL KILLER TARGETING LONDON'S SINGLES. Most of the space below was taken up with pictures of two young women. One had red hair to her shoulders; the other was dark and had short hair. She was huge-eyed and delicate, while the red-head was a stunner with a full mouth and slanting green eyes. Both were slim, both attractive. And dead. My eye fell on a pull quote in bold type: 'They lived alone. No one heard their cries for help.' And then, on the opposite page: 'Mutilated and murdered'.

'It's not our case,' Godley said, to me. 'I've been asked to put together a task force in case they turn out to be connected, but I'm working with the local murder teams and they're still officially investigating them. The victims didn't know one another. They lived in different areas. The first woman died in January. The second was two months ago. This article is just speculation.'

I appreciated the explanation but it wasn't really aimed at me. Nor was Derwent really complaining about me being left out. He wasn't the type to care. He was absolutely the type to make use of a subordinate to get at his boss, though, and he wasn't finished.

'Oh, come on. Of course they're connected.' Derwent leaned over and snatched the paper back, flattening it out so he could read aloud: '"Both Kirsty Campbell and Maxine Willoughby lived alone. They worked within two miles of one another in central London. Friends describe both of them as bubbly and outgoing, but unlucky in love – Maxine had never found the right person, while Kirsty had recently broken off her engagement to her fiancé, Stephen Reeves (28). He describes himself as 'heartbroken' on the Facebook page set up in memory of Kirsty, but declined to comment for this article. Police have cleared Mr Reeves of any involvement in Kirsty's death."'

'He declined to comment but they scavenged a quote from him anyway,' I said. 'I bet the lawyers made them put in the bit about him not being a suspect.'

Derwent read on, this time with more emphasis.

'"And the similarities don't end with how they lived. Kirsty and Maxine were strangled in their homes. There was no sign of a break-in at either address, suggesting that in each case they may have known their killer. Most shocking of all is the anonymous tip-off we received that both women were horribly mutilated, their bodies desecrated, their eyes gouged out. Police had not revealed this grisly detail to the public, but more than anything else it seems to suggest that Kirsty and Maxine were killed by the same person."'

I shuddered. 'That's horrible. I'm not surprised they didn't want that detail revealed. But if no one knew, it can't be a copycat.'

'It's not proof of any connection between the two deaths,' Godley said. Derwent slammed his hands down on the desk.

'Like *fuck* it isn't.'

'I wanted to talk to you about that article, but not out here, Josh.'

'Nothing to do with me.'

'Someone tipped them off. Someone who wants there to be a connection between the murders. Someone not particularly well informed. I don't have to look too far to find someone who fits the bill.' I'd never heard Godley sound so stern. He turned and walked around his desk. Derwent jumped up and followed him. He didn't even glance in my direction as he went past, his face set and pale, his hands clenched. He slammed the door after him, to make it absolutely clear, as if I hadn't known it already, that my presence wasn't required. The newspaper had fallen to the floor, forgotten, and I picked it up. Back at my desk, with one eye on Godley's door to watch for Derwent's return, I read through the rest of the article, and discovered two things. One: I knew the senior investigating officer in the Maxine Willoughby investigation all too well. Two: I had no idea whatsoever why Derwent was so angry.

But I would make it my business to find out.

Chapter 3

'What are you doing tonight?'

I didn't even look up. 'Going home early.'

'Wrong answer.' Liv began tidying my desk around me, humming under her breath.

'Can you stop doing that?'

'It's so untidy.' Liv was the only other female detective constable on Godley's team. She was as elegant and lovely as a Japanese ink drawing; I had never seen a strand of her long dark hair out of place. Her own desk was arranged as neatly as if she'd used a ruler to organise it.

I was basically her exact opposite in every way.

'It's creative mess. I work best like this.' I slammed my hand down on a pile of papers that was beginning to slide sideways. 'That was fine before you started messing with it.'

'If they ever bring in a clean-desk policy—'

'I'll change jobs.' I took the file she was holding and stuck it back in the middle of the muddle.

'It hurts me,' she said.

'Don't look, then.'

'I can't stop myself.'

'It's not that bad.' I rolled back a few inches so I could see what she was talking about. 'Okay. It looks like an explosion in an origami exhibition.'

'Worse than that.' She picked up my pen pot and tipped

the contents out over the desk. 'There. I think that's how it was when I found it.'

I brushed paperclips off the page I had been reading. 'Thanks, that's much better. Why were you asking me about my plans?'

'Come for a drink.'

'I shouldn't.'

'Why not?'

'Rob's going away tomorrow morning. Two weeks in the good old US of A.'

Her eyebrows went up. 'Holiday?'

'An FBI course in Virginia. His boss arranged it.' His predatory, female boss, who had almost caused me to break up with him over the summer, so heavily had she been leaning on him to sleep with her. I'd known he was hiding something and assumed the worst. I'd been absolutely sure he was cheating on me, when the opposite was true. It was like that, with Rob. I kept waiting for everything to go wrong because no one was that perfect, and I couldn't believe he felt the way he said he did about me. To my constant surprise, we were far beyond my usual cut-off for relationships. Most of mine had lasted weeks, not months, but here we were, still together after almost a year.

The course was too good an opportunity for him to turn down, as I'd told him when I encouraged him to go. But I hated that he was going to be gone for so long, and so far away. And I hated that DI Deborah Ormond was going too.

'Two weeks in the States. Nice work if you can get it.' Liv settled down on the chair next to mine, getting comfortable. 'And how do you feel about that?'

'Stop using your relationship-counsellor voice. I'm looking forward to it.'

'Bullshit.'

'No, I am. I'll be able to do whatever I want, when I want. It'll be like being on my own again. Being free.'

Liv raised an eyebrow. 'Still working on the commitment issues?'

'No, because I don't see them as a problem.' I shuffled pages, trying to look busy. 'I just like having options, that's all.'

'How does Rob feel about it?'

'Oh, who knows. He acts as if we've mated for life.'

'What a bastard.'

I glared at her. 'We can't all settle down and get a dog on the second date.'

'It was our fourth,' Liv said, ultra-dignified. 'And not a dog. Goldie is a goldfish.'

'Well, that's totally different.'

She grinned. 'Seriously, though. Is two weeks the longest the two of you have spent apart?'

'Yes, but I haven't seen all that much of him since he left the team.' That was another sore point. He'd had to leave a job he loved because of me. Godley had a rule about relationships within the team and we'd been found out. One of us had had to go. Being Rob, he'd netted a promotion and a slot on the Flying Squad, but it had complicated his life and I knew he missed the old team. I sighed. 'We just never seem to be on the same schedule.'

'It gets a bit like that, doesn't it? Especially in the job.'

'So it seems. If they're not job, they don't understand the hours and stress and bad pay. If they are, you don't get to see them. What's the point?'

'There isn't one. You have to become a nun.'

'I would, but the veil wouldn't suit me.' I checked the time, suddenly aware of the ache in my shoulders and neck from hunching over my desk. 'Where are you going for this drink and who else has signed up?'

'The local, and it's just me and Joanne, and Christine. Please note, I'm not offended by you wanting to know who else is going.'

'Joanne as in your girlfriend? I haven't seen her in ages.'

I'd only met her a couple of times but I liked her a lot. 'Okay, I'm in. Who is Christine?'

Liv shushed me, leaning across so she could mutter. 'Civilian analyst. She's been working for Godley since before I joined the team. Please don't tell me you didn't know who she was.'

'Oh, her. I'd forgotten her name.' I was aware of her, but I hadn't paid much attention. She was young and giggly, addicted to shopping for clothes in her lunch hour and flirting with the male detectives.

Liv tilted her head to one side, like a bird about to peck. 'Don't judge her. You don't know her.'

'Okay. I don't know her. But I don't think we're going to get on.'

'She's sweet. And she's terrified of you.'

'Of *me*?' I glanced over to where she was working, facing away from me so all I could see was light brown hair in a messy up-do and a narrow back. 'But I'm not scary at all. How is that possible?'

Liv sighed. 'You have no idea, do you?' She counted her points off on her fingers. 'You never speak to her. You aren't afraid to snap at the boys if they get out of line with sexist remarks. You're a workaholic and you take your job very seriously. Plus you have a habit of solving our shittiest cases. Most of the team think you're the mutt's nuts and would sacrifice a body part for the chance to sleep with you, which you don't seem to care about. Then again, you do have the finest bloke ever to work here warming your bed, so why would you? She worships you from afar. I made her day by telling her I'd ask you to come with us.'

'You are kidding.' I was feeling deeply uncomfortable.

'Not in the least.'

'She'll be so disappointed when she finds out the truth.'

'What did I say that wasn't true?' Liv patted my head. 'Especially the part about being a workaholic. You really need to have a break now and then.'

I considered that for a moment. By the evening I was usually exhausted, fit for nothing but half an hour in front of the television and then bed. That was on ordinary days, when I wasn't in the middle of a nightmare, headline-grabbing case. I'd been tired for so long, it passed for normal. I only really noticed when I was so fatigued I could neither eat nor sleep.

Now that I thought about it, none of that sounded healthy.

'All right. You've persuaded me.' Liv looked triumphant and I held up my hand to forestall her. 'But just for one drink. Then I really have to go home.'

It was simply amazing how quickly one drink turned to three when you were having fun. I beamed across the table at Liv and Joanne, who were holding hands. Joanne was tall and dark-haired, with clear, freckled skin and high cheekbones. She looked like a model, spoke with a Scouse lilt, and had a high-flying job in the Counter Terrorism Command. Liv had met her when they both worked in Special Branch. The contrast between them was striking. Both were exceedingly attractive, but in very different ways. And they were obviously, transparently in love.

The gin loosened my tongue. 'You know, you two make a lovely couple.'

'Oh, we know.' Joanne smiled at Liv, then back at me. 'Poster girls for Metropolitan Police inclusiveness.'

'The friendly face of lesbianism.' Liv untangled her fingers from her girlfriend's to lift her glass. 'Here's to being a dyke.'

We all clinked glasses, Christine giggling nervously. That was more or less all she had done so far. Sitting beside me, she was facing the bar and therefore had a view, as I did, of most of the team propping it up, drinking as if it was a competition. From where I was sitting it looked as if DS Chris Pettifer was winning. As I watched, he took three goes to get his pint glass back on the bar, then stared at it blearily as if daring it to move again.

'Not a pretty sight,' I said. 'I think Chris needs to call it a night.'

'Poor DS Pettifer. His wife's left him.'

I looked at Christine curiously. 'How did you find that out?'

She shrugged. 'I get to know things about the people on the team. They were having IVF and it didn't work out. They can't afford any more and they're not entitled to another round on the NHS. She's gone off travelling on her own, so I suppose I shouldn't say she's left him, because she might be back and they haven't exactly split up.'

'Why didn't I know any of this?' I asked Liv.

'Because you don't really have time to gossip. You're too busy.'

'That's so sad.' I knocked back the end of my drink. There was another lined up in front of me, fizzing gently. I'd drink it quickly, I thought, checking the time with a twinge of guilt.

'Pettifer?' Liv asked.

'Me. I'm so boring. It's not that I don't like gossip. I absolutely do. It's just that I'm too scared of getting in trouble with Derwent to be caught having fun at work.'

'What's it like?' Christine asked. 'Working with DI Derwent, I mean?'

'A laugh a minute.' I was trying to get at the slice of lemon in the bottom of my glass. Ice slid past my hand on to the table, and I swore.

'Really? It's fun?' Christine had pale blue eyes that were very large, surrounded by a lot of eyeliner and set far apart in a heart-shaped face. She was too pretty to dislike, or take seriously. She had already confided in us that she had always dreamed of being a police officer but having worked for Godley, she wasn't so sure she wanted to be one any more. I imagined myself watching other people do my job while I spent all day reading and colour coding Excel spreadsheets of phone data that meant nothing to me. Hell on earth, I concluded.

I also concluded that Christine and I did not have a lot in common.

I tried to explain what I meant. 'Well, it's sort of fun. In a way. You have to ignore a lot of what he says, and he likes to test me.'

'Test you?'

'Challenge me. I don't know. I can't really describe it.' It was a working dynamic that was as close to dysfunctional as you could get, but we got results. 'I make suggestions and he shoots them down. Or he gives me a hard time for being too good at the job. Or for being a woman.'

'Sounds like a charmer,' Joanne observed.

'I'm used to him,' I said simply.

'I'd rather work with anyone on the team than him. He's a bigoted prick.' Liv sounded extra-fierce and I grinned at her.

'Tell us how you really feel.'

'He hates me because I'm not interested in men.'

'Oh, he hates everyone. Don't take it to heart.' It wasn't often that I found myself defending Derwent, but I knew him better than Liv did. He really wasn't picking on her specifically. There were very few people he liked in the world, and it happened that the majority of that select group were straight white men, just like him.

Christine leaned her chin on her hand and stared dreamily into the middle distance. 'He doesn't have a girlfriend, does he? What do you think he's like in bed?'

'I don't think about that.' I was hoping to stop her before she got too far with that line of conversation.

'But if you did think about it . . .' She sighed. 'I bet he's dominant.'

I pulled a face, appalled at the very idea.

'Energetic,' Liv suggested.

'Go on, Maeve,' Joanne said. 'It's your turn. In a word.'

'Quick.'

The burst of laughter turned heads at the bar. They were wondering what we were talking about, with that prickly suspicion born of being self-conscious. Because of course the four of us had to be talking about the men we worked with.

They were right, as it happened. But we might not have been.

Liv grinned. 'I know, let's play Shag, Marry, Kill. Maeve, who would you pick if you had to choose between Derwent, Godley and . . . Belcott.'

'Too easy. You'd kill Belcott straight away *then* you'd have the party to celebrate. You'd have quite a while before you had to choose between Derwent and Godley.' Belcott was a nasty little man, the same rank as me but going nowhere. I'd seen him in action, taking credit for things he hadn't done and sucking up to anyone who might put in a good word for him with the boss. He'd taken pleasure in the fact that I'd had a stalker who had invaded my privacy, gloating about the fact that he'd seen footage of me with Rob, during private moments. And that was only the beginning of what he'd done to piss me off.

'And?' Liv demanded. 'Marry Godley, shag Derwent?'

'Not so fast.' I was considering it. 'I bet Derwent would worship his wife, in a patronising way, obviously. You'd never hear a word about his cases but he'd bring you flowers every Friday night.'

'And perfume on your birthday,' Joanne agreed.

'Always the same brand . . .' I said.

'The same as his mum used to wear.' Joanne grinned at me.

Liv's jaw had dropped. 'You're not turning down Godley as a marriage prospect, are you? For *Derwent*?'

'I don't know how happy Mrs Godley is. He's married to the job, isn't he? More than any of us. And you'd have to put up with people staring at him as you walked down the street, because the man is beautiful.'

'I'd turn for him. He's on my freebie list,' Liv said. 'Near the top.'

Joanne nodded. 'I wouldn't mind as long as you told me all the details.'

I ran my finger down the side of my glass. 'I don't really want to have sex with him, though.'

'Because you love Rob.' Liv sing-songed the words and I glowered at her.

'Thank you, Disney Princess. It's not that.'

'But you do love Rob, don't you?' Christine sighed. 'I had such a crush on him when I started working here.'

'Who wouldn't?' I made it sound wry, but I kind of meant it.

'Me,' Liv said promptly. 'But only because I love Jo, and he has boy bits, and I knew he was totally head over heels for you the first time I saw you together.' She narrowed her eyes. 'Anyway, get back to Godley. I'm intrigued.'

Even on the wrong side of three drinks I wasn't going to tell them what I knew about Godley, but knowing it had changed the way I saw him. He had been my hero. I had worked my arse off to impress him. I'd been determined to prove he'd been right to whisk me away from Borough CID to work for his specialist murder squad. Then I'd found out the truth about him, and suddenly I couldn't see him any other way.

All three of them were looking at me, waiting for an explanation. Liv and Joanne were too good at interrogations for me to hope they'd drop it. 'I just don't go for older men.'

'Everyone says you've slept with him already.' Three drinks down, Christine had gone far beyond the point where she was capable of being discreet. I'd known about the gossip, but it was irritating to hear it parroted back to me as if saying it would make it true.

'Never. And I never will. Make sure that gets around the squad room when you're passing on things you know about the team.' There had been an edge to my voice, but I was still surprised to see Christine's face crumple. 'Oh, shit.'

'Sorry . . .' Two perfect tears slid down her cheeks.

Liv drew Christine's glass away from her. 'That's quite enough gin for you, dear.'

'I didn't mean to say anything wrong,' she wailed, hunting through her bag for a tissue. Even when she was crying she looked adorable, a fact that wasn't lost on the guys at the bar. Ben Dornton won the race to our table and handed Christine a paper napkin.

'What are they doing to you, Christine? Why do you want to go out drinking with these miserable cows?' He scowled at the three of us. 'Fuck me, it's proper bubble, bubble, toil and trouble over here. Is it Halloween or something?'

'Not for days,' I said.

He seemed genuinely cross. 'Well, you lot are all set for costumes.'

I looked around, noticing that Liv, Jo and I were all in black suits. Christine was wearing a purple cardigan with a butterfly embroidered on the shoulder. *Spot the difference.* I had been too harsh, I knew.

'I didn't mean to upset you, Christine.'

'Don't worry, I always cry when I'm drunk,' floated out from behind the napkin.

'Come and have a drink with us,' Dornton suggested. 'We'll look after you.'

'It's a girls' night out, though.' Christine emerged, looking tragic, as if that was an insurmountable obstacle. The very phrase made me wince.

'I wouldn't say that. Colleagues' night out.'

'Well, that includes us. We're your colleagues too.' Ben gave a little laugh, shooting for casual. It occurred to me that he was trying hard. I glanced up and saw the expression on his face as he stared at Christine: pure yearning. Over at the bar, Dave Kemp was watching us, turning his beer bottle around and around as he brooded. And the brooding wasn't aimed at me. Kemp I didn't know at all, but he was cute if you liked blue eyes, fair hair and a boyish manner. Dornton was all close-cropped hair and attitude, older than Kemp and usually cynical about everything. I'd never seen him look quite so vulnerable before and I hope Christine had the sense not to play them off against one another because I wasn't at all sure Dornton would cope. It reminded me of Rob, all of a sudden, and how he had looked at me before we got together – knowing what he wanted, not at all sure he was going to get it – and all of a sudden I missed him like mad.

'Okay, then.' I stood up. 'I need to get going. We can carry on another time.'

'Oh, what?' Liv began, and Joanne grabbed her knee.

'She's right. We should get going too.' She caught my eye and gave me a wink and I knew she'd seen the same thing I had on Dornton's face. 'Down in one, Maeve.'

It was such a bad idea to knock back my drink, but I didn't even consider leaving it; I did as I'd been told. Slightly high from the gin burning in my stomach, I turned to Dornton under cover of pulling on my jacket and murmured, 'I'm trusting you to look after Christine. Make sure she doesn't get too drunk, and make sure she gets home all right.'

He looked wounded. 'You know I will.'

'I *think* you will, but I'm still making it your job. She needs looking after.' I poked him in the chest. 'And no taking advantage.'

'As if I would.'

'Make sure you don't.' I gave Dave Kemp a long stare to convey the same message, and saw it hit home.

As I stalked to the door, I found myself thinking I could get to like being scary.

Chapter 4

By the time I got home, I'd slid all the way down the helter-skelter from the tough detective who doesn't let anyone intimidate her to the usual version of me, second-guessing every decision I'd made that day and wincing as my feet complained about hours of punishment in heels. It didn't help that I had to take a long route back. Rob and I had moved to a flat in Dalston, in a purpose-built block of no charm whatsoever. It was an easy enough commute to work for both of us, but I was still getting used to the area. I hated the fact that we'd had to leave our flat in Battersea, where we'd been happy, because the stalker I tried not to think about had found out where I lived.

My usual inclination was to stand up to being bullied, but I was scared enough of Chris Swain to follow elaborate precautions in order to avoid being traced. He was a rapist and a coward, a peeping Tom and a technological genius who ran password-protected websites in shady corners of the Internet where like-minded creeps could share their fantasies – and memories. I'd been the one who uncovered the truth about him, and I was his ultimate target, or so he told me. He'd found me before; he could find me again. But I wasn't going to make it easy for him this time. Our land-line was ex-directory and all of our post was redirected to work; I had no magazine subscriptions and wasn't a mem-ber of any organisations that might put me on a mailing list. None of the bills were in my name. I took different methods of public transport home, when I had to rely on it rather than getting a lift. I hadn't replaced my car when it died; Rob parked his anywhere but in front of our flat. I checked, always and methodically, that no one was following me on my walk home, and I never went the same way twice.

Chris Swain had affected every decision we'd made in moving. The area was a busy one, well served by public transport but with a shifting population who wouldn't pay any attention to us. The flat was on the second floor in a modern building with good security and CCTV. It had low ceilings and small, bland rooms: a sitting room that did double duty as a dining room by virtue of the table in the corner, a galley kitchen, a poky bathroom that got no natural light, one bedroom with built-in cupboards and a bed and no room for anything else. We kept the blinds down in the bedroom almost all the time, more aware than most that privacy was an illusion in urban areas. It was a six-month lease and there was nothing to make us leave at the end of those months, but nothing to make us want to stay either. Functional was one word that occurred to me about it. Bleak was another.

It took me three goes to get my key in the door and the first thing I did was fall over the suitcase in the middle of the hall. I landed on my knees with a bang.

'Jesus. Fuck.'

'If that's a request, Jesus is busy. He told me I should stand in.' Rob came out of the bathroom, toothbrush in hand. 'Are you okay?'

'The booze is taking the edge off the pain.'

'Where have you been?'

'I fell among thieves.' Since I was down there anyway, I sat on the floor and pulled off my shoes while Rob finished brushing his teeth. 'Liv made me go for a drink.'

'Twisted your arm, did she?' He said it lightly, but I felt

guilty anyway. When he came back to the hall he put out a hand to me and I allowed myself to be lifted to my feet, smelling mint.

'I hadn't been out for ages. Joanne was there too. And Christine. Do you remember her?'

'The analyst? Yeah, she was sweet.'

'She remembers you, let me tell you.'

He grinned. 'I deny everything.'

'She said she fancied you rotten.'

'That's nice.' It wasn't an unusual event in Rob's life, and not just because he was tall and lean and broad-shouldered, or because of the black-hair-blue-eyes colouring, or the quiet, understated commitment to doing the right thing that had landed him in harm's way once or twice. It was because when he listened to people he seemed to hear more than what they actually said. It gave him an unnerving ability to read minds, which I found inconvenient at times. Like now. He reached out and touched my cheek. 'Don't worry. I only had eyes for you.'

'Who said anything about being worried? I think she fancies Derwent too, so it's not all that flattering.'

'What gives you that idea?'

'She was speculating about what it would be like to sleep with him.'

'And?'

'We speculated.' I blinked up at him. 'Don't make me think about it again. I've been trying to forget.'

'I've heard you talking about him in your sleep.' He imitated me. '"Ooh, Josh, again. Like that. Harder. Don't stop." I think that was it.'

'Yuck. That's a horrible suggestion.'

His eyes were wide with innocence. 'Imagine how I felt having to listen to it.'

'I've never had a dream about Derwent. My subconscious mind is above that sort of thing.'

'I know what I heard.'

'You're making it up.' I looked at him doubtfully. 'Aren't you?'

He laughed at me. 'How is Derwent, anyway?'

'Rude. Horrible. Oh, and weird.' I hadn't noticed him come out of Godley's office; the next time I'd seen the superintendent he'd been alone. Derwent, for once, had gone home early. I told Rob about it and he listened, frowning.

'You know and I know he doesn't give two shits about my career progression. He was using me to get at Godley for leaving him out of the task force he's setting up and I don't know why he would be left out. Or why he'd care, particularly.'

'Maybe because DCI Burt is involved?' Rob suggested.

'Maybe. She does make him crazy.' I sighed. 'He was so angry with Godley, though.'

'He's an angry man.' Rob stretched and yawned. 'I can't believe I'm talking about him rather than sleeping. I'm shattered.'

'Are you going to bed? What time is it?'

'Late. I've got to be up in six hours.'

'I missed your last night.' I rubbed my eyes. 'I am such a crap girlfriend.'

'You have your good points.' Rob looked thoughtful. 'I may need a reminder of what they are.'

I slid my jacket off and leaned back against the wall. 'Where would you like to start?'

'With you taking your make-up off. If you go to bed like that, you'll wake up looking like the saddest clown in the world.' He was standing very close to me, and he started unbuttoning my shirt.

'That is not motivating me to get out the cleanser.'

'What? I'm just helping.' He leaned in for a kiss and I let him do what he wanted with me as his hands roved. The effect he had on me was not wearing off – quite the opposite. He only had to look at me a certain way to make me catch my breath, and when he touched me, I was lost.

'I have been thinking about this all night,' I whispered, the plaster cold against my back as Rob slid the last of my clothes to the floor. His hand slipped between my thighs and I clung to him and shivered, wanting him to keep doing what he was doing. Wanting more.

'It was on my mind too.'

'Oh really?' I pressed against him. 'What were you thinking?'

'I would really rather show you than tell you.' He stepped back, moving towards the bedroom. 'Hurry up, though.'

I came down to earth with a bump as soon as I saw myself in the bathroom mirror. The gin-euphoria had worn off. I was blotchy, with mascara streaked under each eye and my hair was tragic. Sobering up, I scrubbed my face and brushed my teeth until I could no longer taste alcohol. All of the things I was worried about came and stood around me as I wearily, savagely rubbed moisturiser into my face. Why was I so crap? I only had to manage two things: my job and my relationship. Sometimes I felt I was failing at both.

And in the kitchen, as I drank half a litre of water, I saw that he had made dinner for both of us, which made my guilt bite down even harder. It was like him not to mention it. It was like him to say he didn't mind. Sometimes I would have given all I had to know how he really felt.

I found Rob sitting up in bed with his eyes closed, his arms folded across his bare chest, fast asleep. He looked tired too, with dark smudges like thumbprints under his eyes. As usual he was sleeping in a self-contained, composed way, not sprawling or snoring. He was just too perfect.

Too good for me.

I shied away from thinking about it, knowing that I'd touched on the truth but absolutely not wanting to consider it any further because I knew, logically, where it would end: with a break-up. And I didn't want to lose him, even if I didn't deserve him. I turned off his light as quietly as I could and edged around to my side of the bed, intending to get in without waking him.

Some hope. He slept as lightly as a cat. As I slid under the covers, he reached for me.

'Where were we?'

'You don't have to. You're tired.'

'I'll find the energy, believe me.'

I turned over, burrowing into the pillow.

'Don't you want to?' Rob sounded puzzled.

'I'm really, really sorry I missed dinner,' I whispered. 'I'm sorry I missed your last night.'

'Not my last night on the planet, hopefully.' He put on his light. 'Maeve, look at me. If I really minded, I'd have phoned you. I could have gone to bed hours ago. I was watching TV until five minutes before you showed up. I don't mind you going out and having a good time with your mates. I don't expect you to be here if you're not working.'

'But you're going away.'

'And I'll be back.'

'You don't hate me for being selfish?'

He looked startled. 'Who said you were selfish? You're terrible at managing your time, but I knew that before we started going out.'

'And you still find me attractive even when my make-up is smudged and I smell of alcohol.'

The corner of his mouth lifted. 'Then more than ever.'

The thing about Rob was that he had an unerring instinct for the right thing to say, and do. I felt all of my worries slip away as he made me absolutely sure he loved me, despite all of my flaws. Maybe because of some of them. I showed him, because it was true, that I loved him, even though I still hadn't said it, and couldn't, and it turned out to be the sort of sex that makes you smile to yourself when you think about it afterwards, and you think about it a *lot*.

I was almost asleep when I remembered to ask him if he thought I was intimidating, and had to listen to him laughing on and off for the next five minutes, so much that the bed shook, until I turned over and went to sleep in a proper temper.

Some time in the small hours, around the time I usually got a phone call about a dead body, I woke up and reached for him again, curling against him, my knees tucked behind his, my arm around his waist. He held my hand and said my name, and I was almost sure he was asleep but I didn't dare say out loud what I was thinking. *I love you*. It shouldn't have been difficult.

I forgave him everything all over again when I woke early but not quite early enough the next morning to find a glass of water and a couple of Alka-Seltzer on the bedside table, along with a note telling me he loved me and he'd see me in two weeks and of course I could be intimidating if I wanted to be, if that mattered to me.

The flat was tidy, and too quiet, and I wandered around feeling suddenly unmoored. I hadn't lied to Liv. I really did like the idea of being on my own. The reality just seemed a bit brutal.

What I wanted, I realised, was to be on my own with Rob for two weeks. I missed him already.

I hadn't even said goodbye.

FRIDAY

Chapter 5

In the interests of making the best of things, I got into work early. I had a filthy headache, which I refused to admit was a hangover. All I wanted was to sit quietly at my desk, sipping the vat of coffee I'd bought on the way in. I had yet to find a route that meant I *didn't* pass a Starbucks on my journey to the office and sometimes I succumbed, even though I preferred to think of myself as the sort of person who would support small businesses rather than global coffee-pushers. When it came down to it, I just wanted caffeine, and lots of it, with absolutely no conversation on the side, to the point where I couldn't even be bothered to correct the baristas when they mangled my name. That was why I was clutching a cup with 'Maisy' scrawled down the side. I had been 'Midge' and 'May' before, but 'Maisy' was a new one.

The office was practically empty and I sat down at my desk, glad that I had a chance to get through some work before the phone started ringing and people – Derwent, mainly – started to make claims on my attention. His cutting little remark about not reading briefings had stayed with me. I resented it without being able to deny it, which made it worse.

I didn't get very far.

'Maeve, could you come in here, please?' Godley was standing in the doorway of his office, his expression stern.

I jumped up and crossed the room on legs that were suddenly not quite steady. I didn't know whether to be relieved or nervous to discover that Godley wasn't alone. DCI Burt sat in one chair, and DS Harry Maitland in another. Burt looked exactly as normal: plain, abstracted, intense. Maitland's usually cheerful face was serious.

'What's going on?'

'Bad news, I'm afraid.' Godley picked up his coat and began to put it on. 'Another dead woman. Tottenham, this time. It looks as if Josh was right and we are looking for a serial killer. The Commissioner has asked me to get a task force up and running and I want you to be on it, Maeve. I'm not taking most of my team because I'll be in overall command of the two current investigations and I'll have about a hundred officers altogether. No sense in dragging everyone along.' He picked up a folder. 'Ready?'

I was still processing the news that there was another murder. 'How do we know this latest victim is connected? I mean, the timescale—'

'Una can give you the details on the way. You can drive her. Harry, you're coming with me.'

I shot back to my desk and gathered up my things as the others headed for the lift. The four of us crowded in and I fought back a wave of claustrophobia, quickly succeeded by nausea. Maitland was wearing an ancient waxed jacket and it stank of dogs, cigarettes and its own linseed odour. I turned my head away and encountered DCI Burt, who was staring at me with keen interest. Her clever, pale face was scrubbed clean, and she smelled of nothing more glamorous than Pears soap. She was square, mid-forties and sweating slightly in a synthetic blouse she must have had for decades.

'Are you all right?'

'Fine.' I tried to look alert, wishing I could think of something intelligent to say. 'Same MO as the other two?'

'So it seems,' Godley said. 'Glenn is meeting us there.

He did the PMs on the other women, so he should be able to give us a better idea of what happened to her.'

Fantastic, I thought. Glenn Hanshaw was prickly at the best of times. Being under pressure made him less helpful, not more. Godley got on with him well enough, but he was the only one who did. And Hanshaw seemed, for no reason that I could think of, to despise me.

The lift doors slid open on the underground garage. It reeked of exhaust fumes. Godley's Mercedes, sleek and black, was in pride of place nearest the lift. Maitland didn't even try to hide how pleased he was about getting to ride in it.

I picked up a set of keys to one of the pool cars and found the bay where it sat. It was a navy Ford Focus that looked unloved, with mud around its back wheels and dust on the windscreen. DCI Burt stood back, writing something in her notebook, while Godley and Maitland got into the Mercedes. It took off up the ramp with a low, throaty rumble. The car was a high-end tank, indestructible and fast, and I'd been Godley's passenger more than a few times, basking on the leather upholstery in climate-controlled comfort. I had very little prospect of ever sitting in that seat again, though. It was pool cars all the way, with their soft brakes and total lack of poke and breathy heaters that only worked on the highest setting.

So, Maeve, how good does it feel to be right today?

Burt snapped her notebook shut. 'Right. Give me those keys. I don't know why Charles Godley thinks I can't drive myself. You can do the navigating.' She unlocked the car, flung herself into the driver's seat and started adjusting mirrors, frowning with concentration.

'I don't know where we're going,' I pointed out.

'Tottenham. Green Lanes, really.'

'It's not an area I'm familiar with, and I really don't mind driving.'

She bounced up and down, trying to get her seat to slide

forward. 'Do you want me to be blunt? You were obviously out last night, you clearly don't feel the best this morning, and I don't want you driving me in that condition.'

'I'm fine to drive.'

'Legally. But your reaction times will be off. You'll struggle to concentrate on the road as well as what I need to tell you about the case, since you missed the briefing.'

A briefing I hadn't known was going to happen. I opened my mouth to say so, then shut it again. I didn't know Una Burt very well, but I did know she wasn't the type to be moved by self-pity. I got in, wedging the coffee cup between my legs because the car didn't have any cup-holders, unlike Godley's. I just hoped DCI Burt wasn't heavy on the brakes.

'There's the address.' She pushed the notebook at me, open at the correct page. 'Carrington Road.'

The sat nav was out of order, spilling wiring through cracks in the sides where someone had tried, and failed, to tape it together. I pulled out the *A–Z*, grateful for once for Derwent's prejudice against modern technology. He liked to drive and drove too fast. I was capable of plotting routes on blues at the same time as giving a commentary over the radio to the controller and hanging on for dear life. I was fairly sure I could cope with whatever DCI Burt threw at me. Fate and my colleagues often conspired to make me work with Derwent. It was the exact equivalent of altitude training: I felt like vomiting at the time, but he gave me an edge that I'd otherwise have lacked. Just at that moment I needed anything that might impress Una Burt.

I risked a glance sideways. She had flung her jacket into the back seat where it lay in a crumpled heap, tangled up with her coat. Neither was going to look the better for it. Her light brown hair was collar-length and copious. It never seemed longer or shorter, which gave rise to suspicion that it was a wig. No make-up today or ever. No jewellery. She gave not a single shit about what anyone thought of how she looked or what she wore. She had a reputation for being blisteringly clever, mildly eccentric and totally absorbed in her work. The drive would be the longest time I'd ever spent with her, but I was already quite sure I wouldn't know her any better after it. She wore her concentration like armour.

'Better catch up or Charlie will be wondering where we've got to,' she said. *Charlie*. I wondered if she called him that to his face. It was just possible that she did. I couldn't imagine her flirting with him, or anyone, but I could believe she revered him for his professional achievements.

The car eased up the ramp and paused for a bare half-second at the top before it slid into a gap in the traffic. I was still reading the map, working back from the address, but I had enough spare capacity to notice that she was an excellent driver, smooth but unshowy. The car was purring.

We actually made good progress until we landed on the Euston Road. It was moving at its usual rush-hour crawl: eight lanes of traffic going precisely nowhere. Burt tucked the car in behind a red bus that had an ad for its cleaner emissions plastered all over its rear end. Bathed in diesel fumes, I couldn't actually tell that there was much improvement. I hit the button to recirculate the air in the car, and listened resignedly as the fan made a horrible grinding noise.

'You'll have to bear it, I'm afraid,' Burt said.

'I'll survive. At least I'm not in the same car as Maitland and his coat of many odours.'

She half-smiled, then her face went blank again as she returned to her own thoughts. When she eventually looked at me, I could see the effort that went into returning to here and now. Like a diver resurfacing, it took her a second to orientate herself.

'What were we talking about? I was supposed to be briefing you, wasn't I?'

'If you don't mind.'

'Do you know about the other two cases? Maxine and Kirsty?'

The way she said their names made it sound as if she knew them personally. There was nothing like investigating someone's murder to get to know them. None of them would have any secrets left by the time we were finished – no shadows in the corners of their lives. It was what I was trained to do and it still felt, at times, like a violation of the victims themselves.

'I only know what I've read in the papers. Both were single women who lived alone, found strangled. No sign of a break-in in either case. No apparent links between them. Apart from the fact that they were killed by someone they trusted.'

'Exactly. And the killer's signature.'

'The eyes.'

She nodded, satisfied. 'That's what makes us concerned that this latest murder is the next in the series.'

'But that detail was in the *Standard*. Everyone in London read it. It could be a copycat.'

'What it said in the *Standard* was that he gouged out their eyes. Not true.'

'Oh, really?' I didn't know why I was surprised. Journalists rarely got stories absolutely right, especially given the Chinese-whispers effect of secret tip-offs.

'He removes them with a knife. He does it quite carefully.'

'Are they trophies? Does he take them away?'

'No. He positions the bodies in a distinctive way, as you're about to see. In all three cases, they've been found with one eye in each hand. If it was a copycat killer working off the *Standard* article, I think he'd have used his hands to remove the eyes, don't you? Given that they used the word "gouge"?'

'Right. Yes.' My stomach was flipping over and over.

The bus accelerated through the lights in front of us, on the amber. Derwent would have gunned it through on red and ended up squatting on the intersection, causing traffic chaos. Una Burt stopped sedately, well behind the white line.

'Charlie had mentioned to me that we might be involved, so I've already familiarised myself with the files. It helps to be prepared.'

No kidding. It would be nice to know what that felt like. I was distracted by *Charlie*. And people thought I was the one who was over the side with Godley. Una Burt's greatest asset, it turned out, was looking like the back of a bus. They *couldn't* be having an affair. Godley wouldn't. Would he?

Burt was continuing, oblivious. 'And of course we were fairly sure there would be a third. Just not so soon.'

Three was the magic number. Three tipped us into serial-killer territory, with all the hysteria and hype that would bring to the media's reports. And three was what it had taken for the Commissioner to become seriously agitated about the safety of London's young women.

'He's bringing the SIOs to the new crime scene, after we've had a look at this girl, so we have as much information as we can share with them. We're working with them, not taking over. At least, that's the official line.'

'They're not going to be happy,' I predicted.

'Would you be?' She glanced at me. 'Didn't think so.'

I was following my own train of thought. 'Is that why I'm involved? Because I've met Andy Bradbury before?'

'Who's he?' The question came immediately at machine-gun speed: DCI Burt didn't like being uninformed.

'He's a DI. Just been promoted. He's in charge of the Maxine Willoughby investigation.'

'How do you know him?'

'I met him a few months ago at a crime scene.' *And I have absolutely no happy memories from that encounter.*

'Charlie wanted you to be involved because you have more in common with the victims than the rest of us do.'

'Oh.' I looked out of the window, waiting for the sting of disappointment to fade. I was there because of what I was rather than who I was. All the old insecurities about making up the numbers came rushing back.

'Don't take it amiss. You have to know what's normal to see what's not.'

'Fine, but you don't have to be the same as a victim to know what was normal for them.'

'It might help.' She looked across at me again, for longer. 'You know, most people your age and rank would be pleased to be involved with an investigation such as this, especially at such an early stage.'

'I am pleased.' It came out sullen and DCI Burt sighed.

'I don't give advice and I'm certainly not going to pretend to be a mentor to you. But you can waste a lot of time worrying about why you're here, or you can use the time wisely. You should be asking me what we know about what happened last night at number eight, Carrington Road.'

I managed to stop myself from squirming. A headmistress tone came easily to DCI Burt and it was far more effective than any of Derwent's sarcasm. 'That was my next question.'

'I thought it might have been.' She had her notebook open on her lap but she didn't even glance at it as she recited the facts. 'The property is a self-contained two-bedroom ground-floor maisonette with its own front door and side access to the rear of the building. It's owned by Anna Melville, aged twenty-nine, who lives there alone. She works in HR at a bank in the Square Mile. A neighbour heard a disturbance at her home last night at about ten thirty and thought about it for a couple of hours before he called it in as a possible burglary.'

'You wouldn't want to rush into anything,' I said.

'Exactly. Much better to wait until there's absolutely no chance of us catching anyone in the act. A response team was dispatched to the address and found it was secure – no lights on, no answer when they knocked at the door. They spoke to the neighbour and he said he hadn't heard anything since he'd phoned, so they left. The lads on early turn picked up on it in the briefing and decided to check it out in daylight to make sure there was nothing amiss. I gather they've been getting hammered on domestic burglaries so it's a high priority for them.'

'That'll be the recession. Burglary stats always go through the roof when people are skint.'

Una Burt nodded. 'The premises looked fine from the front, but the response officers were thorough. One of the PCs went around to the rear of the property and looked through the windows. Everything seemed to be in order until he reached the main bedroom. It was in a state of considerable disarray, and on the bed he could see what he thought was a body. And so it proved to be.'

'Anna Melville?'

'Yet to be confirmed but we're working on that assumption.'

'And she was laid out as the others had been?'

'More or less. We'll see when we get there.' She frowned to herself and I fell silent too, looking out of the window at the pedestrians who were making better time than us, seeing the young women walking on their own. They were heading to work, for the most part, striding in high heels or scuttling in flat shoes. It was cold, thanks to a stiff easterly wind that came straight off the North Sea, and their hair flew behind them like flags. What they wore and the way they wore it told me so much about them: the ones who dressed for themselves, but with care; the ones who wanted to be looked at; the ones who wanted to hide. What would I look for, if I was hunting? Who would I choose?

Anne Melville had shared something with Maxine Willoughby and Kirsty Campbell, apart from the manner of their deaths. The killer had seen that something, and had known it, and had used it to destroy her. At the moment, he was a stranger to me, a black hole at the centre of the picture. But if I could see what he had seen, I might know enough about him to find him. Una Burt was right. It was far better to be on the team than left out, no matter why I was there in the first place. Every case was another chance to prove I deserved to be there because I was good at what I did – and I *was* good, and I could do it. I sat up a little bit straighter. My hangover slunk away, defeated. I had better things to do than feel sorry for myself.

Like answer my phone. It hummed in my bag and I dug for it, knowing I had six and a half rings before it cut to voicemail. *Two . . . Three . . .* It came out wrapped in an old receipt and I had to waste a second untangling it. *Four . . .* Beside me, DCI Burt's voice was cold.

'Who is that?'

'DI Derwent.' *Of course.*

'Don't answer it.'

I stopped with my thumb poised to accept the call, obedient to the tone of pure command without having the least idea why she'd forbidden it. The ringer cut off and I waited for the beep of a new voicemail. I wasn't actually all that keen to listen to it. A disappointed Derwent was an angry Derwent, and an angry Derwent was even less charming than the usual kind.

'Why can't I speak to him?'

'Because it's not a good idea.'

Which wasn't actually an answer. 'Okay, but he'll be livid. He'll be wondering where I am, for starters.'

'He doesn't own you.' The road ahead was suddenly, miraculously clear – one of those freak moments in heavy traffic when the lights all go your way and no one else does. We were actually making some progress towards the crime scene.

'Of course he doesn't.' *He thinks he does, though . . .* 'Is he meeting us at the house? Or—'

'DI Derwent will not be involved in this investigation.'

I stared at her profile. 'But he was asking about it yesterday. He was insistent.'

'He will not be involved in this investigation,' she repeated, and I didn't know her well enough to be able to tell if she was pleased.

I listened to half of the voicemail before I deleted it: Derwent, ranting about my absence from the office when there was work to be done on the Olesugwe case. It was certain to be the first of many messages. I couldn't imagine why Derwent was shut out, but I knew it was going to be bad news for me.

Chapter 6

When we arrived at the crime scene Godley was standing outside, a still point in the organised mayhem, impossibly glamorous as the low autumn sunlight struck a silver gleam off his hair. The SOCOs were at work already, sealing off the property, and the superintendent was watching from a safe distance. Something about him suggested he was impatient to get into the house, and that he had that impatience under control, but only barely. I felt the same pull myself. There was nothing like seeing a body as the killer had left it, in the place where the victim died. Photographs didn't do the job. Every sense had to be engaged, I had learned. Where a normal person would shy away we leaned in, absorbing every detail. To understand what had happened, you had to allow yourself to relive it, and I was keen to get it over with in Anna Melville's case. I had known what it was like to be afraid for my life, but I had always been lucky, so far. Anna Melville's luck had very definitely run out.

The house wasn't the only focus for the SOCOs' attentions. They had identified her car. It would be taken away for detailed examination, in case she had given the killer a lift, or in case he had opened the door for her, or in case he had so much as leaned against it while they spoke. Like her home it would be ripped apart. There was so much mud to pan for one tiny fleck of DNA gold that could incriminate a killer. Technology meant we needed less and less to prove our cases, but that made it harder on the technicians who had to search for evidence that was literally invisible. There was still a place for good old-fashioned police work to narrow the focus to one person, one man with a dark heart, one killer. Jurors treated forensic evidence with reverence, but more often than not we were the ones who had put the defendant in the dock, and the forensics were just part of the picture.

All of which made me sound like any other copper, I thought. It was a commonplace to complain about not being appreciated, across all ranks, in all branches of the service, across all the different forces. It wasn't a job to do if you liked being praised or if you wanted to earn a lot of money. It was a job to choose if you couldn't see the value in doing anything else. It was a fundamental part of what made me who I was: without it, I wouldn't know myself.

And the reason why I put up with the terrible hours and disappointing pay and sometimes miserable working conditions was staring out of the windows on either side of the road. The neighbours were starting to realise what had happened, staring at the news come to life in their very own street. Later some of them – the more sensitive ones – would think about the fact that a murderer had walked past their doors not long before, on his way to kill. Somehow it was worse to think about him leaving after he had finished, dragging his slaked desire behind him. It made *me* shiver and I didn't have to sleep on Carrington Road. It wasn't my home that had been defiled.

DCI Burt parked the car, humming under her breath. Godley heard the engine and turned to glance in our direction. I saw his eyebrows twitch together in a frown, but I couldn't tell why.

I let her walk across to him on her own as I took a detour to drop my coffee cup in a bin. The wind stung my face and I huddled inside my coat, dropping my chin down to hide behind my collar. Carrington Street was lined with maple trees, which were shedding their leaves as if foliage was going out of fashion. The gutters were clogged and the air had that vinous smell of decay that I associated with autumn. A mordant technician in wellies and a boiler suit was working his way along the road, raking through the piles of leaves, filmed by the handful of news cameras that had made it to the latest crime scene. Someone had tipped them off that it was a murder but so far, judging by the questions they were shouting at me, they didn't know there was anything to connect it to the other deaths. And they wouldn't find out from me. I turned to walk back to the house and my bag vibrated against my hip.

Shit.

I don't know why I looked at the screen because I knew who it was going to be, and why. The ringing was somehow more insistent, the vibration stronger, because it was Derwent on the other end of the line, hating me for making him call back. I simply didn't dare answer it when DCI Burt had specifically told me not to. I looked up and saw she was watching me, as was Godley. I made it very clear that I was rejecting the call, dropping the phone back into my bag with a flourish so they couldn't miss what I had done. The part of me that rebelled against authority and hated working in a hierarchical organisation was outraged that I was obeying orders blindly, without being offered any explanation as to why it was necessary.

If it had been pissing off anyone other than Josh Derwent, I might even have said so.

'I spoke to the uniforms. They'll be around later if you want to ask them anything,' Godley said. 'We shouldn't have too long to wait now.'

On cue Kev Cox appeared at his elbow, a small balding man with a pot belly his boiler suit did nothing to hide and a sweet nature that survived routine exposure to the worst things people could do to one another.

'Two more minutes, folks. Thanks for the patience. You might like to get ready.'

'Gloves and shoe covers?' Godley checked.

'Suits too, please. Got to be careful here.' Kev knew as well as any of us that there would be ferocious interest in Anna Melville's murder. No one wanted to get it wrong.

'Glenn's just been in touch. He's stuck in traffic, but he's on his way.' Godley set off towards the house. Over his shoulder, he threw, 'Keep it in mind, you two. He won't want anyone to touch the body before he sees it.'

I wouldn't have dreamed of it. I went out of my way to avoid it, usually. The loose, yielding feel of dead flesh, especially through rubber gloves, was developing into a phobia. Never a great cook, I had abandoned cooking meat altogether since I'd started working on murders. The raw-meat aisle at the supermarket was the stuff of nightmares, even if it was sanitised in cling-film.

They had set up a tent in front of the door and it functioned as an airlock between the real world and the crime scene. I hurried to get dressed in the protective gear Kev had specified. Beside me, Godley was doing the same. Burt had been about to get changed when her phone rang and she stepped back out to answer it. I wondered if Derwent had started calling her instead. Then I wondered what she didn't want to say in front of me. Then I decided that was pure paranoia, and self-absorbed to boot.

'Where's Harry Maitland?'

'Coordinating the house-to-house. I've got plenty of uniformed officers at my disposal to cover the area but I want them asking the right questions. Maitland's putting the fear of God in them for me.'

I found myself hiding a smile at the unconscious pun. Godley was nicknamed 'God' in the Met not just for his name but also because of his looks and his perfect, untouchable record. It wasn't something he encouraged, and it was used mainly by people who hadn't worked with him. There was nothing grand about the way he did his job – nothing showy – and he had time for the youngest, the least experienced, sometimes the least promising officers he encountered. In turn, he got undying respect and dedication, and very often results no one else would have. And yet he was as dirty as they came. The thought wiped the smile off my face, and when I looked up Godley was watching me. I had the uncomfortable feeling that he knew exactly what I had been thinking.

'Do you want to wait for DCI Burt?' I asked.

'She knows where we're going.' Courteously he held the door open for me, letting me walk into the flat first, and I scanned the hall as I passed through it, starting to form an opinion of Anna Melville from the things she had chosen to keep around her. The hall was painted a faded green and a collection of twelve vintage mirrors hung on one wall, spaced out exactly in rows of four. The floor was polished wood and the cream runner that lay on it was pristine. It wasn't even rumpled. I looked for – and found – the shoe rack by the door. No one was allowed across the threshold without taking their shoes off. If she had let him in, the killer had been in his socks or barefoot, so we wouldn't get shoe treads or soil fragments to match against an eventual suspect. The rack was neatly arranged with shoes that were predominantly pretty rather than functional – delicate, spindly high heels on everyday court shoes, embellished ballet flats for casual wear. Even her wellies were pale pink with silver stars. A girly girl.

'No blood,' I observed to Godley, who nodded. He moved past me into the sitting room.

'Let's start in here. Una will be in soon.'

The room wasn't large but the furniture was expensive. The grey velvet upholstery on the two-seater sofa and armchair looked as if no one had ever sat on it. There was a fireplace, with candles sitting in the grate, and the alcoves on either side of the chimneybreast were shelved. They were filled with vases and ornaments rather than the books or DVDs that might have told us something about her personality. The fact that there weren't *any* books or discs made me think she worked long hours and didn't have time for entertainment. The giant grey wicker heart above the sofa made me suspect she was a romantic. The armfuls of cushions arranged on the sofa itself were impossibly feminine and dainty; I couldn't imagine a man sitting there to watch television. And on another wall, there was a framed poster: the word 'Beauty' in elaborate writing. Pin your colours to the mast, I thought. If that's what matters to you, why not frame it? And what harm was there in any of it? Still, something made me feel I wouldn't have got on with Miss Melville. The array of photographs on the shelves gave me one reason.

'What is it?' Godley was watching me instead of looking around, which made me feel like a canary in a mine. 'You're frowning.'

'Is this her?' There were probably thirty pictures on the shelves and the same dark-haired woman appeared in almost all of them.

'I believe so.'

'She must have been massively insecure, then. Who has framed pictures of themselves when they live alone?' I picked up one which was of a group of girls ready to go out, dressed to the nines. Two of them were talking, their mouths twisted halfway through a word, and one wasn't even looking at the camera. The dark-haired girl was looking right at the lens with a dazzling smile. 'And look at this. She's the only one who looks good in this picture. Why would you choose to frame that?'

'Being insecure isn't a crime.'

'But it makes you susceptible to flattery. The three women lived alone. They were all heading towards thirty and not in a relationship. That has to be one way he could have got in. Do we know if any of them did online dating?'

'I'll ask the other SIOs this afternoon.'

'He's seeing something vulnerable in them. This woman was hyper-feminine and very conscious of how she was perceived. What do you look for in a man if you are like that?'

'Someone who comes across as traditionally masculine,' Godley suggested. 'Someone strong.'

'And forceful. Someone who would take control. Sweep you off your feet. Someone confident.'

'Confidence fits in with murdering them in their own home. He's comfortable in their environment. He takes his time, too.'

'What makes you say that?' I asked.

'How the bodies are left.'

I was staring at the only thing that was out of place in the room: a vase half-filled with greenish water and a few bits of leaves. 'Where are the flowers?'

'I think we're about to find out.' Godley checked his watch. 'Come on, Una. Wind it up.'

She came through the door as if she'd been waiting for the invitation, rustling importantly in her boiler suit. 'Sorry. All done.'

'Are we finished in here?' Godley asked me and I nodded, watching Una Burt scan the room.

'Lead on,' Godley said to her, and I followed her through the hall, past a small bedroom that was primrose yellow and obviously for guests, past a tiny bathroom where the SOCOs were climbing over each other to collect swabs and empty U-bends, past a kitchen with red tulips in a vase on the table and the washing-up neatly stacked on the draining board. No secrets here – nothing that Anna would have been ashamed for us to see. It reminded me of a flat that had been tidied for viewing, down to the matching tea towels hanging neatly on their rail and the cutesy blackboard with 'Nearly the weekend!' written on it, above a shopping list. Organised, careful, feminine, self-conscious. And there was nothing wrong with being like that – I wished I was more like that myself – but I felt it had marked her as a victim and I wondered how he'd seen it, and known her, and calculated how he could have her.

How he had had her was laid out for our inspection in the main bedroom, as neatly and obsessively as everything else in Anna Melville's home. I stopped short in the doorway despite myself and Godley collided with me, then leapt away as if I was burning to the touch.

'Sorry. I just—'

'Don't worry,' he said shortly. 'Take your time.'

Burt had gone ahead and was leaning over the bed, peering intently at the body that lay on it. I skirted the bed, not quite looking at what lay on it. The floor was wood, painted white, and Kev was lying down shining a torch through the cracks between the boards. On the other side of the room another SOCO was doing the same, crawling on hands and knees. I recognised her – Caitriona Bennett, the pretty, soft-spoken technician whose work had led us to a killer during the summer. It was a slight comfort to me to know that Anna Melville was getting the best of everything in death. It gave us a chance to get something like justice for her.

Godley stepped over Kev's prone body. 'Found anything?'

'Dust.' He didn't even look up, working his way along the gap inch by inch. 'Stuff. We'll have these up later to collect anything that seems interesting.'

I stopped beside the window, which was draped in gauzy voile panels. There was a hand-span gap between them where I assumed the uniformed officer had peered. Turning, I saw that the room showed the same feminine attention to detail as the rest of the flat, with a white-painted carved wooden beam nailed to the wall above the bed. Curtains hung down from it, draping the bed head. The bedclothes were white and embroidered with tiny stars, also white, but they had been drawn down to the end of the bed and folded over, out of the way, leaving a clean white sheet underneath the body. A mirrored bedside table had a carafe of water on it, an old-fashioned alarm clock and an iPad that I knew we would be taking away with us. I itched to start looking through it but there were protocols to observe. And a body, I reminded myself, forcing my eyes to where she was waiting.

She lay with her head pointing towards the foot of the bed, her feet together on the pillow. She wore white – a silk nightdress so fine I could see a dark shadow at the top of her thighs and the two faint smudges of her nipples through the fabric. She was small and slim, her bones fragile, her kneecaps sticking up like a child's. Her hands were by her sides, palms up, loosely holding what he had cut out of her head. Her face was horrendous – dark with blood, her tongue protruding – but mercifully for me he had closed her eyelids over the empty sockets. The marks on her neck stood out like splashes of paint on snow. Her hair – her long, glossy dark hair – was gone. He had cut it off close to her head. She looked more vulnerable with her collaborator's crop, and young, and I wondered if he'd cut it before she died or after. Was it to torment her? For his own gratification? Or something more complicated?

'Did he take the hair away with him?'

'Nope. Found it in the bathroom. He dumped it in the bath,' Kev said cheerily. 'But he cut it in here. We found a lot of loose hairs over here in this corner.'

Two candles stood on either side of her head and on either side of her feet – fat ones, about eight inches high.

'Did he bring these, do we think?' Godley asked, pointing at them.

'They're the same as the ones in the living room,' I said, my voice metallic in my ears. Robotic. Emotionless.

'Were they burning when the uniforms got here?' Una Burt asked.

'No. He seems to have put them out when he was leaving,' Godley said.

'Never leave a naked flame unattended,' floated up from the floor where Kev was approaching Godley's feet.

'I'm not sure that was his priority.'

'There were candles at Maxine's house as well. None at Kirsty's,' Burt said. 'So he makes do with what he can find.'

'It makes her look like a sacrifice,' I said. A memory drifted to the surface: helping one of the nuns to prepare the altar for an early-morning Mass. White linen altar cloth. Pure white candles in their low holders. And flowers, rammed by me into a brass container too small for them, because I was bored and wanted to be finished. The nun had taken them from me, tutting under her breath, and cut away the bruised stems with a short, stubby knife she'd produced from the folds of her habit, until the arrangement looked perfect. I moved forward to stand just behind Anna's savaged head and looked down at her. From this angle I could see what I'd missed before: she was lying on a handful of lilies. Their heavy scent drifted up, mingling with the bitter smell of the burnt candles.

'These will be the flowers from the living room.'

'Probably,' Godley said, leaning over beside me. His sleeve brushed mine and again I was aware of him flinching away. Not the way to convince people we weren't having an affair, I thought sourly. Since I had no way of actually saying that to him without stepping a long way outside what was appropriate for my rank, and his, I affected not to notice.

'What do you think the flowers signify?'

'No idea. Part of the ritual, I suppose, along with the candles.'

'Being outside?' Burt suggested.

'Did he do this with the others?'

Godley nodded.

'With lilies? Or other flowers?'

'Other flowers, I think.' He frowned. 'I have crime scene photos in the car.'

'We should have a look,' Burt said. 'With the other SIOs.'

'How did he know there would be flowers here?' I bent down: from what I could see of the petals they didn't look fresh. One or two were brown and coming away from the flower. Even allowing for them being crushed under the victim, they weren't in the best condition. 'Did he deliver these, maybe, earlier in the week? Is that how he saw her first?'

Una Burt didn't hide her scepticism. 'Why would she let him in again, though? There was no sign of a break-in. Even if she recognised him, she'd never let a delivery man into her house.'

'Unless he was carrying something heavy.'

'Like what?'

There was no evidence of anything having been delivered and I subsided, feeling squashed. But Una Burt was right, and she wasn't trying to put me down, unlike Derwent. She was just saying what she thought.

'What did he use to cut her hair? Scissors?'

'Not that we found.' Kev surfaced beside the bed. 'If you ask me, looking at the way he left it, he used a knife.'

'The same knife he used on her eyes?' Burt suggested.

'It's possible.'

'Did she fight?' I asked. 'What did the neighbour hear?'

'Unusual noises, he said. Moving furniture. Thumps and bumps.' Godley scanned the room. 'Not that you'd know.'

'If he made a mess, he took the time to tidy up afterwards. This was important to him – making this image.' I stepped back to look at it as he might have, wondering what he wanted us to see. 'He took the hair out of this room. He could have left it.'

Godley was using his torch to examine the woman's face, peering at it from a distance of a couple of inches.

He looked disturbingly like Prince Charming leaning over Sleeping Beauty, ready to wake her with a kiss.

'Stop. Go back.' Something had caught my attention. 'Where you had the torch before – I saw something.'

He turned it back to the side, shining it across her bloodless skin, and again I saw a glint.

'There's something under her neck. A hair.'

'Not surprising,' Godley said, disappointment colouring his tone very slightly. 'You'd expect him to miss a few.'

I reached over and took the torch out of his hand, shining it directly on what I had seen. Caitriona swooped in with tweezers and drew the hair out, holding it up so she could slip it into an evidence collection envelope. Now that I could see it properly, I could tell it was maybe fourteen inches long. It hung in an elongated 'S', the bottom curling out and up as if it had been styled to flick up. It was pure gold in colour.

'Not one of hers,' Kev said happily. 'Where did that come from?'

'Him?' I said, dubious. My mental image of a serial killer didn't really include styled, shoulder-length hair.

'One of the other victims?' Burt suggested.

'They weren't blondes either,' Godley said. 'Let's hope it's relevant.'

'We'd have got it on the bedclothes,' Caitriona pointed out, as defensive as if someone had told her she'd failed. 'We were going to take the sheets away once the body was moved.'

'No one is moving anything without my say-so.' Glenn Hanshaw's voice was grating as it cut through the room. We scattered away from the bed like cockroaches surprised by a light going on. 'I'm sorry I'm late.'

He didn't sound sorry. He sounded livid. I edged back, towards the door, as he folded his tall, bony frame into a crouch beside the bed and began unpacking his equipment. I appreciated that he was good at his job, but the snap of his rubber gloves going on and the rattle of the thermometer as he took it out of its case made me clench. He was exceptionally professional but his patients were beyond feeling and he was businesslike about the way he examined them, quick and somehow brutal. I felt it was uncomfortably close to a violation and as I watched him lever Anna Melville's legs apart – moving quickly because he was late, and angry, and she was beyond caring if he was gentle – I felt a wave of unease that was close to distress. I went and stood in a corner of the hall, taking deep breaths, waiting for my heart rate to drop.

'Are you okay?' Una Burt's face was close to mine when I looked up.

'I hate that bit.'

'So do I. But it's not Hanshaw's fault. He's not the one who put her there.'

'I know.' And I did know it. 'I don't blame him. It's just – this case feels a bit close to home. You were right. I do feel something for these victims. Not that it could be me.' Although it nearly had been me when I'd thought my stalker Chris Swain was just a friendly neighbour. He had got closer than I liked to recall. 'It could be someone I know. One of my friends. Someone more trusting than me.'

'You think he gains their trust.'

'She wasn't tied up. She wasn't beaten up. She was killed. How did he control her before that? The only thing I can think is that he had some authority over her. She did what he said because he asked her to.'

'You could be right.' She looked away from me, into the room where Anna Melville still lay, and the next thing she said proved I wasn't following her train of thought at all, because I couldn't tell why it had occurred to her. 'If DI Derwent attempts to talk to you about this case, refer him to me.'

She was gone before I could ask why.

Chapter 7

I was just about to go back in to confront the body and whatever Glenn Hanshaw was doing to it when I heard voices outside the front door. I scooted down the hall to see four men pulling on protective suits, watched by a crime-scene technician who had his arms folded. His name was Pierce, I recalled, and his voice was both camp and carrying.

'It's even more important for you guys to be careful about what you're walking into the property, given who you are. One of you brings in some material from another crime scene and we are screwed, do you know what I'm saying?'

'Yes, I think we have the idea.' The testy response reminded me how uncharming I found Andrew Bradbury. He was thin and unsmiling behind glasses with heavy frames. Some men made going bald look good: Bradbury was not one of them.

'I'm sorry if you don't like it. I'm just doing my job. I'd be skinned alive if I let you in.' If anything, Pierce sounded rather pleased to have a reason to tell the detectives what to do. I cleared my throat and he twisted around. 'Oh, here's DC Kerrigan. She'll look after you.'

I was expecting some glimmer of recognition from Bradbury but it seemed I had made no impression on him at all. Since I encountered him he had been promoted, though he'd been one of the least impressive detective sergeants I'd ever met. Getting him out of harm's way by pushing him up the ladder, Derwent had suggested. Derwent had given him quite a hard time, and Bradbury had conceded in a hurry to the alpha male. If Derwent had been there, Bradbury would have thought twice about pushing past me. As it was, he didn't even say hello.

'Where's Superintendent Godley?'

'The bedroom at the back, on the left.'

He barrelled past me and down the hall. I let him go, addressing the three who remained outside the door.

'Thanks for coming. I'm Maeve Kerrigan – I work with Superintendent Godley.'

'Nice to meet you.' The speaker was lugubrious, sallow and in his mid-forties. 'DI Carl Groves. This is DS Burns. Frank by name and nature,' he added.

The sergeant waved a gloved hand at me instead of shaking mine. 'Thanks for laughing at the boss's little joke. I did too, the first thousand times I heard it.'

I grinned at the pair of them. They were a double act – one fat, one thin, around the same age, old in their very souls and as cynical as murder detectives are supposed to be. The third man introduced himself as James Peake, a detective from the East End where Andy Bradbury worked and where Maxine Willoughby had died. He was about my age, a big handsome redhead.

'Did you want to speak to Superintendent Godley first, or . . .'

'Probably more use to have a look round, isn't it?' Groves said. 'That's why we're meeting here, after all.'

I agreed with Groves. Only Bradbury, it seemed, had missed the point.

They were quiet as soon as they entered the flat, taking in everything it could tell us about poor Anna and her aspirations. DI Burt appeared in the kitchen, dispatched by Godley, and there was another round of introductions.

'Are you seeing similarities?' she demanded, and all three nodded with varying degrees of enthusiasm.

'Same type of victim, definitely.' Burns lifted a fold of curtain material and weighed it. 'Better off than Kirsty, I'd say.'

'Didn't she live in Blackheath?' I had noticed it in the *Standard* article because it was a nice part of south-east London, close to the river at Greenwich and rich in green open spaces. It was on my list if I ever managed to save enough money for a deposit for a place of my own, assuming – as I tended to – that I was buying it alone, Rob having gone the way of all men. It was emphatically not the sort of place where you expected to be strangled in your bed.

'It was Blackheath in estate-agent speak. It was more like Lewisham.'

'Lewisham's all right,' Groves said. 'What's wrong with Lewisham?'

'Where do I start?' Burns rolled his eyes. They'd be doing a music-hall number next. Una Burt could see the warning signs as well as I could and cut in.

'What about Maxine Willoughby? Where did she live?'

'She had a one-bed flat in Whitechapel,' Peake said. 'This place is a big step up from what she could afford.'

'Anna was in HR in the City,' I said. 'I'd imagine she was earning a fair bit.'

'Living simply, though,' Una Burt said. 'Quietly.'

'Not attracting attention to herself,' I agreed.

'Whether she wanted attention or not, she attracted the wrong kind,' Groves said.

'The worst.' Burt looked around. 'Shouldn't DI Bradbury be in here too? I thought he was following me. Where's he got to?'

'Have a look in the superintendent's arse,' Peake suggested, very quietly, so that only I could hear, and I smothered a laugh, converting it into a cough that made everyone stare at me. To do something worthy of everyone's attention since it was on me anyway, I asked about the vase. Kev Cox had made sure it was removed since Godley and I had noticed it, but I described it.

'Did you have anything like this in either of the other flats?'

'Flowers, yeah.' Groves's face was twisted in thought. 'Don't know if we ever worked out where they came from.'

Peake was flicking back through a folder of photos he'd been carrying under one arm: pictures from Maxine's flat. I looked over his shoulder, seeing rooms that were neat but IKEA-unimaginative, and all painted the same shade of cream.

'There. On the draining board.' I put out a hand to stop him as he flipped past the kitchen. 'That's a vase, isn't it?'

It was turned upside down, as if it had been washed out.

'Do you think he left it like that?'

'Could be. He definitely cleaned up after he'd finished with Maxine. He wasn't in a hurry to leave. He even vacuumed the place, we think, and took the bag away with him. He must have been feeling very confident. If there was more noise here – didn't you say a neighbour called 999? – maybe he didn't feel it was worth his while to tidy up after himself.'

'You could be right.'

Groves and Burns were conferring in low tones, and concluded that there might have been a vase. They couldn't remember.

'What's your theory?' Peake asked.

I squirmed. 'I don't really have one yet. Maybe he delivers them and that's how he gets to check out the victims and their homes. Or maybe he brings them flowers to get them to trust him.'

'Well, he must be fucking charming is all I can say. They let him in. They don't fight back.' Groves shook his head. 'Maybe he buys them chocolates too.'

'And offers to fix a few things around the house,' Burns suggested. 'And tells them he hates football.'

'But he loves shopping.' Peake was grinning.

Burt looked as entertained as I was, which is to say not very. *Poor silly women, pinning their hopes on Prince Charming, trusting the wrong man.* 'I hate to interrupt, but I think we'd better move on. Dr Hanshaw is going to want to move the body, so if you want to see it in position . . .'

The three of them fell into line and we toured the rest of the flat, including the small bathroom, now SOCO-free, where I noticed the shower curtain was decorated with tiny yellow ducks. It was the kind of detail that reminded me why we were there. The person who had chosen it and hung it up and looked at it every morning was now stiff and dead and lying exposed to anyone's view in her own bedroom, because someone else had decided she should be.

The bedroom itself was getting crowded and I hung back, watching Caitriona extract herself from the room with the urgency and purpose of a cross wasp fighting its way out of a bottle. Glenn Hanshaw had finished and Godley was listening, patiently, to Andy Bradshaw's self-important account of the Maxine Willoughby crime scene and how it had been different.

'I thought we'd discuss this at the local police station. I've asked them to let us have a room,' he said when he could get a word in. 'We need to see your crime-scene photos. And I'd like everyone to hear what you have to say, not just me.'

'Of course.' Bradshaw sounded as if that was only natural, not appreciating perhaps that it was meant to apply to everyone.

'Then, Kev, I think we're finished here. Can you let them know they can take the body?'

Kev nodded cheerfully. 'We'll finish up.'

As I followed the others out of Anna Melville's flat I felt

bleak. Someone would come and tidy it up, once we'd taken all of the evidence we required. Someone would decide to throw out or sell or keep the things Anna had chosen. The flat would be sold to a buyer who wasn't squeamish or didn't know what had happened there. Someone would take Anna's job. She had no children to mourn her. She had been an only child and her parents were dead: the next-of-kin contact we had been given for her was a godmother who hadn't seen her for five or six years. Anna's life would be undone and she would be gone.

It just didn't seem fair.

Chapter 8

The room at the local police station was on the small side but it had a projector and, importantly, blinds to cover the windows and the glass in the door. It would be a very bad idea indeed to let anyone else see or hear what we were discussing. We sat around the table like well-behaved children at a party. The heating was on full and the room was stuffy even before we'd begun. I started to undo the buttons on my jacket but changed my mind halfway through, when I noticed Peake looking at me with a little bit too much interest. I would have to swelter.

'Right. I think it would be useful to go through what we know from the beginning,' Godley said, taking charge. 'Carl?'

Groves flipped open the file in front of him. 'Kirsty Campbell. Lovely girl. She was twenty-eight. Broke up with her fiancé a few months before she died but it was because they'd grown apart, not because he was cheating or she was or anything of that sort. We considered him as a suspect, obviously, but he had an alibi and a new girlfriend and he wasn't the type to do something like that.'

Burns was nodding. 'Stephen Reeves, his name was. We interviewed him twice, just to make sure. Never got a bad feeling from him. Honest and straight down the line.'

'What about Kirsty? Had she found anyone else?' Burt asked.

'That's the question, isn't it? We asked, believe me. Some friends said yes, others not. She'd said she didn't want to date for a while – she was hurt that the ex had moved on as quickly as he did. She broke up with him, but it seemed like it was worse for her than for him.'

'Biological clock ticking,' Burns said wisely.

His boss carried on as if he hadn't spoken. 'According to her colleagues, she cried at work sometimes.'

'Which was where?' Godley asked.

'Westminster Council. She was a planning officer.'

Being a planning officer meant she had to see people face to face. 'Did you manage to trace all of the applicants she'd been dealing with at work?' I asked.

'We went back twelve months,' Burns replied. 'Didn't find anyone with a grudge against her, or anyone who acted weird when her name was mentioned. A few had criminal records, but for fighting and fraud, not stalking or anything sexual. We did follow them up.'

Godley smiled. 'No one is suggesting that you missed anything, Frank. I want to make that clear to you too, Andy. This isn't about going over old cases to see what you didn't do. It's about finding common ground for the victims.'

'What was Kirsty like as a person?' I asked.

'Gentle. Soft-spoken,' Groves said. 'She was from Edinburgh originally. Not a strong accent, though. One of her colleagues said she had the most beautiful speaking voice he'd ever heard.'

'Bit of an odd remark,' Bradbury said.

'Do you think so?' Groves's face wrinkled as he thought about it. 'He was an older man, her boss. Married. Nothing dodgy going on with her. And I think he was actually out of the country when she died.'

We had so little to go on, we were chasing the slightest hint of a lead. Godley drew Groves back to the point. 'Was she popular at work?'

'Very. No one had a bad word to say about her. She was

very attractive.' Groves held up a picture of her, not one I'd seen before, and proved his point. The main impression was of tumbling red hair and a smile that was shy but endearing. 'She worked hard. She volunteered for a charity that works with inner-city kids on improving their reading.'

'And we traced everyone else who was involved with it, and the teachers she met, and the parents of the kids she worked with,' Burns added.

'Her parents said she was always a credit to them. Very stable background. We spoke to all her ex-boyfriends and there weren't that many of them. They all said the same thing: gentle, fair-minded, a perfectionist. Much harder on herself than anyone else.'

'Any history of depression or mental health issues?' I asked.

'Why do you ask, Maeve?' Godley said.

'Being a perfectionist, crying at work, being hard on herself – that all sounds as if she was quite fragile. She broke up with her fiancé, but then she took it harder than him. Maybe she thought she wasn't good enough for him.' *I wonder how that feels.*

'That's what her mum said,' Groves agreed.

'They were planning to get married and then suddenly they weren't. That changed how her life was going to be, completely. Maybe she needed counselling. Or a support group,' I suggested.

'She wouldn't necessarily have told anyone she was doing that kind of thing,' Peake said. 'She might have hidden it.'

'We didn't think of that,' Groves said.

'Look into it,' Godley said to me. 'Check out the area near to her home. Local churches and the library.'

'Can we look at the pictures from her flat?' Una Burt asked.

Burns got up and fiddled with his laptop, which he had

linked to the projector. 'I hope this thing works.'

'It was easier in the old days,' Grove said. 'When we were young. Stick some pictures up on the wall and no one had to worry about technology. I've yet to see anything that's actually improved by computers.'

The screen flickered and a desktop appeared. We watched as Burns slowly, painfully tracked the cursor across to the folder of pictures on the desktop. He was breathing heavily, concentrating as if he was doing something exceptionally difficult. There was a universal sigh of relief when he succeeded in double-clicking it.

'Ground-floor flat in a purpose-built block,' Groves said, as the first picture in the slideshow appeared. 'She'd lived there for six months.'

'Since the break-up?' Burt asked.

'Exactly.'

The block was red brick and rather nice, with grey-framed windows and some low shrubs around it.

'Communal hallway. The front door was supposed to be locked, but the lock wasn't working.'

'Suspicious,' Peake commented.

'Yeah, it was. The contacts were damaged so it didn't engage the magnetic lock when the door was closed. It broke a couple of days before the murder. The managing agent had been told, but they hadn't actually done anything about getting it fixed. Wasn't the first time it had gone wrong, so no one was too bothered. Each flat has a front door and they weren't allowed to keep personal belongings or bikes in the stairwells anyway.'

'How big is the building? How many other residents were there?'

'There were six flats, nine other residents. All checked out. No one heard anything. No one made it on to the suspects' list.'

The image on screen was a front door, green-painted but inlaid with frosted glass. 'This is Kirsty's.'

'CCTV?' Bradbury asked.

'No.'

'Shame.'

'Yeah, it was.' Groves waited for the next image, a close-up of the door locks. 'No damage here. No damage to any of the windows.'

'She let him in.' Godley sounded grim.

'Indeed she did.'

'Do we know where she'd been the evening before she died?' I asked. 'What day of the week was it?'

'A Friday. She went for a drink after work with a colleague who was celebrating her birthday. Didn't stay long, apparently. Wasn't drunk. Got the train back. We have her on CCTV walking through the station and later passing her local pub. No one seems to be following, for what it's worth.'

A living room. Bookshelves. A huge collection of DVDs and maybe twenty novels.

'Was she in a book club?' I asked.

'Don't know.' Groves looked at Burns, who shrugged.

'Try and find out, Maeve,' Godley ordered. 'What else did she do?'

'Went to the gym – one in Blackheath. She didn't have a car, so she walked everywhere. She'd joined a knitting group, believe it or not, in a local pub, but she'd only been to a couple of sessions and no one really remembered much about her.'

'Knitting?' Peake rolled his eyes.

'It's very trendy, apparently,' I told him.

'Not the sort of thing you do if you want to meet blokes.'

'I thought we'd established she didn't.'

'Settle down, you two,' Bradbury said. 'She liked knitting.'

'Didn't travel much,' Burns said. 'She went to Edinburgh to see her folks when she had time off. Liked baking.' The picture on screen was the kitchen, a bland pine one accessorised with red tea towels, a red teapot and red storage jars.

'Anna was very feminine too,' I observed.

'That plays into them doing what they're told,' Una Burt said. 'Used to taking orders from men.'

The next picture was the bedroom door, left ajar, a glimpse of the bed beyond offering a clue to the horror that was the reason for our knowing anything at all about Kirsty. There was a vacuum cleaner on the floor outside the door, tipped over, and a bucket with cleaning products in it.

'It was her cleaner that found her. She was actually one of the other residents in the block who was looking for a bit of cash because she was a single mum and Christmas had cost a lot. Kirsty got her to do her ironing and cleaning. Bit of charity, I reckon. She said the place was always spotless.'

'Had she cleaned the rest of the place before she got to the bedroom?' Godley checked.

'Yeah.'

There was a groan around the room and Groves nodded. 'We didn't have much luck with this one. We got nothing on the forensics, even in the bedroom itself. What she didn't clean, the killer did.'

'And on the body?'

'Nothing. He didn't have sex with her, either with a condom or without, with permission or without. He only touched her to kill her.'

The next few pictures were of the bedroom and the body, both from a distance and in close-up. Her bedclothes had been blue, but he had piled them in the corner of the room and spread a white sheet on the mattress. She wore white too, something that looked like a sundress, with ties on the shoulders and a tiered, mid-calf skirt. Her head had been roughly cropped, as in Anna's case. It was pillowed on roses, white ones, the petals splayed and the leaves brown at the tips.

'Those flowers aren't fresh,' I observed. 'Do we know where they came from?'

'No. It was the thirtieth of January and all the florists were on a post-Christmas comedown. They'd have remembered someone buying roses, but no one did.'

'Where did he leave her hair?' Burt asked.

'In the bin in the kitchen. In a bag. Neat, like.' DS Burns sounded sour.

Her injuries were very similar to Anna's. I asked Bradbury, 'How does this compare to how Maxine was found?'

'She was dead too.'

You arse. 'I mean the level of violence he used.'

Peake answered for his boss. 'Bruising to the neck, where she was strangled, and he cut her around the eyes but we think that was while he was removing the eyeballs and it was after she died.' He held up a picture from his file, one from the post-mortem, a close-up of the woman's face. I wouldn't have recognised her as the same person I'd seen in the newspaper. Her skin had a pearly quality, like the bloom on a plum. Dark hair, like Anna.

'That's pretty minimal violence,' I pointed out. 'No defence wounds. No bruises or scrapes. He's very controlled.'

'Nothing that will ruin the image in his head.' Burt picked up the photograph Peake had been holding and looked at it, then at the screen. 'That's what he's doing, isn't it? Painting a picture but with dead bodies.'

'I don't want any talk about him being an artist, or anything else that glorifies what he does.' Godley's voice was hard. 'He kills women because he gets a thrill out of it. He does it because he likes it. If we start taking him at his own estimation, he's won.'

'We need to understand why he's doing this,' Burt objected.

'We need to know how, and who. Not why.' I'd never heard Godley speak so abruptly to Una Burt. He was courteous as a rule anyway, and particularly towards his brilliant but difficult chief inspector since it set a good example to the rest of the team. But I had noticed before what little patience he had for the idea of a killer with a mission, a serial murderer acting out an elaborate game. He was a realist. The people he hunted were indulging their darkest desires, but that didn't mean he was going to play along. A killer was a killer and that was that.

'Did he cut Maxine's hair?' I asked.

'No, she did. She wore it short. Started getting it cut that way about six months ago and liked it, according to her best friend.' Bradbury sounded as if that was just about the most outlandish idea he'd ever heard. But she'd had fine, small features, like the other two women, and short hair had suited her.

'So he didn't bother cutting her hair for the sake of it. That must mean there's a practical reason for him to do it,' I said. 'He didn't need to, with Maxine.'

'Maybe the short hair attracted him to her in the first place,' Peake suggested.

'That's the trouble, isn't it? We don't know what attracted him.' Godley sighed. 'You've had less time than this lot to look into your victim's life, Andy, but tell us what you know anyway.'

The inspector's ears coloured slightly as everyone turned to look at him. He liked being important but not being put on the spot, I thought. Power but not pressure.

'Maxine Willoughby was twenty-nine. She was Australian, from some tiny town in the middle of absolutely nowhere, and she'd been living in London for nine months. She worked near Covent Garden, in the marketing department of an insurance company. She didn't have anything to do with clients or the public – it was more of a backroom job. Her colleagues liked her. She worked hard, and long hours. No boyfriend and it became a standing joke with her colleagues that she needed to find a good Englishman. She didn't seem to be trying to meet anyone. The word her colleague used was "asexual". When she joined the company, the single men all tried it on with her but she wasn't interested or didn't notice.'

'Maybe she wasn't interested in men,' I suggested.

'Not a lesbian. I asked. One of her colleagues was, and Maxine found the whole subject agonising in case she said the wrong thing.'

'Both Kirsty and Maxine had accents,' Burns said.

'Everyone has an accent. You have an accent. There's no such thing as a neutral voice.' Una Burt didn't even look to see if the sergeant minded being corrected. I was starting to realise that she wouldn't have been upset to be told she was wrong so she assumed everyone else felt the same way. The important thing to her was being accurate.

Burns cleared his throat. 'I mean, they were both from places with distinctive accents. Maybe he spoke to them on the phone.'

'Does anyone know about Anna? No?' Godley turned to me. 'Make sure you ask her friends and colleagues about the way she spoke. We can get the phone records for all three and see if there are any common numbers.'

That sounded like a fun job. I didn't mind asking the question but I would rather poach my eyes in lighter fluid than spend days reading reams of numbers.

Bradbury continued. 'Maxine wasn't your stereotypical Aussie. She was shy and reserved, young for her age. The big city intimidated her. She picked Whitechapel as a place to live without knowing very much about it and she found it hard to settle in.' I thought of the street stalls that lined the main road in Whitechapel, the market sellers shouting in hundreds of languages, the sense that thousands of lives were being lived all around you. Coming from a quiet rural community, Maxine must have been dazed.

'Why did she stay there?' Godley asked.

Bradbury shrugged. 'She could afford it.'

'I think she was too proud to admit to her folks she'd made a mistake in moving there,' Peake said gently. It was a sensitive reading of Maxine's decision to stay where she was. I knew people who loved Whitechapel, who wouldn't live anywhere else, but I still thought she'd have been happier elsewhere.

'I don't have this on a PowerPoint display, but these are the crime-scene pictures.' Bradbury skimmed them across the table, laying them out so we could all see them. 'Carnations underneath the body. White, of course. But she was naked.'

She was covered with a sheet, not exposed. The bed was surrounded with tea lights this time, ten or twelve of them, all burnt out. The carpet was cream and not new, marked in various places with stains that didn't look recent. Her room was neat but the furniture was as cheap as it gets.

'Any DNA?'

'Nothing.' Bradbury corrected himself. 'Nothing fresh.'

'They could at least have replaced that carpet between tenants,' Groves muttered.

'No sign of a break-in. No mention to friends or family that she'd recently met someone, as far as we can tell. Unlike Kirsty, she didn't seem to have any hobbies. She wasn't the kind to go out and join clubs.'

There was something desperately pathetic about the girl who'd travelled to the other side of the world to live in a grotty flat in Whitechapel, alone, and work hard at a job where her colleagues thought her awkward and immature. It was a rite of passage for young people from Australia, New Zealand and South Africa, but they tended to flock together, taking over whole neighbourhoods and creating their own version of London. Maxine hadn't made it to her own group. And lone animals were more vulnerable outside the herd.

'Okay. Wait.' Burns was snapping his fingers. 'I'm getting an idea.'

'Brace yourselves,' Groves said.

'Colours. Places.'

'What are you talking about?'

'*Black*heath. *White*chapel. *Green* Lanes.' He looked triumphant. 'What do you think?'

'I think there are a lot of places in London with colours in their names,' Groves said. 'A hell of a lot.'

'And it was Lewisham, you said, not Blackheath.' Una Burt was flipping back through her notes to check, her forehead puckered.

'Greenwich. Redbridge. Limehouse. Blackfriars. Bethnal Green. Wood Green. White City.' Groves sounded as if he was going to go on all night, and Godley spoke over him.

'Is there anything else anyone would like to share? Any ideas?'

'Plenty of ideas, but they don't lead anywhere,' Peake said. 'Every time we come up with a way to find him, he's already thought of it and avoided it. Everywhere we look, he's missing. No DNA. No CCTV. No parking tickets. Nothing that links the victims. Nothing that tells us why he chose them and not someone else. He hasn't left us anything but dead women. It's like he knows how we think.' I could hear the bitterness in his voice, the frustration at two months of getting nowhere. 'It's like he's better at this than we are.'

We were all thinking it, but Bradbury said it.

'It's like he's one of us. A police officer.'

Godley shuffled his papers, looking down so I couldn't catch his eye. I switched my attention to Burt, who had a bland, inscrutable expression on her face. The smallest suspicion was starting to form in my mind.

But it was clearly ridiculous.

'He could be a copper,' Groves said. 'We thought of that. He could have got in by pretending he needed to ask them questions.'

'It would fit in with them doing what they were told,' Una Burt said.

'He'd be used to ordering people around.' Burns was looking bleak.

We contemplated the idea in silence, until Groves spoke again.

'The gaps are getting shorter. Seven months to two months. He's getting more confident. You know what that means.' We all did, but he said it anyway. 'We don't have long before he does it again.'

Chapter 9

Having wimped out at the house when Dr Hanshaw was doing his worst, I made a point of attending Anna Melville's post-mortem and managed not to disgrace myself by fainting or throwing up or acting as if it bothered me to see her turned inside out. I found it was easier in the morgue, where she was out of her own context. It turned her body into an object of scientific interest rather than something that had once lived and felt and breathed. And Hanshaw was on better form in his own environment as he methodically unravelled all of Anna Melville's secrets. I stood beside Godley, my hands in the pockets of my coat, well back from the action but with a grandstand view nonetheless. I had been at enough post-mortems to know what to expect, so none of it came as a surprise.

Except for one part.

'Your victim was *virgo intacta*. No sign of sexual assault, no sign of sexual activity at all.'

'At her age? Seriously?' I was struggling to believe it.

'So it seems. Maybe she was saving herself for the right man,' Hanshaw suggested.

I batted it back. 'But she found Mr Wrong.'

'Please, don't. All we need is for the papers to start calling him that.' Godley was looking pained, as well he might. The news had got out that there was another death, which meant there was a serial killer stalking single women. That

81

was a headline-grabbing development in itself, but then, at the press conference Godley had reluctantly given, a tabloid reporter had christened him the Gentleman Killer.

Godley *hated* it.

Now he shook his head. 'I don't get it. We know he doesn't interfere with his victims but there has to be a sexual element to it – dressing them up like that, cutting the hair. He gets a kick out of what he does.'

'Maybe he can't have sex with them,' I said. 'Or maybe he isn't prepared to risk leaving body fluid and skin cells on the victims, if he's scared we'll find his DNA. He was extra-careful about cleaning up, which suggests we have him on file somewhere. When I'm back in the office, I'll have a look through the CRIS reports for anything that sounds similar in any respect – strangulation and not necessarily to death, cutting hair, removing eyes – all the combinations.'

'You'll be swamped. There'll be too much for you to review alone.'

'I can get someone to help me. Colin Vale would be good.' It was the sort of task that was pure grinding tedium. That made Colin light up with excitement.

'Colin's busy.'

And I decide who does what on my team, I filled in silently.

'He must be very controlled,' Dr Hanshaw said, and I was grateful to him for breaking the awkward silence that had fallen. 'This would be the high point of his sexual gratification, if that's why he does it. Not touching them, not touching himself – doesn't that spoil it for him?'

'The crime scenes suggest someone in command of the situation, someone prepared to take their time to achieve what they imagined. I don't pretend to understand the psychology but I know there's a kind of killer who gets off on reliving the thrill afterwards, like Ted Bundy. Killing is the risky part, with the highest likelihood of being caught. Once he's done it and got away, he can indulge himself at his leisure.' Godley sighed. 'Maybe fiddling with them isn't the point of what he's doing. But I would dearly love to know what is.'

'It might just be killing them. And leaving them for us to find as he wants us to find them,' I risked.

'Controlling how we see them.' Godley nodded. 'The hair depersonalises them. Maybe that's what he wants. It's a pretty powerful signifier of femininity. Cutting it off, dressing them in white, lighting candles, women who have sworn off men – what does that say to you?'

'Becoming a novice.'

'A bride of Christ,' Godley said.

'You know, He wasn't on my list of suspects up to now.'

It was a joke, but Godley didn't laugh. 'That's rather the trouble. There doesn't seem to be a list. These three women – nothing overlaps.'

'There'll be something,' Hanshaw said, lifting a glistening object out of her chest and placing it into a bowl to be weighed. 'He's not picking them at random.'

'What makes you say that?' Godley asked.

'I saw how he left the others. He's a perfectionist. He wants conformity. So they'll have something in common that attracted his attention, even if you can't see it yet.'

'I never thought I'd wish for a common-or-garden murderous rapist,' Godley said. 'At least it's easy to understand what motivates them.'

'But if we can understand what he's trying to do with the way he leaves the bodies, we should be a lot closer to finding him,' I pointed out. 'It's the common-or-garden murderous rapists who go undetected for years because they just do their straightforward raping and killing and fade away into the night. This guy is making it complicated, which gives us more to go on.'

'How do you know he hasn't been killing for years? Decades, even?' Godley's voice was cold. 'Kirsty Campbell is the first one we can link to him directly, but she won't be the first of his victims. He'll have done something to someone before that, even if it wasn't murder. And you should know that, Maeve.'

Out of the corner of my eye I saw Hanshaw glance at us, then share a look with his assistant. *Not you too . . .*

I kept the hurt out of my voice. 'That's why I wanted to look at the CRIS reports. He's specialised in his MO to the point where we should be able to find a pattern and watch him escalate. He's making that easy for us.'

Godley's jaw was tight. 'He's making it a hell of a lot more complicated. If you knew—' He stopped.

'If I knew what?'

'Not now. Not here.'

I knew better than to argue with a superior officer so I shut up and watched the completely routine remainder of the post-mortem while I tried to think of a polite way to tell him everyone thought we were shagging and could he please stop making cryptic remarks all the time as it was making a bad situation worse.

I failed.

When the PM was over, Godley went back to the office but sent me in the opposite direction to Anna Melville's place of work in the City, so I was alone with my thoughts and several hundred strangers on the Underground. It was a long, dull journey. The train was slow, held up by signal problems way up the line, and we stopped between stations. I tested how much I could find out just by looking at my fellow passengers. What they read, and what they carried, and what they wore. Work ID cards were a gift: name, job title, office address . . . what more could you need? It was the perfect environment for hunting, proximity allowing fleeting intimacy. And it was so easy to follow someone without being noticed in the surge of people coming and going through the maze of corridors and escalators at every station. I wondered if that was all the killer had needed to do – sit on the train and wait. Look for the feminine, submissive kind of woman, the sort who stood back to let others get on first. The ones who blushed if you stood beside them. The ones who read books about falling in love. The ones who couldn't help staring at kissing couples wistfully, when everyone else in their immediate environment was trying not to yak. The ones who would make ideal, obedient victims.

I got off the train at Bank and came out into the fresh air in the shadow of the venerable Bank of England itself. I noticed, as always, the sudden upsurge in wealth that distinguished the Square Mile from the rest of central London. The bars advertised twenty types of champagne, the women wore immaculate suits and carried bags worth multiples of my salary, everyone walked fast and talked loudly in acronyms that were meaningless to me. The City was all about money, making it for other people and for yourself, and it was so far removed from my world that I felt as if I'd landed in another country. Disorientating too was the sense that the glass-and-steel modernity was just the latest layer of development. The history of the place lived in the street names and the idiosyncratic angles they took along medieval byways. Pudding Lane, where the Great Fire had started in 1666. Cheapside. Tokenhouse Yard. Threadneedle Street. The old thriving life of the city seemed to stir in the shadows, the names a reminder of a time when trade was in the things that kept you alive, like bread and poultry, not futures and securities.

I walked towards the Monument, thinking about Anna Melville and how she had journeyed to work, and the other women and how they had lived. Kirsty had been a planning officer with Westminster Council. Maxine was in an insurance company just off Long Acre. It wasn't surprising that they worked near one another given that central London was quite compact and, during the working day, densely populated. It was a truism to say Londoners tended to know small areas in minute detail but have the haziest idea of the rest of the city. My frequent changes of address made me more conscious than most that London was still a collection of villages, as it had been in the dim and distant past, and you could live in your village quite happily without ever needing to go much further afield. Covent Garden was within walking distance of the City and Westminster, but it would be unusual for someone to be familiar with all three areas, unless they were a taxi driver.

He could be a taxi driver. I made a note to mention it to Godley. Assuming, of course, that the superintendent was willing to listen to anything I had to say. I'd been determined to do my job, regardless of what I knew about him. I knew he was a good police officer and I loved working on his team. But I hadn't allowed for how awkward it was going to be.

Kirsty Campbell had loved her job too. Maxine Willoughby had lived for hers. If Anna Melville had been dedicated to her work too, that was practically the first and only thing I'd found they had in common. The more I looked, the less I found that they shared.

Except for being dead, of course.

I found Anna's office and asked for Vanessa Knight. The receptionist stared at me covertly while I waited for Anna's boss to meet me.

The lift doors opened and a blonde woman shot out, her heels skidding a little on the polished floor. She rushed over to me.

'You're the policewoman. Come with me.'

When the lift doors closed, she looked at me. 'I'm sorry. I'm nervous. I've never spoken to the police before about anything.'

'I just have a few questions about Anna.'

'How did it happen?'

'I'd rather not talk about it in the lift.'

'No. Of course not. Of course.' She jabbed at the buttons. 'Oh God.'

'Are you all right?'

She leaned against the side of the lift with one hand pressed against her chest. Her rings sparkled in the lights as she took deep, quivery breaths. 'I just get very nervous. I'm being so rude. Oh help.'

'Mrs Knight, there's nothing to be nervous about. Just try to calm down.'

'Okay. Yes. You're right.' She looked at me piteously. 'I'm going to be lost without her, you know. Anna. I don't know how I'm going to cope.'

Which was very different from, 'I'm going to miss her.'

When the lift doors opened she hurled herself out. 'This way.'

She led me to a small conference room and spent ages fiddling with the blinds, trying to block out the low sun that was shining across the table and making me screw up my eyes. I clenched my jaw to stop myself from telling her to hurry up, waiting until she was seated opposite me to start asking questions.

'Did you know Anna well? Had she worked here for long?'

'About five years.' She tilted her head from side to side, thinking. 'Yes. Five.'

'Would you say you were friends?'

'Close colleagues. We had a good working relationship.' Vanessa laid a slight emphasis on the word 'working'.

'Would you know what was happening in her personal life? Any boyfriends?'

She shook her head. 'She went on a couple of dates but nothing serious. She wanted to get married, not have a boyfriend, and it was a bit hard to have one without the other. She was quite well off, you know, and someone had told her she'd be a target for gold-diggers.'

'What about her social life? Friends? Classes or groups that she went to after work?'

Vanessa's face was blank. 'I really don't think so. She watched television a lot. And she shopped.'

I'd looked through Anna's wardrobe before leaving the flat and it was all colour-coded and neat and dry-clean only. None of it was showy, though. If anything, she'd dressed so subtly as to be almost invisible, and the clothes seemed to be made for someone older than she was. Looking at Vanessa, languid in grey cashmere with a pencil skirt, I thought Anna had been dressing to impress her boss.

'How did she travel to work?'

'No idea.'

'Was she popular at work?'

'Of course.'

'Did she ever make people redundant?'

'She helped to process redundancies, but it wasn't her responsibility to do it alone.'

'Was she involved in disciplinary proceedings?'

'Sometimes.'

'Did she have any enemies that you know of?'

'Of course not.'

'What sort of person was she?'

'Efficient. Competent. Dedicated.' The words came without prior thought and I realised I was getting the short form of the eulogy that would be emailed around the office along with confirmation that the rumours were true, it really was Anna Melville from the sixth floor who had been murdered . . . 'She was liked by everyone who knew her,' Vanessa finished, as if that was the last word on the subject.

'Would you describe her as attractive?'

'Yes. Of course. I mean, I never thought about it.'

'Did she ever have meetings with anyone from outside the company?'

'Not that I can recall.'

'What was her speaking voice like?'

Vanessa stared at me, floored.

'Did she have a regional accent?'

'No. She sounded normal. Totally normal.' Vanessa herself sounded extremely posh, nay for no and yah for yeah. I was getting more nays than yahs, I thought.

'There were two other murders in London in the last twelve months that we're looking into. There may be a connection with Anna's – it's one of our lines of inquiry. Did Anna ever mention knowing anyone who'd been murdered? Did she ever mention the names Kirsty Campbell or Maxine Willoughby?'

A slow headshake.

'Did she ever spend time south of the river, or in the East End?'

'I have no idea.'

'Did she ever say she was scared of anyone?'

'No.'

'When was the last time you saw her?'

'Yesterday, around four. I had to leave early. I'm supposed to be going on holiday tomorrow. Anna was going to look after things while I was gone. I just don't know how I'm going to manage to get away now.'

I wrapped things up pretty quickly, asking if I could have a look at Anna's desk. Without enthusiasm, Vanessa led me through a corridor of glass-walled offices to an area filled with cubicles, where every head was bent over a desk and every single person was aware of every move I made. Vanessa stood beside the cubicle, watching me, which didn't really help my concentration either. I thanked her for her time and told her I would be in touch if I had any other questions.

'You need a widget to make the lift work and I don't have a spare one I can give you. When you want to leave, just mention it to . . .' She looked down at the cubicle on her right.

'Penny,' a voice supplied from within the cubicle.

'Yes. Penny. Of course. She'll show you out.'

I nodded my thanks and waited until she was out of

sight before starting to go through Anna's work station. She had decorated the wall of her cubicle like a hermit crab, sticking random bits and pieces on it as they took her fancy. A sample of Chanel Mademoiselle from a magazine. A pair of dangly pearl earrings – costume jewellery, but pretty. A postcard from the Maldives seemed to be from a friend and I pocketed it so I could pass it on to Harry Maitland. He was working through her address book and email contacts. I hoped he was having more luck than me.

I sat in her chair to go through the drawers of the desk, finding neat stationery, an empty notebook, a zipped make-up bag and hairbrush, dry shampoo, a toothbrush, high heels, flat shoes . . . all the essentials for someone who spent long hours at work. Or someone who went out after work on dates. I swivelled on the chair, swinging from side to side. It wasn't completely professional, but it always helped me to think. I spun around 180 degrees and looked straight at an interested face that was peering over the side of the cubicle. She was young and fair-haired and had a wide mouth that made her look sulky and a little bit cheeky.

'Penny?'

'Just checking you didn't need anything.'

'Not at the moment.'

'Okay. Let me know if you do.'

I watched her disappear. 'Penny.'

'Yep.' She bounced back as if she was on a spring.

'Do you know the password Anna used for her computer?'

Instead of answering, she disappeared again and I heard scuffling before she arrived beside me, holding out a crumpled Post-it. 'I had this stuck to my monitor. She gave it to me the last time she was on leave in case I needed to look at her files. I don't know if she's changed it since, but the IT department creates them and we're not supposed to change them.'

I took it from her. 'Thanks.'

'Do you need anything else?'

'I don't think so.' Lowering my voice, I added, 'Unless there's anything you know that you think might be useful for us to know.'

'About who killed her?'

'Ideally. Or about her life. Anything strange or out of character she did.'

Penny shook her head regretfully. 'She was so straight it was unbelievable. She never did anything strange or unexpected.'

'Did you know her well?'

'Yeah, I suppose. I worked with her for two and a half years.'

'Did you like her?'

Penny had been speaking quietly too, but now her voice dropped to something close to a whisper. 'I couldn't stand her. She was so self-centred. Really precious and self-absorbed. She used to suck up to Vanessa but she'd never even talk to anyone else. She never so much as asked me if I'd had a nice weekend.'

That was the base level of in-office communication; it was what you said to the receptionist, the post-boy, your boss, the managing director when you bumped into them on a Monday morning. Even Derwent had been known to ask me that question, though I always felt it was in the hope of getting some salacious details about what Rob and I had been up to. Not saying it was pretty much a mortal sin.

'What about her love life? Do you know if she was seeing anyone recently?'

'I presume so.'

'Why?'

'Because she made enough of a fuss about the flowers he sent her last week. White lilies.' Penny wrinkled her nose. 'That's a funeral flower, I always think. And the smell. They stank the office out.'

'I quite like them,' I said.

She shuddered. 'Not for me, thanks. But Anna was delighted.'

'When did the flowers arrive?'

'Umm . . . Thursday?'

'Was there a card with them?'

'I don't know.'

'Did she know who they were from?'

'I think so. She wouldn't say, though. Someone said—' Penny laughed, then looked guilty and a little scared.

'What did someone say?'

'That she might have sent them to herself.' She looked edgy. 'Sorry. That was mean.'

'Well, she might have. But I think she probably didn't.' *I think they were a prop disguised as a gift. I think they were window-dressing for her corpse, a present from her killer.* 'What sort of a person was she? What words would you use to describe her?'

'Cold. Manipulative.' Penny thought some more. 'But sweet too, in a fake way. Needy.'

I asked Penny a few more questions but got no further and let her go, clutching one of my business cards. She might remember something, or she might not. I hoped she would try, even though she hadn't liked Anna.

I turned to the computer and looked at the Post-it Penny had supplied. A_Melville, with Xanna0Melv underneath. I put them in the required fields and lo, my brilliant detective work was rewarded with access to all of Anna's files. I worked through folder after folder looking for anything personal and finding nothing remarkable. In some cases, finding literally nothing. The Internet history had been wiped, which made me curious. Everyone used the Internet for something, whether it was work-related or personal. I checked with Penny, who confirmed that it was Anna's habit to wipe her history every day 'in case her identity was stolen or something'. On a hunch I checked the preferences and found that she had forgotten or not known about the cookies that tracked visits to websites. I scrolled through at speed, seeing lots of shopping websites and fashion blogs. Internet banking. A couple of newspapers featured. YouTube. Amazon. Ebay. It was like a greatest hits of the Internet, and nothing I saw was remarkable.

Except.

I had scrolled past it before I registered that I'd seen it, because it was so familiar to me. Familiar to me, but I didn't know why it would be on Anna's computer. Without the Internet history I was missing the whole story and I didn't know enough to be able to track it back any further, but alarm bells were ringing loud enough to deafen me.

Three days before she died, starting at 5.53 p.m., Anna Melville had spent twelve minutes looking at the website for the Metropolitan Police.

Chapter 10

I didn't go back to the office after my trip to the City, though I'd planned to. I called Una Burt first.

'I don't think she was all that popular in the office. A bit self-absorbed and cold. She was more focused on work than interested in her colleagues.' Too late I realised I could have been describing DCI Burt herself, who was legendary for her lack of interest in other people's lives, unless they were dead. If she noticed, she didn't mention it.

'Sounds quite different to the others, then. Kirsty was gentle and sociable. Maxine was reclusive and immature.'

'Anna was stuck-up and self-centred. Mind you, none of them was having much luck with men.'

'Don't assume that's why they let him in,' she said sharply. 'Everyone in that room this morning thought they were desperate old maids, but it's got us nowhere with this investigation so far. Think of the other things they had in common.'

Desperate old maids . . . I wondered if this was all a bit too close to home for the chief inspector, who was single and had apparently been so for ever. I felt I was letting her down even by just thinking that. There were plenty of police officers her age who were unmarried but it wasn't worthy of comment if they were men.

Besides, the victims had more in common with me than with Burt. I was their age, more or less. I could have walked into Kirsty's place and set up home without changing a thing, from what I'd seen in the crime-scene pictures. Usually the crime scenes I visited were the places no one wants to go – the festering one-bed flats in bleak, poverty-stricken areas, the sad, dated homes of forgotten pensioners, the back alleys and abandoned buildings and bits of secluded waste ground where bodies were dumped. Murder was a great leveller and I had been to lavish, multi-million-pound properties as well as the dives where you didn't want to touch anything, where you knew if you sat down you'd stand up with fleas. But I had never been so conscious of the hair's-breadth difference between me and the victims as on this case. I was luckier, and hopefully wiser, and I was very definitely not single any more, but I didn't have to work too hard to know these girls.

'Did you get the results from the technical examination? Did they find anything on Anna's iPad?'

'It was wiped. The history was cleared.' I could hear the frustration she was feeling. 'They're trying to retrieve data from it but they told me there wasn't likely to be much. It was almost new, apparently.'

'Do you think it was the killer who cleared the history?'

'We can't speculate about that. We'll never know.'

I felt reproved. She was right, of course. Unless we found the murderer and he was cooperative enough to tell us if he'd done it. 'It could have been Anna. It was her habit to clear it at the end of a session. Her computer at work was the same.'

'Was it? Damn.'

'Yes, but it's still worth recovering and examining. I've told Anna's colleagues not to touch it until someone comes to collect it. Because guess what Anna had been looking at before she died.'

Burt listened as I outlined what I had found, the trail that led to the Met website. Without seeing her face I couldn't even guess what she thought about it. There was something massive about her silence, something more than concentration. But her only comment when I had finished was, 'Where are you going now?'

'Back to the office. I've got some paperwork to do, and—'

'What about following up those leads in Lewisham? The book club and support groups.'

'Oh,' I said lamely. 'I could.'

'It may seem insignificant to you but it's the sort of legwork that can make a case. And it was your idea.'

'No, I think it's definitely worthwhile. It's just that I wasn't planning—'

'You might think it's not time-sensitive given that Kirsty has been dead for almost a year, but we have an active serial killer at work in the city and I don't need to remind you that the intervals between murders are getting shorter. Make no mistake about it, this needs a prompt response.'

'Yes. Of course. I understand that. But I thought it was a bit of a long shot.'

'This late in the day, they're all long shots.' Burt sounded tired. 'Get it done. And Maeve?'

'Yep.'

'I thought the others did a good job, from their presentation, even though they didn't make this particular connection. They were thorough. Make sure you don't tread on any toes while you're on their patch.'

I rolled my eyes. Being lectured on politeness by Una Burt was like taking make-up advice from Barbara Cartland. 'I'll keep it in mind. But I think if we have problems with anyone it will be Andy Bradbury.'

'Why do you say that?'

Because he's a dickhead. 'Because he's recently promoted and he seemed defensive at the meeting earlier.'

'So he did. Was he like that when you met him before?'

'Pretty much.'

She made a noise that after a moment of sheer disbelief I identified as a chuckle. 'Rest assured I will take great

pleasure in going through his work on this case and finding out what he has done wrong.'

'Without treading on his toes.'

'Some toes deserve it.' She hung up without saying
goodbye.

I'd armed myself with a few pictures of Kirsty Campbell,
given that she'd been dead for nine months, but I didn't
need to remind anyone in Blackheath about her. The article
in the evening paper had brought her right to the forefront
of most people's minds. Anna's death had led the news all
day and there was a strange, unseemly excitement in the
air, a kind of suppressed thrill that something was actually
happening, right there and then, something potentially
historic in a Jack the Ripper sort of way. I was too close to
the reality of violent death to see why it was exciting.

I walked from the station to the flat where she'd died,
following in her footsteps, seeing what she had seen. More
than ever I found myself identifying with her as I walked
along the busy main street and into the quieter residen-
tial roads where the lights were starting to come on in the
houses. I recognised the block of flats from some way off
and walked around the outside of the building. There was
no value in demanding to see the flat where she'd died.
I was too late to see it as she'd arranged it, and I had the
crime-scene photos to study. But I noted that Kirsty's flat
was at the front, and not overlooked. The security on the
building wasn't all that impressive either. I wondered if the
killer had started with where she lived when he was thinking of choosing a victim. It had been pretty much perfect
for his purposes.

I made some progress once I started talking to people,
finding the place where she had her dry-cleaning done and
the shop where she always bought the paper on Saturdays.
A smart, newly painted pub with squashy leather sofas
and a huge collection of board games was the venue for

the knitting club Kirsty had briefly attended, though the landlord couldn't remember her.

'We get so many in, you see.' He eyed me, as much on edge as if I was going to blame him for what had happened, and take away his licence.

'Do you have any other groups that meet here?'

'Rugby club on a Tuesday night. Bitching Stitching on Wednesday, which is the quilting group – their name for it, not mine,' he said, noticing the look on my face. 'Knitwits is on Mondays. Thursday to Sunday we're too busy to spare the space.'

'No book clubs?'

He shook his head. 'The library might.'

I thanked him but not effusively. Derwent would have said something sarcastic to him about joining the Met with brilliant ideas of that sort. He hadn't been much help. Kirsty was a pretty, nicely spoken woman and it bothered me that he couldn't recall her, probably because she'd been gentle and polite and hadn't made a fuss about anything.

Maybe that was what the victims had in common, I thought, walking on down the street as a double-decker bus tore past, swaying as it went, apparently seconds from overturning. They were the kind of women who could be overlooked, despite being conventionally attractive and reasonably successful. They were introverts and being singled out for attention was such a change for them it made them drop their guard. Because they had to have done that to let their killer in. I couldn't escape the conclusion that he'd made them trust him.

Or they were too scared to do anything but follow his orders. I shivered, imagining myself in their shoes. I couldn't fool myself that they had been anything other than terrified at the end, when they knew they had no way out. I'd have bargained, and fought, and begged, and done anything at all to save my life, but maybe they had done all that and more. Or maybe they had abandoned hope in the face of implacable evil. Only the killer knew now.

At some level I had decided I would find what I was looking for at the library, so it was a disappointment to discover that there wasn't a book group there, at least not for young women. They had a group for the pensioners, and a club for schoolchildren.

'We've been forced to reduce our opening hours to save money so we can't offer any evening sessions,' the librarian explained. 'That means we're not really able to reach the younger professionals who might be interested in that sort of thing.'

'Do you know if there is a book group locally? The sort of place Kirsty might have wanted to go?'

The librarian tilted his head to one side. He seemed fearsomely competent, and had been brisk in dealing with the large queue. I was holding things up. There were about twenty people standing behind me, and it was five minutes to closing time. The library was intensely hot, too, and I wished I'd taken off my coat when I went in.

'I'm not aware of a book group. Leave me your contact details though, and I'll check with my colleagues.'

'What about a support group? For bereavement, or eating disorders, or—'

He was shaking his head.

I gave him my card and went to stand outside, the cool air a pleasant shock after the tropical heat. They could save on some costs if they turned the thermostat down, I thought. I was tired, and frustrated. This whole trip had been a huge waste of time.

'Excuse me. Sorry. I was in the queue behind you and I couldn't help overhearing . . .' The girl was standing about two feet away from me and I hadn't noticed her at all. She was wearing a hand-knitted scarf with long tassels, and a matching hat that she had pulled down over her eyebrows. 'You're the police, aren't you?'

'That's right.'

'Investigating Kirsty Campbell's death?'

'Among others.'

'I heard about the others. That one in Tottenham, today.' She plaited the tassels and undid them again, her fingers flying. She was tall and slender, slightly ungainly, and young in a way that had nothing to do with her actual age.

'Can I help you with something?' I didn't sound encouraging. She would want advice on staying safe, reassurance that there was no reason to be afraid. My patience for that sort of thing was not infinite, and I was tired.

'I knew her. Kirsty.'

'Really?'

She nodded. 'From church.'

I tried to remember if we'd known Kirsty was religious. 'I didn't know Kirsty went to church.'

'She didn't. Not really. Neither do I. But the vicar at St Mary's did a series of lectures that we both went to.'

'What were the lectures about?'

'Personal empowerment.' She flushed a little. 'It was about taking control of your life. Not depending on anyone else for fulfilment. I think the idea was that we were supposed to start depending on Jesus or something, but that didn't really happen.'

She'd just gone from potential nuisance to potential lead, and I felt my heart rate pick up. 'What did you say your name was?'

'I didn't. I'm Ruth Johnson. But everyone calls me Jonty.'

'Has anyone spoken to you about your friendship with Kirsty since she died? Anyone from the police, I mean?'

'No.' She squirmed. 'I didn't think anyone would be interested. We weren't friends really. I mean, I only met her three times.'

'It all helps. Especially if there's something that's been bothering you.'

'Well. Maybe. I don't know. It's probably not important.'

I'll be the judge of that. 'Look, is there anywhere around here that we could talk?'

'Bon Café is nice.'

I didn't care about nice. I cared about whatever Jonty Johnson had been suppressing for nine months because she didn't have the nerve or the notion to go into the police station and ask to speak to whoever was handling Kirsty Campbell's murder investigation. I wasn't going to let her out of my sight until I'd found out what it was.

Bon Café turned out to be devoted to ultra-organic vegetarian food – pulses and quinoa – and was painted green in a fairly literal-minded way. I sat on a bench that was just the wrong height for me and backless so I couldn't even slouch. The muddy liquid they called coffee came in a thick earthenware mug that was rough to the touch and quite startlingly unpleasant to drink out of.

Jonty had chosen a herbal tea that came in a glass, which was an improvement on what I had. It smelled, however, like tomcats' bottoms. That didn't seem to put her off. If it was the reason her skin glowed, it would almost be worth drinking it, because she had the radiance of someone who habitually washed in melted snow. Under the hat she had thick fair hair that she'd plaited and twisted and attached to her head somehow. She had narrow eyes that she'd made smaller with black liner, and her eyebrows were straight and thick. Her teeth were very white, and small, and spaced out like milk teeth. I was aware of the guy behind the counter staring across at her, admiring the effect. Jonty herself seemed oblivious. She was looking everywhere but at me, fidgeting in her seat, checking her phone and her watch. Now that we were indoors and face to face, her confessional urge had sputtered and died. I started with an easy one.

'Tell me about the lectures.'

'Um – it was a three-week programme. Once a week,

fifty minutes long. Non-denominational, but I think you were supposed to want to go on to do the Alpha Course and become a fully fledged Christian.'

'When was it?'

'January. It started right after Christmas. For everyone who'd resolved to get their lives in order, I suppose.' She sounded ironic.

'Was that why you did it?'

'Oh yeah. Time to stand on my own two feet and stop depending on other people. My parents, specifically. I needed to cut the apron strings.'

I thought of my own parents with a qualm. My life choices were so clearly not what they had wanted for me, from my job to my unmarried status. I went my own way and I made my own decisions, but basically I was still trying to make it up to them that I hadn't done what they expected. I was still hoping that they might one day be proud of me. Most of my friends didn't seem to have this problem. I had a feeling it was an Irish thing.

'Did you manage it?'

'Not really. My parents are very controlling. They're rich. They bought my flat. I just can't afford to walk away from them yet.'

'What job do you do?'

'I'm a singer. I write songs for other people too.' She sipped her tea, then anticipated my next question. 'I don't make a living out of it or anything. I keep going because it's what I want to do.'

'How did you find out about the lectures?'

'I saw the course advertised outside the church and it just seemed like it might be interesting, you know? It was one of those "Keep Calm" posters, like the wartime information ones.' She laughed a little. 'Typical – they're not exactly trendsetting at that church. Like, those posters are so overplayed. But this one was "Keep Calm and Find Happiness". And then underneath it said, "You can be everything you need". It just spoke to me. I was feeling really frazzled and stressed out and down and like I should just give up, and all I wanted was to take a moment for myself. I wanted to find myself without having to go off and travel the Far East for a year.' The tea slopped over the side of her glass as she turned it on the saucer. 'Again, I mean. Anyway, it was free.'

'How many people signed up?'

'About fifteen. There was this little circle of chairs and I was just so embarrassed to even be there that I sat down in the first one I got to and it happened to be beside Kirsty.'

'And the two of you got talking?'

'Not then. Afterwards. We came out and I didn't feel like going home straight away, because all these ideas were just buzzing around in my head and I didn't want to be on my own staring at the walls, you know? And I suppose Kirsty felt the same way because she came over and asked if I wanted to get a drink and talk about why we were there and what we wanted to get out of it.'

'What did Kirsty want?'

'She was trying to put her life back together after breaking up with her fiancé.' Jonty sighed. 'It was really hard on her. She was so brave to break it off. They were all involved in planning the wedding and inside she was just like . . .' She dragged her fingers down her cheeks, her mouth open in a silent scream.

'Why?'

'She didn't love him enough, she said. She felt smothered. She felt like he was going to run her life for her, or try to. It made her uncomfortable. She wanted to be on her own for a while to work out what she actually wanted to do.'

I'd had that smothering sensation myself. I knew exactly the chord of guilt, frustration and resentment that it struck, and it was the death knell for relationships. Rob was very careful to back off when he noticed I was getting claustrophobic. He was almost too good at backing off. Hence the paranoia.

I dragged my mind back to Kirsty. 'So, she wanted to be on her own. She wasn't trying to meet men.'

'No. Well, not then.' Jonty looked down at her tea. 'This is disgusting. I wonder if it would be better with sugar.'

She reached to take a packet from the jar on the table and I put out my hand and stopped her. 'Okay, firstly, no, it wouldn't help. Secondly, what do you mean by "not then"?'

'Because of the guy.'

'What guy?' I was leaning forward.

'The guy she said she was meeting the last time I saw her.' Jonty drew one leg up onto the chair and retied the laces on her Doc Marten. I bit the inside of my cheek hard enough to taste blood, fighting the urge to tell her to hurry up. 'The third week she couldn't come for a drink. She said she had to meet someone afterwards, and she was really sorry but it was the only day he could do.'

'A date?'

'I don't think so. I said "ooooh", you know, as you do, when she said she had to meet someone and she was really short with me. She just said, "Not like that" and then she gave me her number and told me to give her a call if I was at a loose end and wanted to meet up. Look.' She flicked through her contacts until she came to Kirsty's name and showed it to me, like a child proud of her homework.

'When was this?'

'Towards the end of January. The twenty-sixth.'

'And she died—'

'On the thirtieth.' Jonty nodded. 'I saw it in the paper. I couldn't get my head around it. I almost texted her – can you believe that? Even though I knew she was dead? Crazy.'

'It's not that unusual. People call their loved ones' phones after they're gone. They leave messages for them to say the things they didn't get the chance to say.'

'That makes me feel a bit better. I thought I was mental.'
She gave me a rueful grin.

'Can we get back to the man? Had she mentioned him
before?'

'Definitely not.'

'Did you see him? Did she tell you anything about him?
A name? How they met?' I made myself stop. I could see
the barrage of questions was confusing her.

'I didn't see him. She was meeting him somewhere else.
She didn't tell me why they were meeting but it seemed
more like something she had to do than something she was
excited by. Like he was a chimney sweep or a plumber or
something and she had to let him in.'

'To her flat?'

'I don't know.' Jonty frowned. 'That was just the impression I had. When she said he couldn't do any other night
she sounded a bit irritated but business-like.'

The flats' management company was supposed to sort
out tradesmen for the tenants. I made a note to check with
them to see if she had made any complaints in the couple
of months before her death.

'And you're sure she didn't use a name.'

'She might have, but I'm crap with names.' Jonty gave
a tiny, panicky laugh, knowing that it was a terrible name
to have forgotten. 'It was something short and simple. Not
a foreign name. Geoff or John or something. But it wasn't
Geoff or John.'

I wrote them down anyway. Not foreign, one syllable,
possibly with a 'J' sound. 'Jack. James. Jim.'

'None of those.' She shook her head. 'I can't remember.
I've tried and tried.'

'It doesn't matter.' I succeeded in keeping the frustration
out of my voice. Mostly. 'One of those things. Just let me
know if it comes back to you. You've been really helpful.'

'Have I?' She looked piteous. 'I wanted to help but I
thought it would just be a waste of everyone's time.'

'Far from it,' I said. 'Would you be willing to give a statement to the local detectives who investigated Kirsty's death?'

'I don't mind.' She looked terrified.

'They're nice. Nothing to be frightened of. Let me call and check when they'd like to see you.' I rang Groves, who was pleased to hear from me but went quiet when I explained what I'd found out. He wanted to speak to Jonty immediately, he said. At the police station, if she could present herself there. He'd try not to keep her too long.

I passed it on to Jonty who agreed without any difficulty, being the good girl she was. Her eyes were troubled, though, and she drained her glass of tea without apparently remembering it was disgusting.

She was winding her scarf around her neck again in long, misshapen loops when she asked the question I'd been dreading.

'Do you think the man she mentioned was the one who – you know.'

'Killed her?'

A nod.

Yes. 'I don't know.'

She swallowed. 'Do you think I should have come forward earlier? When they were appealing for witnesses?'

'You're not responsible,' I said, seeing where this was going. 'You didn't make him kill anyone else. You could have come forward earlier, but I don't think it would have made any difference.'

In the overall scheme of things, a small lie sometimes made more sense than the truth. It might have made a huge difference, but she didn't need to know that.

Chapter 11

It was late by the time I got back to my desk, getting on for nine. The office was emptying out after a busy day. It smelled stale, despite the air conditioning, and the large windows were filled with dark skies and bright lights like sequins on velvet. Nightfall changed the atmosphere in the office. The desk lamps – so much better than fluorescent overhead lighting – marooned each of us who remained on our own individual island, and the noise level had dropped to a murmur of a few phone conversations, most of them winding up.

The door to Godley's office stood open. His desk was vacant, but his coat still hung on its hook and his computer was on. Una Burt's desk was similarly unoccupied, and she wasn't answering her mobile. I hoped I would see them before I left for the day, so I could share what I'd found out in Lewisham. There was no reason to dash home, anyway. I had had the best of intentions about how I would live while Rob was away: eating properly, going to bed early, painting my nails and writing emails to friends I hadn't seen in ages, catching up on reading books that had sat beside my bed for months. It was the first day and already I could tell my intentions were going to fall by the wayside. I would eat when I could and work as much as was humanly possible and the books would remain unread.

Too bad. There were more important things than manicures.

Being out of the office all day meant that I had to deal with what seemed like thousands of emails. I skimmed through them, trying to keep track of cases that had no press attention, no clamour for a result. Princess Gordon's death had passed almost unnoticed, and not just because it had been solved so quickly. There was no media interest in a young black woman being beaten to death by her partner, even if she had been pregnant. But she was just as dead as the Gentleman Killer's victims.

DS Burns had come up trumps with the number for Method Management, the company that looked after Kirsty Campbell's apartment building. I was gratified to discover that they had an emergency hotline number and I rang them straight away, even as I was reading through the rest of my emails, to ask about Kirsty's property. I explained who I was to the bored-sounding man who answered the phone.

'Is it possible to check if Kirsty had any issues with her flat, or the building? Any complaints?'

'In what period?'

'Let's start with December and January.'

'I'll have to look it up. Do you want me to call you back?'

'I'll hold on.'

He put the phone down beside his keyboard and I listened to the tapping, hoping he was doing what I'd asked rather than updating his Facebook status.

'I've just got to go and check something.' He didn't wait for me to reply, dropping the phone again with a clatter. His chair squeaked as he pushed it away from his desk and I imagined him walking across the office, giving him a crumpled white shirt that was pulling out of the waistband of wrinkled trousers and scuffed shoes. My version of him needed a haircut and had a weakness for pies. He was probably whippet thin and bandbox neat in real life.

While I waited I dealt with the remaining emails. Just as I was getting to the end, a new one popped into my inbox. It was from James Peake, the DS on the Maxine Willoughby case, which in itself wasn't that odd; I had given him my card when I was distributing them to all and sundry after the meeting. The bit that made my heart sink was the subject line. *Drink?*

'You still there?'

'Yep,' I said, dragging my mind back to Kirsty.

'Just to say, I've had to speak to my boss about releasing this information and he wants me to make sure you realise that we aren't liable for anything.' *Anyfing.*

'That's not why I'm ringing. I just want to know her concerns.' I wiggled my pen between my fingers, tapping the end on the desk. The tapping was getting faster the longer he delayed.

'He wants to speak to you.'

'Fine. Give me his number.' I would speak to anyone if they could just tell me something helpful.

The phone didn't even ring before he picked up with a sharp-sounding 'Hello?'

'This is Detective Constable Maeve Kerrigan.'

'I'm Kevin Montrose, the owner of Method Management.'

Good for you. 'I'm investigating the murder of Kirsty Campbell.'

'So I'm told. Just so you know, there was no damage to the property and no sign of forced entry.' He sounded anxious as well as sharp. Something was up.

'I'm aware of the lack of damage.'

'There was going to be an investigation of Miss Campbell's concerns and we were actively engaged in organising that at the time she died.'

'I see. And what were those concerns?'

'According to the file, Miss Campbell raised some issues about the quality of the locks used on the external doors and the internal front doors in the building. She was also concerned about the window locks and the provision for escape from the property in the event of a fire. Obviously we are very careful to maintain smoke alarms and carbon monoxide monitors in the properties we manage, as I informed her.'

'When did she contact you about this?'

'Twenty-seven one.'

It took me a second. 'The twenty-seventh of January? Three days before she died?'

'I believe so.'

'Was there anything else?'

'She said she had been advised we should have CCTV fitted on the outside of the property, to cover the front and rear exits and the car park area. There is a bike rack at the flats too and she was worried about bikes being stolen from there. I told her a determined thief won't be put off by locks or CCTV but she wasn't impressed.' He gave a thin laugh. 'And she wanted us to install a video entryphone so the residents could see who they were buzzing in to the building.'

'That's recommended on the Metropolitan Police website.'

'Well, they can come up with the money, then. I told her it would cost a fortune and I also told her she'd have no chance of persuading everyone else in the building to pay their share. The landlords don't want to be bothered with that sort of thing and the owner-occupiers have enough to worry about with the basic charges.' He sounded smug as he said it, and since his company set the charges, I could see why he might.

'Anything else?'

'Letterbox shields on the back of the door to stop people fishing through the letterbox. Security lighting outside. And she wanted the doorframe reinforced on her flat.'

'It sounds as if she was desperately concerned about her security.'

'Something had made her aware of potential security issues.' Montrose's version was a much blander, safer one than mine.

'Did you speak to her yourself?'

'The call was transferred to me at Miss Campbell's request.'

'How did she seem? Was she upset?'

'No. It wasn't an unpleasant call. She was calm. It was as if someone had given her a list and she was just working through it. She didn't seem to know or care if it would be expensive to make those changes.'

'Maybe she thought it was worth any money to be safe in her own home,' I said. 'But she wasn't safe. And you had no intention of making any of the changes she requested.'

'That's not so. We listed them as I've just proved since it was all in the file, and we were working on a costing when her body was found.'

'Do you have the costing on file?'

'I think we didn't complete it. Under the circumstances—'

'I would have thought the circumstances would have made it more urgent, not less.' *And it's 'in the circumstances', you greasy little twerp.* 'I was at the flats today, Mr Montrose. Do you know what I saw? No CCTV. No security lighting. No video intercom at the front door. I didn't examine the locks but I bet they're the same ones that were in use when Kirsty Campbell was alive.'

His silence told me I was right.

'If you were taking her seriously, you would have gone ahead with the changes the tenants agreed to make. You would have done a proper costing and circulated it to all the residents and it is possible that not all of the security measures would have been adopted but some of them would have gone ahead. You heard she was dead and as far as you were concerned the problem had gone away.'

'She didn't die because the locks weren't adequate,' he blustered. 'There was no sign of a break-in at the address.

We were in close contact with the officers who were investigating the murder back in January and they were absolutely clear that there was no damage to the building, the locks, the doors or the windows.'

'What about the fact that the front door lock was broken?'

'What about it?'

'That had been reported to you, hadn't it? Not just by Kirsty. By the other residents. You'd had complaints, I gather, before the murder.'

'A couple.'

'When was the first one logged?'

'Four days before the murder.'

'Four days,' I repeated. 'And you hadn't got it repaired.'

'We were bringing in a technician.'

'From where? China? While the door was broken, the tenants were at risk of burglary or worse. And Kirsty *died*.' My voice had risen and I glanced around, suddenly self-conscious. The room had emptied out while I was talking. With the exception of the new detective, Dave Kemp, I was on my own. 'What was the hold-up?'

'I'm not sure.'

'Pretty standard, was it?'

'I'm not sure I should answer that.'

'This isn't a civil court, Mr Montrose, and you're not in the witness box. I'm just trying to find out the facts. I'm not going to sue you on Kirsty's behalf.'

'There are no grounds for suing us.' The reply came too quickly. I really doubted Kevin Montrose slept well at night.

'Did Kirsty mention being afraid of anyone or anything in particular?'

'No.'

'Did she mention where she'd got this list of security measures?'

'No.'

'Did she mention anyone else at all? Other residents?

Friends? A boyfriend?'

'No. The police asked me all this at the time.'

'Well, I'm asking you about it again.'

'Is that because of the other girls?'

I didn't answer him straight away, wondering how to play it, and he went on.

'I saw it in the paper. Now there are three of them. Terrible, isn't it? You know, you're giving me shit about not having sorted out the security measures, but it seems to me the Met are more at fault than anyone.' He was angry, and getting more confident by the second. 'If you'd caught him back in January, two women would be alive who aren't now. That's a lot worse than being a bit slack about fixing a door.' He hung up almost before he'd finished saying 'door', afraid that I'd find some way of hitting back so he wouldn't get the last word.

'Pillock,' I said under my breath anyway and put the phone down so I could click on James Peake's email. I'd been putting it off while I was on the phone but I hadn't forgotten it; I'd seen it out of the corner of my eye the whole time I was enduring my conversation with Kevin Montrose. It didn't take long to read it.

> *Thought we should meet up to discuss the case.*
> *Might be useful to talk about it one-to-one.*
> *JP*

I felt less tense. Just a friendly invitation to go for a drink. And perhaps an indication that he felt as enthusiastic about Andy Bradbury as I did. Maybe there was something he wanted me to know about how the new inspector had been handling the investigation and he couldn't say so directly on his work email. He'd never grass Bradbury up to a senior officer like Una Burt or God himself, no matter how annoying Bradbury was to work for. I was low enough to the bottom of the pole to be unthreatening, yet I could pass the word on to the bosses that Bradbury was out of his depth. It all made perfect sense. I rattled off a reply suggesting that we meet the following night and leaving the venue up to him. It meant we would be meeting on a Saturday, which made me slightly uneasy, but I would be working all weekend and so would he. He would know it was strictly business.

I sent the email without another thought about it, except the vague relief that I wouldn't be left to my own company. So much for wanting to enjoy spending time alone. I checked my phone again, hoping for a message from Rob, but there was nothing. I'd had a text to say he'd arrived, but that was it so far. Punitive roaming charges meant he was unlikely to use his mobile. I couldn't help looking, though.

'What are you doing?'

I must have jumped a foot in the air. 'N–nothing.'

Derwent was standing directly behind my chair. I hadn't heard him coming; the carpet had made his footsteps completely silent. His face was shadowed, his expression equally dark, and I twisted awkwardly in my chair to keep him in view. He was looking at my desk, and the notes I had written while I was on the phone with Kevin Montrose. Kirsty's name straggled in capitals across the top of the page, and the rest was a tangle of dates and phrases. It made sense to me, but I doubted anyone else could follow it. Nonetheless, I pulled a file across the page to hide it from Derwent's view.

It was like snapping my fingers to wake a sleepwalker. His attention jumped to me, and his face hardened. 'Covering up your work? Afraid I'll copy you? Don't tell the teacher, will you?'

'What's up?' I said calmly, ignoring his tone. My heart was racing.

'I was going to ask you the same thing. You've been avoiding me. Screening my calls.'

'No, I haven't.'

He leaned across me and snatched my phone off the desk. 'Voicemail. No new messages, no saved messages.' He showed me. 'But I've called you eight times and left messages every time. That means you've been deleting them.'

'It was an oversight.'

'It was a big fucking mistake, I'll tell you that for nothing.' He leaned in and I could smell the doublemint chewing gum he liked, and something else that was sour underneath it, as if he hadn't eaten for a while. 'Don't ignore me.'

'I was busy. DCI Burt—'

'Don't give me that. Don't mention her name.' He was still leaning over me and now he knocked the file to one side so he could see my notebook again. 'Kirsty Campbell. The girl who died in Lewisham in January. Are we investigating this now?'

'*We* aren't.'

He straightened up as if I'd pushed him, staring down at me with surprise and enough hurt for me to feel sorry for him, and guilty, and unsure of myself.

'What are you saying? You are but I'm not, is that it?'

'The boss asked me to work with Burt on it. She's had me running around today. I didn't have time to call you.' And I hadn't wanted to face his anger. It was like standing at the door of a blast furnace. The heat of it was withering. He stared at me for what felt like endless seconds.

'Whose idea was it? Who cut me out?' He grabbed the arms of my chair and turned it around so he was right in my face. 'Who told you not to talk to me?'

'I did.'

I had never, ever been so pleased to hear Una Burt's voice. She was at the door to the office, quite far away, but there was something reassuringly calm about the way she said it.

'You.' Derwent had turned to see her but he was still

leaning towards me, his face inches from mine. I pressed my head back against the seat, trying to make more space between us.

'That's right. If you want to intimidate anyone, try me.' She stomped in and across to her desk, putting her handbag down on it with a thud. She wasn't even looking at Derwent any more. She'd turned her back on him, which was more than I'd risk when his eyes were so wild. At long last, he straightened up and I sucked air into aching lungs, realising I'd been unable to breathe while he was in my face. Behind her, Dave Kemp shrugged into his coat and headed for the door, careful not to look at any of us as he mumbled a goodbye. Sensible not to want a ringside seat. I wished I could do the same.

'What gave *you* the right to tell *her* not to answer my calls?'

'She's engaged with a sensitive case. It wouldn't be appropriate for her to speak to you about it.'

'I work with Kerrigan. We've got cases together. And I know all about sensitive cases. I know all about this one.'

'I'm sure you do.'

'What's that supposed to mean?' He came out from behind my desk and started moving towards her with that faltering sleepwalker step that told me he was blinded by rage. The red mist. A killing fury. Call it what you wanted, but it was controlling Derwent now, making the decisions for him. His rational mind had stepped out of the building, along with Una Burt's sense of danger, apparently. I stood up too, not really sure what I could do. Clobber him with something, maybe. I started to look around for a suitably heavy object and came up short. The stapler wasn't going to do it. I really wished I had my Asp, the extendable baton that I'd used to win friends and influence people while I was on the street. Twenty-one inches of steel tended to end arguments pretty quickly.

'Was this your idea?' Derwent demanded, still getting

closer to Una Burt, who was reading a file, completely unconcerned, as if nothing was going on. 'Was it your suggestion to shut me out?'

'It was Godley, if you must know.'

'No, it wasn't.' Derwent stopped.

'It was.' She twisted around to look at him and I felt even more uncomfortable when I saw how much she was enjoying this. 'He was quite clear about it. You're to be kept well away from this investigation.'

'Why?' The way he said it was almost plaintive.

'I think you know.'

I heard footsteps in the corridor and Godley appeared in the doorway. He stopped dead. 'What's going on?'

'Just finding out why I'm not in the gang, boss.' The bitterness in Derwent's voice was searing.

'It's not like that.'

'It is,' Derwent insisted.

'I have a small team working on this inquiry. I don't need another DI.'

'But you need Kerrigan. And *her*.' He pointed at Una Burt.

'And Harry Maitland. And one or two others.' Godley moved a little closer to Derwent. 'I've got officers coming out of my ears on this one. I don't want to take people like you away from the other cases that are going on. They matter too.'

'I've asked you. I've *begged* you.'

'Not going to happen. And you need to leave now, before you make a serious mistake.' Godley took another step forward. Because he was so civilised, I tended to overlook the fact that he was tall and physically fit. He'd done his time on the street too, back in the day. Standing near Derwent, his eyes watchful, Godley looked as if he could handle himself in a fight. I saw him shift his feet to adjust his balance and I suddenly felt sorry for Derwent – sorry and scared.

'It's all right,' I said, not really knowing what I was going to say next.

Godley's attention switched to me for a second before he focused again on Derwent. 'Go into my office, Maeve.'

'Sir, I hadn't returned DI Derwent's calls. I hadn't been communicating with him. He needed to talk to me about the Gordon case, urgently.' Derwent was staring at me as if he'd never seen me before or heard the name Gordon. 'I'm sorry,' I said, tailing off. *Please take the hint. Take the exit strategy I'm giving you. Everyone knows what I just said is total bullshit, but it means you can keep your dignity at the very least.*

Derwent looked back to Godley and it was as if something in him had died. Not the anger. More like his pride. His voice was dull. 'That's right. I needed to talk to her about the Gordon case. Follow things up.'

'Another time.' Godley's face was unreadable. 'Maeve, go and wait in my office and shut the door. DCI Burt and I want a word with you before you go home.'

I took the long way round rather than walk past Derwent. When I'd closed the door I sank into a chair, feeling like I wanted to cry. I didn't understand what was going on. I didn't know why Derwent was behaving that way, or what they were saying to him. Through a gap in the blinds I could see the three of them standing in a tight little triangle as Godley talked to Derwent. He was looking at the floor, not at the superintendent. While the boss was still speaking, Derwent turned and walked out of the room. Burt and Godley stood together, watching him go. By the time they turned back and started to walk towards the office, I was far away from the gap in the blinds, leafing through the newspaper from the day before as if I was completely engrossed. I doubted I was fooling anyone.

'Right, Maeve. Tell me about Anna's workplace. What did you find out?' Godley was aiming for a normal tone of voice but it came out too hearty, too honest and direct. *You can trust me . . .* Except, of course, I couldn't.

I explained again about the trail of cookies on her computer leading to the Met website. A meaningful look passed between Burt and Godley so quickly that I almost missed it. But I didn't.

'The tech guys have already recovered the computer. They're talking to the IT department at the office to see if there's any other record of what people have been browsing on their work computers,' Burt added.

'There's bound to be in a place like that, I should think.' Godley nodded. 'Good. What else? You went to Lewisham, didn't you? Anything new?'

'Nothing on the book club, but I did find out that Kirsty Campbell was planning to meet a man a few days before she died and she was worried about her home security.' I told them about meeting Jonty, and the conversation I'd had with Montrose.

'Do we think she was being stalked?' Burt's eyebrows were drawn down in a thick, bristling line. I found I couldn't quite look at her. No one had mentioned Derwent, but I couldn't get his shattered demeanour out of my mind.

'It's possible. But according to Montrose, she was calm on the phone.'

'Check with Groves. See if her friends and colleagues had picked up on anything. I'm sure they've asked the question already.'

'Even if they've done nothing else.' Burt sniffed. 'Maeve's been following up leads for half a day and she's already found out more than they have in nine months.'

'You're doing well,' Godley said to me, and I forced myself to smile. They were both watching me. They were both trying to see if I was on their side, I thought. I could play this game. I could cooperate and get another inch or two up the ladder.

I could lose my self-respect.

'About DI Derwent.'

Twin expressions that were the opposite of encouraging.

'I think it's time you told me what's going on.'

Silence.

'Okay then.' I stood up. 'See you tomorrow.'

'Where are you going?' Una Burt demanded.

I gave the pair of them my best sunshiny smile. 'If neither of you is prepared to start talking, I'll just have to go and ask him myself.'

Chapter 12

I'll say this for Godley and Burt: they were realists. They knew I wasn't joking and they knew the only thing they could use to stop me was the truth. If they'd been in my place, they'd have done the same. So they came clean.

Not, however, without a warning from Godley.

'There was a reason we were trying to keep this from you, Maeve. This sort of thing – you can't unknow it. You have been working with DI Derwent; you may have to work with him in the future. You must not reveal to him what you know, if he asks you about it. Can you do that?'

'I have quite a lot of practice at being discreet.' And let Godley take that however he pleased.

'It's vital that you keep this to yourself, as well. I don't want this being talked about. The more people discussing it, the more problems we're going to have.'

'I understand. And I don't gossip.'

'Everyone gossips,' Godley said flatly. 'This is the main reason why I'm keeping the team's involvement in the serial killer investigation to a minimum. I want to know exactly what's going on with it but I don't need everyone else to know about Josh. Do you understand?'

'Sort of.' I had remained standing by the door, but now I came back and sat down. 'I can't really say I understand when I don't know what the issue is.'

'It's pretty straightforward. When Josh was a teenager,

his girlfriend was murdered. He was the number-one suspect but he was never charged.'

'No evidence,' Una Burt chipped in. 'I've read the file.'

'He had an alibi.' Godley glared at her. 'There was no question of him being responsible for her death. It didn't stop him from being accepted when he applied to the Met, and they wouldn't have considered him for a moment if he was a potential murderer.'

'So you say.' She didn't sound convinced.

'I know you don't like him, but—' Godley seemed to remember I was there and broke off. 'Where was I?'

'Murder. His girlfriend.'

'Right. Well, there are some . . . similarities between the girlfriend's murder and the recent deaths.'

'Such as?'

'Angela Poole was strangled. Had her eyes gouged out. But it happened in her back garden, not her bedroom.' Burt's voice was matter-of-fact, even when she added the last detail, the one that made me wince. 'She was fifteen years old.'

'Did they get whoever did it?'

'No one was ever charged,' Godley said. 'And Josh has spent the last twenty years trying to find out who killed her.'

'So Derwent is obsessed with his dead girlfriend, and the case is superficially similar to the current killings.' I still wasn't seeing the problem.

'The killings aren't similar. They are identical in many respects,' Burt said.

'I didn't want Josh involved from the start,' Godley said. 'There's a good chance he'd say or do something inappropriate – you saw him just now. He's not himself.'

Burt snorted. 'I think that was the real him, Charlie.'

'I know him better than you do.'

'I'd rather not know him at all.'

They were bickering like an old married couple. I

cleared my throat. 'So is that it? That's the reason why he's not allowed to know what's going on? Why I'm not even allowed to *talk* to him?'

Godley looked down, not meeting my eyes. 'At the meeting today, there was speculation about the character of our killer. And about his job.'

'He could be a police officer. Or pretending to be one,' I added.

'It makes sense, doesn't it?'

'Yes, but it doesn't have to be Derwent.'

'Tell her about the profile,' Burt said.

'What profile?'

Godley started to leaf through his in tray. 'I had Dr Chen profile the killer a couple of weeks ago. Obviously she based it on the information we had, which was from two murders. It's worrying, Maeve.'

'I don't believe it. You're hanging Derwent out to dry because of a forensic psychologist's profile?' Forget diplomacy; I was outraged. God knows, I didn't like Derwent, but he was a committed police officer and loyal in his own way to those he chose to care about, which included Godley. Moreover, I didn't believe he could be responsible for the crime scene I'd seen that day. Killer was possible – cold-blooded was not.

'Just listen before you make up your mind,' Godley said, and started to read aloud. 'The subject is aged between thirty and forty-five and has a dominant personality. He is confident with women and probably works in a position of authority. He is single and lives alone. He is obsessive about detail and a perfectionist. He can be manipulative and has sadistic traits but he is controlled in his behaviour, able to suppress this aspect of his personality much of the time. He could have a military background or experience of being in a highly controlled environment such as a strict boarding school, young offenders' institution or prison. He is employed in a job where he has considerable personal freedom and may work for himself rather than a private company. He may have spent time outside the UK. He is well-spoken, middle-class and superficially attractive but he has serious sociopathic traits.'

I snorted. 'Derwent is an arsehole. That may not be what the psychologists would call him, but it's true. He's not a sociopath.'

'It's more common than you'd think. One per cent of the population, they estimate. No ability to empathise. No guilt about committing violent acts. No morality,' Burt said.

'Derwent is one of the most moral people I know.' By his own standards, obviously; he wasn't winning any prizes for equality campaigning.

'If he is a sociopath, he's an expert at disguising it,' Burt said. 'And you know very well he's bright enough to look up the traits that distinguish a sociopath so he can create the opposite impression. Weren't you listening, Maeve? Most of that profile might as well have his picture beside it.'

'I don't know that a profile is the best way to find a killer. I prefer to rely on the evidence. And there isn't any.'

'No, there isn't,' Godley said. 'But you see why I can't take the risk of letting him know too much. I shared my initial concerns with Una when Josh first raised the possible connection with Angela Poole's death—'

'And it was my idea to consider him a possible suspect,' she finished.

Godley winced. 'I don't like to suggest it's a possibility but I can't just defend him because I like him. I've got to keep it in mind. He's on leave for the next two weeks and I've warned him not to come near the office, or you, or anyone else who's working on the investigation.'

'So if he does approach you, tell us.' Burt ran her tongue over her upper lip and I turned away again, sickened at the look of anticipation on her face. She hated Derwent almost as much as he hated her. She must have noticed that I was upset. 'Look at what you've found out just today, Maeve, that points at Josh Derwent. Anna was looking at the Met website. Miss Johnson thought the man who Kirsty was meeting had a name that could have been Josh.'

'She didn't say that.'

'She suggested it.'

'I think you're seeing what you want to see. With respect,' I added, recalling that she was a DCI.

'He is obsessed with this case. He is obsessed with being involved in the investigation. Angela's murder changed the course of his life – you know his parents kicked him out, don't you, before he joined the army? It was because they were so ashamed of him. Imagine how they must have felt to cut him off like that. *They* thought he did it.'

'That's just speculation,' I protested.

'It's a theory but it makes sense.' Burt leaned towards me. 'I heard about what happened yesterday. Derwent lost his temper because he wanted to know about the investigation into Kirsty and Maxine's deaths. A few hours later, Anna was dead. Why then? Why so soon after Maxine? He was angry last night and today we have a murder. It's possible that he was angry in January, and in August, before the other two women died.'

'This is Derwent we're talking about,' I said. 'He's angry all the time.'

'Has he ever spoken to you about Angela?' Godley was watching me.

'We don't really have that kind of relationship.' By which I meant I would rather crawl over broken glass than talk to him about my private life and he didn't volunteer much about his, except stories about his sexual exploits that he knew would make me edgy. Sadistic tendencies? Well, maybe.

Godley pushed the file across the table towards me. 'This is a copy of the case file. Take it. Read it. Get familiar with the facts of the case and draw your own conclusions.'

'You cannot believe that he is a killer. You wouldn't have him anywhere near your team if that was the case.' I held Godley's gaze, challenging him.

'Honestly, I don't know what to think. He's been obsessed with this murder for as long as I've known him – talking about it, talking about her.'

'I've never noticed anything.' But even as I said it, I was remembering incidents from other cases – his prudishness, unusual among cops, where young girls were concerned. I remembered him throwing up at a crime scene where the victim was a teenager and blaming it on food poisoning. I remembered him being surprisingly tender when it came to persuading a troubled young woman not to set herself on fire. I remembered him saying he wasn't in touch with his parents, and not wanting to talk about it. I remembered him taking a positive and wistful delight in my so-close-it's-claustrophobic family. All of the times Derwent had surprised me, it seemed, could be traced back to this. He walked around with it like a shadow.

'You know Josh.' Godley's voice was quiet, the effect hypnotic. 'You know what he's like. He gets an idea in his head and he has to carry it through, no matter who he hurts or what goes wrong in the process. It could be him, Maeve. And even if it's not – and I hope and trust it's not – I can't have him rampaging through this case causing mayhem. Now read the file. Take it home. I don't want you to look at it in the office, for obvious reasons.'

I stood up and took it from Godley. The file was thin for a murder investigation, even one that had happened twenty years ago. Too thin to be a reason to sabotage someone's career.

'Give it back to me tomorrow. Come and see me at ten. You too, Una.'

I couldn't get out of Godley's office quickly enough. The file fitted in my shoulder bag but there wasn't any room for my notes from the current case. I switched off my computer and light, grabbed my coat and headed for the door. DCI Burt was back at her own desk and I was aware of her watching me as I strode across the room.

'You were the one who wanted to know.'

'I don't mind knowing.' *I mind the way you're enjoying all of this.*

'I'm glad you do know now. For your own sake. And safety.'

I laughed. 'I'm hardly in danger from Derwent.'

'You don't know that. Just be on your guard.'

She reminded me of the people who'd mobbed public hangings for entertainment in the nineteenth century. I wasn't yet on Derwent's side but I was also very far from being on Burt's. I would make up my own mind.

I set off down the stairs, hurrying, because I was madly curious to read about what had happened to Angela Poole. It was the best way to find out what had made Derwent the man he was. A normal, happy upbringing didn't produce anything as complicated as him. The building was hushed, so quiet I could hear the lift shuttling up and down beside the stairwell. My heels echoed on the tiled steps, a quick staccato. I was already planning my route home. I'd get a bus, I thought, at least some of the way. Changing methods of transport was a good way to check I wasn't being followed. Thank God for free travel, one of my perks as a police officer. I had my ID in my hand as I nodded goodnight to the security guard and pushed through the revolving door onto the street. Force of habit made me take the measure of the people passing, the cars on the street, the safety or otherwise of my surroundings. No vehicles I had seen before. No one giving me a second look. Nothing suspicious. I paused to wrap my scarf around my neck, tucking it in under the collar of the expensive coat that had been a Christmas present from the well-heeled boyfriend before

Rob. Behind me, the revolving door made a noise like a quick intake of breath as someone else emerged. I barely registered it.

So it was a shock to be grabbed from behind, one arm held in a way that suggested the person who had taken hold of me wasn't going to let go for anything – not tears, not swearing, not violence. For one brief moment I still considered trying all three. I had known who it was the moment he touched me, without even looking; it was surprise and outrage that made my heart pound, not fear. He steered me down the street, walking beside me, so close that most people wouldn't have noticed the way he was grasping my arm. It was expertly done.

He guided me down a one-way street not far from the office, one of the little forgotten lanes of Westminster, too narrow to allow cars to park on it, a cut-through for taxis, a breathing space between buildings more than a street in its own right. And it was deserted. We walked halfway along it before Derwent stopped. He was wearing his dark overcoat buttoned, the collar turned up as usual to ward off the sharp east wind that was ruffling his hair and whipping colour into his cheeks.

I found my voice. 'What the hell do you think you're doing?'

'Bit of kidnapping. Nothing fancy.'

'Get off.' I leaned away from him, or tried to. All the feminism in the world couldn't give me enough heft to move an inch.

'Where are you going in such a hurry?' He sounded jittery, the nerves masked by a horribly unsuccessful attempt at being jocular.

'Home.'

'Home,' he repeated. 'And what's this? Taking work with you? Little bit of extra reading?' He twanged the strap of my bag and I couldn't stop myself from clenching my arm against it.

'It's just some stuff I wanted to go through. You know I never have time to read the briefings properly.'

His eyes glittered in the streetlight, the half-smile less convincing by the minute. 'Was that why you stayed late, Kerrigan? Printing them off like a good girl? Showing Burt and Godley you're more dedicated than the average detective?'

'If you like.'

'It's not about what *I* like. *I* don't matter any more. You've got someone else to suck up to now.'

It wasn't the first time I'd been scared by Derwent, but I knew him better now than on the last occasion, and this time I was angry too. 'Spare me the self-pity. And I'm not like that. I've never tried to suck up to you or Chief Inspector Burt. You wish I would so you could enjoy upsetting me when you put me down.'

He looked surprised. 'Why would I want to put you down?'

'I wish I knew.' I took the opportunity to try to pull my arm away again, and failed. 'Look, what do you want?'

'To talk to you.'

'You don't have to behave like a thug.'

'I did try calling you.' His jaw was clenched.

'Is that what this is about? You want to have another go at me for not returning your calls? You really need to work on how you handle rejection.'

'Shut up.' A black cab turned into the street, its orange light on. The throaty diesel engine sounded loud in the narrow street. Derwent leaned into the road and held up his hand. The driver slid to a stop within inches of us and Derwent yanked open the door. He pushed me forward. 'In there.'

'I'm not going anywhere with you.' I meant it, too.

'Why not? Don't you trust me?'

I looked up at him, about to say something cutting, but the words faded out of my mind as I realised he actually meant it. His face was set, the strain showing around his eyes and his mouth.

'What do you want from me?' I asked, very quietly. 'What do you think *I* can do?'

'I don't know. It's just – I don't know what else to do.' No attitude. No belligerence. Derwent was actually asking me for help, in his own awkward way.

'Look, mate, what's the problem?' The driver was staring at us with frank interest. 'Everything all right, love? Want me to get this gentleman to leave you be?'

I was aware that Derwent was silent beside me, waiting for me to answer. 'No,' I said. 'It's fine.'

'Are you getting in or not, then? Only I've got a living to make.'

Derwent let go of me completely and stepped back. 'Up to you. Are you in or out?'

I would have liked the time to read the file first. I wasn't sure I could trust him. I'd been specifically warned against talking to him. The cautious approach would have been to put him off.

I'd never been a great one for caution.

I got into the cab.

Chapter 13

The address Derwent gave to the driver was in London Fields, which was actually not all that far from where I lived, though I didn't feel like starting a conversation about it. He sat on the fold-down seat opposite mine and looked at me with puppy-dog eyes.

'Do you understand why I had to do it this way?'

'Not really.'

'Godley warned me to stay away from you,' Derwent said.

'And yet here we are.'

'I want to know what's going on with the case.'

'I'm not supposed to talk to you about it.' I folded my arms over my bag. 'You know you're a suspect, don't you?'

He glanced over his shoulder at the back of the driver's head. 'Keep your voice down.'

'You targeted me because you thought you could bully me. You knew Burt and Godley would shut you down as soon as you started asking questions, but I'm not in a position to tell you to get stuffed.'

'Well, I'm on leave. At this moment I'm not your supervisor. You can say what you like as long as you're honest with me.'

'I'm not going to talk to you about it.'

'Because you agree with them.'

'I don't know enough about it yet.' I looked at him. He

filled most of the other side of the taxi, bracing himself with the grab handles as the driver took corners at speed. His shoulders were wide and he was all muscle; it took a lot of determination to move that kind of bulk over 26.2 miles, as he did for fun. He was ruthless in fighting the softening that came from too much time in cars eating junk food, his stomach flat and his jawline firm. And as he'd just proved, he was stronger than me. Physically, he was intimidating. His personality was controlling. He was unpredictable and brutal when it suited him. I was more wary of him than I wanted him to know. The possibility that he was a killer made my stomach flip every time I thought of it, as if I'd missed a step and was halfway to falling. I didn't believe it – I didn't want to believe it – but that didn't mean I was sure of him. The one thing I knew about the killer we were hunting was that he was good at making women trust him. So despite the way he was looking at me, I wasn't going to let my guard down.

'Why are we going to your place?'

'Because I didn't think you'd let me come to yours.'

'One hundred per cent correct.'

He grinned, a flash of the old Derwent appearing for a moment. 'I like feisty. You can keep that going.'

'You haven't even seen feisty, mate.'

The grin widened. 'I almost wish your pal Burt was here to see you. She thinks you're made of sugar and spice.'

'Did she stick up for me?'

'Told me to fuck off. In those words.' Derwent shook his head. 'I didn't think she had it in her. I thought she'd *never* had it in her.'

'Is that a sexual reference?' I pulled a face. 'I've changed my mind. I'm going home.'

'Don't.' The appeal was instant, unpremeditated.

'Una Burt was using me to get at you. She doesn't actually think I'm all that fragile.'

'What did I ever do to her?'

'Where should I start? You've been undermining her since she arrived on the team. The real question is what you've done to piss Godley off. I'd never have expected him to take his cue from her.'

'He's not pissed off with me. He's just trying to avoid trouble. And I'm trouble.' He looked lost, bereft. For someone so used to knowing their place in the wolf pack, being an outcast was torture. And he was still defending Godley, still loyal even if the superintendent wasn't. 'Look, I don't want to drop you in the shit because you're talking to me. I do need to know what's going on. They've told you about Angela, haven't they?'

I nodded.

'Right.' He took a deep breath and blew it out, looking away from me for a moment. Struggling for composure or pretending to be? 'Well, I've always wanted to find whoever did that to her. That's why I became a copper.'

'Then you should be working cold cases, not murder.'

'No one is ever going to reopen Angela's case.' He sounded definite. 'There was nothing to go on.'

'Forensics?'

'Not here.' He rubbed a hand over his face. 'I'll tell you about it, but not here. All you need to know is that this is the first chance there's been to find out what happened to her.'

'Do you really think it's the same killer?'

'I don't know. Because I've been shut out, haven't I?' He thumped the door with a fist and the driver slowed for a moment, looking back to see what had made the noise. 'It's driving me mad, Kerrigan. I've waited for this for twenty years. Everything I've done in my adult life has been about this. And now I can't get close enough to know what's going on.'

'It's not the same guy.'

'Why do you say that?'

'It's been twenty years. Why would the killer start again now?'

'He could have been in prison. He could have been abroad.'

'It could be someone else.'

'How can it be? I'm only going on what I've read in the paper and heard on the news, but it sounds like her. The eyes.' His voice broke on the last word and he cleared his throat, annoyed with himself. 'Look, if I was working this case, I'd want to compare it to the original murder. It feeds back to that. Crack Angela's case and you find this guy.'

'If there's a connection.'

'There has to be.' He held my gaze. He had everything staked on me. I could get him in a world of trouble if I told anyone what he'd done. I could get him fired.

'So you want me to tell you what I know.'

'Please. Like I said, I don't know what else to do.' He was hunched in his coat, the picture of misery.

I made up my mind. 'Okay. Here's the deal. You tell me about what happened to Angela. Everything.'

A nod.

'I'll share with you what I know about the other murders. But there's no guarantee I'll know what you want to know.'

'I appreciate that.'

'And this stays between us. Godley would have me back on Borough CID before I had time to say I was sorry if he found out about this.'

'Strictly off the books.' He was looking better already, the tension easing a little. Give Derwent what he wanted and he always cheered up.

I hoped like hell I was doing the right thing.

One of the compelling reasons for wanting to help Derwent was the chance to see where he lived. From the outside, it was a neat enough place, an end-of-terrace Victorian house in a street where most of the properties were in good condition. It wasn't the best in the street and it wasn't the worst.

He had his own front door to one side of the building, where there was a small hallway before a steep flight of stairs led up to his flat. Slinging his coat on a hook, he stood back to let me go up the stairs.

'You know where you're going,' I said, and stayed where I was. Now that we were alone together, I was seriously doubting I'd made the right decision. He was volatile, and I knew he had a temper, and the army had trained him to kill people. I couldn't make myself believe he was the Gentleman Killer but I was staking a lot on that, and I definitely didn't feel safe. It was too late to back out now, though, so I'd carry on, but I didn't want him behind me on the stairs. Nor did I want to take off my coat. He didn't comment, beyond flicking on the lights above us, and I followed him up the narrow stairs with no very clear idea of what to expect.

'Living room.' He pointed. 'Have a seat.'

It was small and not showy, but incredibly neat. He'd been in the army and it showed: everything was spotless. One sofa, one armchair. A vast television, all the better to watch endless hours of sport. A complicated music system. A coffee table with remote controls lined up like soldiers. No cushions or rugs; blinds at the windows rather than curtains. No ornaments. No pictures. It could have been bleak but it wasn't, somehow: it was comfortable and everything was chosen to be functional. The central heating was on and I felt my feet thawing for the first time that day. I perched on the edge of the sofa, my bag leaning against my legs, and went as far as loosening my scarf.

He came back into the room having shed his jacket and tie, rolling up his shirtsleeves. 'Drink?'

'This isn't a social occasion. You don't have to play the host.'

He shrugged. 'I'm not cooking dinner. But a drink's easy enough.'

'What have you got?'

'Beer.'

'And?'

'Whisky.'

'And?'

'Beer,' he repeated, giving me the widest version of his grin. In his own environment, Derwent was a lot calmer. I just hoped he wasn't going to take off any more clothes.

'Glass of water,' I said.

'Boring.'

'Again, not here to have fun.'

He came back with a bottle of beer for himself and a pint glass of water for me. The glass was wet and he fussed over finding a coaster.

'God forbid I should leave a mark on your coffee table.'

'Just try not to.' There was an edge to his voice. So we had got to the end of Derwent being nice, I diagnosed, and felt obscurely reassured. I even went as far as to take off my coat. I caught the whiff of alcohol on his breath as he moved the table closer to me. A shot of whisky in the kitchen to give him Dutch courage? Two shots? More?

'Where do you want to start?' He turned off the main light, leaving only a single lamp on beside me. He sat in the armchair. 'I feel like I'm talking to a therapist.'

'Have you ever spoken to one?'

He squirmed. 'A couple of times. When I was ordered to. Waste of time.'

I could imagine he was impervious to guidance from others, especially if they weren't superior officers. 'Why do you think they think you're a suspect?'

'Fucked if I know.' He drank from his beer.

'That's not an answer.'

'Because of what happened to Angela.'

'But you were never charged.'

'Exactly. I was just a bystander.' He put the bottle on a table beside him, placing it carefully on another coaster. 'They'd have stuck me on for it if they could. And I've no doubt they'd do the same now, for this, if they had the evidence.'

'Godley wouldn't.'

'Godley absolutely would. In a heartbeat.'

He was right, I thought. For the sake of solving the case. Or maybe he wanted to get rid of Derwent because he knew him better than anyone and might spot that Godley was on the take. You couldn't appeal to Derwent for mercy if you'd done wrong. He was a lot tougher than me. For a moment I considered telling him what I knew, tempted to share the burden with someone who would act on what I'd found out, but I stopped myself. Now was not the time to tell Derwent what I knew about Godley, if there ever was a time for that conversation.

'I can tell you this. It's fucking weird being a suspect again. Makes me feel like I'm seventeen. And not in a good way.' He tried for a laugh but it didn't quite work.

I sat back on the sofa. 'Okay. Tell me about the last time.'

'Where do I start?'

'Tell me about Angela,' I said patiently. 'Whatever you can remember.'

'I remember everything.'

'Then tell me everything.'

Rather to my surprise, he did just that.

In the summer of 1992, Angela Poole was fifteen. If anyone had ever deserved the name Angela, it was her, because she was as close as you could get to an angel on earth. She had heavy, honey-blonde hair and eyes the colour of a summer sky. She was small, and slim, and giggly. She wasn't the best academically but she wasn't stupid either, and she worked hard. She was a good girl, a sweet girl, and the only thing she ever lied to her parents about was her boyfriend.

*

'Me, obviously.' Derwent looked sheepish.

'Bad influence,' I commented.

'Always.'

Everyone in Bromley knew who Josh Derwent was. He was a troublemaker, cheeky – a cocky little shit. He was always hanging out around the shops giving backchat to anyone who tried to tell him what to do. He went to school because he liked it and he was bright enough to be top of the class or thereabouts without making too much effort. He liked that he never got grief for being a swot because he was good at football – good enough to have a trial for Arsenal's youth team.

'Which didn't go anywhere, as you might have noticed.'

'Imagine if you'd become a footballer instead of a copper. This would be a mansion.'

'And I'd be retired by now.'

'But your knees would be knackered. No marathons for you.'

He raised an eyebrow. 'I'd survive.'

How Josh had persuaded Angela to go out with him was no mystery. He was best mates with her brother Shane, and Angela had worshipped him for years. He was good-looking, funny and good at fighting. She was not the only girl who wanted him to notice her, but she was special. He'd watched her grow up without thinking anything of it – she was just a kid – until suddenly the day came when she wasn't a kid any more. She walked into a room wearing tight jeans and a clinging top and he just about lost his mind. Couldn't speak. Couldn't think. He spent a year trying to convince himself she was too young for him, too sweet, too innocent, but no matter how many other girls he snogged, even when he was allowed to play with their tits, even if he was allowed the confusing and exciting treat of fingering them, he couldn't stop thinking about her.

'This is so romantic.'

'This is how seventeen-year-old boys think. I'm sure you encountered your share of them, Kerrigan.'

'I wasn't allowed to know that sort of boy.'

'Neither was Angela.'

Shane and Josh hung around with Vinny Naylor, and Vinny's sister Claire. Vinny was the wise one, the one who called a halt when things were going too far. He had a good head on his shoulders and a genius for fixing things that were broken. Claire was a tomboy, one of the lads. Flat as a board, hard as nails. She and Vinny were born eleven months apart and did everything together, always; if Vinny was in the gang, so was Claire. Shane wasn't all that thrilled about Angela coming along too, but there wasn't much he could do about it. Josh was the one who called the shots. Shane went as far as warning him not to take advantage of his sister, and Josh thumped him for suggesting she might be prepared to have sex with him.

'But you were hoping she would.'

'I wasn't trying to persuade her,' Derwent snapped. 'Fuck, I had this at the time. I didn't want to corrupt her. I was in love with her. I wanted to wait. She was the one who—' He broke off. 'I'm getting ahead of myself.'

'Get on with it.'

All that summer, during the long days when they weren't at school, the five of them wandered around getting into trouble, having a laugh. During the nights, Angela and Josh spent every moment they could together, aching for each other. They had no money and nowhere to go. Josh had a part-time job washing dishes in a café in town. The only reason he kept it was because the owner was mates with his mum and he didn't dare play up too much. The only reason he wanted it was to have enough cash to take Angela out now and then, to the cinema or into London to wander around. They couldn't go to a pub because even if Josh could pass for over eighteen, Angela didn't have a hope of fooling anyone. They couldn't go to Josh's house because his mum didn't approve of him having a serious girlfriend at his age and she'd have flayed him alive if she thought they were even thinking about kissing, let alone having sex. Then there was Josh's little sister, Naomi. Five years younger, she was a pain in the balls. She never left him alone when he was at home, and when he wasn't there, she was always in his stuff. He got in trouble for shouting at her too. They couldn't go to Angela's because Shane would be there, glaring at him. Besides, Angela's parents weren't all that keen on him as a mate for Shane, let alone a boyfriend for their beautiful daughter. Claire and Vinny were two of the eight children in the Naylor family.

'They were Catholics, as you might imagine. Irish background. Same as you.'

'I'm one of two,' I pointed out.

'So your mum's frigid or your dad couldn't get it up more than twice. That wasn't Mr Naylor's problem.'

'It sounds more like Mrs Naylor's problem. Eight pregnancies is hard work.'

'More that that. She had hundreds of miscarriages too. It was a four-bedroom house so God knows where they got the privacy to have sex.'

'Or the time.'

'Anyway, it was a madhouse, so we couldn't go there.'

'Where did you go?'

He had the grace to look shamefaced. 'The cemetery.'

It was a good summer that year, no hardship to be outside.

And the cemetery was easy to climb into, and had secluded corners where the trees and bushes grew close together, and had benches in it where you could sit for hours, staring at the stars. It was, by definition, quiet. They could be alone together which was more than you could say for any of the local parks. They were full of teenagers drinking and carousing once the sun went down. Josh didn't really want an audience when he was with Angela. It might damage his reputation if people saw him handling her like she was bone china.

She was the one who made all the running. She was the one who whispered the things she'd like to do to him. She was the one who stroked his cock through his jeans, who went out with no bra on so he could see her nipples through her top, who bit his lip when they kissed and left purple love bites on his neck. She was the one who sat on his lap, straddling him, and ground her pelvis against him until he came in his pants.

I blinked. 'You're really not holding back, are you?'

'You need to understand how it was.' He picked up his beer but stopped before he drank from it. 'That hasn't happened since, obviously.'

'Obviously.'

Josh got in the habit of bringing a rug and a bottle of wine when they went to the cemetery. He was careful not to let Angela drink too much because she wasn't used to it and it made her silly. She had to face her parents when she got home and they were wary enough of her being out at all hours without her being blind drunk when she came back. She always left the house looking modest, with a cardigan hiding whatever skimpy top she was wearing to excite him, and her hair in a little-girl ponytail. Somewhere along the way she shed the cardigan, the hair-tie and her inhibitions. It scared him, sometimes, the way she was. It worried him.

He was the one who tried to slow things down. But Angela had other ideas.

'She wanted to pop her cherry before we went back to school. She had a thing about it. One of the reasons she was with me was because everyone knew I'd shagged around a lot.' A long swallow of beer. 'Which was a total lie. I'd never done it. I didn't mind, obviously, because it was a lot better for my reputation. And the girls didn't mind because it was a status thing to have shagged me – no one wanted to admit I hadn't done it with them.'

'Why didn't you?'

'I don't know.' He started peeling the label. 'I couldn't admit that I hadn't. I couldn't take the risk that when I lost it, whoever I did it with would tell everyone I was crap. I was scared, basically. Vinny had done it a few times, with a few different girls. Shane had a girlfriend called Mags and she was into all sorts. She had a copy of the Kama Sutra and she was making him work through it.' He grinned suddenly. 'Poor bloke. She wouldn't let him skip anything. I still remember him saying, "Sometimes I just want a hand shandy and a nice lie-down".'

I laughed with him. 'Are you still in touch with Shane?'

'No.' The answer was quick, the change in his mood instant. The room felt colder and darker.

'Back to the story,' I said.

Josh wasn't going to tell Angela he was a virgin too. There was plenty of time to confess when they were older. He'd already decided he was going to propose to her on her eighteenth birthday. If he trained as an electrician, he'd have to do an apprenticeship but then he'd be earning good money. There was always a demand for sparks in the building trade. His uncle was an electrician; he'd told him about it. The careers teacher at school shook her head over it because she wanted him to go to university, but he told her he'd made up his mind.

'I thought the sun shone out of Angela. I'd have done anything for her.' He sounded bemused. 'Never felt that way about anyone before or since.'

'The first time you fall in love is special.'

'It was going to be the only time,' he said coldly.

'You were very young.'

'I knew what I wanted. It was her.'

I nodded, thinking of my first serious boyfriend, Gerard, and how very glad I was that we hadn't got engaged. He had cried every time we had sex.

Every. Time.

The charm of that kind of thing wore off after a while.

'Anyway,' Derwent said. 'We were serious about each other is what I'm saying. And I'd have killed myself rather than hurt her.'

'So what happened?'

'I'm going to need another beer.' He stood up and bolted out of the room and I could only wonder what was so bad that he wasn't prepared to share it with me, given everything else he'd said without turning a hair. He came back with two bottles and handed me one.

'I know you said you didn't want one—'

'But now I do.'

He opened his, then threw me his keys so I could use the bottle opener on his key ring. It was in the shape of a pair of handcuffs.

'Cute,' I observed.

'It was a present.'

'From someone who knows you well?'

'Someone I was going out with a while back. She liked shagging a copper.'

'Did you have to use your cuffs on her? Wear your uniform?'

He smirked so I knew he had, and I concentrated on swapping the bottle for the glass on the precious coffee table. *Never ask a question if you don't want the answer.*

'I appreciate you doing this, you know,' Derwent said.

'Noted.'

'Do you need to call Rob to tell him where you are?'

'No. He's not my keeper.' No need to tell Derwent he was thousands of miles away, I thought. 'Where were we?'

'Young. Happy. In love.' He sighed. 'Then everything turned to shit.'

I sat and listened while Derwent told me about the end of Angela Poole's short life. I kept my mouth shut this time and let him tell it his way. And after the first couple of minutes, I think he'd even forgotten I was there.

1992

The mirror in the bathroom was steamed up, which wasn't all that surprising after the – Josh checked – twenty-three minutes he had spent in the shower. The bathroom was tropical and he'd used all the hot water. He swiped at the glass with a towel and succeeded only in smearing it. He still couldn't see himself clearly enough to risk shaving.

'Fuck my luck.' He ran a hand over his chin, feeling the velvety fuzz of a day's growth. It wasn't so bad that he had to shave, not really. But he had a bit of a thing about showing respect for Angela. When they spent as long snogging as the two of them tended to, any stubble at all made her skin go blotchy, which made her folks suspicious, and made him feel guilty.

So. Shaving.

He grabbed a towel and wrapped it around his hips, as low as he could sling it without it sliding off altogether. Then he leaned over and opened the bathroom window wide, resting his elbows on the sill. A lawnmower whined in the distance and some kids played on a trampoline in the garden behind, singing pop songs at the tops of their voices. Summer made him happy.

Angela made him happy.

The mirror was drying off and he could see himself in it again. He looked at his torso critically, wondering if it was his imagination that his chest and shoulders were bigger.

He'd worked on them enough. He curled his arm, staring at the bulge of his biceps. Not bad.

He shaved quickly, without cutting himself, pulling faces in the mirror for his own amusement. God, it was boring. A lifetime of this, unless he grew a beard, but Angela wouldn't like a beard. So no beard. He finished off with a handful of Cool Water, the aftershave she loved. It stung like a bastard on his skin and he swore, his eyes swimming in sudden tears. It was good pain, though. Part of the ritual, like wearing a clean T-shirt or checking the condoms were in the side pocket of his backpack.

The condoms. If she'd known they were there, they'd have done it the previous week. He didn't know why he hadn't said they were in the bag. He wanted to do it – God, he wanted it so much the anticipation sat in the middle of his brain, blocking all logical thought. He had to think around the sides of it as best he could. But when it came to it, he couldn't just *say* it to her. Now, in the bathroom, he couldn't understand why he hadn't. She wanted to as much as he did, if not more. She'd have been delighted.

But tonight was the night. At last. He gave a shiver of anticipation and stared at himself again, wondering afterwards if he would look different or just feel different.

He was looking good, he decided. He was tanned. His hair hung down from a centre parting as far as his eyebrows. From the nape of his neck to halfway up his head he had a blade two cut. Mrs Beale at school had told him he looked like he should be in a boy band with a haircut like that, and he'd just looked at her without saying anything until she went red and walked off. It was common knowledge that she fancied him, undoing an extra button on her blouse before his class came in for their geography lesson. He didn't mind. He never minded when women liked him. He liked saying things to see if he got a reaction from them – a catch in their breath, the blood coming to their cheeks, their pupils dilating. And it was so easy.

He tilted his head back to give his tough-guy stare, his come-and-have-a-go-if-you-think-you're-hard-enough look. It looked good, he decided. It wasn't a shock that he was popular with the girls, when all was said and done. But he was still young. No hair on his chest to speak of. He ran his finger down the trail that went from his belly button to beneath the towel, imagining Angela stroking the hair with her small, perfect fingers. His cock sprang to life instantly and he held it, thinking about later. Thinking about what she'd said to him the previous week, her hand sliding up and down on it the way he'd shown her.

'I want to suck it.'

He hadn't allowed her to. She'd be disgusted with herself afterwards, he thought. And he didn't want her doing that kind of thing, not at her age. Fifteen was too young to be giving blowjobs. But the *idea* of it – her tongue flickering around the tip, her pretty mouth stretched wide to accommodate him as he thrust, his hand on her head, pushing her down on it . . .

Fucking hell. He groaned, checking his watch. He had time, he thought, for a wank before he finished getting ready. It was a good idea to relieve some of the pressure.

And it wouldn't take long.

He felt ten feet tall, walking along her street with his backpack slung over one shoulder. He'd got a bottle of wine from a mate who worked at an off-licence in town and the bag was heavy. She was outside her house already, sitting on the brick pillar beside the gate. Her father had grown a massive hedge in front of the house, for privacy, and it needed cutting back. All he could see of her at first were her feet, crossed at the ankle, neat in white Converse. He liked that about her – that she didn't feel the need to mince around in stupid heels when they had walls to scale and grass to trudge through. She was brave, he thought, and steady. Not a squealer. She was like him.

He got right up close to her before she realised he was there. 'All right, babe.'

'Josh!' She went to slide down off the pillar but he got there in time to stop her, sliding between her knees and reaching up for a long, greedy kiss. She wrapped her legs around his waist, laughing a little as her denim miniskirt edged up towards her hips.

'This is risky.'

'Is he in?'

'Yeah. Getting ready to go.'

'He' was her dad. He drove buses, and this week it was the night bus. He worshipped Angela. If he knew the truth about what they'd been doing together he'd castrate Josh with rusty scissors and smile while he did it. Then he'd never speak to her again.

Josh didn't give a fuck at that precise moment. She was so warm, so real in his arms. He kissed her again, her tongue teasing his and he remembered what she'd said, and how he imagined her running that tongue over his bell end, and he was rock hard, which she could feel, which made her laugh, again. He turned his head to let her nuzzle his neck – she had a thing about it, especially when he'd just shaved – and his eyes wandered to the house next door, and up to the front bedroom, where a figure was standing in the window, watching them. Fat Stu. Fifteen, like Angela, but that was all they had in common. He was short and podgy with a feathered fringe, like Princess Diana, and buck teeth that would pay for an orthodontist's five-star beach holiday if his parents weren't too mean to get them fixed. He wore black at weekends and listened to the Smiths, very loud, which was enough for Josh to be sure he was gay. He looked like a beaver, Josh thought, and that was what he called him – beaver boy. Or Fat Stu. Or dickhead. Or gaylord. Or anything else that came to mind.

Josh held Fat Stu's gaze while he took a good handful of Angela's arse and squeezed it, his fingers sliding towards the cleft of her buttocks. He ran the other hand up her back, the middle finger extended. *Go fuck yourself, beaver boy.* Even at that distance he could see the colour rushing into Stu's cheeks before he turned away and disappeared. What was he doing, anyway, standing there in his mother's bedroom? Probably trying on her clothes. Josh had a vision of him wearing high heels and stockings with suspenders on his invisible bottom half, and had to turn his head to bury his face in Angela's hair so she wouldn't notice him grinning and ask why. He didn't want to talk about Fat Stu.

The distraction had at least taken his mind off sex so his erection had subsided enough to allow him to walk down the street.

'Are you ready?'

She nodded.

'Sure about this?'

Another emphatic nod.

'Let's go.'

It was nine by the time they got to the cemetery and the sun had set but only just, the sky still streaked with pink and purple clouds. *Red sky at night, shepherd's delight.* August was a funny month: hot, but the nights were getting longer, and the trees were starting to turn here and there. Summer wasn't going to last much longer. Josh didn't want to think about that, though. Didn't want to think about A levels and university versus apprenticeships and homework and stress from his folks and not seeing Angela. They'd have to abandon their cemetery soon and he couldn't think where else to go. Keeping the gloom to himself, Josh helped Angela climb the wall, her skirt riding high as she scrambled over. He swung himself up and over, landing on the grass beside her with a thud.

'Usual place?'

'Where else?'

The usual place was the far side of the graveyard, away

from the houses, in an area that was mainly old grave-
stones. They were mossy, broken, the inscriptions faded
away by years of polluted rain. Long ago, grieving families
had planted trees around their loved ones' graves, and they
had grown tangled and unkempt, draped in ivy, climbing roses blossoming on briars that threaded through the
branches. Sensibly, the council hadn't attempted to fix it.
The health and safety types had stuck a notice up warning
about entry at your own risk and someone had donated a
bench to go under the largest tree, and there was a patch
of flat ground in front of it that was just right for the rug. It
didn't *feel* like they were in a graveyard, there.

The hardest part was getting across the graveyard in the
gathering dusk. Josh had eyes like a cat and didn't mind it,
but Angela often stumbled. They had to go fast in case anyone saw them. He didn't fancy explaining what they were
doing to a nosy groundsman, or a neighbour, or even the
police. This time, they made it without difficulty, though
his heart was thudding in his chest like a heavy bass beat.

That would be excitement, a detached part of his brain
observed. He looked at Angela, whose chest was rising and
falling rapidly, and grinned at her.

'So here we are.'

'Yeah.'

'Drink?'

'Yeah.' She smiled, sliding the bag off his shoulder and
unzipping it, taking out the rug and unfolding it.

She was complicit in her own downfall.

She was happy.

Later, much later, and the sky had darkened to a brilliant
blue that was as clear as glass. Angela's knickers were
on the ground beside them, her top pushed up, her skirt
around her waist. She smiled up at him, her eyes hazy with
lust and alcohol, and let her knees fall apart.

'Do it.'

'Ange.' He was breathing hard.

'Go on.' She propped herself up on one elbow and ran a hand up his chest to stroke his face, then down again to his cock. 'I want you in me.'

He'd never moved so fast. He leaned across to the bag and dug around for the condoms which he knew were in there, which had now disappeared. He'd taken them out of the box so he could get at them quickly. Nothing he touched felt like foil and it was too dark to see where they were.

'What's wrong?'

'I can't find the condoms.'

'It doesn't matter.' Her voice was soft, beseeching. She held on to him. 'I don't care. I want to feel *you*, not some rubber.'

He felt light-headed but there was still some reason in him, something detached from the maelstrom of desire that was making him shake like he had a fever. 'You could get pregnant.'

'It's fine. It's not the right time.' She took his hand and put it between her legs. 'Feel how much I want you. *Now*, Josh.'

He assumed she knew what she was talking about and it was all right. He was a virgin and so was she, so he didn't have to worry about STDs. If he didn't get inside her soon . . .

As he was thinking it she moved his hand away and lifted her hips, offering herself to him and he lost all his reason as he lowered himself onto her, into her, finding the right place by luck rather than skill. It was more difficult than he'd expected to get into her and he pushed, pressing against her until something gave. He stopped moving when she gave a gasp that was definitely pain, not pleasure, but she dug her nails into his arse.

'Go on. Do it.'

So he kept pushing, and suddenly all of him was in her, and she was wet and warm and tight around him and he fucked her, his breath coming in gasps, thrusting hard as she pulled him towards her, scratching his back, moving to let him get even deeper though her face was twisted like it hurt, a lot. He didn't care. He couldn't. He was almost coming and then he was coming and he made a noise he'd never made before, a sound that was like choking and then he collapsed down to one side of her, bruising his cheek on the hard ground.

The euphoria lasted for about as long as it took him to get the power of speech back. Then the fear kicked in.

'Oh Jesus. Angela. Are you okay? Did I hurt you?'

'It's fine.' She wasn't looking at him. She was staring up at the trees above them, with a strange little smile on her face.

'Are you sure? Ange, if I hurt you . . .'

'Don't be stupid.' She wrapped an arm around his neck and patted his shoulder. 'It's okay.'

He was used to being the one in charge, but suddenly he felt as if she was older than him. Decades older. Centuries.

'Was it not—' *Good*, he was going to say, but she stopped him with a kiss.

'It was lovely.'

'Are you sore?'

'I'll survive.' That smile again. Then, 'Did you bring any tissues?'

He hadn't. It hadn't occurred to him. He'd thought all the mess would be in a condom, tied up neatly and thrown away. He gave her his socks, in the end, and she did her best to tidy herself up while he turned away, pretending he needed to do something important with the bag, with what was in the bag, until she'd finished and put her knickers back on.

She stood up and again he had the feeling that things had changed between them. She was in charge now, even though he'd had her. He couldn't understand it. 'It's time to go.'

'Sure. Of course. I'll walk you home.'

'Thanks.'

They walked to the place where they'd climbed in. Usually they stopped to snog before they went over the wall again, back to reality. This time, Angela shinned up the brickwork without even waiting for him to help her, let alone a kiss. He followed in silence, his trainers loose on his bare feet. He was on the point of asking what was wrong but he couldn't, afraid to hear the answer. It hadn't been good. *He* hadn't been good. The buzz from the wine was gone. He felt sober, and tired, and he really wanted to be back at home, in bed, asleep, instead of walking along a pavement on the other side of town beside the girl he adored but somehow didn't know any more.

They came to the point where Josh would have turned off if he was going straight home, and Angela stopped.

'You might as well go. There's no need to walk me all the way.'

'I will, though.'

'Come on. It's ten minutes.'

'Exactly.'

'But that's twenty minutes for you, there and back.' She was looking away from him, down the street. She hadn't looked at him since, he realised.

'Do you want me to go?'

'*I* don't care.' The way she said it made it sound as if he'd asked something so unreasonable, so outrageous, that the only possible response was mockery.

'Ange . . .'

'What?' She looked at him then, with that pitying half-smile. 'What is it, Josh?'

'Are you all right?'

'I told you, I'm fine.'

'You're acting like you're pissed off.'

She looked away again and sighed. 'I'm not.'

'I thought it was what you wanted.'

'It was.' She slid a hand around him, leaning against him, her head under his chin. 'I'm tired.'

'If that's all.'

'Of course.'

'When will I see you again?'

'I don't know.' She did sound tired, he thought. 'I'll see you tomorrow, maybe. Are you working?'

'Breakfast and lunch.' He had to be up at half past five to do the morning rush, the builders and scaffolders and taxi-drivers. They put away vast quantities of food in short order. Clearing away plates, up to his elbows in hot water, the muscles in his arms complaining as he hefted trays of mugs around. 'I'll be finished at two.'

'I'll come and find you.'

'Don't come to the café. I'll go home and change.' He was sensitive about the smell of the place, the grease that made his skin and hair reek. He didn't want her associating it with him.

'Three o'clock at your house, then.'

'Yeah.' He turned her face up to his and kissed her, but it was a chaste kiss, no tongues. Her lips were pursed against his. 'Look, let me walk you home.'

She shook her head. 'We've already said goodbye.'

'Angela.'

'Tomorrow, Josh.' She slipped out of his grasp and walked away from him, down the street, moving carefully as if something hurt. But she'd said she was fine, he thought. His own legs were quivering as if he'd just done a fast four miles. Maybe that was the problem.

He waited until she'd gone out of sight before he turned to lope away. He would never forget that. He would never get over the guilt about the main thing he felt, watching her walk away from him.

Relief.

Chapter 14

It was one in the morning when Derwent ran out of words, around the same time Angela had run out of luck in his story. His voice was raw from talking, his eyes red from fatigue. I wouldn't have dared suggest it was emotion. At some point he had switched from beer to whisky, pouring a glass for me. Scotch was not my usual drink but I drank it slowly, feeling the warmth spreading down to my toes with every sip. He knocked it back in gulps, not noticeably affected by it. Practice, I presumed, and added that to my list of things to worry about. An alcohol-dependent Derwent was not going to be an easier colleague.

After he fell silent he stared into space, lost in memories that were two decades old, and I felt my jaw creak with the effort of not yawning. It was a lost cause. My mouth sprang open as if it had been spring-loaded and I covered it with the hand I wasn't using to take sketchy notes.

'Tell me if I'm boring you, won't you.' Heavy on the sarcasm. Back to the Derwent I knew and loved.

'Sorry. It's late.'

'I'm fucking pouring my heart out here and you're yawning.' He shook his head. 'I thought better of you, Kerrigan.'

'What happened after that?'

'She was strangled to death.'

'I know that. To you, I mean.'

He shrugged. 'I went home. I slept. I went to work the

155

next day. Didn't hear from her and didn't think anything of it. This was before teenagers had mobile phones, you realise. We're going that far back. I hoped I'd see her at my house around three, and she never turned up. But two fat detectives did.'

'And interviewed you?'

'Arrested me. Took me to the local nick and interviewed me. Gave me a hard time.' He sipped his drink meditatively. 'Course, I was lying my arse off at that stage. They said she was dead and I thought it had to be a set-up. Her dad's way of finding out what we'd been up to. One of the coppers was a mate of his, going way back, so I didn't really believe him. Besides, I was petrified to say what we'd done. She was fifteen so it was statutory rape. Took me a long time to believe what they were telling me was true.'

'How did they convince you?'

Another gulp and a wince as he swallowed. 'Showed me pictures from the scene.'

'Her body?'

He nodded, looking down into his glass, his face bleak.

'Did they really think you'd killed her?'

'Definitely. No question about it. Longest twenty-four hours of my life.'

'But you weren't charged.'

'Nope.'

'Why not?'

'I had an alibi. Someone saw me walking through town on my way home. Again, there wasn't a lot of CCTV around back then, so I was bloody lucky there was a witness to back up my story.'

'Whoever saw you must have been absolutely definite about the ID.'

'He was. Believe me, he'd have liked to say different, but he was a fair man.'

'Who was it?'

'Angela's father.'

'Wow.'

'Poor bloke. I was on my way home through the town centre. Typical teenager, thinking I was immortal. I walked out into the road right in front of his bus. He had to stand on the brakes in a hurry. One of the passengers fell over and cut his head. The guy was too pissed to hold on properly but it was still Charlie Poole's responsibility. He made a note of the time it happened, as he was required to do, and since I'd been that far away from him,' – he held up his hands about two feet apart – 'and waved at him, cheeky little fucker that I was, there was no doubt about the ID. It happened at two minutes to midnight and that was right about the time she died.'

'Don't tell me the pathologist was prepared to give an exact TOD.'

'They didn't need the pathologist for that.' Derwent smiled bitterly. 'They had a witness.'

'Who?'

'Stuart Sinclair. Fat Stu from next door. A noise woke him at 11.56 p.m., which he noted because his clock radio was beside his bed. He looked out and saw nothing. A few minutes later he got up again to make sure there was nothing wrong, and saw a male walking through the gate of the garden next door and down the road. That was at one minute past midnight.'

'Did he give a description?'

'Yeah. Me. Down to the colour of my T-shirt.'

'But it couldn't have been you.'

'That's what I said. And they had to accept it, after a while.'

'Didn't Stu retract his statement?'

A slow headshake.

'But he had to admit it was nonsense.'

'He was adamant about it.'

'Not your biggest fan,' I suggested.

'No. He had a thing about Angela. Not that she'd have dreamed of looking at him. And he hated me because I was a shit to him.'

'Poor Stu.'

'He was a twat,' Derwent said, outraged. 'Poor Stu tried to fit me up for murder.'

'I take it he wasn't a suspect.'

'No. His hands were too small to have left the marks on her neck. Mine would have done, but I was already getting towards six foot. He really was just a kid. Still waiting for puberty to kick in.' He laughed. 'I think he was even a vegetarian, just like Morrissey. He sang in the school choir. Definitely not murderer material.'

'Okay. But he was muddying the waters for the investigation.'

'The waters were muddy enough as it was. They didn't get much further with it once they ruled me out. I've looked it up. In the five years before and after there were plenty of deaths by manual asphyxiation in the greater London area but nothing with those distinctive elements.'

'The eyes.'

'Specifically.' He rubbed a hand over his face. 'Where were we?'

'How you went from golden boy to chief suspect to being ruled out.'

'By the police. Not by public opinion. Everyone knew I'd been picked up and that someone had seen me nearby. They assumed the police had just fucked up. Our house was vandalised. Then a gang of girls thumped my sister on her way home from school because they thought she was sticking up for me too much. That was it. By then I'd come clean about the sex, because they'd found semen in Angela and told me they could match it to me, which would have taken weeks, probably – but by then I was cooperating with everything they asked me. Proper broken by it. So everyone knew what we'd done too. My parents were disgusted with me for it, and scared for my sister. I don't really blame them for what they did.'

'Which was kick you out.'

He nodded. 'Vinny's parents let me stay with them for a bit, but they didn't have room for me really and I didn't want to be a nuisance. I was under eighteen so I was entitled to go into care and I ended up in a home.'

'Not known for being pleasant.'

'It was all right.' His face was shuttered and I knew he wasn't going to tell me what it had really been like. I also knew that meant it had been bad. 'I was in a bit of a state because of what had happened to Angela. Vinny and Claire were still talking to me but Shane couldn't stand the sight of me. He threw up when I tried to tell him I was sorry about what had happened – literally chucked up, right in front of me. I stopped going to school. Then someone told me I was old enough to join the army. I didn't think about it. I just did it. My way out. I rang home to tell them and my dad put the phone down on me and I haven't spoken to them since.' He drained his glass then refilled it with a practised swoop. 'The army took me in and fed me, housed me, clothed me and paid me for years. It was my family. Better than my family.'

'But you still left.'

'I realised what I wanted to do with my life. I quit, studied for A levels, got my exams, got into the Met and the rest is what you know. Brilliant career, inspector by thirty-six. All-round sex symbol and winner of popularity contests.'

'Sorry, who are we talking about now?'

He grinned. 'Watch it, Kerrigan.'

'Have you got a picture of her?'

'Yeah, I do.'

'Can I see it?'

He was reluctant to say yes, I could tell, but he knew he would have asked the same thing if he'd been in my place. 'Wait there.'

159

He disappeared into the room next door and I heard a drawer open and close. He didn't keep it where he could see it, but not because he didn't care. I doubted there was a day he didn't think about Angela.

When he came back he handed me a framed photograph and stood beside me, looming. 'Ange. Me. Vinny. Claire. And that's Shane. It was his girlfriend who took it.'

It wasn't a great picture; the focus was a bit off and the colours muddy. They had been at a barbecue, in a back garden, the background an anonymous fence. An impossibly young Derwent sat on a white plastic garden chair, leaning back so the front legs were off the ground. He looked innocent and cheeky and I stared at him for a long time, trying to match it up with the present-day version. A girl sat on his lap, petite and pretty, her head leaning against his, her arms around his neck. Possessive was the word that sprang to mind. Insecure, maybe. They all wanted him and she had him, even though he was two years older and her brother's friend. I bet she couldn't believe her luck, which was a strange thought in connection with Derwent. Her brother was darker than her, and built like a brick shithouse. He stared at the camera as if he was daring it to capture his image. Claire sat beside him on another chair, one leg pulled up, drinking from a can so I could hardly see her face. She was long-limbed and very slender, with short dark hair she had tucked behind her ears. One arm had a collection of leather cuffs on it and she was wearing the Nirvana Nevermind T-shirt.

Vinny was at the back, standing, his arms spread wide, his mouth open as if he was cheering. He and Shane and Derwent were dressed identically in layered T-shirts, baggy jeans and Vans trainers, and Vinny had the same haircut as Derwent.

'It wasn't a good era for fashion, was it?'

'You can say that again. Seen enough?'

I nodded, letting him take it out of my hands. 'Is that the only one you've got?'

'Do you need to see another?' He glowered at me and I shook my head. The thing with Derwent was to know when you should stop pushing your luck. I got it right some of the time. He left the room and the drawer opened and closed again. Everything in its place. The words from Dr Chen's profile repeated in my head in Godley's voice. *He is obsessive about detail and a perfectionist . . .*

I stuffed the thought to the back of my mind in case Derwent could tell what I was thinking. While he was gone I stood up and put my coat back on. It went down predictably well.

'Where do you think you're going?'

'It's late.'

'And?'

'And I have to be in the office early.'

'You owe me. Time to start talking, Kerrigan.' He folded his arms. 'We had a deal.'

'And I'm going to honour my part in it.' I pulled my bag onto my shoulder. 'Look, I don't have the file on the murders with me and I'm still getting my head around it myself. I'm meeting up with Bradbury's DS tomorrow to hear about what they've found out. I can come here after that and give you the whole picture.'

He stared at me, trying to decide if I meant it. 'Do you promise?'

'I promise. And no need for any kidnapping shenanigans this time.'

'Do you believe me?'

'Would I volunteer to come back if I didn't?'

He was too clever not to pick up on the fact that I hadn't answered him. He nodded, as if I'd proved something to him.

'How are you getting home?'

'It's not far,' I said.

161

'Where do you live?'

'Dalston,' I admitted.

'Seriously? How did I not know that?'

'I keep it to myself.'

'What else are you hiding?'

Not as much as you, I thought. He hadn't told me everything, not by a long shot.

He went down the stairs in front of me and took his coat off the hook. I stopped two steps from the bottom.

'What are you doing?'

'How are you getting home?'

'I'll get a cab. There's an office near here, isn't there? I saw it from the taxi.'

He shrugged his coat on. 'Right. I'll walk you there.'

'There's absolutely no need.'

'Fuck's sake, Kerrigan. Did you listen to *anything* I said?'

'I don't need you to protect me.'

'Yes, you do.' He came towards me, the little hallway suddenly feeling very small indeed. 'Do you think you're invincible or something just because you're a cop? If someone wanted to attack you – a man – what would you do? Fight him off?'

'I've had combat training.'

'Didn't do you a lot of good this evening, did it?' He took another step and it was with difficulty that I resisted the urge to flee back up the stairs. 'This is why I hate women's lib. You're not equal. You're not independent. The minute you walk out there, you're prey, pure and simple.'

'You're overreacting.'

'I don't give a fuck.' Massive in his coat, he was standing between me and the door. His face softened. 'Look, Kerrigan, I have to do this.'

'I'm not Angela.'

'I know that.'

'What happened to her wasn't your fault.'

'I don't agree.'

'Someone killed her. *You* didn't. Someone chose to end her life and that's on them.' I was arguing against two decades of conditioning and I could tell from his face I was getting absolutely nowhere. I sighed. 'Okay. Walk me to the cab office.'

'Finally.' He headed for the door, happy again. 'I thought I was going to have to follow you.'

'You say that like it would be a reasonable course of action.' I saw the look on his face. 'Please tell me you don't follow women around.'

'When they're on their own and it's late. Just to make sure they're safe.'

'Christ almighty.' I followed him out. 'I mean, really.'

He locked the door after me, not one little bit abashed. 'So what? Most of the time they don't even know I'm there.'

Chapter 15

It was a short run back to the flat but it felt endless. The driver had taken offence at Derwent asking him his name, checking his licence and ostentatiously noting the number of his car. I sat in the back, fuming, as Derwent lectured him on maintenance of his tyres and cross-examined him about whether his MOT was up to date. By the time he got back in the car, the driver's mood matched mine. He turned up the radio as he accelerated away from where Derwent was standing, watching, and I was blasted with bhangra music all the way home. I over-tipped, despite the surliness and the soundtrack, and was rewarded with a tirade of hurt, semi-comprehensible English about how he was a good driver and trustworthy and he had daughters himself.

The taxi drove away eventually, the street quiet as the noise of the engine receded into the distance. There was no one around, no noise in the building as I trudged up the stairs to the flat. I felt the tension of the day hit home, leaving me exhausted. I wanted to sleep more than anything, but I had to look at the Angela Poole file while Derwent's account of what had happened was still fresh in my mind. I felt hollowed out. Today had taken all I had to give, and more. Alcohol on an empty stomach had left me with a headache and heartburn. I needed food and caffeine. I would spend an hour reading through the file and no more. Four hours' sleep – that was a complete cycle. Into the office, to face Godley and Burt. To defend Derwent, maybe, if I had the nerve, and if I could do it without revealing I'd spoken to him. If nothing else, the evening's adventures had confirmed one thing: he was just as deranged as I'd always suspected. But not, I thought, a murderer.

Probably.

The stairs made me breathless but the reason I ground to a halt on the landing by my front door was not so I could catch my breath. Leaning against the door was a fat bunch of red roses, a tied bouquet with a little reservoir of water inside the cellophane to keep them alive while they waited for me to return.

It was all kinds of sad that my first reaction was fear. My second reaction was anger. *Not this again.* Flowers by the front door made me think instantly of Chris Swain. It was just the sort of romantic gesture he knew would terrify me.

I pulled on the blue latex gloves I carried in my bag and approached the flowers as warily as if they were hiding a fully grown tiger. There was a little white envelope taped to the plastic and I ripped it off carefully to preserve the tape. SOCOs loved tape. It was good for trace evidence and fingerprints and matching the ends to a roll if you ever tracked down a suspect. The envelope wasn't stuck down and I edged the card out, trying not to touch it. A hastily written message in biro, presumably dictated over the phone to the florist who'd made up the bunch, because I didn't recognise the writing.

'I'll miss you. Be good while I'm gone. Love, Rob.'

Relief made me irritable. 'Be good'? That was unusually patronising of him. And having flowers delivered to the flat was against the rules, especially when they were addressed to me by name. I picked them up and sniffed the one nearest me. They'd been bred for looks, not scent, but it was still faintly sweet, and my irritation faded. He missed me. I missed him. He must have known coming back to the empty flat was going to be hard. I was smiling as I carried them in and ripped off the cellophane, then shoved them in a vase, still tied with the straw-like twine. It was good that he'd chosen an arrangement that didn't need much input from me because I was not the type to spend hours fluffing a flower arrangement. But then, he knew that.

I made toast and a pot of coffee, then set my phone to ring at three thirty to remind me to go to bed. Already in pyjamas, I sat down on the sofa with the file and spread out its contents on the table in front of me. I put the news on to check the headlines: we were still the lead story. They had found some file footage of Anna Melville presenting a bunch of flowers to Princess Anne. It was strange to see a younger version of the victim walking and smiling – strange and unsettling. Godley looked as film-star perfect as ever in his press conference. And of course, the Gentleman Killer name got full play. After the report was over, the newsreader went through the morning editions of the papers: front page after front page featured the case. We didn't know if the publicity would encourage our man or put him off, but there was nothing we could do about it anyway.

The second story after Anna Melville's death was a Dads Matter demonstration in Liverpool where a police officer had been hit over the head and concussed. Philip Pace gave a smooth statement managing not to apologise and suggesting it was the officer's fault. I switched the television off rather than listen to any more of it and turned my attention to the file.

First up was the MG5, the summary of the case written by the officer in charge, the OIC for short. Inspector Lionel Orpen was his name. I set the pages to one side, looking for witness statements and piling them up. Stuart Sinclair would be Fat Stu's real name. His statement matched Derwent's story, as I glanced through it, and the timings did rule Derwent out. Charles Poole's statement, complete with an alibi for Derwent. Josh Derwent's own statement where I found the story he'd told me but in official language. 'I last saw the victim at 11.39 p.m. on AUDERLY Road, proceeding in the direction of KIMLETT Road.' Disappearing from him for ever. The Orpheus and Eurydice of Bromley. It was the statement agreed after hours of interviews, after all the suggestions and insinuations and repeated questions had battered their way to the truth. The tale was told without emotion, without comment. I was glad I'd heard Derwent's story first. I could read exhaustion in every line of the statement. Broken was the word he'd used himself. And he'd rebuilt himself in the army, in an environment that was comfortably intolerant of difference, whether it was difference of race, sexuality or gender. Why was I surprised he was a twat?

I put the rest of the witness statements to one side and found what I really wanted: the forensics from the scene and a sheaf of colour-photocopied pictures, recent copies of the originals, which had held up well enough themselves to the passage of time. A house, taken from the other side of the road: a small 1930s semi-detached one, four-square like a child's drawing, with two windows above a door and a bay window on the ground floor, visible through the gate that made a gap in the hedge. The hedge, as Derwent had described it, towering ten feet. It was dense and spilled over the front wall. Moving forward, the path to the front door. The photographer had worked around the house, tracking along the path made in grass that was helpfully overlong and showed the dragging struggle that had taken Angela to her death. To the right of the front garden, by the hedge that ran between it and the Sinclair house next door, there was a small beech tree. Underneath it there was a sweep of greenery dotted with tiny white flowers on delicate stems. And in the middle of the flowers, under the tree, lay Angela Poole, in a denim mini and a white low-cut vest top. Her hair was tangled in the grass, blonde locks gleaming in the light of the flash. Her pale pink cardigan was balled up nearby. Her legs were apart, but as she had fallen rather than in a deliberate attempt to display her. What was deliberate was the removal of her eyes. This was gouging, I thought, staring at the gelatinous mess that had been left to one side of her head rather than in her palms. No knife. He improvised.

The photographer had included a few generous close-ups of Angela's face. I had no personal involvement with her; I'd seen one picture of her and heard Derwent's highly coloured account of how perfect she had been and neither had made me feel like I should care about her. But there was something unspeakably dreadful about the purple bruises on her throat, the red flecks on her skin caused by blood vessels bursting as she struggled for air. Her mouth was open, her teeth white. Her lips looked bruised but I thought of teenagers kissing for endless hours and remembered my own mouth tingling as I crept into the house, unable to stop smiling, after getting off with Brian O'Neill at the Krystal disco when I was fifteen. Without eyes, her eyelids sat oddly, puckered and deflated. The lashes were still clotted with mascara. I wished for the crime-scene pictures from Kirsty, Maxine and Anna so I could compare them, but I knew what I would see. There were differences – he worked inside, not in the open air. He had moved on from this death, making it his own with the candles, the dying flowers, the white sheet under the body. But Derwent was right. This was where it started. This was the beginning. And it demanded that someone take another look at Angela Poole's murder.

The next pictures made me jump: seventeen-year-old Derwent looking back at me with the flawless skin and lean features of youth. His hair was ridiculous, hanging down on either side of his forehead like curtains, and he hadn't mentioned the double line he'd shaved in one eyebrow.

'Vanilla bloody Ice,' I said aloud, grinning. If I had the nerve I'd give him a hard time about it when I saw him next.

In the first picture he stared down the camera like it was a gun. His eyes looked angry and wary, with the dangerous bewilderment of a cornered animal, and the skin around them was puffy, as if he had been crying. Next, the photographer had got in close with the camera to focus on a scuff on one cheek and I remembered what he'd said about bruising his face. Another shot was his neck, with a yellowing mark just under one ear: an old love bite, healing now. The next picture was of his back and a handful of long, deep scratches raked across his tanned skin. You could see where they were going with this. It was hard to tell, sometimes, if they were love marks or wounds made by the victim. In Derwent's version, there was an innocent explanation for every injury. It was as if he'd tailored his story to account for them.

Or it was the truth. That was the other possible explanation.

The next picture was an A4 blow-up of Angela alive, unmade-up and very pretty in school uniform, posing for her picture as if butter wouldn't melt. Innocent. Virginal. Reluctantly virginal, as it turned out. Assuming that the sex had been consensual, and I hadn't seen anything yet to say it wasn't. I flipped through the remainder of the shots: exhibits such as Derwent's bag, the unused condoms, the cardigan spread out on a table with a close-up of a tear in one sleeve. There was a list of items removed from Derwent's house: the bag and its contents, notes from victim, tape made by victim, pictures . . . the whole history of their relationship, everything that she had touched. They'd taken her away from him all over again. And a set of photocopied pages from Angela's diary showed that she had been a typical teenage girl. She wrote a lot about Derwent, usually in the kind of code that takes no time at all to crack. She sounded very enthusiastic about what they'd got up to, I noticed.

I was grateful for a map of the area and returned to Derwent's statement to plot his journey, and Angela's. If there was time the next day I'd do them on an overlay so I could see where they had been together, and where they had parted.

More interesting still was the floor plan of the house and the one next door, with Stuart Sinclair's room marked on it. I went back to the pictures which showed the side of the house with the hedge and tried to imagine what Stuart Sinclair could have seen. I'd have to go there and imagine the hedge was still at the height it had reached in the summer of 1992. It would be worth checking whether the Pooles still lived there. I didn't want to disturb them unless I really had to.

I was too tired to plough through the fine detail of the post-mortem report though I did get the gist: manual strangulation. The removal of the eyes had taken place before she died, which made me stop reading for a moment. Her vaginal area was abraded and there was a trace of blood on the anterior vaginal wall. The pathologist noted the presence of a quantity of semen inside her and on her underwear, but her underwear had been in the correct position and it was the pathologist's view that the injuries were consistent with consensual sexual activity. As usual, everything came with a hefty dose of prevarication.

My eyes were closing. The last pages got the quickest glance, just so I knew what I was skipping. A report on scrapings from under the victim's fingernails. A statement from the bus passenger who had fallen. A statement from Shane Poole and one from his mother about when they'd last seen Angela. A statement from Derwent's mother, who had washed his clothes early the following morning. It was her habit to get the wash on before breakfast, she had explained, outrage in every line of her statement. He hadn't asked her. She'd picked his clothes off the bedroom floor, as usual.

It didn't look good for him that she'd done the laundry but there was nothing to find on the clothes; his alibi was sound. So said Lionel Orpen in his summary, listing the many ways they'd tried and failed to prove Derwent's guilt. They had looked for other suspects, of course. Sex offenders. Murderers on parole. Men the local prostitutes identified as liking to choke them during sex. They'd done the rounds looking for their man, and hadn't found him.

My phone burst into life, playing the jaunty little tune that made me want to fling it against the wall most mornings. I flicked through the statements, seeing names I recognised, longing to keep reading. I was out on my feet, and tomorrow would be a big day. I shovelled everything back into the folder and headed for my cold, empty bed, glad that I was too tired to think, too tired to be aware of being alone.

In spite of my unsettling evening, or maybe because of it, I slept like the dead.

SATURDAY

Chapter 16

'The killer does not see his victims as human beings. Their role is to assist him in creating a scene that has some personal significance, either a memory or a fantasy that he wants to make real.' Dr Chen was sitting in a corner of Godley's office, her legs crossed neatly at the ankle, her hands folded in her lap. She had a soft speaking voice and the three of us – Godley, Burt and I – were all leaning forward, trying not to miss anything. It created a strange atmosphere in the room, I thought. An intimacy, as if we were listening to a prophecy about our futures instead of a scientific analysis of a criminal's likely background and status. Usually, she would have been addressing a larger group, but Godley's policy of keeping the Derwent angle confidential meant that there were just the four of us in the room.

'Is it likely to be something he's experienced himself? Or could it be something he's seen, like a photograph or a film?' Una Burt, making sure that Derwent could still fit this profile, even if she couldn't bend time to make him a suspect for Angela Poole's murder.

'It could be. It would be something of enormous importance to him though. This is an experience that has defined him. He wants to relive it, or recreate it.' Dr Chen was wearing her usual red lipstick and a cherry-red cardigan over a white shirt; she looked immaculate. 'You can look for similarities between the women but it's possible that they are only connected by the fact that he was able to convince them to trust him.'

'What if he's pretending to be a police officer?' I said. Emphasis on *pretending*.

'That would work. It would fit in with how he presents himself too. Trustworthy but able to control their behaviour. I find it interesting that none of them seem to have mentioned him to their friends or family. He managed to persuade them to keep him a secret. Or they didn't want to talk about him for other reasons. They were embarrassed, perhaps, or they didn't want to jinx a potential romantic partner.'

'They were all waiting for their happy ever after. Only it didn't work out that way.' Godley shook his head.

'There was no sexual assault in any of these cases. Is that significant?' Burt asked.

'I should say so, yes. There is a sexual component to this, even though there is no sexual assault. The strangulation can be very arousing to killers of this nature.'

'Is this something that girlfriends or partners would be aware of?' I asked. 'The choking, specifically?'

'Possibly. But it's extremely likely he is impotent with women in ordinary sexual encounters. Or you may find he has been able to maintain medium-term relationships with women that include a healthy sex life. But he will most likely have been using pornographic material or encounters with prostitutes as an outlet for his less mainstream desires.'

'So he could be impotent, or perverted, or into porn, or normal.' *Not exactly narrowing it down for us.*

Dr Chen picked up on my implication and she flushed. 'Killers share characteristics and we can make educated guesses about this one, but when you find him you will find some parts of the profile are exact and others less applicable. This is designed to help you rule suspects out.

A profile on its own won't find you a killer, no matter how accurate it is.'

Which is why the police still have jobs instead of handing the hunt over to the psychologists.

'So strangling them is arousing but he can control himself. He doesn't touch them,' Burt said. 'Knows too much about forensic investigation to risk it.'

'More than likely he waits until after the body is arranged and masturbates. He may take photographs so he can revisit the scene in his own time.'

'But he's cleaned up too well for the SOCOs to find anything.' Burt made a note. 'We'll keep it in mind for the next one.'

'Una.' Godley's tone was a reproof.

'Well, there's going to be another one. He's not going to stop now.' She turned over another page. 'Unless he gets spooked and runs. But I'd say there's time for another.'

Godley ignored her and went back to Dr Chen. 'What about the way he leaves them? The white clothes, the flowers, the candles?'

'The way these victims are left is very deliberate but it's not designed to shock those who see them. A lot of killers will humiliate their victims by leaving their genitals and breasts exposed.'

'This is the opposite,' I said, thinking of Maxine draped in a sheet, covered from neck to knee.

'Yes. His fantasy involves them being pure. The bodies are clean. There's no blood. The cut hair is tidied away.'

'And the mutilation?' I said. 'It's the only damage he does, aside from killing them. Why?'

'Ah, that's interesting,' Dr Chen said. 'The fact that it's post-mortem means it's not to torture them. The Victorians believed that the last image a dead person saw remained imprinted on their retina after death. In this case, that would be their killer. They took it seriously – they tried to photograph the eyes of one of Jack the Ripper's victims.

That's what I thought of straight away when I heard about the eyes.'

'Don't mention Jack the Ripper in connection with these crimes, please,' Godley said. 'A serial killer operating in London with a victim in Whitechapel – the ghouls will be circling anyway.'

Dr Chen's mouth became a scarlet line: she did not enjoy being told off. Hastily, I said, 'What about the hair?'

'Traditionally, cropping the hair is a punishment. It's possible he tempts them into what he would consider indecent behaviour – maybe they offer him sex as a way of placating him, but it has the opposite effect. Then he cuts their hair to make them atone for their sin. Or he could do it after they're dead.'

'It makes them look like mannequins. Dehumanises them.' Burt tapped her pen on her teeth. 'Or it could be that it makes them unfeminine.'

'It makes them look younger,' I pointed out. 'They're all quite short and very slim. Anna looked like a child.'

Dr Chen looked at her watch. 'I'm sorry to break this up but I need to go.'

'Of course.' Godley stood up. 'Is there anything else we need to know?'

'Chief Inspector Burt is right. He will continue killing unless he feels threatened. He's not a risk-taker. At the moment, the odds are heavily in his favour. But if you can reduce those odds, you might find he stops, or moves on. If he stops killing in London, it will be worth keeping an eye on murders in other parts of the UK or even other juris-dictions within Europe and the US.'

'That won't happen,' Godley said. 'We'll get him before he moves on.'

You won't if you can't look past Josh Derwent, I thought.

Ever the gentleman, Godley walked Dr Chen out. I went over to the noticeboard and looked at the pictures of the three dead women that Godley had pinned there.

'You look tired,' Burt said.

'I am. I was up late.'

'Reading the Angela Poole file. What did you make of it?'

I shrugged. 'I'm not sure yet.'

'Do you think it's relevant to this case?'

I opened my mouth to say yes, then changed my mind. 'I don't know. It could be a wild goose chase.'

'What makes you say that?'

'Look at the differences. She died out of doors. These women are killed in their homes. Our victims are in their late twenties and she was fifteen. They're left lying on beds, not the ground. She wasn't wearing white and her hair wasn't cut. Someone followed her and killed her – that didn't take a lot of planning or ritual, and these deaths did. There's a twenty-year gap with no deaths. We can't be look-ing for the same killer. It doesn't make any sense.' I rubbed my eyes, suddenly exhausted. 'Derwent is obsessed with Angela and he sees similarities with every murder of a female by manual strangulation. He wants there to be a connection and you're going along with it, but that doesn't make it true.'

'What about the eyes?'

'What about them? You heard Dr Chen. Maybe the killer is superstitious. Anyway, Angela's eyes were gouged out while she was alive and left to one side. The three victims in our case have them removed after their deaths with a knife and are positioned holding them. That's a Masonic symbol, isn't it – the eye on the palm of a hand. Maybe we should be looking for a Freemason.'

'Maybe we should.' Godley had come in behind me while I was talking. He was leaning against the doorframe with his arms folded. 'You think we're seeing what we want to see, Maeve.'

'I do. And I think you're being unfair to Derwent to let him think there's a connection. He's losing his mind over this. Probably,' I remembered to add. *Because* I *haven't seen him since you told him to leave me alone.*

'What do you think, Una?' Godley asked.

'I can't agree.' She glared at me. 'You're just as wrong to try to make the facts fit your theory that he's not guilty.'

'If there were any facts, that might be true.' She looked furious. I reminded myself I was speaking to a senior officer and carried on in a more measured tone. 'If you're right and there is a connection between these deaths and Angela Poole's, why are you assuming Derwent is responsible? Angela's killer was never found.'

'Angela's killer is probably dead. We're looking for someone who has spent his life thinking about her.'

'You're narrowing the search down too quickly.'

She slammed her hand down on the desk. 'You're making excuses for someone who wouldn't do the same for you.'

'It doesn't matter what he would do or not do. This isn't about a personality. It's about the truth.' My voice had risen too. Heads were turning outside Godley's office.

'That's enough.' Godley stepped between us. 'Una, you had somewhere else to be, I think.'

'Whitechapel. I'm reinterviewing Maxine's neighbours.' She shut her notebook with a snap and stared at me. 'Want to come?'

No.

'No.' Godley gave her a bland look. 'Maeve has other things to do. Take Belcott with you.'

She didn't look thrilled, but I didn't blame her. Belcott was not a lot of fun at the best of times. I was annoyed with Una Burt but I wouldn't have wished Belcott on her. She stumped out of the office with a frown and Godley shut the door behind her.

'What do you really think?'

'I don't know. At all. But I don't think Derwent can be involved.'

'I never thought I'd see the day when you'd be sticking up for him.' He sat down behind his desk.

'And I never thought I'd see the day when you'd be trying to drop him in it. This is Derwent we're talking about. His one quality, the one thing that makes him decent, is that he is totally loyal. He'd literally die for you. And you're trying to tie him into a serial murder.'

Godley's jaw was tight. 'At the very least I don't want my case interfered with by someone who is a stranger to doing things by the book.'

'I didn't know doing things by the book was so important to you.'

'What does that mean?'

'You know what it means.'

He stood up, his face white. 'I will not be blackmailed by a member of my team. If you have a specific complaint to make about me, there are official channels for handling that.'

'I don't want to make a complaint and I am not blackmailing you. I just feel you're not being fair to Derwent.'

'I would think very carefully about whether you want to use your undeniable advantage for Derwent's benefit.'

I could feel my hands shaking, partly from anger, partly from tension. Get this wrong and I'd be back to local CID if I was lucky. Get it really wrong and I'd be in a traffic car writing tickets for bald tyres. 'This isn't about me. Or you. I still don't understand why you would risk your reputation and your career for money but I meant what I said when we spoke about it before – it's none of my business. And I am not the sort of person to try and turn that knowledge to my advantage. So please, stop assuming that I'm two seconds away from threatening you with disgrace.'

Godley fiddled with his pen, still on edge.

'Look, I'm just pointing out that nobody is perfect. I can understand why you don't want Derwent involved but I can't see why he has to be sent away in disgrace. And you know DCI Burt can't stand him. You know she's taking every opportunity to make him suffer. Neither of you seriously believes he's guilty, do you?'

'I don't know. Did you read the file?'

'Yes.'

'All of it?'

I thought about it. 'I – yes. Not in detail. I didn't have time. I didn't get in until after midnight.'

His eyebrows shot up. 'You must have taken a long way home.'

Shit. I'd forgotten he knew when I'd left. 'What was it you think I missed in the file?' I asked quickly.

'He was a different person then.'

'He was seventeen years old. Anyone is entitled to change in twenty years. And he's been in the army. He was shot at.'

'Exactly my point. He hasn't had an easy time of it. You know him well enough now, Maeve. You know he's not stable.'

'He's not always *pleasant*.'

'You don't want to believe the worst of him. Neither do I.'

'I'll believe it when I see the evidence.'

'All right,' Godley said. 'All right. You know, I like Josh and I like working with him. I take your point about Una – she is enjoying this. But she is a professional, as am I. We both think there is enough of an issue here to be concerned about him. He is off-balance at the moment, and these murders are pushing him in the wrong direction.'

I thought of him jumping on me the night before. 'I agree.'

'You seem to think I'm trying to harm him, but I'm not. If anything, I'm trying to protect him. I want to sit on the Angela Poole thing until we're sure that it is connected, or sure that it's not. If we start investigating it alongside the three current murders, people will talk. It needs to be done quietly.'

'May I look into Angela Poole's death?'

'Are you able to be objective about him?' Godley asked.

'Of course.'

'Do you consider him a friend?'

'No.'

'An enemy?'

'No.'

'Do you consider yourself to be neutral?'

It was hard to be neutral about Derwent. 'He's a colleague. I admire some things about him. I dislike others. I don't need him to be my friend to work with him.'

'All right. Keep it quiet. Report to me. I'm bringing some other members of the team on to the investigation into the current murders, but I'd rather keep the details of the Poole murder between us. Josh still works here, and as I said before, I don't want gossip about him.'

'What about Chief Inspector Burt?'

'She's liaison with Bradbury and Groves. She's busy with the current cases. She's read the file and formed her own opinion and she thinks we'll get our man if we start at this end, not in the archives of an unsolved.'

'Do I talk to Derwent?'

'Stay away from him.'

'He might be able to help.'

'He might be dangerous.' Godley gave me a warning look. 'Don't even think about it, Maeve.'

'I have his statement anyway,' I said, which was true, but not actually relevant.

'Talk to the witnesses. See where she died. Keep it quiet. Report to me. I can tell Josh we're looking into it and mean it.' Godley sighed. 'You don't think there's a connection between the two cases, and you don't think we should be worried about Derwent. I hope you prove yourself right on both counts.'

Chapter 17

I spent the day reading the Angela Poole file in detail and dealing with paperwork, and my head was aching by the evening. I was glad to have a reason to leave the office, and besides that I was looking forward to seeing James Peake again. He was a lot more charming than his boss, though that wasn't difficult. I also liked the idea of getting the inside track on Maxine Willoughby without having to ask Una Burt about it. I thought less of her for being vindictive towards Derwent. It was ironic that Derwent was the prince of vindictiveness. In her position, he'd have done the same and worse. Still, I had my standards, and Una Burt was not meeting them, currently.

Peake had picked a hotel bar in Kensington, a place with lots of mirrors and glass and low-slung designer armchairs and dim lighting. It was busy but the noise level was pleasantly muted, the conversations pitched to a murmur. He was sitting at a table at the end of the room when I got there and he waved, looking exactly like a DS who'd just come off duty in his suit and woeful tie. I hoped I was looking a bit better than him. I was wearing a Liv-approved charcoal-grey trouser suit, low heels, hair down but more or less under control. Businesslike. Not flirtatious in the least. But I couldn't quite suppress a small, guilty glow of pleasure when Peake watched me walk all the way to the table, his expression telling me that he liked what he saw. The glow faded as I contemplated exactly how awkward it would be to encourage him to think of me as anything other than a colleague. And of course I had no interest in him, beyond finding out what he knew about Maxine Willoughby. No interest at all. The old me, before Rob, would have been quivering with lust, but I was totally unmoved.

'Thanks for coming.' He stood up and pulled out a chair for me. 'What'll you have?'

'Tonic water, please.'

'With gin or vodka?'

I smiled. 'Not when I'm still working.'

'Yeah. Of course. Maybe later.'

He headed over to the bar and leaned against it, taller by inches than the men on either side and a good deal broader. He looked as if he'd expect to win an arm-wrestling competition with anyone there. His hair was really properly red, which I happened to like. From the looks Peake was getting from ladies – and quite a few men – all around the bar, I wasn't alone in noticing that he wore it well.

He came back juggling a beer, a bottle of tonic water, a glass for me with ice and a plate of nuts and crisps.

'Brain food. Here you go.'

I crunched a pretzel, suddenly ravenous. 'Do they know you here? How come we've got this and no one else has?'

'I was nice to Magda.' He looked back at the girl who was working our end of the bar and grinned at her, getting a lopsided smile in return. 'She's from Krakow.'

'I think you made her night.' She was now polishing a spot on the bar that probably hadn't needed a two-minute shine but it allowed her an unimpeded view of Peake. It wasn't altogether surprising, I thought. He was pleasant, handsome, and I found him attractive. I reminded myself firmly that my boyfriend possessed all three characteristics in truckloads, and concentrated on sipping my drink.

'So what did you do to annoy my boss?' Peake raised one eyebrow slowly. 'Anything I should know about?'

'I didn't think he remembered meeting me. Why, what did he say?'

'He said you were arrogant.'

'Just arrogant?'

'An arrogant bitch.'

I nodded. 'Nice.'

'Sorry.' He drank his lager. 'I hadn't planned to say so much.'

'Christ, don't ever commit a crime. The interview would be pitiful.'

'What can I say? I can't lie to you.'

I looked away, smiling politely.

He moved on without further comment. 'So I thought we should get together and have a chat about this case minus my twat of a boss and your . . . Chief Inspector Burt.'

I wondered what choice phrases he had decided not to use. It was wise of him not to slag her off, as he didn't know how I felt about her. The funny part was that I didn't know either.

'What's been going on? How did Bradbury get this case when he's only just been promoted?'

'No one else wanted it. Everyone assumed it was a domestic gone bad, an easy one that Bradbury could handle. They didn't make the connection with the other woman until after the post-mortem, when Dr Hanshaw said he'd seen something similar. And then Groves and his fat friend came along and looked over our shoulders.'

'They're quite the double act,' I observed.

'They've been dying to take over. Not that I blame them.' He finished his beer in one long swallow and caught Magda's eye, holding up the glass. 'Changed your mind?'

I'd barely touched my drink. 'I'm fine. What's been the problem with the investigation? Why do they want to take over?'

'Bradbury doesn't want to listen to anyone. I mean,

anyone. He took some convincing to admit it was the same killer.'

'Hadn't he seen the crime-scene pictures?'

'Yeah. He wasn't prepared to admit they were identical straight away. I think he was afraid the case would get taken away from him.'

'He must be just delighted at how things have worked out, now that Godley's taken over the lot.'

'Actually, I think he is. He's glad to have an opportunity to impress your boss.'

'Please, God, don't let him impress Godley so much that he gets him to join the team.'

'Godley's got to know better than that.'

'You'd think, but he doesn't filter out the tossers.' I stirred my tonic water with the totally unnecessary swizzle stick, jabbing the ice viciously. 'As long as they're good coppers, they can join the team.'

'Rest easy. That leaves Bradbury out.'

'Is he actually fucking it up or is he just dragging his heels?'

'Fucking up. He put everyone's backs up at Maxine's work, asking questions about her sex life and everyone else's in the office. He upset her parents – did a video link interview with them and they were so steamed up about what he was suggesting that they complained to our boss.'

'What was he saying, for God's sake?'

'He got it into his head that she was working as a hooker to make some extra cash. Don't ask me what gave him that idea, because there was no evidence that I saw. A hunch, apparently. Gut instinct.'

'Always reliable.'

'I think it was the address that made him think that.' He went quiet while Magda put a fresh coaster and glass in front of him, with a flourish. She got a smile for her trouble and looked thrilled. Once she was out of earshot he went on, 'It's flats, right, and the one upstairs was being used by

187

a part-time prossie for work. Prearranged meet-ups only. She didn't solicit on the street and bring unknown punters back and she didn't live there herself. We found her when we were tracing the tenants to do interviews.'

'How did she advertise her services?'

'Escort websites. She waited to give the address until she was sure she was willing to go ahead with that particular client. Said she's good at picking out the wrong ones.'

'Until the time she doesn't,' I said. 'Did she ever arrange to meet someone there but get stood up?'

'All the time.' Peake grinned. 'Apparently a lot of men lose their nerve the first time. When they've been once, they tend to go back. This is what she told me,' he added. 'I'm not speaking from personal experience.'

'I'm just wondering if someone got the address by pretending to be a client and then got the flat numbers confused.'

'That was something we looked into, but we didn't get very far with it. Bradbury decided that Maxine got the idea to be a hooker from her and started working the streets without having the local knowledge or the smarts to stay safe.'

I thought of the crime-scene pictures. 'She really doesn't seem to have been that kind of girl.'

'That's what her parents said. Anyway, the girl said she'd never even seen Maxine, let alone advised her on a career in prostitution. She only saw regulars in the time Maxine was living there. She's a student, by the way. This is how she's paying her tuition fees. She'll probably end up being a lawyer and earning five times what I do.'

'She could probably earn that now if she wasn't so picky about her clientele.' I frowned. 'If the killer thought Maxine was a prostitute, maybe he was trying to redeem her from her life of sin. Maybe that's what he's doing.'

'Cutting off the hair. Dressing them in white. It's possible.'

'Any link with prostitution in Kirsty's case?'

'None that I know of.'

'Did Groves and Burns look into it?'

'You'd have to ask them.' Peake looked pained. 'Bradbury insisted that all queries go through him. I hadn't been allowed five minutes to talk to them on my own until we got to Anna Melville's house.'

'I should always bring Godley along. He's the highest-ranking officer Bradbury is likely to meet. He made for him like a dog finding the only lamppost for miles.'

'Bradbury would absolutely piss on his leg if he thought Godley would like it.'

'Not having much fun working with him?'

'You know when someone is wrong, and you tell them they're wrong, and just being told they're wrong makes them determined to stick to what they said?'

'All too well,' I said, thinking of Derwent.

'He's a twat.' Peake took a handful of peanuts and started working through them. 'I hate coming to work with him. If he'd been more open-minded and less shitty about Maxine, we wouldn't have to reinterview everyone now. Your chief inspector has got him where she wants him – he's actually terrified of her. So that's something.'

'No better woman.'

'She worked out that Bradbury was out of his depth about two seconds after she started dealing with him.' He shook his head. 'Godley has a good eye for female talent.'

'She'd made her reputation long before Godley took her on,' I said calmly, ignoring the implicit compliment.

'I bet you're glad she's there. It's proof he doesn't just go on looks.' He looked down, then up again, pretending to be awkward when he was nothing of the sort. 'Sorry. But you know, you're very attractive. You must have had people saying that you got where you are because of that.'

'Oh, they said it. And then they took it back.'

'I'm sure they did.' He leaned forward. 'I'm glad you

were able to come out tonight. I've been wanting to get to know more about you since I saw you.'

It wasn't often that I was aware of the significance of choosing one course of action over another. The images clicked through my head like a slideshow. Option A: go home, be glad you have a nice boyfriend, be grateful that you have the sense to know when you're in danger of trampling all over the things you care about. Option B: keep talking, keep drinking, allow yourself to flirt just a little bit, here and there. End up getting to know the dashing DS Peake better. Do something you regret just to prove to yourself that you're still free to make mistakes, even if you are in a serious relationship. Dispel the feeling of being trapped. Behave like the old Maeve. Be the person you used to be.

Option A was safe. Option B had its dangerous attractions. The risk-taking part of me yearned for it. The rest of me was terrified at the prospect.

I picked up my bag. 'It'll have to wait for another time, I'm afraid. I've got to go.'

He looked genuinely surprised. 'You've only just arrived.'

'I've got to meet someone now.'

'A date?'

'No. Work. Like this.'

His face darkened, then cleared. Peake had too much pride to admit he was annoyed, or disappointed. 'Another time, then. Somewhere a bit less formal, maybe.'

'This is nice.' I stood up. 'Quiet.'

'And there are rooms upstairs if you don't feel like heading home.' His eyes held mine, then dropped to my mouth, then skimmed over my body. My cheeks burned.

It was my cue to say, *Actually, I have a boyfriend, so . . .* I couldn't bring myself to do it. I hated excusing myself like that – *I'm the property of another man, so I can't stay in spite of how much I want to.* It wasn't the only reason I wasn't going to stay for another drink, so why mention it?

I smiled, composed again. 'That is convenient. If you find out when Magda finishes work, you might get to try one.'

'I don't think so,' he said softly, and I hoped he didn't think I was jealous. 'You pick a place next time. I'll leave it up to you. Let me know when you're free again and I'll be there.'

It was too awkward to say something about Rob now, or make a weak excuse about working late a lot. I hesitated, left it too long to reply, stammered a goodbye that sounded breathy rather than decisive and walked out, wondering why it was so damn hard to tell men to back off when they couldn't or wouldn't notice the not-interested signs. Be too brutal and they called you a bitch. Be too nice and you ended up giving them your phone number or agreeing to see them again.

And then there was the one who wouldn't take no for an answer, who persuaded you to trust him. The one you let into your home so he could murder you and dress you up for kicks.

Suddenly I missed Rob, a lot. I rang his mobile, knowing that it probably wouldn't work. It clicked through to voice-mail which I wasn't sure he could pick up in the US. I left a message anyway, thanking him for the flowers, telling him I was busy but looking after myself. Coping fine without him. Missing him a bit.

Half-truths.

He knew me well enough to know better.

I hung up and had no regrets at all about leaving hand-some, charming James Peake sitting on his own in the bar. He wouldn't be alone for long, I thought, and he was free to get up to mischief with whomever he liked.

But not me.

Chapter 18

Derwent opened the door with the positive mental attitude of a boxer heading into the last round of a must-win prize fight. His first shot was a haymaker. 'What time do you call this?'

'I had to work. Then I had to meet someone. Then I had to go back to the office to collect these.' I was standing on one leg, my arms full of files, one knee supporting them as they threatened to slide out of my grasp. 'Can you take these? Or let me come in?'

He grabbed the top two files and started flicking through them. I was still standing on the doorstep.

'Excuse me.'

'What is it?' He hadn't even looked up.

'I'm still out here. On the street. And it's cold.' I shivered as the wind cut at my ankles. 'Let me in, for God's sake.'

'The choice was between taking the files and allowing you into my flat again.' Still reading. 'I have made my choice.'

Seething, I dumped the rest of the files at his feet. 'Fine. Enjoy. I want them back in the morning.'

I was ten yards down the street when he caught up with me. 'I was joking. Come on, Kerrigan. I didn't mean it.'

'I was going to tell you about everything that's *not* in the file,' I said coldly. 'But you don't deserve it.'

'I know. I'm an arsehole. But you love me anyway.'

'You're half right.'

'Come on.' He took my arm. 'Don't make me kidnap you again.'

I pulled away from him. 'Don't touch me. I'm here because I choose to be and I can choose to go home just as easily.'

'I know. I'm sorry.' He tilted his head to one side, considering me. 'Why are you choosing to be here?'

'Because you're not getting a fair deal.'

'Lucky for me you love an underdog.'

'Yeah, it is. And it's also good for my career if you're right about Angela's murder being connected to the three killings this year.'

'That's more like it.' He looked relieved. 'Ambitious as ever, Kerrigan.'

'You'd be the same if you were in my position.'

'Very possibly.'

The wind blew my hair around my face and I pushed it back, shivering. 'Are we going inside or what?'

'Of course.' He hesitated. 'You know I was only taking the piss.'

'I know. But I can't understand why when you also want me to help you.'

'I'm my own worst enemy.'

'Despite considerable competition.'

He stared at me, deciding how he was going to react, before he threw his head back and laughed. 'You know, Kerrigan, I'm starting to see the point of you.'

'Then I can die happy.' But I muttered it as I followed him to the flat, and I was pretty sure he didn't hear me. I'd gone just about as far as I could go with Derwent and the next smart remark would earn me a snarl.

It was warm in Derwent's flat and this time I let him hang up my coat downstairs, as a token of something – what, I wasn't sure. Trust wasn't quite the word. I wasn't feeling at home, exactly, but I was getting used to being around him.

We were halfway up the stairs, both carrying files, when Derwent stopped without warning. I almost collided with him. 'Who else is on this investigation?'

'Generally? Burt, Maitland, Colin Vale, me . . . oh, Peter Belcott was out with Burt today. Then there are the teams in Whitechapel and Lewisham.' I propped the files I was carrying on the step nearest me, since Derwent didn't seem to be moving any time soon.

'And they all know about Angela? And me?'

'No!' I suddenly understood what he was getting at. 'Absolutely not. Godley wants to keep it quiet to protect your reputation in the team.'

'So who knows? Burt does.'

'Yes, but she's senior to you.' It was the simple truth but I saw him flinch; he hated that it was true and I quite liked reminding him. 'I'm the only other person who's seen the file. I don't think anyone else has even heard Angela's name.'

'The file?'

Belatedly, I realised the trap I had dug for myself, and also realised that I was peering up from the bottom of it.

'You've got Angela's file?' He was staring at me.

'I've seen it.'

'Read it?'

I nodded.

'Can I see it?'

'Why would you want to do that?'

'Don't.' He shook his head, warning me. 'You know better than that.'

'Okay. All right.' He was leaning over me, looming, and I took a step back, flustered. 'I'll have to ask Godley.'

'He'll say no.'

'Not necessarily.'

Derwent hit the banister with the side of his hand, thinking. I know he could tell that I was spooked enough to take the files I'd been carrying and go. And he wanted to know about the other victims too. He had enough control to weigh it up and make the right choice.

'Okay. Run it by him first. That's how I've been train-ing you to behave. No independent thinking. Chain of command.' He punctuated the last three words with a fore-finger poking my head.

'I'm not going to show it to you just to prove I'm capable of making up my own mind.'

'Exactly what I'm saying. I'd be disappointed if you did.'

I followed him into the sitting room, still very much on my guard.

Derwent lined up the files he'd been carrying, two inches from the edge of the coffee table, in a straight line. 'Drink?'

'Ever the perfect host. Tea, if you're making it.' I stacked mine on the sofa to watch his face work as he tried to quell his OCD. No chance.

'Gimme those.' He put them beside the others, nudg-ing them into position like a sheepdog coaxing recalcitrant ewes. 'And I'm not making tea. No milk, for starters. You can have instant coffee.'

'You spoil me. Coffee's fine.' *Anything hot*, I almost said, but stopped myself. That was the sort of open statement he was likely to punish.

He left and I heard him opening and closing cupboard doors down the hall. I followed the sounds to a small, tidy kitchen – white units on two sides, with a fold-out table under the window and two chairs stacked beside it.

'That's nifty.'

'What? The table? I made it.'

'Really?'

'Yep.' He wiped some non-existent drips off the counter. 'Can't stand eating in the living room.'

'A place for everything and everything in its place.'

'What's wrong with that? First rule of life is don't eat where you shit.'

'Please tell me you don't shit in your living room.'

'Obviously not. But I've extended it to cover sleeping and watching TV too. No crumbs in the bed, no marks on the upholstery.'

'I guess it depends on how messy you are.'

'No, it doesn't. Food belongs in the kitchen and that's where you should eat it.'

'But TV snacks are surely exempt.'

He looked me up and down. 'Yeah. That's how you'll get fat.'

'Excuse me?'

'You've got the height advantage and your metabolism is ticking over now, but you hit your mid-thirties and it's all going to go. Sitting on your arse watching telly eating crisps is the quick way to becoming obese. Mindless consumption.'

I folded my arms, feeling the familiar slow burn of rage that Derwent usually provoked. 'I am a long way from obese.'

'Now, maybe. But give it some time.' He picked up the mugs. 'Finished snooping?'

'We were having a conversation,' I pointed out.

'You were nosing around.'

I opened my mouth to argue, then closed it again. He was right, basically. Busted. Taking a leaf out of his book, I went on the attack. 'Takes one to know one.'

'Occupational hazard. Coppers don't do casual chats.' He grinned, then thrust one mug at me. 'Come on. I'm not your slave. Carry it yourself.'

Back in the living room, he sat down. 'How do you want to do this? Stay while I read, or pick them up tomorrow?'

'I thought we could go through them together. See what jumps out.' I opened the nearest one, which was Maxine's. 'You know, everyone's been looking at them to see the similarities. I think we need to look at the differences too.'

'Floor?'

'Floor.' I helped to move the coffee table out of the way,

and then joined Derwent in taking the files apart. The space filled up quickly: victim pictures I hadn't seen before with the three women full-face and smiling, crime-scene photographs, maps, floor plans, diagrams of the victims' injuries, post-mortem close-ups, forensic reports. Witness statements. Interviews. Phone records. Bank statements. Paper, and lots of it. Three dead women generated a lot of words.

'These are just the edited highlights,' I said. 'I left most of it at work.'

'It's a start.' Derwent was scanning the post-mortem report on Anna Melville, scrawling notes as he went. 'Let's see how far we can get.'

For the next couple of hours, we read. I hadn't had time to go through the paperwork for Maxine and Kirsty in detail and I was glad to have the chance to familiarise myself with it. Derwent talked to himself as he worked, which I had never noticed before. I found it strangely endearing.

I was sitting on the floor on the opposite side of the room, looking at a floor plan of Maxine's flat, when Derwent stretched. 'This is doing my head in.'

'Problem?'

'Just trying to get it all straight in my head.'

I put down the plan, realising that I'd ended up in a very uncomfortable position. My neck was aching. 'Do you want to have a break? Talk it through?'

'Yeah. What did you say? Focus on the differences?' He flipped to a new page in his notebook. 'Go for it.'

'Right. Well, I don't think there's any doubt they were killed by the same man.'

'*Differences*, Kerrigan.'

'I'm getting to that,' I said, with dignity. 'From what I can tell, they each had very different personalities. Their jobs were completely different and none of them worked or lived near any of the others. No connection between their backgrounds – Kirsty grew up in Scotland, Anna in

Hampshire, Maxine in Australia. So we really don't know where our man found them or why he chose them.'

'Something made his psycho radar ping,' Derwent said. 'Something they did, or said, or the way they looked.'

From where I was kneeling the three pictures of the victims were upside down. I glanced at them and then looked again. 'Hold on.'

'What?'

I grabbed three pieces of paper and made a frame that I laid over Kirsty's head, hiding her hair. 'One.' I made another and put it on Maxine's picture. 'Two.'

'What is this, kindergarten?'

'Bear with me.' I covered Anna's hair. 'They look alike now. That's the same smile.'

'You think they smile at him.' Derwent did not sound convinced.

'That could be enough.' I frowned, remembering, then scrambled across to the forensic report on Anna Melville, which I hadn't had time to read yet. 'Bingo. We found a hair on Anna's body. This report says it was a synthetic one. From a wig. He crops their hair so they can wear the wig.'

'What colour?'

'Fair.'

'Like Angela?'

I really wanted to compare them too. I had to make a quick decision. Instead of answering Derwent I got up and found my bag, pulling out Angela's file. 'Don't go mental.'

He was up on his knees, trying to see what I was holding. 'What's that?'

I laid the school photograph of her beside the other three. 'Perfect match, I'd have said.'

'Is that Angela's file?'

'Yes, but concentrate on this. This is important. He sees them – doesn't matter where. He makes a connection. They were all about the same height – five two, five three – with a physical resemblance to Angela. The wig makes them identical. You're right. This is all about her.'

'Give me the file.' Derwent's eyes were fixed on it.

'You're not listening.'

'Give it.'

I held it against me, my arms folded across it. 'Not yet. What did you pick up? I heard you mumbling.'

Derwent glowered. 'Enjoy this moment, Kerrigan, because you're not going to be in charge for much longer. When things get back to normal, you're going to get a reminder that you're a very junior detective.' He picked up the crime-scene pictures from Maxine's flat and Anna's bedroom. 'Right. Look at these. Why is Anna Melville lying with her head at the end of the bed?'

'Don't know. So you can see her through the window?'

He made a buzzer sound. 'Good answer but wrong. Why did the killer move Maxine's bed?'

'Did he?'

'Definitely.' Derwent pointed. 'That's the bedside table over there. That's the line from the headboard on the wall. That mark in the carpet is from the castors on the bed. This isn't where the bed was supposed to be.'

I checked Kirsty's pictures. 'This one wasn't moved.'

'No need. Do me a favour. Look up the crime-scene pictures from Angela's file.'

I did as I was told. 'And?'

'He leaves them with their heads to the east. I bet Angela's the same.'

He was right. I chewed my lip, thinking. 'So he's making them into Angela all over again. That suggests he killed her, too. Why the twenty-year gap?'

'No idea. You'll have to ask him.' He looked pointedly at the file. 'You know, it would be a good idea to compare the original crime-scene pictures with these.'

I slid them out of the file and hesitated, weighing them in one hand. 'Are you okay to look at these?'

'It was a long time ago, Kerrigan.'

'Even so.'

He held out his hand. 'Come on. I've seen them before, anyway.'

'When was that?'

'When Leonard Bastard Orpen was interviewing me.' He fanned them out, his hands steady. 'Right. What have we got?'

'The flowers and greenery match our new victims.' I looked across the images. 'Candles, though. There weren't any at the Poole crime scene.'

'It would have been dark there, at that hour of night. The less light he has in the room, the more it resembles Angela's death. A few candles give him enough light to see his victims. He can't open the curtains or blinds in case someone sees him, and electric light isn't going to make it seem real for him.'

'Candlelight flickers,' I said. 'The light might make it seem like they're moving. If he's acting out a scene, I mean.'

We sat for a moment, imagining our killer and his conversations with the dead. Because dead women can't answer back. Out of nowhere, I recalled Derwent telling a joke at a domestic murder scene, the victim lying on her kitchen floor in a pool of blood.

What do you say to a woman with two black eyes?

Nothing. You've already told her twice.

'And the eyes,' Derwent said. 'What about them?'

I told him Dr Chen's theory about the retinal image.

'Jack the fucking Ripper.' He shook his head. 'I don't think so.'

'He does it differently now. I don't know if that's relevant. Knife rather than by hand.'

'More squeamish.' He tapped the recent crime-scene pictures. 'This is all more tentative, isn't it? He doesn't have the nerve to do them outside. Angela's death was quick and dirty. He took a big risk, killing her beside the house.'

'Why did he kill her in the first place? She wasn't sexually assaulted, according to the file.'

'Maybe he didn't have time. Got interrupted.' Derwent blew out a lungful of air. 'I'm not imagining the connection, am I?'

'I don't think so. Are we looking for the same killer?'

'Fuck knows. Maybe.'

'A twenty-year gap and it's not quite the same MO, is it? But he's using the same signature as Angela's killer. Reliving it.'

'We could be looking for a twenty-something killer in 1992 who's been in prison or abroad and now that he's forty-something he doesn't have the stomach for killing out of doors, or gouging out eyes with his hands. Or back then he *wanted* to use a knife on Angela and he didn't have one. He'd have *preferred* to be indoors but had to go with being outside when the opportunity presented itself. Works both ways. Maybe he's perfecting his technique, not imitating what happened in 1992.' Derwent was pacing back and forth along a narrow strip of carpet that was all that remained uncovered by the drifts of paper.

'I'll go through the files again. See if anyone who was sent down for a long stretch in the year after Angela's death has been released recently.'

'Or if anyone's just come off probation. That might be making him cocky, now that no one's looking over his shoulder.' He snapped his fingers. 'Speak to probation officers too. See if there's anyone they're worried about for these killings.'

It would take roughly a million hours to cover all of the paperwork. 'The geographical spread doesn't help,' I said tentatively. 'We have no way of knowing where he actually lives. He seems happy to operate wherever the victims live.'

'I like him for being ex-army. He adapts according to the territory. That's a military mindset.'

'It could equally apply to a chess player.'

'We're not looking for a fucking geek, Kerrigan. Nerd boy who loves chess isn't going to be out there strangling and mutilating women. He's an alpha male, this guy. He takes control. He knows what he wants and he makes it possible to get it.'

'You sound as if you admire him.'

He shook his head. 'Admiration is not what I feel for this turd. But you have to admit, he's doing a good job. Three murders and we've got nothing. There isn't one credible suspect in that pile of interviews, just like last time. I was the only one they had and I was just lucky to have an alibi because otherwise I'd have gone down for it.'

'What about this time round?'

'What do you mean?'

'Have you got alibis for the nights the murders took place?'

He glared. 'Probably. I haven't checked.'

'Maybe you should.'

'Why?'

'In case someone makes the same connection as us and comes asking. Andy Bradbury would love the chance to make you sweat in an interview room.'

'That tosser.'

'Yeah. That increasingly senior tosser.' I started to sort out the pile of pages nearest me. 'Someone has already suggested we might be looking for a police officer.'

'We might. But it's not me.'

I glanced up at him and found that he was staring at me with the peculiarly intense blue gaze that meant he was irritated. 'Of course not,' I said, a little too late.

'So what happens now? You said Godley's keeping it quiet. Are you and Una Burt the only people actually working on comparing Angela's case with the three recent deaths?'

'That's not quite right,' I said cautiously. 'Una Burt is tied up with organising liaison between the different teams.'

'So it's just you.'

'And you know you can trust me.' *Look on the bright side . . .*

'For fuck's sake.' Derwent paced back and forth again. 'I'm going to have to get involved.'

'No, Josh, you have to stay out of it.' I stopped for a second, surprised that I'd used his first name, but he didn't notice.

'I'm not staying out of it. I'm in it. It's my story, for fuck's sake. This is about me.'

'It's about three dead women. Four, including Angela. And you can't be involved because Godley would sack us both, and he'd be right. Look, I'll tell you everything I find out. I'll discuss interview strategies with you and let you know who I'm talking to. You just can't be there.'

'Kerrigan . . .'

'No.' I put Angela's file down on the sofa. 'It's late. I'm going to go home. I'll leave you this because I think you should read it, no matter what Godley says. You need to stay in the background but you can absolutely advise me, and between us, I think we might be able to get somewhere.'

He was shaking his head. 'You can't buy me off with the file.'

'Okay, then I'll take it away and you can talk Godley into letting you be officially involved.' *Which will never happen.* His shoulders slumped and I knew I'd won, though it didn't give me all that much pleasure. 'I'm trying to help you, you know.'

'I know.'

'I want to find out what happened too.'

'Yeah.' He looked out the window at the street below. It was deserted, except for a rangy fox scavenging on the other side of the road. He watched it until it disappeared. Almost to himself, he said, 'I'd just like to know.'

SUNDAY

Chapter 19

I don't know if I'd have recognised him in the street, but when I saw him in the bar he owned, my first thought was that Shane Poole hadn't changed all that much since he was seventeen. He was broader in the shoulder and softer around the middle, and his hair had a startling amount of grey in it considering he wasn't yet forty, but the basic elements were the same: a tall, hefty guy with big hands and a serious expression. He reminded me of Derwent, but I couldn't have said why – his voice, maybe, and his demeanour, and a little bit his appearance. I wondered if it was just growing up in the same place or if Poole had been so influenced by Derwent's example that it was still, after all these years, how he chose to carry himself.

His business, the Rest Bar, was in a side street off Brick Lane, something that had pinged my radar when I tracked him down. Brick Lane was curry-house central, popular for office outings, open until late and the very definition of vibrant. It was close to the City where Anna had worked, closer still to Whitechapel where Maxine had lived. It was a place where my victims might plausibly have gone, where they might have met their killer. A killer who was obsessed, it seemed, with Shane Poole's sister and how she died. I went to meet him with a long list of questions and the uncomfortable feeling that Derwent was standing right behind me, looking over my shoulder, watching my every move.

At nine on a Sunday morning the Rest Bar was empty except for a man slowly sweeping the wooden floor. It was a bleak place at that time of day – too quiet without the hum of conversation and music, too bright when the sun was shining through the windows on grey leather seats that looked unpleasantly sticky. Everything would look a lot better at night when the great copper pendant lights over the bar were switched on. As it was, nothing could make up for the smell of spilled wine, stale beer and bleach. I'd expected Shane Poole to speak to me in a back office but he sat down in one of the booths, stretching out an arm along the top of the banquette as if he was relaxed. He was anything but, I thought, noticing the tremor in his right eyelid and the rapid tapping of one finger that he couldn't seem to suppress.

'Thanks for agreeing to see me.'

'You said it was about Angela.' He had a raw-edged voice, throaty and pitched a little too loud. The cleaner looked up when he spoke, then quickly bent his head over what he was doing. I thought the man looked scared and wondered if it was because he was scared of Shane or because he thought I was there to check the employees' visas and send him straight back to Lagos on the first available plane.

'We're trying to work out if there's a connection between Angela's death and three murders that we're currently investigating. Kirsty Campbell, Maxine Willoughby and Anna Melville.'

He pulled the corners of his mouth down and shrugged, as if to say the names meant nothing to him.

'They were strangled in their homes in the last nine months.'

'Sorry to hear it.'

'There are . . . circumstances that made us want to compare them with Angela's death.'

'Do you think it's the same guy?'

'It's possible.'

He leaned forward with his elbows on his knees, staring at the floor instead of at me. 'I thought I'd left all this behind. It's years since we've heard anything from you. Years.'

'You' in this context meant the police, I understood. 'Sometimes there's nothing to tell the families in unsolved cases. Sometimes it's better to wait until a proper case review instead of bothering you for no reason.'

'It would have been nice to know someone still cared.'

Someone had cared. Someone named Josh Derwent had cared, a lot. I wasn't ready to mention his name, though.

'There were no new developments. Solving a murder can be a waiting game but I understand it's hard to be patient if you feel nothing is being done.'

'My mother waited. My mother was patient with you. She's dead now. She died three years ago come December.' He rubbed a hand over his face, rasping stubble. 'She never got over it, as you might expect. Never forgave herself for not stopping it. Never could rest, knowing you hadn't caught him.'

'It wasn't an easy case,' I said quietly. 'There wasn't a lot to go on.'

'There was an obvious suspect and they let him go.' Shane looked at me, his eyes watery but defiant. 'Now he's one of you lot.'

'He had an alibi. Your father—'

'My father. Do you know where he is?'

I shook my head.

'In a home – not far from where we used to live, though he doesn't know it. He's got dementia. Doesn't know what day it is. He was probably going that way back in 1992 – he had to retire two years later. Mum tried to look after him but it was hopeless. We sold the house to pay for his nursing home and she had to move in with her sister.'

Shane pointed a finger at me, a little too close for comfort. 'Don't tell me he couldn't have made a mistake. Got confused. Mixed up one young lad with another. One person was responsible for what happened to Ange. One. And he walked away from it.'

'He was ruled out as a possible suspect early in the investigation.'

'He was my *friend*. He raped my sister.'

I squirmed. 'I am the last person to be an apologist for a rapist, believe me, but if it was rape it was only in a technical sense. From what I understand there was consensual intercourse.'

'She was fifteen. He was older than her. It was rape.'

'The Crown Prosecution considered it at the time and decided prosecution wasn't in the public interest.' I hesitated, wondering if I should go on. *In for a penny . . .* 'I read the file. Statements from her friends. Transcripts from her diary. There was a lot of evidence that she was a willing participant in whatever sexual activity took place up to the night in question. Obviously she was killed before she could talk to anyone about what had happened, or write about it, but—'

His nostrils flared. 'He took advantage of her and then he killed her, and as if that wasn't enough he *mutilated* her.'

I wasn't going to argue with him any more; he'd had twenty years to resent Derwent and I couldn't change his mind in twenty minutes. 'What happened to Angela was horrible. As I say, I've read the file. I am more sorry than I can say that the murderer wasn't caught. I'm not discounting what you've told me about who was responsible, but I think it's worth investigating other angles too.'

'If you can't or won't see the truth there's nothing I can do to help you.' His tone was final and I was afraid he was going to get up and walk away.

Quickly, I took out three pictures and laid them on the

table in front of Shane. 'Can you look at these and tell me if you recognise any of them?'

He glanced at them. 'Who are they?'

'The recent victims.' I didn't identify them beyond that. Let him try to put a name to a face if he recognised someone. He leaned over and stared at them for another few seconds.

'Did any of them drink here?' I tried.

'You'd have to ask my staff. I don't spend a lot of time talking to the customers.'

'But you're here when the bar is open.'

He spread his arms out. 'I live here. I've got a flat upstairs.'

And he hadn't invited me to see it, preferring the public space of the bar. I could almost have felt hurt. Except that I would have wanted to do the same thing, if the police had been interviewing me.

'You might have seen these women even if you didn't talk to them. Look again.'

When he reached out and picked up Maxine's picture, I felt a brief flutter of excitement, but he laid it down without making any comment.

'No one ringing any bells?'

He shook his head. 'Leave them here if you like. I'll show them round the regulars and the staff. See if I can find someone who knows any of them.'

I was surprised. 'That's very helpful of you.'

'I have a personal interest in making sure killers get caught. Seems to me you need all the help you can get from the general public.'

I dug out a stack of business cards and handed them to him. 'If anyone thinks they remember any of the women, they can get in touch with me.'

He put them to one side and raised his eyebrows. 'Anything else?'

'Going back to 1992. Angela's death. Do you mind

talking about it a little? I don't want to bring back unhappy memories but if there is a connection with the recent killings, we need to find out as much as we can.'

'What do you want to know?'

'Before Angela died – do you remember anything strange happening? Someone you didn't know hanging around, or a strange car driving by the house more than once?'

'Nope.'

'Do you recall anyone behaving oddly around the time Angela died? And afterwards – did anyone's behaviour change? Did you think anyone was particularly affected by her death?'

'Everyone was. It knocked a fair few people for six.'

'But no one stands out?'

'I told you who killed her,' he said heavily. 'I don't know why you're bothering with these questions.'

'Bear with me, please.' I changed tack. 'What do you remember about the night she died?'

He sighed, looking away from me again. 'I don't know. Bits. I was out that night with some mates and I'd been smoking a bit of weed. When I got home I saw police cars outside the house and I got it into my head that they were there to arrest me. I tried to hide between two parked cars, if you can believe that. What a twat.'

'When did you realise the police weren't there for you?'

'There was an ambulance too, which I thought was weird. The paramedics were talking about Mum, giving her a sedative and stuff. I thought something had happened to Dad. And then one of the coppers spotted me so I gave myself up. I was all sweaty and shaky and paranoid, but I think Mum and Dad were too upset to notice. The cops weren't interested in arresting me for smoking marijuana given what was actually going on, but one of them had a quiet word a week or two later. Recommended that I knock the smoking on the head. Which didn't quite work out, but he was doing his best.'

'Did you see Angela?'

'Then? No. I went with Dad to identify the body later. Mum couldn't do it. I didn't want him to go on his own.'

'Where was that?'

'The local hospital. In the morgue.' He shuddered. 'Horrible place.'

'Did you ever see pictures from the crime scene?'

'No.'

'Do you know if there were press photographs of Angela's body, either in the garden or in the morgue?'

'Don't think so. Why do you ask?'

'I'm just trying to narrow down the number of people who saw her body at any stage. Sometimes photographs like that get passed around – at school, for instance.'

He flexed the muscles in his chest and shoulders. 'No fucking way would I have allowed that. Not for a second.'

'What else do you remember?'

'The funeral. All the girls in her year crying, holding on to one another. They were supposed to be doing an honour guard but they were a fucking embarrassment to the school and themselves.' He shook his head and I was suddenly reminded of Derwent again: the disapproval, the scorn for weakness of any kind when there was a duty to be performed.

'It must have been very upsetting for everyone.'

'Last funeral I went to. Never again.' He looked at me again, briefly. 'You'll be able to find this out easily enough, so I'll tell you. Josh came to speak to us at the funeral. Tried to shake my dad's hand, and mine. I threw up. All over the floor of the church. It fucking stank. That's what I remember from Angela's funeral. This massive arrangement of lilies on the coffin that reeked, mixed up with the smell of sick.' He almost gagged at the thought and I didn't blame him. He stood up, looking green. 'I need some water. Do you want a drink?'

'I'm fine.'

When he sat down he had more colour in his face and he gave a wry smile. 'I remember the next time I saw Josh too, at school. I punched him in the face. I really regret it.'

'Oh,' I started to say, 'I'm sure he doesn't remember—'

'I should have hit him harder,' Shane interrupted. 'That's what I regret.'

I could see how you might feel that way about Derwent. 'And then he stopped coming to school.'

'That's right. Joined the army. Disappeared off to drink and fuck and wave guns around in Cyprus or Germany or wherever. Playing soldiers and calling himself a hero.'

'What happened to everyone else?'

'Everything went out of control. There was a little group of us – Josh, Ange, me, our mate Vinny and his sister. It affected each of us differently. I started doing a lot of drugs – pills and coke, everything except smack because I didn't like needles, thank fuck. Claire, Vinny's sister – she disappeared for a couple of years. Went to live with their aunt in Birmingham. I think she wanted to get away, so she could get over it in her own time.' He shrugged. 'Dunno. When she came back she'd been engaged to some Brummie, but he'd broken it off. She had a little kid by him. The kid took up all her time so we never saw her. She was only young but she was determined to be a good mum. I think she got pregnant on purpose. I think she had something to prove. She wanted to get a lot of living in because Ange didn't get the chance.' His eyes were wet suddenly and he looked at the corner of the ceiling fixedly until he'd got himself under control again. I pretended not to notice.

'What about Vinny?'

He half-laughed, then coughed, still fighting for composure. 'Vinny and me finished in school, and then he went travelling. I couldn't go because Mum and Dad needed me around. Good thing too because I'd have OD'd somewhere along the way. Vinny went around Thailand, Cambodia,

Laos, Vietnam – just wandered through Asia, basically, living on rice and sleeping in cheap dosshouses. He did a bit of kickboxing in Thailand, fought a few bouts. He thought about staying there and turning pro but he came back instead. He couldn't keep a job here – got bored too easily. He had no patience for authority, so it was a big joke when he went into the army too.'

'To be like Josh?'

'It was a different regiment.'

I wanted to say *same difference* but I knew better. 'Okay. But it seems quite similar to how Josh dealt with Angela's death.'

'Maybe. I dunno. I never lost touch with Vinny, though. Josh disappeared, much to my relief. Vinny was always there for me, even if he was on the other side of the world.'

'How can I get in touch with him?' I asked, and saw him flinch.

'You can't.' I somehow knew what he was going to say but I let him say it anyway. 'He's dead.'

'When did he die?'

'Last November. Almost a year ago. Afghanistan. Stepped on an IED. A car battery wired to some leftover Russian plastic explosives by a fucking goatherd in the worst country on earth.'

'How awful.' I meant it.

Shane nodded. 'He was my best friend.'

'I didn't realise. I'm sorry for your loss.'

'I miss him a lot,' he admitted. 'There. That's Vinny.' He had taken a picture out of his wallet and he showed it to me: a formal portrait, full dress uniform. Vinny had been handsome, in a square-jawed, tough way. His neck was wider than his head.

'And that was in November,' I double-checked.

'As I said.' The photograph went back where it belonged and he tucked his wallet away.

'Who else should I speak to? Your father . . .'

'Don't waste your time. He doesn't remember me or Angela, let alone what happened to her.'

'Who else?'

'Claire, I suppose. She's back in Bromley. Not married – she's still Claire Naylor. Manages a card shop.'

'I'll find her.'

'She'll tell you the same as me, but you might as well hear it from her too.' He stood up, making it clear that he'd said all he had to say and our interview was over. 'Yeah. Talk to Claire.'

Chapter 20

I tracked Claire Naylor down by calling the four card shops in Bromley. As luck would have it, she was the manager of the fourth, and was off sick. I insisted on getting an address out of the very hassled deputy manager. The reduced Sunday opening hours were a nice idea in theory, but it just made the shops busier for a shorter space of time. It was, the deputy manager told me bitterly, the run-up to Christmas. Already.

I decided it was worth a trip to see Claire in person rather than a phone call. I drove a pool car that had an iffy clutch, got stuck in traffic on the way and spent an hour touring Bromley before I spoke with her, by which time I was in the blackest of moods.

I found Derwent's old home, now inhabited by an Asian family, and the cemetery where he and Angela had shagged, though I didn't make a pilgrimage to the exact spot. There was unlikely to be a plaque, I thought. I drove from there to Kimlett Road and the Pooles' old house. From what Shane Poole had told me, it had changed hands years earlier so there was no need to worry about upsetting family members. Even so, I kept a low profile, standing near the gate and looking into the garden to see where Angela had met her end. The tree was gone, the hedge between the houses had been replaced by a high wooden fence and the house had acquired a large conservatory that took up most of the garden. The house next door, however, looked much the same as it had in the pictures. Stuart Sinclair's house. It was worth ringing the doorbell, I thought, and did so. A child opened the door, a girl aged nine or ten whose face fell when she saw me. Her mother came hurrying towards me down the dark hallway. She was stocky, with heavy features and very dark straight eyebrows that made her look fierce.

'Sorry. She thought it was her friend.' To the girl, she said, 'Into the sitting room, Milly, quick. I've told you before not to answer the door.'

She waited until the girl had gone out of sight before she said, 'I don't buy at the door.'

'I'm not selling anything,' I said quickly, showing her my ID as she started to close the door. 'I'm a police officer. DC Kerrigan is my name. I just wanted to ask you if Stuart Sinclair still lived here, or if you had an address for him or his family.'

'He's the landlord. Dunno where he lives.'

'How do you contact him then?'

'I don't.' She sighed. 'Look, I can ask my husband. He's the one who handles all that.'

'Is he here?'

'He's away. A stag weekend.' She rolled her eyes. 'At his age.'

I gave her a business card. 'It's really important that I get in touch with him. If you could get your husband to call or email me, I'd appreciate it.'

'I'll see what we can do.' No enthusiasm.

'Can I just make a note of your name?'

'Sharon Parsons. My husband's name is David.' She watched me write the names down, peering as if she was suspicious I'd write something else or spell them wrong.

I started to turn away, then changed my mind. 'Would it be possible for me to have a look upstairs? I just want to see the view from the windows, not anything in your house.'

She was already shaking her head. 'Absolutely not. It's private.'

'I understand. I only ask because I'm involved in a murder investigation, and—'

The word 'murder' usually provoked a reaction of some kind. Not here. Her expression didn't waver. 'I can't help, I'm afraid.'

There was nothing else I could do; I couldn't compel her to let me into her house. I left with more questions than ever and very little hope her husband would be in touch.

It took a further twenty minutes to locate Claire's house. She lived on an ex-council estate that was constructed around long, winding cul-de-sacs and I got more than enough practice at three-point turns before I found it. I rang the doorbell and while I waited, I turned to look at the immaculate strip of lawn, the clean but elderly Fiat on the driveway. A perfectionist.

'Can I help you?'

There was no doubting that Claire deserved to be off sick: her eyes were glassy, her skin pale and the end of her nose was scarlet. Unlike Shane she looked a good twenty years older than the photograph Derwent had kept, if not more, with lines across her forehead and her hair dyed a harsh blue-black. She was huddled in a dressing gown and looked as if the last thing she wanted was a long chat.

'Claire Naylor? I'm Detective Constable Maeve Kerrigan. I was hoping to ask you a few questions about Angela Poole.'

'Angela?' She wrapped one hand around her waist, the other clutching the neck of her dressing gown. 'Why do you want to ask about her?'

'Angela's death may be relevant to an ongoing investigation.' The woman didn't move. I took a leaf out of Derwent's book and put my foot across the threshold so she couldn't shut the door on me. 'Can I come in? I'll try not to take up too much of your time.'

'I don't . . . Oh God.' She rubbed her forehead. 'I've got the flu.'

'I'll keep it short.' *And I'm not going anywhere so you might as well let me in.*

She must have seen the resolve on my face because she stepped back and I went past her into the hall. It was as spotless as the front garden, so tidy that it was almost bleak. I moved towards the door to the living room, assuming that's where we would talk.

'Wait! I want to tidy up first. Give me a second.'

She pushed past, closing the living room door behind her, and I listened to sounds of drawers opening and closing as she moved quickly around the room. After less than a minute she opened the door again.

'You can come in.'

I walked into a room that had never been untidy as long as Claire Naylor had lived there. She seemed obsessively house-proud, because the walls and shelves were practically bare. One drawer of the sideboard in the corner of the room was sticking out a little, as if it had been closed in a hurry, and I would have given a lot to see what was in it. As if she knew what I was thinking, she stood between me and the sideboard, holding on to the back of an armchair.

'Please, sit down.'

I did as I was told, getting out a notebook.

'Would you like anything to drink? Tea? Water?' She coughed, a rattling sound that shook her narrow frame.

'No, thank you.' I waited until she sat down too, perching on the edge of the armchair, ready to flee at any moment.

'You said it's about Angela. I don't understand. Why do you want to talk to me?'

'We're looking into Angela's death because it seems to be connected to a series of murders that have taken place in the last few months.' I showed her the pictures, naming each of the women in turn, and she nodded.

'I read about them in the paper. Strangled, like Angela.' She looked up at me. 'Just like Angela?'

'There are similarities.'

She shuddered. 'Don't tell me any more. Do you think it's the same murderer?'

I hesitated. 'We don't have any definite suspects at the moment. That's one reason why I've come to talk to you. I know it must seem unlikely but we need to see if there's anything you can tell us that might send us in the right direction.'

'I don't think I can help,' she said flatly. 'I don't really know why you're here.'

'It was Shane Poole who suggested I speak with you.'

'Shane? I haven't seen him for years.'

'Your brother was in touch with him, I understand.'

'Vinny was.' She sniffed and I couldn't tell if it was because she was upset or because of the flu. 'I moved away, after what happened. Shane and Vinny stayed close but I didn't want to. It just felt as if I was reliving it all the time.'

'You were friends with Angela.'

'We were all friends. Vinny and Shane and Angela and me.'

'And?' I prompted.

'Josh Derwent.' She said his name in a toneless voice and I couldn't tell how she felt about him. She looked at me sharply. 'He's a policeman now. Do you know him?'

There was no reason to pretend I didn't. 'I work with him. But he's not involved with this investigation.'

'Does he know where I live? Have you told him you're speaking to me?'

'No, no. I won't, either, if you'd prefer me not to.'

'Don't tell him. Please.' She started to smooth the skirt of her dressing gown over her knees, fidgeting. 'I don't want to see him. I haven't since that year and there's no reason to start now.'

'He was the main suspect in Angela's death, but he was

ruled out during the original inquiry,' I said gently. 'He had an alibi.'

'I know *that*.'

'So it's not that you're scared of him.'

'Of *Josh*?' She laughed. 'No. I just don't want to go back there.'

'When was the last time you saw him?'

'A few months after it happened.' She paused to cough again. 'I stuck by him afterwards. I didn't believe what everyone was saying about him. I knew Angela was the one who'd wanted them to sleep together. It wasn't Josh's idea. And he worshipped the ground she walked on. He'd never have hurt her. He'd never hurt a woman.'

'Does that mean he didn't hesitate when it came to hurting a man?'

'If you know Josh, you'll know it was his solution to fight his way through anyone who said he was guilty, which was everyone. And his family kicked him out. He was a lost soul.'

'It sounds as if you really felt for him.'

'I did.' She'd been gazing into the middle distance, her expression wry, but now it snapped back to serious. 'That doesn't mean I want to bring him back into my life. I'm happy with things the way they are. I supported him when he needed me, and I'm glad I didn't let him down. We were just kids, though, and he'll be different now. I know I am.'

'I gather you became a mum. You must have had to grow up fast.'

'Who told you that? Shane?' She coughed again. 'I met someone in Birmingham – Mark, his name was – but the relationship was never going to last. I got Luke out of it and that was enough for me.'

'Does Luke live here with you?' The living room was so pristine I couldn't imagine a teenager sprawling on the sofa watching television, but there was a PlayStation behind the TV, the leads unplugged and wound in neat loops.

'He's away. He's a student. At Cambridge,' she added. 'Studying engineering.'

'He must be bright.'

'Very.' She looked proud.

'Does he take after you? Did you go to university?'

'Not once I was pregnant. They had crèches and my mum would have helped look after him but I was too wrapped up in him to think about studying.'

'That's a shame.'

'It was a lot more important to concentrate on Luke than to indulge myself. I wanted to be a lawyer but I gave up on the idea of having a career.'

'You work, though.'

'Just to put food on the table. I don't love it. No one cares if I run the best card shop in Bromley. They don't think about whether I'm a good manager or not. I can miss a day or two and nothing bad will happen to the shop, probably – I'll pick up where I left off and no one will notice I was gone. But Luke needed me to be there every second of every day, and I did it, and I don't regret it.'

She was self-possessed in a way that I thought was rare – prepared to defend her decisions, devoted to doing the right thing no matter what it cost her.

Claire frowned. 'How is this relevant to what happened to Angela?'

'It's not. Sorry. I just have a habit of asking questions.' I'd been trying to set her at her ease by talking about generalities. And I had my mother's need to put people into context, analysing every twig in their family tree until the subject was exhausted.

'Well, that's your job, isn't it?' She tightened the belt of her dressing gown again. 'I don't mean to be rude, but you did say you'd be quick.'

'Can you tell me what you remember about Angela's death? How did you find out what had happened to her?'

'Shane rang our house at four in the morning to talk to

Vinny. None of us had a mobile phone – funny, isn't it? It doesn't seem like that long ago, but they were still a rarity. So he called up on the house phone and woke half the family.' She paused, remembering. 'You know when you hear a phone ring and you know, even before anyone's answered it, that it's bad news? Yeah. It was like that. No reason for anyone to be calling us then unless it was that someone had died. But I never thought it would be Angela.'

'Did you see her body?'

'No. Of course not.' She looked affronted. 'It was a closed coffin.'

'Did you have any suspicions about who was responsible?'

'I knew it wasn't Josh. Beyond that, no.'

'How did you know?'

'I told you, it couldn't have been him.' She sounded definite. 'He was . . . sweet. Not the brooding type. He had a temper but it was the sort of thing where he'd shout or punch someone and then spend half an hour apologising. If he was upset it blew over quickly. He'd never have strangled her, even if she'd provoked him.'

Something in her voice made me ask, 'Were you and Angela close?'

'Not exactly.'

'But you all hung around together.'

'Vinny and I were like that.' She held up crossed fingers. 'I got on well with Josh and Shane, but they were Vinny's friends first and it took them a while to accept me. I was a tomboy. We were like a bunch of lads together – same sense of humour, same interests. Angela wasn't really part of the gang. Well, she was because Josh wanted her there.'

'But no one else did.'

'Vinny didn't like her. He thought she wasn't right for Josh. He told me she was always trying to flirt with him when Josh wasn't there. She just needed boys to fancy her, I think, so she'd know she was attractive.'

'Did anything happen between them?'

'No. He'd never have touched her because his first loyalty was to Josh. Anyway, he really didn't like her, but we
were stuck with her. Shane was seriously fed up to have
his little sister following us around and I ended up spending more time with him and Vinny while Josh and Angela
went off together. Shane didn't want to see them kissing.
He was the big protective older brother, but then he adored
Josh, so he couldn't really get his head around how he felt
about them being together. Conflicted, you'd have to say.'

'He's not a fan of Josh, even now.'

'Yeah. Well, Shane wasn't the brightest.' She sniffed.
'Vinny was the only one who could really talk to him. Do
you know about Vinny? Do you know he's dead?'

'Shane told me.'

'Such a waste.' Her eyes filled with tears. 'He should
have had kids. He should have been around for a lot longer
than thirty-eight years.'

'He must have liked the army, though, to stay in for so
long. If he died doing what he loved—'

'It's still a waste. Anyway, Vinny was just a creature of
habit. He stayed in the army because he couldn't think of
anything better to do. They fed him and housed him and
sent him to the ends of the earth and he never had to make
any decisions for himself once he'd chosen to join up.'

'But he did choose that life. He'd travelled, hadn't he?
He'd had a chance to see the alternative.'

'He was never going to do anything else once Josh did it.
All he ever wanted was to be like Josh. Shane too.'

'Like *Derwent*?' I couldn't keep the surprise out of my
voice.

'You don't know what he was like.' She shrugged.
'Maybe he's different now. He was . . . he was funny and
mad and everyone wanted to be him, or be with him. There
were people who didn't like him, but all he had to do was
snap his fingers and they'd change their tune. They didn't

like him because he had no time for them, but they wanted him to notice them. He had a real gift for making anyone and everyone fall for him.'

'Did you?' I asked and got a glower.

'We were friends. That's all.'

'And you never thought he was guilty.'

'Never.'

'Did Vinny?'

'No.'

'Did you have any idea who might have been responsible?'

She sighed. 'I thought about it a lot. I talked about it with Vinny. Not Shane – he was too raw about the whole thing. You couldn't say her name or he'd fly off the handle. But Vinny and I – we tried to work out what had happened, and we came up with nothing. I always assumed it was a stranger who happened to see her walking home and followed her, and did whatever he wanted to do.'

'Had you noticed anyone hanging around? Any cars you didn't recognise that you saw more than once, or anyone on foot?'

She shook her head, but then stopped for a moment, staring at the ground. 'There was a guy who got talking to us in the park one night. He said his name was Craig and he was older than us – twenty-eight, he said, but I thought he was shaving a few years off, even though he was wearing pretty trendy clothes. He was trying too hard to look like one of us. You know how teenagers think everyone is ancient, though, so I wouldn't put too much faith in my opinion.'

I was inclined to believe her, all the same. She'd been seventeen, not a child, and if she had thought he was in his thirties she'd probably been right.

Almost to herself, she said, 'Funny – I didn't think anything of it at the time, but now I'm wondering why he wanted to hang out with a bunch of teenagers.'

I was writing it down, knowing that it was probably going to be a dead end. At least it was new information. 'Can you remember anything else about him?'

'He had really good gear.' She grinned and I saw a flash of the tomboy who'd been best friends with Derwent. It was only for an instant, though, and then her expression turned serious. 'Not much else. He was really interested in us – the girls, that is. He sat between me and Angela and asked us about school and boyfriends. He seemed nice, not creepy. That was about ten days before it happened.'

'And did you see him again before Angela died?'

'Around town, once. Not to talk to. He waved.'

'And after?'

'Never. He said he was just passing through. He was heading south.'

'To where?'

'France, he said. On from there. He wasn't planning on settling anywhere.'

'Could you describe him?'

'Tall. Long neck – he had a really prominent Adam's apple. White. Brown hair.' She shrugged. 'That's really all I remember. I don't think I could describe him in more detail.'

'What about a photofit?'

'No. I don't remember the shape of his face, even.'

'If I showed you some pictures, would you be able to pick him out?'

'I really doubt it.' She saw the look on my face. 'It's not that I don't want to help. It was a long time ago, and it was dark, and we were high. I'd forgotten it, you know?'

'Did you mention him to the police at the time?'

'No. I'd never have said anything to an adult about smoking drugs.' She shifted her position. 'I wouldn't get too excited about it. He was probably lying about his name and his age, if he was the killer. And if he wasn't he was just some sad sack who you'll never trace.'

'You could be right, but it's a start. Can you remember if he told you anything else about himself?'

'He said he'd been up north but it was too cold for him there. He said he could speak French but it was rubbish – he just knew a few phrases and busked the rest. Angela and I took the piss out of him all evening. But he didn't talk about himself all that much. He was more interested in us. And we were flattered, I suppose, and young enough to talk about ourselves a lot and think that was all right.' She coughed for a long time. 'Speaking of talking a lot, this is killing my voice.'

'I know. I'm sorry. I'll go soon.' I hesitated. 'Is it all right to come back if I think of anything else?'

'Sure. But alone. Not with Josh.'

'I'll respect your wishes, I promise.'

'Thanks.' She rammed a knuckle under one eye, catching a tear before it spilled over. 'I don't expect you to under-stand but I left that part of my life behind a long time ago. And I wouldn't want him to see me like this. Not having achieved anything with my life except turning into a hag.'

'I don't think that's what he'd see, for what it's worth.' But I could hear Derwent's voice in my head. *Shit, she's got old. How hard is it to slap on a bit of moisturiser now and then?*

'Is he married?'

I shook my head.

'Girlfriend?'

'Not this week, as far as I know.'

She sighed. 'Do you know him well?'

'I work with him a lot. I wouldn't say I know him well. He's senior to me.' *And he's a wanker, so . . .* 'We're not really friends. It's a working relationship.'

'Is he good at his job?'

'Very,' I said, without having to think about it.

'Is he still funny?' She sounded wistful.

'He has a unique sense of humour,' I said truthfully. 'He's not like anyone else I know.' *Thank God.*

She nodded. 'Sorry for asking you about him. I'm just curious. I don't want to see him but I'd like to know how he turned out. Don't tell him I asked.'

'I won't.'

She followed me to the door and watched me walk to my car. Her expression was worried and I knew she didn't trust me.

Over the time I'd spent in Bromley my bad mood had faded to mild melancholy. There was no one else to hear, so I tuned the radio to a Golden Oldies station and crooned along to love songs all the traffic-clogged way back.

MONDAY

Chapter 21

I'd done the Parsons an injustice. My mobile rang before I'd even left the flat the following morning. In contrast to his wife, David Parsons couldn't have sounded more eager to be helpful.

'Sorry for calling you so early but the wife said it was urgent. I've got a number for Stu Sinclair but it's not a landline and I don't know where he lives.'

'Mobile will do,' I said, scrambling for a pen. He read out the numbers slowly, checking that I'd got it right by making me read it back to him.

'You'll probably have to leave a message because he never answers it but he's pretty quick to get in touch usually.'

'Thanks for your help.'

'He's not in trouble, is he? Only we were wondering. The wife said it was a murder investigation you were looking into.' Curiosity, raw and undisguised. I kept the smile out of my voice.

'It's an old case and he was a key witness, that's all. I do need to speak to him, though, so I'm very grateful.'

'Any time.' He sounded as if he meant it too.

I hung up wondering how two people could have such different personalities and yet be married. As he had promised, there was no answer from Stuart Sinclair's number but I left a message on his voicemail. The office was where I needed to be anyway; the paperwork had been piling up and I had a few phone calls to make. Once again, I found myself thinking about Derwent's criticism of my failure to keep up with briefings. I wished I could point out to him that my current problem was investigating his girlfriend's death in my spare time.

Before I left the flat I hesitated over the window in the sitting room, which was open a few inches. With Rob gone, and since I was out all the time, I'd noticed the flat was developing a stale smell. I'd checked the fridge for horrors and emptied the kitchen bin but there was still an unpleasant undertone to the atmosphere. We were too high up to be afraid of burglars but I still didn't want to take the risk and leave it open – locking all the doors and windows was part of the security routine that left me able to sleep at night. I slammed it in the end and double-locked it. Smells I could deal with; my own fears were not so easy to tolerate.

I got my head down to work once I got into the office. It was after eleven before Stuart Sinclair got back to me and it took me a second to change gears when the phone rang. I sounded vague rather than competent.

'Oh. Right. Yes, it was regarding—'

He interrupted. 'You rang me, originally. I hope you know what it was about because I haven't got a clue.'

I was used to Derwent; Stu Sinclair didn't stand a chance of flustering me. 'As I was saying, I would like to interview you regarding the witness statement you made in 1992 about the murder of Angela Poole.'

I heard him blow out a lungful of breath. 'Going back a bit. I was just a kid then. Any particular reason why this is urgent now?'

If he had been more pleasant I might have told him it was connected to the recent murders. 'I've been carrying out a review of the case file and there are some anomalies. I'd like to speak with you in person. Today, preferably.'

He sounded borderline scared when he replied, which was good: it was the reaction a normal person should have to being involved in a murder investigation. Something had told me the hard-arse routine was a fake. 'Oh, okay. It was a long time ago and I don't remember everything in as much detail as I did then, obviously, but if you think it would help, I'll try. I'm actually looking after my kid this afternoon so if you don't mind interviewing me with a toddler running around, you could come to my house.'

'That's fine. What's the address?'

'Eighty-two Danbury Road, West Norwood. That's SE27.'

'I know the area,' I said, writing it down. 'Two o'clock?'

He hesitated. 'Make it half past. And I can't let you stay for long, I'm afraid. If it's going to take longer than half an hour or so, we'll have to rearrange it.'

'I'll be quick,' I said, meaning it. I had a short list of questions for Stuart Sinclair, but they were important, and I'd have promised him the moon and stars if it meant I could see him sooner rather than later.

Danbury Road was a terrace of Victorian houses, but not the grand, four-storey kind – the narrow ones built by the hundreds and thousands for high-ranking clerks and managers with small families. Roads like it snaked through London's outer suburbs, the late Victorian middle-class desire for a bathroom and garden manifested in red brick. Norwood had never been fashionable and Danbury Road was indefinably shabby, but quiet. Lots of families with small children, I thought, noticing pushchairs parked in the bay windows of several houses as I walked to number 82.

Without giving it too much thought I was expecting to see a grown-up version of Fat Stu, the buck-toothed unfortunate Derwent had described to me, so when a dark-haired, well-built man opened the door I immediately assumed I'd got the wrong address. His first words made it clear that I was in the right place.

'Bang on time. I'm impressed, DC Kerrigan.'

'Mr Sinclair?'

'None other. Come in.' He stood back and I hurried into the narrow, dark hallway where a jumble of wellies and tiny shoes told me the house was run for and by the child who lived there.

'He's still having his nap,' Sinclair explained in a low voice. 'We might be able to talk uninterrupted.'

I nodded and followed him into a heroically untidy sitting room, with wall-to-wall toys littering the floor and a pile of sofa cushions in the corner.

'Sorry. We were playing hide and seek after lunch.' He started dismantling the stack and I muttered something about there being no need to tidy up, distracted by his appearance. It wasn't the muscles flexing in his forearms or his lean, gym-honed torso that made me stare as he rearranged the room. It was more the fact that, like Shane Poole, he had conformed to the Derwent template as he grew into adulthood. I tried to work out what made them look similar. He was better-looking than Derwent but his hair was cut the same way and his clothes were the sort Derwent wore off duty, as I now knew. He had a very white, very perfect smile, an ad for his orthodontist if what Derwent had said was true. Despite the resemblance to Derwent I thought he was attractive – a handsome face with blue eyes, a square jaw and a straight nose. He turned around at just the wrong moment and caught me staring: I deserved the smirk I got. I sat down on the restored sofa and took my time over getting my notebook out, spending ages looking for my pen although I knew exactly where it was. Derwent would never let me live it down if I let Stuart Sinclair get the upper hand, I thought, and sat up a little bit straighter.

'Thank you for agreeing to see me at such short notice.'

'Glad to help,' he said, sitting down in an armchair and propping his right ankle on top of his left knee. I could hear Derwent's opinion of that: *only a total plonker sits like that, Kerrigan, no matter how pretty he may be.* He wore thick-soled boots and I wondered if he was sensitive about his height. He was a shade shorter than me – five nine to my five eleven, a difference that was negligible when he was wearing such heavy boots. Far from small, anyway, but I remembered Derwent's description of him and while diet and exercise could put manners on your genetic heritage, height was pretty difficult to change. Being tall myself I couldn't quite understand why anyone would care; it wasn't all that amazing to be leggy.

Quickly, I filled him in on the possible connection between Angela Poole and the three current murders. Each victim got a two-second look from under eyebrows twisted with pity, but no reaction beyond that.

'And what makes you think there's a connection?' He handed the three pictures back to me.

'The MO. That's modus operandi.'

'I know. I watch a lot of crime dramas.' A big grin. 'Bet you avoid them.'

'Like the plague. I don't know how much you remember about Angela's death—'

'More than I thought,' he said promptly. 'I've been thinking about it since you called. It's all coming back.'

'Great. Because you're one of the only people who might have seen Angela's killer, and I was wondering if you'd managed to recall anything that you didn't tell the police at the time.'

He shook his head. 'I told them, and I'm telling you now, I saw her boyfriend walking off, just after midnight. Something woke me up a few minutes before that – must have been the poor girl screaming, I suppose.'

There was something dispassionate about how he spoke about her, especially compared to Derwent's raw grief.

It had been a long time since she died, though. 'Did you know her? Angela?'

'She was the girl next door. I knew about her more than I knew her.'

'Did you have a crush on her?' I saw him look surprised for the first time and explained what I'd meant. 'Because she was the girl next door. That's what's supposed to happen, isn't it?'

'I don't remember that.' He smiled. 'Anyway, she wouldn't have looked twice at me. I was short and fat and ugly. And as I said, she had her boyfriend. The one the police wouldn't arrest for killing her.'

'He had an alibi.'

'That must have been wrong. He did it. I saw him.' His eyes were unwavering. He sounded sure and I had to resist the urge to argue with him, to defend Derwent.

'What exactly did you see? When you got up, before twelve – did you see anything in the garden?'

'No. Or hear anything. It was summer and my window was open. I leaned out, didn't hear anything, gave up. That's why I went back to bed.'

'And then . . .'

'I got worried. I thought I'd go and look out of another window.'

'At the front.'

'Yeah.'

'That's the main bedroom, isn't it? Your parents' room?'

'My mum's. My dad had left us.' A flash of the white teeth. 'I've got over it now, but I missed him at the time.'

'So you went in and looked out.'

'Yeah.'

'And she was in bed, asleep, or . . .'

'I don't remember.' He raised his eyebrows. 'You're very interested in the details, aren't you?'

There was no easy way to say it. 'I don't believe you really did look out of the window upstairs at the front.'

'Are you calling me a liar?' His voice was still pleasant but his fingers were digging into the uppermost leg, his knuckles white.

'I think you've told the story so often you almost believe it yourself, but you didn't see anyone walking away at a minute after twelve. You didn't like Angela's boyfriend and you wanted him to get into trouble, so you said you'd seen him. You didn't know about his alibi, and once you'd said it, you had to keep saying it.'

He was shaking his head. 'No. Wrong.'

'He was mean to you, wasn't he? He bullied you. Called you names. You had a massive grudge against him but you were scared of him and this was your chance to get him into trouble like you couldn't believe. You were fifteen – you probably didn't even realise how serious it was and that the last thing you should do was lie.'

'Oh, spare me the psychology.' His face was red now. 'I saw someone and I thought it was Josh Derwent. It looked like Josh Derwent.'

'In what way?'

'He was tall. Moved fast. He – I don't know. I was expecting it to be Josh. I thought it was him.' He looked at me again, back to the wide-eyed sincerity. 'I really thought it was him.'

'Thinking again, can you add anything to the description that you didn't say before?'

'Nope.'

'You'd seen Der— Josh Derwent earlier in the evening. Did you describe the clothes you'd seen him wearing? Or was the person you saw really wearing the same colour T-shirt as Josh Derwent and similar jeans? Could you tell, in the streetlight, when he was walking away from you at speed?'

'Okay. Okay. You're right. I just saw a silhouette, really. He might have been wearing black. Dark colours, anyway.' Stuart touched a hand to his upper lip and looked at it. 'I'm actually sweating. You're pretty good at this, aren't you?'

'I do all right.'

'But you gave something away. You started to call him by his surname. You know him, don't you? Josh Derwent? He's a copper, I know that much. Are you mates?' He waited a beat. 'Lovers?'

'I know him. I work with him sometimes. But I'm here because my guv'nor wanted me to find out about Angela's death, not because of Derwent.'

'You must get asked that a lot. If you're in a relationship with him, I mean.'

'Surprisingly often,' I agreed. 'Especially since he's not my type.' The understatement of the decade.

'I'll do you the courtesy of believing you if you'll do the same for me. I really did think I saw him. I wouldn't have been able to keep lying about it.' He shuddered. 'I'd almost forgotten that guy – Orpen, his name was. He was a beast. A real old-fashioned copper. I was terrified every time he spoke to me. He always seemed to be trying to stop himself from lashing out. Met him?'

'A pleasure that awaits me,' I said with a smile.

'You're in for a treat.' He checked his watch. 'Wow. Time marches on. Is there anything else?'

I ran through my usual questions about seeing strangers or strange cars, to which he replied in the negative.

'Do you recall anything else from that night? Even after the body was discovered? The noise and lights must have disturbed you.'

'They must have. I don't really remember.'

I found that very hard to believe, but then I had been fascinated by the police and their work since I was about five. A murder next door would have been more entertaining than the best soap opera. 'Did you see the police? The ambulance?'

'Yeah. I did.'

'What about Angela's body?'

'No.' He looked edgy. 'Why do you ask?'

'There are similarities in the crime scenes we've been processing. It looks as if someone familiar with how Angela's
body was left is perpetrating these crimes. I'm just trying
to work out how many people could have seen her there.
But you said you couldn't see anything from the window.'

'No.' He pulled at his lip. 'Is this important?'

'Very. Do you know if there were photographs circu-
lating in school, or outside it? Were you aware of people
talking about it, even?'

'No. But . . .' He went into the hall and came back with
a brown leather messenger bag, an expensive man bag that
Derwent would have described, instantly and implacably,
as gay, and would not have meant that as a compliment.
He took out a battered iPad and tapped at the screen before
handing it to me. 'If you want to know who's seen Angela's
body, you'd better see this.'

I stared at it, not understanding for a second. There, filling the entire screen, was the close-up of Angela's face that
I'd seen in the file, her hair caught up in flowers, her eyelids drawn down over empty sockets. 'What the *fuck*?'

Instead of an answer a long, miserable wail cut through
the air and I jumped.

'It's the monitor. Oliver's up.' Stuart picked up a white
handset and poked at it until the noise stopped. 'Thank
God for mute.'

In the distance there was a faint shadow of a scream,
coming from the top of the house.

'Do you think you should go and get him?' I asked.

'Probably.' He was still staring at me, trying to read me.
'You know what that is, don't you?'

'A crime-scene picture of Angela Poole.'

'Scroll down. There's more. I could not believe it when I
saw it. I'm sure you feel the same way.'

I did as he suggested, distracted by the crying from

upstairs. It was getting louder and more high-pitched by the second. 'How did you find this? What is this website?'

'It's a blog called Crime-scene Shots. I'd never heard of it. After we spoke I was thinking about Angela and I don't know, I just thought I should search for her name online to see if there had been any developments I didn't know about, and *that* came up.'

I swore under my breath as pictures slipped down the screen, images I hadn't even seen in the file. 'Anyone could have seen this.'

'Anyone with access to the Internet,' Stuart agreed. Reluctantly, he edged towards the door. 'Better go up.'

'Yeah, I'll wait.'

'Well.' He checked his watch again. 'It's just that my wife will be coming back, and I didn't tell her you were going to be here.'

'I'm good at explaining things,' I said, not moving.

'I don't want to have to tell her about Angela. It's history. Nothing to do with who I am now.'

'I'll be gone in five minutes,' I promised and he looked as if he was about to say something else, but then changed his mind and left. I heard him taking the stairs two at a time.

He was back quickly, holding a red-headed boy of about fourteen months with his thumb lodged in his mouth. The child was wearing a vest and nappy and still had tears on his cheeks, which were flushed. *Teething*, I thought, remembering my nieces and their misery as the incredibly sharp baby teeth cut through their gums.

'Is he all right?'

'Fine.'

'Is it his molars? They're awfully sore when they're coming through.'

Stuart shrugged. 'Could be. It's always something.' The boy was leaning away from him and he bent down to let him stand on the floor. 'There you go, Oliver. Find a toy. Plenty of them about.'

Oliver looked at me, then turned around to check the rest of the room. Finding no one else, he collapsed to the floor and gave an anguished howl.

'Missing Mummy,' Stuart said over the noise. 'I definitely come second compared to her. Was there anything else?'

'Do you remember anyone behaving differently after Angela's death? Erratic behaviour, seeming upset, or changing their routine?'

'Yeah. One person. Josh Derwent.' He shook his head. 'I know you don't want to hear this, but I still think he was guilty.'

'If he was, there would have been some evidence to prove it.'

'He had an answer for everything. He made up a story and got away with it, but he killed her.' On the floor, Oliver was coughing and crying alternately, snot running down his upper lip in two grey-green rivers. Stuart bent down to him and ruffled his hair. 'Come on, Oliver. Belt up. She'll be back soon.'

'If you think of anything else—'

'I'll call.' He snatched the card I held out to him and shoved it in his back pocket. 'Right. I'll show you out.'

He left Oliver in his puddle of misery and disappeared into the hall. I couldn't just walk past him. I crouched down beside the boy.

'It's all right. Your mummy will be back soon. Daddy will play with you once I'm gone.'

Oliver stared at me, his face blank. I dug in my bag for a tissue and swiped it across his face, heaving slightly as I folded the soggy tissue up. There was no bin in sight so I had to put it back in my bag and I hoped like hell I'd remember it was there before I went looking for something and put my hand in it.

Stuart was standing in the hall, impatience obvious on his face. When he saw me emerge from the sitting room he opened the door. No long goodbyes, then.

As I stepped onto the doorstep, a small dark-haired woman was striding up the front path, neat in a grey suit and carrying a briefcase. She stared at me, then looked past me to Stuart.

'What's going on?'

'She's just leaving.'

'Who are you?' There was a cry from inside the house and her attention switched to Stuart before I could answer. She was already moving past me. 'Was that Oliver? Is he okay? When did he wake up?'

'Just now.'

'Shit. I thought he'd sleep for another half-hour at least.' She turned and glowered at me again. 'Who are you? Did you say?'

'Jehovah's Witness,' came from behind her and I saw Stuart pulling a face, like *what could I do?* 'I did try to discourage her.'

'I don't do God,' the woman said to me. 'Stu, honestly. I leave you alone for an hour and you let random people into the house. You're hopeless.'

'You know me. I can't be rude.' Over her head he widened his eyes at me. *Go away.*

I walked off without saying anything to back him up or undermine him. Behind me, I heard Stuart ask, 'How was the interview?' The door closed before I could hear a reply. It made sense that he wasn't usually left in sole charge of Oliver. He really didn't seem used to the messy end of parenting. Typical dad, loving the toys and games, hating the snot and nappies, I thought, and couldn't suppress the thought that the fair-weather dads had the right idea. Wiping snotty noses was not my idea of fun.

I hoped Stuart didn't get into too much trouble. If I'd been his wife I would have known he was lying, and I'd have been going through him for a short cut at that very moment. Maybe it was easier to pretend she believed him, given that they had a child. Maybe she didn't even care that he'd been alone with a relatively nice-looking woman, or that he was prepared to try to mislead her about it.

Or maybe I was vastly overrating my personal attractiveness. It wasn't my favourite option, but it was probably the most likely.

TUESDAY

Chapter 22

I sat in the car waiting for a traffic light to change to green and wished myself absolutely elsewhere. I'd have been nervous enough about interviewing Lionel Orpen, Detective Inspector (retired) on my own. Having to take Derwent along was positively the last straw.

'Tell me again what he said.'

'He told me to bring you with me. He said he wanted to see how you'd turned out, and he wanted to tell you some things about the investigation that he'd never told anyone else.' I was beyond bored now with repeating my phone conversation with the retired police officer. Gruff wasn't the word for his phone manner. Once I'd explained who I was, all he wanted to know was whether I knew Derwent.

'And then?' Derwent prompted.

'And then he said he wouldn't talk to me at all unless you came with me.' I shot a glance at him. 'Happy now?'

'Intrigued.' He grinned. 'Glad to be back in the saddle.'

'You're not. That's why you're not driving.' The car tore away from the lights and I braked, then bit my lip. The accelerator needed to be practically on the floor before the car would move and it was easy to misjudge it. Easy for me, as Derwent had said two minutes after I picked him up. A *normal* driver would have been fine, apparently.

'Remember, you mustn't tell anyone you were with me. I'm supposed to be doing this on my own.'

'You need someone to hold your hand, Kerrigan. Firstly, because Lionel is fucking scary. Secondly, because you let Fat Stu run rings around you. *And* Shaney.'

I hadn't told him I'd seen Claire; I hadn't even mentioned her name. Undoubtedly I would have got that interview wrong too, somehow. Derwent was the worst kind of back-seat driver and not just in the car. I was glad to have him along if it made Lionel Orpen more forthcoming but I was seriously considering dumping him by the side of the nearest main road on my way back.

'Remember, I'm not telling Godley you came with me today. If you let it slip, I'll get in a ton of trouble.'

'Relax,' Derwent said, opening the window and sticking his elbow out. Icy wind blasted across my face, blowing my hair into my eyes.

'Hey! Shut it.'

'I need air.'

'It's like having a dog. Do I need to take you for a walk before the interview or do you think you can wait until afterwards?'

'Very funny,' he said, without shutting it. I gritted my teeth and concentrated on getting to Kensal Rise, where Lionel Orpen was living out his retirement in a small ter-raced house.

There was nowhere to park on Orpen's street so I drove around the corner and left the car beside a small park with a playground. The day was cool but bright and the park was busy with mothers and small children, who were run-ning around shouting at top volume. I thought of Oliver Sinclair and wondered if Stuart would be allowed to look after him on his own again after letting a strange woman into the house.

Derwent squinted across the top of the car looking pained. 'Do they have to make so much noise?'

'It's a key part of having a good time when you're little.'

Two small boys ran past us on the other side of the railings, scuffling with one another.

'Give them fifteen years and they'll be being arrested for fighting outside pubs after closing time.'

'Well, that won't be your problem any more. You'll be retired by then,' I said.

He pulled a face. 'Not quite. Anyway, they'll have extended retirement age to seventy to save on pensions. Or I'll keep working for free. I'm not exactly thrilled at the thought of doing fuck all every day for the rest of my life.'

'I don't think fuck all is obligatory. You could find something worthwhile to do.'

'What sort of thing could I do? What else would I want to do? The crossword?' He snorted. 'Come on. Let's go and see how it's done.'

Good policeman or not, Lionel Orpen was no poster boy for retirement. He opened his door and peered out at us suspiciously, two days of stubble frosting flabby thread-veined cheeks. He'd been a big man in his time but now his clothes hung off his body, apart from where a substantial gut pushed against the thin wool of his jumper. Even before I smelled the alcohol on his breath I knew he was a drinker. It was half past ten and he was weaving as he led us into a living room piled high with newspapers and books.

'Excuse the mess. I'm writing my memoirs. This lot is the raw material. Sources, and such.' He sat down in a thread-bare armchair by the gas fire, leaving us to find somewhere to put ourselves. Derwent perched on the arm of the sofa, which was loaded with yellowing magazines and otherwise unusable. I stood near the door, not wanting to touch anything. The house smelled of mildew and I was afraid to disturb any of the piles in case something jumped out at me. A movement at the back of the room made me whirl around, my heart thumping.

'Gave you a fright, did he?' Orpen patted his lap and

a cat threaded his way through the stacks of books, uttering low cries. It was a round-faced tom with tattered ears and a scarred nose. It jumped up on Orpen's knee and he scratched it under the chin. 'Poor old Rudolf.'

'As in the reindeer?' Derwent asked.

'As in Hess.'

Derwent glanced at me and I could see what he was thinking. *Oh, here we go . . .*

'You're wondering why I named him after a Nazi. Well, he reminded me of him. He used to be free – I fed him now and then, when he came into the garden. He had a great life, fighting and screwing and chasing rats. Then he got picked up by the do-gooders next door and taken to a rehoming centre, as if anyone would want him. He was on death row when I found out where he'd gone. I got there in time to save him but he'd been de-balled. The way he looked at me, through the bars of the cage – it was Hess at Spandau all over again.'

'Oh. That's—'

Orpen interrupted Derwent. 'You didn't come here to talk about Rudy. You came to talk about Angela. Don't bullshit me. I spent long enough doing the job you're trying to pretend you're capable of doing.'

'All right.' Derwent shifted position on the arm of the sofa. 'Tell us about Angela.'

'You first. What made you join the Met?'

'It seemed like a good career.'

'Bollocks. The truth.'

'I wanted to help people.'

'You're wasting my time.'

'I wanted to fuck up the people who think they can do what they want with other people's lives.'

Orpen's eyes lit up. 'That's what I liked about you, Joshua. You understood what we were trying to do.'

'You were trying to fit me up for murdering Angela,' Derwent said with commendable restraint.

'It was obviously you. All the evidence pointed to you. Except that you couldn't have done it.' He gave a rattling, wet cough. 'We put Charlie Poole under plenty of pressure to take back his statement but he wouldn't. Said it wasn't fair. He wanted justice, not revenge on you for putting his darling daughter in the wrong place at the wrong time.'

'He was a good man.'

'Oh, do you think so?' Orpen leaned back in his chair to let the cat surge up his chest and lie against his shoulder. 'He had no love for you.'

'Not surprising. Men tend to have trouble with their daughters' boyfriends.'

'He thought you were a fool.'

'He was probably right.' Derwent smiled. 'I was a teenager.'

'You weren't the worst. Not as clever as you thought you were, but cleverer than most.' Another cough. 'I knew you joined the army, you know. I kept in touch with your social worker. Found out when you left and decided to become a police officer.'

'I'm flattered.' Sarcasm was so much a habit with Derwent that I couldn't tell if he meant it or not.

'Don't be. I kept track of a few lads. The ones I couldn't lock up, for whatever reason. Some of them turned into killers and rapists, just as I'd thought, and got sent down. Some of them got on the straight and narrow. You're the only one who joined the Met, I'll tell you that much.'

'I'm not surprised. You weren't the best example I could have had.'

'I. Did. My. Job.' He slammed his hand down on the arm of his chair, his face livid with rage, and I actually stepped back even though he wasn't speaking to me. The cat took offence and jumped off, sliding under the chair instead. Orpen was depleted now, a shadow of what he had been in his prime. It must have been truly terrifying to be inter-viewed by him when he was in the full vigour of middle age.

Derwent folded his arms, outwardly unmoved. 'Yeah, but you didn't. Because you never locked anyone up for Angela's death. Who did you like for it, apart from me?'

'The dad, initially. That went nowhere. The two of you cancelled each other out, didn't you? Alibied each other.' Orpen burped, loudly, and went on as if he hadn't. 'The local troublemakers. We had a couple of sex offenders who were living nearby who seemed right, but then there wasn't a sexual assault.'

'Why do you think that was?' I asked, too interested to stay silent.

'Dunno. Maybe he lost his nerve. Couldn't get it up. Got disturbed and ran off.' He looked at Derwent with a glint in his eye. 'Didn't fancy sloppy seconds.'

I saw it hit home. It was only the smallest shift in his pos-ture but it was a giveaway nonetheless and Orpen didn't miss it either.

'Still sad about her, aren't you? Still wish you'd walked her home.'

Derwent was the last person to need rescuing, usually, but in this instance he seemed defenceless and I found myself stepping forward to stand beside him.

'Mr Orpen, I spoke to Stuart Sinclair yesterday. He admitted he'd lied to you in his original witness statements.'

'About seeing this fellow?' Orpen pointed a long, wrinkled finger at Derwent. 'I knew that. He was a real mummy's boy. His mother kept her door locked at night to stop him from coming into her room.'

'Fucking hell,' Derwent said. 'You mean—'

'Not like that.' Orpen raised a hand to stop Derwent from going on. 'Don't get too excited. The Sinclair marriage had split up earlier that year. Stuart was going through a bad time and he'd stopped sleeping. He wandered around the house all night. Drove his mother mad. She didn't want him bothering her.'

'So he didn't see anything from the front window,' I said.
'No.'

'And you knew he was lying at the time.'

'Yeah, but he wouldn't budge. Said he'd seen what he'd seen.'

'Did you go into his bedroom?' I asked. 'What sort of view did he have of the garden next door?'

Orpen's face went slack and he gazed into the corner of the room, trying to remember. 'He could see a bit, I think. His room was on the left at the back.'

'Could he have seen Angela with her killer from his bedroom?'

'He said he didn't.'

'He lied about seeing Derwent,' I pointed out.

'There was a tree in that corner of the garden. It was in full leaf. He wouldn't have been able to see much, if anything.'

I thought about it, trying to imagine myself there. A sleepless fifteen-year-old, attracted by the noise of a scuffle, seeing movement under the trees. Assuming it was the girl next door and her boyfriend. Assuming they were having sex, there and then, only feet from him. And he hated Derwent. Certainly enough to want to disturb them.

'You know who didn't have an alibi?' Orpen was watching Derwent again, his expression wry. 'Your mate. What was his name? Vinny. He said he was with Shane, but it was bullshit.'

'Why didn't you arrest them?' I asked.

'No evidence.' He sucked his teeth. 'And Shane *did* have an alibi in the end. Some girl he wasn't supposed to be seeing. That's why he lied. He dragged Vinny into it to back him up – that was their story.'

'So Shane was out. But why didn't you arrest Vinny?' I asked.

'I wanted to. It was just a hunch, though. No evidence. I interviewed him twice and didn't get anywhere. Got told to back off by my boss because he was a juvenile and his parents were getting antsy.'

'Who was the girl?' Derwent demanded.

'Now you're asking me.' He went looking through a stack of papers by his chair, wetting his thumb the better to flick through them. 'Here we are. Claire Naylor. You should talk to that Vinny again. Find out if he knows anything about these killings you're investigating.'

Derwent didn't say anything. He was staring into space. I assumed it was too hard for him to tell Orpen what had happened to Vinny, in the end. He had walked away from me when I told him – just turned and left before I could say I was sorry.

'Vinny died, Mr Orpen. In Afghanistan,' I said.

'So he's probably not your killer, then.'

'Probably not.'

'He wouldn't have hurt Angela.' Derwent had recovered. 'No way.'

'Well, someone did. And you asked me what I thought, and that's what I thought.'

'Do you remember if you showed the crime-scene pictures to many people when you were doing interviews? Do you recall who saw them?'

Orpen winced. 'Bit of a sore point, the pictures. We lost a set.'

'What do you mean, lost them?' Derwent demanded.

'They went missing. They were in the police station, on a desk, and someone misplaced them.'

'Or they were stolen,' I said.

'Who'd want to do that?' Orpen asked. 'Anyway, why are you asking me about them?'

I explained about the website Stuart had shown me, and the relevance to our murders. Orpen shrugged.

'Can't help you. Didn't know who nicked them at the

time and I'm certainly not going to be able to tell you now. Any more questions?'

'Just one,' I said quickly. 'Do you recall any intel coming in on a guy called Craig? He was passing through the area around the time of Angela's death.'

'First name or last name?'

'No idea.'

'Description?'

I told him what Claire had told me and he shook his head. 'Where did you get that?'

'I came across the name,' I said vaguely.

'Never heard of him before. And good luck with tracking him down twenty years on.'

'Thanks.'

Orpen nodded at me. 'She's a bright one, Joshua.'

'Never thought you'd fall for a pretty face,' Derwent said, dismissing me as usual.

'Not my type. Too tall. But she's got something.'

'Yeah. Ears.' I glared at the pair of them. 'Can you stop talking about me as if I'm not here?'

'Take it as a compliment, lovely.' The old police officer gave a wheezing laugh that degenerated into a cough.

Derwent turned so Orpen couldn't see his face and looked from me to the door. I took the hint and said good-bye, leaving Derwent behind. He joined me on the doorstep a few minutes later and blew his nose.

'Good to go?' I asked.

'Yeah. I am.' He set off towards the car and I hurried after him.

'Are you okay?'

'Of course. Got dust in my sinuses. That place is a health hazard.' He blew his nose again, and took the opportunity to wipe his eyes. 'Oh, fuck it. I must be getting soft.'

A lorry with a skip on the back of it blasted past, taking the speed bumps along the road far too fast. The skip flew into the air and thumped back down after every bump. I waited until it had gone by, with a thud and a crack that sounded like a gunshot, before I tried to ask anything else.

'What did he say to you?'

'He told me he was proud of how I'd turned out.'

'Aw. That's nice.'

'Don't,' Derwent said, shaking his head. 'Just don't.'

'I knew you were sentimental but that's astonishing. I bet he never made you cry when he was interrogating you.'

'You're right, he didn't.' Derwent sniffed. 'Don't tell anyone about this. Ever.'

'You're not here, remember?' I took out the car keys. 'So no one will ever know.'

We turned the corner so the park came into view. The children were still screaming, sounding shriller than ever. I glanced across at the playground, about to make some remark to Derwent about it, and stopped. I was aware of him pausing too, looking in the same direction. Something was wrong, I thought, trying to work out what it could be. I couldn't see any of the children or mothers at first, just a lot of abandoned prams and buggies, but I could see a man standing in the middle of the park, all in black.

And as he turned towards us I saw the gun in his hand.

Derwent and I started running at the same time. Towards, not away.

It didn't occur to either of us to do anything else.

Chapter 23

Being fitter and quicker, Derwent got ahead of me, but not by much. I sank down behind the car nearest the park gate, a couple of seconds after he had done the same thing.

'Stay here. Call it in. Tell them to send SO19.'

'I won't need to tell them to do that,' I said, not unreasonably. A gunman in a playground would get every resource available to the Met. I had my phone out and was dialling already. Derwent turned and prepared to move.

'Hey,' I hissed. 'Where do you think you're going?'

'I'm not going to stay here and wait for him to start killing kids.'

'And what do you propose to do about it? Talk him to death? You're not armed.' I got through to the police control room before I could say anything else to Derwent and he took advantage of that to dart out from behind the car and slide through the gate. I moved along a bit further, still crouching, still on the phone, so I could keep him in view, see the gunman, and monitor the distance between the two of them. It was not enough and narrowing all the time.

And then Derwent whistled, a jaunty two notes to attract the man's attention.

'All right, fella? Lovely day for it.'

The gunman turned, his free hand stretched out towards Derwent as a warning. 'Go away.'

He was older than I'd thought – forty, at a guess. White.

Fair hair, thinning a bit. Deep lines scored his forehead and bracketed his mouth. Staring eyes: I could see white all around the irises even from where I was lurking. The gun was rock-steady in his right hand, though.

'Come on, mate. You don't want to wave one of those around.' Hands in his pockets, Derwent was walking towards him, slowly but inexorably. The gunman stepped back a pace.

'Fuck off, *mate*. This is none of your business.'

'What's the problem? What's going on?'

Through his teeth, the man hissed, 'I was looking for my bitch wife and my little boy.'

In my ear, the operator was repeating all I'd told her and checking the address, her voice calm and nasal. I was riveted to the scene in front of me.

'We'll get backup to you ASAP. Trojans are on the way. ASU is lifting. Stay on the line.'

I wasn't going to argue with her but I needed both hands. I put the phone in my jacket pocket, still on so she could hear what was happening, and moved forward to the gate. Derwent was about thirty feet away from me, getting closer to the gunman and, crucially, his weapon. Beyond him, I could see a group of about ten women and maybe fifteen children, huddled together in a tight group. They were looking at Derwent as if he was their only hope.

'The two of you not getting on?'

'We split up. A couple of months ago. She threw me out.'

Derwent tutted. 'What's your name, fella?'

'Lee.'

'This isn't going to help, is it, Lee? You don't want your little boy seeing you with a gun, do you? Not for real.'

'I don't know where he is.' Lee swung back to face the group of children and women, waving the gun in their direction. 'They won't tell me.'

'Maybe he's not here. Maybe he's gone home.'

'Not without his mother.' A ghastly grin. 'She's not going anywhere.'

I saw it at the same time as Derwent: a body lying on the ground. From my angle, all I could see was a pair of legs in skinny jeans and flat brown leather boots. They weren't moving. She was lying on her front, just beside a brightly coloured climbing frame in the shape of a giraffe.

'What did you do, Lee?' Derwent's voice was sharp. 'Did you shoot her?'

'Sometimes you've got to stop talking and start doing. She never listened. I warned her about it and she never changed. Anyway, what do you care?' He held up the gun again, pointing it straight at Derwent's chest. 'Fucking stop moving or I'll shoot you too. I told you before, go away.'

'Not going to happen, mate.' But Derwent had stopped. 'I'm not going anywhere. She needs help and you need to put the gun down.'

'I want my son. That bitch took him away from me. She poisoned his mind against me. She made him say he didn't want to see me. Me! His daddy.' Lee was shaking his head, incredulous. 'It broke my heart. If no one's going to listen to me, and people like me, it's time to take control. It's time to do something that can't be ignored.'

'This isn't the right way to go about getting him back,' Derwent said. 'This is going to fuck up your chances something chronic unless you stop shooting and start thinking. Give me the gun and let's get an ambulance for the lady.'

'She's a whore and she deserved what she got.'

I was close enough now to see that the weapon was not a handgun, which made sense because they were illegal and hard to come by on the street. It was a modified starter's pistol – still illegal but much cheaper and easier to get hold of. It would be unpredictable even in an expert's hands, and risky to use. His aim would be rotten. There was a very good chance he'd have bent the firing pin with his first shot, making the gun useless. Then again, he might not. I doubted he was using heavy ammunition, but at close range a small projectile could kill. I wished I could see more of the woman on the ground. I took out my phone and murmured a report to the operator, telling the paramedics to expect at least one gunshot victim.

'This isn't going to help,' Derwent said again. 'This was a bad idea and you need to start thinking about how you're going to walk away from it.'

'This is what I was driven to do. The courts don't listen to men. They don't listen to honest, straight-talking people. They don't value fathers, except as a source of income for lazy sluts like Marianne.'

Marianne, I assumed, was the woman lying on the ground.

'You sound like Philip Pace,' Derwent said. 'That Dads Matter guy.'

'Philip Pace is the only person willing to stand up to the feminazi left-wing cunts who are running this country.'

I tried to think of a woman of any political persuasion with real power, currently, and failed. Somehow, I didn't think Lee was in the mood for a discussion about it.

Proving that he was the worst negotiator possible, Derwent was getting annoyed. He dropped the all-in-it-together matey tone and spoke in his usual trenchant way. 'Pace is an egomaniac. He's in it for the attention and the fame. He doesn't care about you.'

'He's the only one who cares. The only one.'

'Mate, you are fucking deluded. But then again, you must be if you're standing in the middle of a playground waving a gun around.'

'Have you got kids?' Lee asked. 'Do you even understand what I'm trying to do here?'

'I don't think you even know what you're trying to do. This was never going to go well, was it?'

'I don't care what you think. It's none of your business.'

'You've made it my business. I don't give a flying fuck through a rolling doughnut about your marriage problems, but I do want to see everyone make it home in one piece.'

'It's a bit late for that now.'

'It's not too late. It will be when the firearms officers turn up and shoot you because you're armed and dangerous. They don't mess about. They will kill you.'

'I don't care.'

'Course you do. You want to see your little boy grow up. That's what this is all about, according to you. You can do that if you put the gun down and give yourself up.' The thud-thud-thud of a helicopter sounded overhead, approaching fast. Derwent spoke louder to be heard over it. 'You're about to get into a world of shit, mate. I reckon you've got about three minutes to get this sorted. The thing about firearms officers is that they spend their lives training for this moment, and they're trained to shoot to kill. Head, chest, boom. You know they're going to take the shot if you give them the opportunity. Be smart about it.'

'Are you a copper?'

'Yeah.'

'Why aren't you in uniform?'

'I'm CID. An inspector. So I know what I'm talking about.'

I decided that was my cue and moved forward. 'These women and children have nothing to do with you. It's time to let them leave.' They would have to walk past him to get to the gate, unfortunately. The railings around the park were designed to keep people out. They were high and not climbable.

The gunman looked at me for the first time, then swung around to check on the group huddled behind him. The screaming had stopped but someone was sobbing, a dry and terrible sound that made my stomach contract. 'They're not going anywhere.'

Derwent shook his head. 'Not helping anyone, my friend. Buy yourself some time. Let them go.'

'No.'

'You don't need them. They're just one more thing to think about.'

I risked a look over my shoulder and saw that the promised backup had arrived, though I couldn't yet see the distinctive blue boiler suits and body armour of the Met's firearms unit, SO19. I could see three officers from where I was standing, all more or less camouflaged behind cars, which meant there were a lot more I couldn't see, but they would have tasers at best. Too far away to help at the moment.

And the only consolation was that if they had been armed, I'd have been standing in the middle of their field of fire.

'I want to take a hostage,' the man said. 'One of them has to stay.'

'Not a chance. Move towards them and I'll have to stop you.' Derwent sounded very sure of himself. The helicopter hovered overhead, not so low that we could feel the wind from the rotors, but low enough that it was necessary to shout.

'You wouldn't dare.'

'I'd have to.'

'I'll shoot you,' Lee promised, pointing the gun at Derwent again. 'You know I will.'

Derwent took a step closer, getting into position. 'Get them moving, Kerrigan.'

I went past the two of them quickly, not even acknowledging the possibility that it might be dangerous, though fear was a heavy weight in the pit of my stomach. I was less afraid for myself than for the children. And Derwent, who hadn't the sense he was born with, who lived to be a hero.

I chose an older woman who looked calmer than the rest and had two little girls by the hand. 'Walk, don't run, and small groups. You three first.'

She nodded and led them across the playground towards the gate, not running but not dawdling either. I sent another two after her, and then four, watching to make sure they made it. The first woman crossed the road and disappeared around the corner and I knew the officers were directing them from their hiding places behind the cars, sending them out of sight to safety. Another four. Three. Five together, taking a chance but they were all holding hands, two women and three children. The group was dwindling now and as I got down to the last few they were getting more agitated. One of them was holding a squirming little boy. She was on the verge of hysterics.

'I can't do it. I can't.'

'Calm down.' I put a hand on her shoulder and held on while I sent another two women to safety, carrying their children. 'You'll walk with me.'

'Don't make me. Please.'

'It'll be all right.' Her panic was starting to affect the others who were left: two women who looked like a mother and daughter and a little girl who was clinging to the younger woman like a koala. 'You've seen everyone else do it. It'll be fine.'

Derwent was talking to the gunman all the time, his voice low and calm. I knew he wanted me to hurry up: I could practically hear him thinking it. I made myself be patient.

'All right, ladies. We'll all go together. No crying, no screaming, no running. Let's not frighten the children.'

'But I'm scared,' the panicking woman wailed, and I saw Lee turn around. Derwent leaned forward, still talking, trying to get his attention back, but he was focused on us now.

'Walk,' I said through gritted teeth and took her by the arm, marching her towards the gate as if I was taking her into custody. I took the side closer to Lee, shielding her from him as I strode past, but he leaned forward and saw her.

'Izzy, you cow. This is all your fault.' He grabbed my arm and pulled me back so he could reach her, lifting the gun to point it straight at her head.

I still had a firm hold on Izzy and I dragged her with me, turning away from the gun so I was between the two of them, staring at her terrified face and the small head of the boy she was holding against her, his face buried in her shoulder. I was glad I couldn't see the gun any more and I was glad I wouldn't have any warning when he fired. Everything seemed to have gone quiet and I felt detached from gravity, floating in the moment.

Out of the corner of my eye I saw a movement: Derwent charging the last few feet to grab for the gun. Too slow. Too late.

When it came, the shot sounded like the end of the world. Izzy dropped to the ground and I went with her, sprawling on the rubberised surface. Behind me, Derwent staggered, off balance. I could see his lips moving but I couldn't hear anything because my ears were ringing from the shot, and I couldn't tell if I was hurt or Izzy was or God forbid if the boy was injured. I checked them both and found they weren't shot after all and the sound was starting to come back as if someone was turning up the volume, the low tones of the helicopter first, and screaming, and a voice shouting instructions to the gunman.

I looked around and saw Derwent still on his feet but only just, stepping back and back, trying to remain upright and failing. Falling. It seemed to happen in slow motion, and I'd never thought I'd see him defeated but his face showed it: resignation. He hit the ground hard, falling back onto one shoulder, his head smacking a paving slab that was concrete, not the soft, yielding surface of the playground. I had no time to think about him because I was still turning and saw Lee, his face the colour of ice, and he lifted the gun again even as I looked up at him, pointing it at my face. He'd swapped hands, I saw. Blood was dripping from his right hand. Even money the gun had misfired that time. It was probably wrecked. Useless. He'd be right-handed, at a guess, and his reactions would be slower when he was using his left. I could rush him. Grab the gun. Disable him, as Derwent had intended to.

I couldn't move.

Behind me, Izzy scrambled to her feet and ran, holding her boy. I counted her steps, visualising the path to the gate, to the pavement outside, the sanctuary of the police cordon. They would help them.

No one could help me.

'No shot, no shot.' Pure frustration: between the playground equipment and the civilian coming through the gate with her child, the armed officers were at the wrong angle to take Lee out. A shout came in response, and a bit of basic training resurfaced at just the right moment. I got low, wrapped my arms around my head and waited as something rushed past me quicker than any human being could move, flying through the air with one intention. To kill.

And I heard Lee scream as he hit the ground with eighty pounds of Belgian Malinois on top of him.

It was moments before the handler caught up with his dog, followed by what seemed to be the entire SO19 team, but it felt like for ever. I uncurled myself and remained wary, remembering the question one of my fellow recruits had asked of the dog handler the day we got our training in working with canines.

'How do they know not to bite police officers?'

'They don't. They've got a high prey drive. To them, we all look like legitimate targets.'

'Can't you train them not to bite people in uniform?'

He had shrugged. 'Why bother? Keep your distance. They like doing their jobs. They get excited. Get in their way and they'll bite you.'

Lee was the ultimate legitimate target and on this occasion the dog was taking great pleasure in teaching him a lesson. One of the firearms officers retrieved the gun as the rest of them kept a respectful distance. The handler tried, not very hard, to persuade the dog to let go of Lee's arm.

'Come on, Bruiser. Good lad.'

Bruiser wagged his tail ecstatically. His jaws remained

clamped on Lee's biceps. Lee was still making a fair amount of noise, but it was terrified moaning now, not screaming or invective. It made a nice change.

I didn't stay to watch the show. I was more worried about Lee's victims. The paramedics were crouching around the woman who was now on her side in the recovery position. The ground where she'd been lying was saturated with blood but she was talking to the paramedics and it was her left shoulder that was injured rather than any vital organs. I ran over.

'Marianne? Where's your son? Where's your little boy? Is he all right?'

She looked up at me, huge-eyed. 'I told him to hide. I didn't want him to see Lee like that.'

'Where is he?'

'In the ladybird.'

I looked around wildly, then saw what she meant: a big red plastic ladybird with steps up the back and a slide down the front. It was hollow and there was an opening in the side to a space underneath.

'What's his name?'

'Alfie.'

I went over and crouched beside the ladybird. 'Alfie? You can come out now.'

'I'm playing hidey seek. Wiv Mummy.'

'That game's over. It's time to come out. Mummy's waiting.'

'You have to *count*.' A furious face appeared at the opening: his mother's eyes, his father's mouth, white-blond hair. He was three or four and he was livid. 'I been waiting for *her*. For *ages*. If you want to play, you have to *count*.'

One of the paramedics came and crouched down beside me. He was a fatherly type, mid-forties and he winked at Alfie before muttering to me, 'I'll take care of this. I think you're needed over there.'

I looked where he was pointing and went cold. Derwent

was still on the ground, with another team of paramedics gathered around him, and uniformed officers standing behind them, looking grave. I flew across the playground and shouldered my way through the sightseers, dropping to my knees beside Derwent's head. He was awake, sheet-white and quivering with pain.

'What happened? Where did he get you?'

'He's been shot in the thigh,' a young woman replied. She was a doctor, according to her high-visibility jacket, and she was preparing a syringe. 'This will help, Josh.'

'What is it?' he ground out between gritted teeth. 'Morphine? I don't want it.'

'It will help with the pain.'

'I can cope with the pain.' Typical macho Derwent. He was sweating.

'You don't have to cope with it. We can take it away.'

He waved a hand at her, very definitely saying no, and looked at me. 'What a fuck-up.'

'You took one for the team,' I said.

'It fucking hurts.' He grabbed my hand and held on to it, digging his fingers in. 'Sorry. It helps.'

'I don't mind.'

'I can't believe he shot me.'

'He did warn you.'

'Yeah, but I thought he was faking.' He looked up at the sky. 'You win some, you lose some. How does it look?'

I glanced down at his leg. They were holding a pad over the entrance wound and had slipped another under his thigh, so I couldn't see how bad the damage was, but it looked nasty. I kept my voice light. 'I think your trousers have had it. You'll probably keep the leg, though.'

'Of course he will.' The doctor glowered at me. 'It's a through and through. I think the bullet grazed the bone which is why he's in so much pain.'

'Did you get that?' I asked Derwent, who had shut his eyes.

'Every word.' He squeezed my hand again. 'Sorry I didn't do a better job.'

'You were amazing.'

'If I had a pound for every time a woman's said that to me . . .'

'You'd have a pound,' I finished.

'Got it in one.' Derwent winced. 'Jesus God.'

'Just have the morphine. You've done enough heroics for one day.'

'One lifetime.' He shook his head. 'No, thanks. I don't like morphine. It makes me say what I really think.'

I regarded him with awe. 'You mean there's usually a filter? I can't imagine what you stop yourself from saying given the stuff you come out with.'

'Just as well.' He lifted his head up and eyeballed the doctor. 'I mean it. Put the needle down. I'll survive.'

'Yes, you will,' the doctor said crisply. 'But we need to move you now.'

I let go of Derwent's hand.

'Hey,' he said, protesting. 'Come back, Maeve.'

'There's no room in the ambulance,' one of the paramedics told him.

'I'll see you at the hospital,' I promised.

'You'd better.'

I watched them lift him onto a stretcher and wheel him to the waiting ambulance, and I was so busy staring at that I completely missed the black Mercedes stopping beside the park. Godley was standing beside me before I registered he had arrived.

'What's going on? What happened? What was Josh even doing here?'

I looked up at Godley. 'He called me Maeve. He never calls me Maeve.'

Then, to my eternal shame, I burst into tears.

WEDNESDAY

Chapter 24

'Christ, you look worse than I do.'

'That's debatable,' I said, dropping my bag on the end of Derwent's bed and perching beside it. 'Anyway, why wouldn't you look well rested? All you've had to do for the last twenty-four hours is lie in bed.'

'I was shot,' he protested. 'I'm injured. I had to have a blood transfusion.' He looked seedy, as it happened, with untidy hair and a greyish tinge to his skin. He needed a shower, a shave and a juicy steak, in that order. A lunch tray on the table told its own story: untouched macaroni cheese congealing on a plate, and a bowl full of something covered in custard. Two slices of white bread sat on a side plate, the edges curling up in the dry, over-heated hospital air. It was pale food that was plainly not going to do the job, and I didn't blame Derwent for not trying it.

'Never mind. You're well on the mend, according to the doctors.'

'What happened to patient confidentiality?'

'Don't blame them. They had to make a statement.' I bent down to retrieve the other bag I'd brought with me and took out a stack of newspapers. 'Have you seen these?'

'Just what's on the TV.' Derwent struggled to sit up and I went to rearrange his pillows. 'Oh, give it a rest, Florence. I can manage.'

'Fine.' I retreated. 'You'll find your picture on the first five pages of every tabloid and most of the broadsheets, but they don't really do you justice. They're mainly ultra-fuzzy long-distance shots from yesterday or old pictures. The *Guardian* is running a special poll on whether the police should be armed, but you don't need me to tell you the answer will be no. The *Mail* is campaigning for us to be given tasers as standard kit. And *The Times* has dug up your military background as well as your achievements in the Met. I didn't know you were a sniper.'

He flinched. 'I don't talk about that.'

'You might have to in future. Everyone wants to interview you. You're quite the star.'

He was staring at the front page of the *Sun*, which was a dramatic but blurry shot in which he was falling backwards. Izzy and her son were in the foreground, running for cover. She looked terrified and her son was crying. It was a still from a video one of the neighbours had taken with a phone, and the film had been running on every news bulletin, along with footage from the police helicopter's camera. Derwent had the TV on with the sound turned down; he must have seen it. But there was something compelling about the single instant they had selected. High drama, caught in colour.

'Where were you?' Derwent asked.

'Behind the gate. Not shown, anyway.'

'That's not on.' He shook his head. 'You were there too.'

'Oh, please. I'm more than happy for you to get the credit for tackling Lee.'

'You should be on the front page, not relegated to page . . .' He flicked on. 'Nine. Jesus, look at your hair. Was that the best you could do?'

The picture was a formal uniformed portrait taken when I passed out of Hendon. I did not look my best. Mad hair was about the least of it.

'I don't need the attention.'

'Your mum will be furious if there's nothing for her scrapbook.'

'She'll be furious anyway. With me.' I shuddered. 'I dread to think what she'll say about us blundering in to confront a gunman. She might blame you for leading me astray.'

He looked genuinely upset at that prospect. Derwent liked my mother, for reasons he had yet to explain to me. The home cooking helped. And, it occurred to me for the first time, he probably missed his own mum. It was awful to think that she was the one who'd cut off contact. He'd deserved better than that. Another tiny bit of my dislike of Derwent crumbled and fell away, much to my own surprise.

'I can't believe you haven't spoken to her yet,' Derwent said. 'Don't you call her every day?'

'Not if I can help it. Anyway, I haven't been home. The answering machine is probably full already, just from her calls.'

'She must have your mobile number.'

I groaned. 'Yes, but I dropped it in the playground and some jobsworth SOCO bagged it and tagged it as evidence. I spent hours trying to get it back yesterday. Even the SIM card would have done. But no luck.'

'Butterfingers. Why haven't you been home? Did you go clubbing or something?'

'I've been a bit busy being debriefed by everyone you can think of.' He probably hadn't noticed but I was still wearing the same clothes as the previous day, now creased and limp with added blood on one knee from tending to the fallen warrior.

'Who debriefed you?'

'Godley. The commander of SO19. The heavies from the DPS to make sure we did things by the book.'

Derwent rolled his eyes. No one liked to attract the attention of the Department of Professional Standards, the bogeymen of the Met. 'Hope you told them to fuck themselves.'

'Not in so many words.' I knew he'd like the next bit. 'The Independent Police Complaints Commission sent a team round, just in case Lee makes a complaint.'

'I'd like to see him try.'

'Some lawyer is probably talking him into it at this very moment.' A yawn threatened to crack my jaw.

'Bored? You've only just got here. Imagine what it's like for me.' He rolled his head from side to side. 'I'm climbing the walls. How come it took you so long to visit me?'

'You're supposed to be recuperating. We were leaving you alone to rest. Anyway, the investigating officers have been letting me read the witness statements for the last few hours.' I yawned again. 'I'm shattered.'

'Anything interesting?'

'What you'd expect. Lee and Marianne had a stormy relationship – lots of arguments, a history of domestic violence on both sides. Izzy was the one who persuaded Marianne to leave him, which is why he had such a massive reaction to seeing her walk past him. The break-up turned nasty when Lee was months late paying his child support. Marianne went to court and stopped his visits to Alfie back in August. It took Lee this long to set up his little stunt, but he was planning it for a while. Marianne knew Lee was looking for her because his brother warned her. She wasn't expecting the gun, though.'

'A starter's pistol. Not a real gun.'

'It fired real bullets,' I pointed out. 'Luckily, Lee only had four, so he didn't do any practice shots. He was aiming for Marianne's heart, she said, but the shot was high and to the left.'

'Too close for comfort. Where did he get it?'

'He bought it in a pub car park in Gravesend, he says. He got a tip-off from a friend of a friend of a friend and we're never going to be able to trace it back to the armourer if you ask me. Anyway, it wasn't much good. According to the ballistics report, by the time he shot you the gun was practically falling apart. It was about half as effective as it might have been and it seriously damaged Lee's hand when he fired it. He probably wouldn't have got another shot off.'

'Lucky for you.'

'And lucky for you he didn't shoot you before Marianne, or aim a bit better. If he'd hit your femur and the gun had been in full working order you'd be walking with a limp for rest of your life and living off a disability pension.'

'Instead of being released later on today.'

'Already?'

Derwent grinned. 'I'm talking them into it.'

'I bet they can't wait to get rid of you.'

'What are you talking about? The nurses love me.'

The door opened behind me and Godley walked in, carrying an elaborate flower arrangement in one hand and a bag of grapes in the other. 'They said you were ready for visitors.'

'Not flowers, please. Makes me feel as if I'm dead or gay or something.'

'I think it takes more than a couple of flower arrangements to change your sexual orientation,' I said.

'I'm not taking any chances. Go and find the prettiest nurse you can see and give them to her instead, boss.'

Godley dumped the grapes on the bedside locker and took the flowers back out to the hall.

'This is why you're popular with the nurses,' I said.

'That and the friendly banter.'

'God help them.'

'Just because you don't appreciate it, Kerrigan.'

'It's growing on me,' I admitted, and Derwent looked smug.

'They all fall for it eventually.'

Godley came back. 'The nurses' station looks like a florist's shop. All your doing, apparently.'

'I don't want them. I told them to give anything that came in to people who didn't have any.' He shifted against the pillows, obviously in pain. 'I don't know why anyone would send flowers.'

'Well, I didn't. They're from Marianne Grimes.' Godley sat in the single armchair by the bed. 'She's very grateful.'

'So she should be. She had the sense to play dead but that wasn't going to work for ever. How's the kid?'

'Confused,' Godley said. 'He doesn't know what happened except that his mum is a bit unwell and staying in hospital. He didn't see Lee so for the time being everyone is keeping their mouths shut about it. He's too young to understand.'

'That's something, anyway,' I said. He'd find out eventually, though.

'Speaking of not understanding things.' All the warmth had left Godley's voice. 'Josh, would you like to explain what you were doing there in the first place?'

'Kerrigan needed me.'

'For my interview with Lionel Orpen,' I clarified. I'd told Godley this already. And the DPS. I had yet to work out how much trouble we were both in, though.

'He wanted to talk to me,' Derwent said.

'He insisted.'

'It wasn't Kerrigan's idea.'

'It was just for that one interview.'

'No one else was ever supposed to know I was there.'

'I thought it would be all right,' I said. 'It was all about Angela, not about the current murders.'

'That wasn't your call to make.' Godley looked at Derwent. 'And you. Where do I begin? You should have said no. You were on leave. I warned you.'

'Yeah, but—'

'I don't want to hear it.'

'If I hadn't been there,' Derwent said, ignoring the interruption, 'Kerrigan would have had to deal with Lee on her own. Someone would have died – a kid, or Marianne. Kerrigan, even.'

'So we were really lucky that you both disobeyed direct orders and you were both prepared to lie about it, is that it?' The sarcasm in Godley's voice made me wince.

'It was the right thing to do.' Derwent wasn't backing down.

'You should have asked me for permission.'

'You'd have said no.'

'If you think that argument is persuasive, being shot in the leg has affected your brain.'

'Look, boss, we needed to talk to Orpen. He's a miserable old git. He would have said no to Kerrigan.'

'He *did* say no,' I interjected.

'Leaving Lee aside, it was a good morning's work. I'm sorry it happened that way but it was worth it.'

Godley raised his eyebrows. 'The end justifies the means? Really, Josh?'

'What do you want me to say?'

'An apology would be a good start.'

'I'm very, very sorry.'

'Sorry you got caught,' Godley said, and Derwent grinned at him.

'You can't stay angry, can you?'

'If it ever happens again, Josh, you're out. No more second chances. I mean it.'

'Understood.' A look passed between the two of them that was, on Derwent's part, an acknowledgement that he'd been wrong, and on Godley's that he wasn't going to stand for being messed around any more.

'And as for you, Maeve—' Godley began.

Derwent lunged for the remote control, his attention fixed on the TV screen. 'This is us. Look. We're on again.'

I half-glanced at it then turned away. I had seen that particular report more than once.

'Come on, Kerrigan. Watch it. Your big moment is

coming up.' Derwent turned up the volume so we could listen to the commentary. The reporter's voice was solemn.

'The moment a father lashed out against society . . . and the brave police officers who stopped his murderous rampage. Lee Grimes had a grudge against his ex-wife – and an illegally held firearm. The modified weapon was unreliable, but it had the potential to be lethal.'

In order to spin out the visuals for longer they had slowed it down so every frame of the blurry footage got full value and I had seen myself trying to block Izzy from Lee, and watched Derwent fall to the ground too many times. Knowing how it ended didn't make it easier viewing.

'Wait for it. This is my favourite bit.' Derwent was grinning. I glanced back at the screen in time to see myself dissolving into tears while Godley supported me.

'I was in shock.'

'You were worried about me. I made you cry.'

'I had just come very close to being shot. I think I was entitled to get a bit upset.'

'Now, now,' Godley said. 'Settle down, you two.'

The report was now dealing with the emotional scenes as parents clung to their mostly uncomprehending children.

'I hate this,' Godley said, wincing. 'As soon as you have children, the thought of them being injured or even upset is unbearable. You hold them a bit closer for a while.'

'Do you feel sorry for him?' I asked. 'Lee, I mean?'

'A bit. I hope I wouldn't behave the same way, but he sounded desperate to see his son.'

'They should have been safe in a playground on a sunny autumn afternoon, but only chance – and two unarmed police officers – stood between them and a potential massacre,' the reporter intoned.

I snorted. 'Again, he had four bullets. Four. And he'd used one on Marianne already.'

'He could have finished her off, killed Alfie and turned the gun on himself. He could have killed Izzy for interfering.

He could have shot at random and killed some of those children.' Godley shook his head. 'Four bullets could have done plenty of harm.'

'I didn't exactly come out of it unscathed,' Derwent pointed out. 'I don't know when I'll be able to run again.'

'Or work.' Godley stood up. 'I came to tell you, you'll need to be passed as medically fit to return to work. It'll be weeks, not days. Make some plans for your time off if you get bored in here.'

Derwent, predictably, exploded. 'Fuck that. I don't need my leg to solve cases. Look at Ironsides. He was in a bloody wheelchair.'

'You know that was a TV programme, don't you?' I said.

'I know I've wasted enough time on the sidelines recently and I want to get back to what I do best.' Derwent's attention was caught by the news again. 'That bastard.'

The screen was filled with a face that was instantly familiar, even without the banner on the bottom of the screen. Philip Pace looked tense but still handsome in a slick way. His tan was too deep, his hair too groomed for my liking. He was wearing a dark suit and a cobalt tie, which he touched while the newsreader was introducing him.

'That's a giveaway. He's nervous,' I said.

'So he should be.' Derwent threw a grape at the screen and missed. 'This is his fault. Whipping people up. Telling them they're victims.' Another grape hit the target and bounced off onto the bed. 'If Lee Grimes had really cared about Alfie he'd have paid the child support on time instead of pissing off his wife and making her play hardball in the family courts.'

'This just goes to show the desperate situation of men in an uncaring society, one that doesn't recognise their rights as fathers and as *people*.' Philip Pace's eyes glistened with sincerity.

'*People* who are still paid more for doing the same job as women,' I said.

'Right and proper,' Derwent said. 'They don't go off and take a year's paid leave any time they like to have babies.'

'Which they do by themselves, of course. No men are involved in the process.'

'Don't rise to the bait, Maeve. He's teasing you.' Godley stretched. 'I wish I could stay longer, Josh, but I have to get going.'

'So does Kerrigan.' Derwent threw another grape, this time at me. 'Don't you have work to do?'

'I was just leaving.' I gathered up my bags.

'I think as a society,' Philip Pace said, 'we need to understand why we're demonising a loving, caring father because he missed his little boy.'

'I can't watch this.' I reached over and switched the sound off. 'Most loving, caring fathers don't try to kill the mothers of their little boys.'

'Most fathers would die for their children,' Godley agreed.

'Not all,' Derwent said. 'Some people shouldn't be allowed to breed. You should have to get a licence.'

Godley had got as far as the door, and was just raising a hand to salute Derwent when his phone rang.

'Don't tell me someone's gone and killed someone,' Derwent muttered to me. 'Don't they know I'm off work?'

I half-smiled, but I was watching Godley's face and try-ing to work out what he was being told. He checked his watch. His side of the conversation was mostly yes and no so I couldn't make much of it.

'Text me the address. I'll be there in half an hour. Yes. She is. I will.' He hung up and looked at me. 'I know you've had a tough twenty-four hours but you should probably come with me.'

'What is it?'

'Another woman. Strangled.'

'When did that happen?' Derwent demanded. He was

trying to sit up again, and his face had lost the colour it had gained during our conversation.

'The last time anyone spoke to the victim was ten thirty last night, and she was found at lunchtime.'

'Which puts you in the clear,' I said to Derwent. 'You were here, surrounded by adoring nurses.'

'Talk about your silver linings.' Derwent still looked ashen.

'We need to go,' Godley said to me. Something had happened to flip the switch in him; he'd gone from total composure to simmering excitement and I couldn't work out why news of another dead woman was making him giddy. 'Get better soon, Josh.'

'Yeah.' He sounded distracted and I knew he wasn't paying much attention as I said goodbye. For all three of us, the only thing that mattered now was the new victim, and what her death could tell us about the man who killed her.

Godley set off down the corridor at a blistering pace, leaving me to try to keep up while dodging around patients and trolleys. He was whistling under his breath, though I doubted he was aware of it.

'What's her name, guv?'

'Deena Prescott.'

I thought hard, but it didn't ring any bells for me.

'I can't believe it's happened again. And so soon after the last one.' I was doing my best to keep my voice down because the last thing we wanted was an entourage of reporters. 'Are we sure it's the same guy? Is it the same MO?'

'More or less.' Godley pressed the button for the lift, then changed his mind and headed for the stairs, as if he had to keep moving. I went through the door after him and grabbed his arm. It was something I would never have done normally, but I was tired, and confused, and deeply unsettled.

'Stop! Just for a second.'

I waited for a couple of visitors to trudge past us. I could hear footsteps approaching from the floor below, and someone was talking on the floor above, so we didn't have long. I half-whispered, 'I don't understand. He's killed again in the space of days, not weeks or months. Why are you pleased?'

Godley leaned close to me so his words didn't carry through the echoing, busy stairwell, his mouth almost grazing my ear. 'Because this time, we've got a lead.'

It was my turn to feel the adrenalin rush, so intense that it made me dizzy. As I followed Godley down the stairs, I wondered if the killer felt the same thrill when he knew he'd found a victim – if it was as addictive for him as it was for me. There were times I felt almost too close to the criminals I was hunting. He was born to be a killer. I liked to think I was born to catch him.

Chapter 25

There was an element of déjà vu about our arrival at Deena Prescott's tiny modern townhouse in Walthamstow. As at Anna Melville's home the street was clogged with police vehicles. The media were pressing against hastily erected barriers a hundred yards in either direction from the house, and as Godley's car was waved through a hundred camera flashes went off, half-blinding me. I put my hand up to shield my eyes.

'Jesus. Can you see enough to drive?'

'I'm used to it.' He parked and headed for the crime scene, not hanging around. I scrambled to follow. Godley started up the steps to the front door, which had already been screened off. Before he reached the top, the canvas screen parted and Una Burt appeared, rotund in a protective boiler suit. She pushed the hood back and her hair was flat against her head, damp with sweat. It was quite amazing to me that she had no personal vanity, but it seemed that she really didn't care.

What she did care about was her job. Without preamble, she said, 'I think he panicked.'

'Our killer?'

'Yes.'

'Are we sure it's the same guy?'

'Yes and no.'

'Explain,' Godley said.

'Not yet.' She didn't say it in an argumentative way, but you could tell there was absolutely no chance of persuading her to change her mind. She looked at me and her expression darkened. 'I want a word with you.'

'Not now, Una,' Godley said. 'Let her view the crime scene.'

'That's not why she's here. She needs to explain why Josh Derwent was with her yesterday.'

'I've already spoken to her. And Josh, indeed.'

Burt wasn't going to be put off so easily. 'I suppose we'd never have known about it if you hadn't run into trouble.'

'Probably not,' I admitted.

'You were specifically told not to allow him access to any part of this investigation.'

'With respect, I wouldn't have been able to conduct that interview without him. And he's got an alibi for this murder, so your concerns about him were unfounded anyway.'

'Some of them may have been unfounded. Not all.' She was still glowering. 'Was it useful? The interview?'

'Oh. I think so.' I struggled to think back to what Orpen had told us. There were things to follow up, if I ever got the chance, but I couldn't tell yet if they would help.

Godley was getting impatient. 'This isn't the time or the place, Una. Can you drop it for now?'

'For now.' She stood aside to let him go past her and then moved to block me. 'Don't think I'm going to forget about it, though. You deliberately disobeyed an order and you were prepared to lie about it. I thought you were better than that.'

I felt the colour rise in my cheeks. 'Look, I didn't have a choice. I—'

'You did. You chose Josh Derwent. I hope you won't regret it, but I can't see how you won't.'

'I don't see that there's a need to take sides.'

'Then your judgement is even more unreliable than I thought.'

I followed her into the house, shaking my head when her back was turned. It was a first for anyone to make me more annoyed than Derwent, but she was getting there.

'You need a suit, please, Maeve-y, and shoe covers,' said Pierce, Kev Cox's assistant, who was in charge of supervising access again. He handed me the protective gear I needed. 'Kev is pretty twitchy about this scene.'

I put the suit on, hurrying to catch up with Godley and Burt. I could hear them talking in the first room off the hall on the left, a sitting room, and I strained to hear the conversation. It was about the crime scene, not me, for which I was truly grateful. I couldn't have endured Godley standing up for me, or – worse – damning me as Burt had.

'No staging,' Godley said.

'Not this time.'

'Any sign of forced entry?'

'No. She let him in. Or at least she opened the door – he may have forced his way in.'

'And they came in here. Were the curtains open or closed when the body was found?'

'Closed. Lights on.'

'Which explains how he was able to kill her in here without being seen. And suggests she was killed last night, not this morning.'

I passed Pierce's inspection and rustled into the sitting room, where the first thing I saw was an overturned table, and the second a body on the floor, Godley crouching by the head. She was lying at an awkward angle, one arm thrown up over her face, and her torso twisted so her hips were flat on the floor but her right shoulder was supporting the weight of her upper body. She was dressed in pyjamas but the top was unbuttoned, the bottoms halfway down her hips, exposing most of her torso, which was bruised and scratched, as if he had lost control and ripped at it with his bare hands. It made her look pathetic and I had to resist the urge to pull her clothes back into place. I couldn't work out if the killer had left her like that to demean her or because he couldn't be bothered to dress her as he had the others. She was small but busty and her hair was henna-red. He had cut it off, as he had done with the others, but it lay in tangles around her body, scattered all over it. I wondered about that too.

Godley was peering at her face, which was bruised and bloodied. 'He lost it, didn't he? He stabbed her in the eyes rather than removing them.'

'That's not the only difference.' Burt leaned across to point. 'There's blood all over that wall and the floor. He beat her first. Slammed her against any hard surface he could find.'

'Angry because just killing them isn't enough any more?' I asked.

'Good question,' Burt said. 'But I think I know why Deena's death was different. When I got here, I had a very interesting conversation with Elaine Bridlow, her best friend. She's the one who found the body. She'd been try-ing to get in touch with Deena all morning and was worried enough to dash here during her lunch hour to check on her.'

'This is the lead you were talking about.'

She nodded. 'She was pretty hysterical, but from what I can gather, Deena rang her last night, quite late. She was sounding confused, but she said she'd just seen the news and she thought someone she knew was in hospital and she didn't know what to do.'

'Did she explain?'

'She'd seen the footage from the playground. Derwent's little adventure. According to Elaine, she said, "I think it's the same guy, but I'm not sure. I only saw him once."'

'*What*?' Godley and I said it at the same time.

Burt nodded. 'She told Elaine she'd met someone who said they were a Met inspector called Josh, and he'd said he worked on homicide investigations. He followed her home, she said, one night last month, when she came back late from work, and she noticed it and challenged him. He told her there was a dangerous criminal operating in the area and he wanted to make sure she got home all right. He asked her not to tell anyone about him because he could get in trouble for warning her and he wanted to keep it between the two of them.'

I was recalling what Derwent had said about shadowing women to safety, with or without their knowledge, and a prickle of unease ran down my spine.

'Did she say anything else?'

'He'd been in touch with her, calling and emailing. He was supposed to be coming around to check her security arrangements. She thought he'd been flirting but she wasn't sure if he was just being friendly.'

'Kirsty Campbell made a list for her building's management company,' I said. 'Maybe that's how he gains their trust. He tells them he's a police officer and they need to let him into their homes so he can advise them on their safety. But really, he's just stringing them along while he gets to scope the place out from the inside.'

'Elaine asked why Deena hadn't told her about him before and she said she hadn't had any reason to mention it. It was a chance encounter and so far it hadn't come to anything. Deena was a real romance addict, according to Elaine. She said she hadn't wanted to jinx a possible relationship by talking about it.'

'He has a real gift for finding the right women,' I said.

'It couldn't have been our Josh,' Godley said firmly. 'He was in hospital when she died.'

'It could have been someone covering for him,' Burt said.

'No way,' I said. 'It's not Derwent.'

She whipped around. 'You are hopelessly biased. You won't admit the evidence in front of your own eyes. There are major, striking differences between this killing and the others, and one explanation is that it was not the same person but it was supposed to look like the same person.'

'Because it's so easy to find someone to do your killing for you if you need to establish an alibi.' I didn't even bother trying to hide my disbelief. 'You can't be serious about this.'

'I've never been more serious. And Andy Bradbury agrees with me.'

'That should be your first clue that you're completely wrong,' I said, my voice pure ice. 'Bradbury is a moron.'

'And how does he know about it, anyway?' Godley asked.

'I told him.'

'You did *what*?'

'He's put in a lot of time on this investigation and he deserved to have the full picture. It was wrong to keep something back, especially when it could be the most important element in the case.'

'Does no one listen to me any more?' Godley was livid. 'I ordered you to keep it to yourself, Una. You're as bad as Derwent.'

'That's grossly unfair. I felt you were exhibiting an unusual lack of judgement and I stepped in.'

'Look, keep it down,' I said, noticing that the conversation was attracting some interest from the SOCOs working in the hall. Pierce's ears were flapping.

'This discussion is not over,' Godley said. 'But I am not going to talk about it over this poor woman's body.' He glared at Burt. 'You need to reconsider your tone, too.'

'I'm just saying what I think.'

'I noticed.'

'What are the differences between this murder and the others?' I asked, partly to keep the peace but also because I really wanted to know. 'He cut her hair but threw it on top of her. He didn't arrange the body. He beat her. He killed her quickly. What else?'

'He put her clothes in the bath and poured bleach on them.'

Now that Burt mentioned it, I noticed a strong chemical smell. I looked around at the room. It was smeared with fingerprint powder that had highlighted swirls and sweeps and smears and smudges but no actual fingerprints. 'Did he wipe the place down?'

Kev Cox answered me, leaning in from the hall. 'He cleaned up in here, the hall and the kitchen. Didn't bother with her bedroom upstairs, which suggests he wasn't in there, except to get her clothes. The bathroom is like an operating theatre – spotless.'

'What does this say to you?' Godley asked, looking at me.

'Damage control. He must have been scared she was going to give the game away. This one wasn't about living out his fantasies. He wanted her dead.' I stared at Una Burt. 'That doesn't mean it wasn't the same killer as for the other three.'

'This is a pale imitation of the others.'

'He likes to control the women and the crime scenes,' I pointed out. 'He likes to use minimal violence. There's something almost artistic about the way he leaves the bodies. Now, if Deena challenged him – if she argued, or fought with him, or if he wasn't prepared as he wanted to be for her death – he might have killed her differently. I think he sees it as an honour to be selected by him. She didn't deserve the treatment the other victims got. She betrayed his trust.'

'He probably didn't know about her phone call to Elaine. He might have thought he could come here and kill her before she spoke to anyone,' Godley said.

Burt looked stubborn. 'It was someone acting on Josh Derwent's behalf.'

'Who? Who would?'

'A friend. Someone he met through work – someone he arrested, maybe.'

'Because that's the best way to make friends.' I turned to Godley. 'This is insane. Isn't it?'

'I respect Una's opinion,' Godley said slowly. 'I don't agree with her, but I'm not writing it off just yet. I can't be sure my objectivity isn't affected by my friendship with Josh.'

Lack of sleep was making me slow-witted. I felt as if I was lost in a fog. 'Derwent was in hospital. How would he arrange for this mythical person to come and kill Deena for him?'

'He wasn't unconscious. He had his phone. I'm going to get a list of all the calls from and to that number over the last twenty-four hours, and all the calls to and from his hospital room, and I'm going to prove that Derwent was able to make contact with someone who, for love or money, was prepared to kill at his request. He could have briefed them over the phone – not in detail, maybe, which explains the differences.' She looked at Godley. 'You've known him for a long time. You know he's capable of killing. He did it in the army. He shot people—'

'That's different,' I objected.

'Yes, it is.' She didn't even turn her head. 'He doesn't have a girlfriend. He lives alone. Who knows what's in his flat? We need to get a search warrant while he's still in hospital and go through it.'

I snapped. 'Okay, first of all, I've been in his flat recently and I doubt there's anything to find. Do you really think if he was a killer Derwent wouldn't have the sense to keep everything relating to that in a different location? A storage unit or a lock-up garage? He's seen enough practical examples of what not to do, hasn't he? And anyway, he's not going to be in hospital for long. He might be out already. Do you really want to tell him you think he's a killer?'

'Absolutely not,' Godley said. 'Una, this needs to stay between us for now. If you're right, I want Josh to think he's free and clear. We'll check his phone and bank accounts and get surveillance on him.'

'What about the other investigators?'

'We'll have a conference with them in the next couple of hours. Set it up. I don't mind talking to them behind closed doors because it's worth considering every possibility, but I don't want you talking to Bradbury or anyone else about it when I'm not there. Not a word.' He turned to me. 'Maeve, I know you don't agree with this approach to the investigation. I'm not going to insist you come to the conference. You have other work to do on this case, don't you? Leads from the Orpen interview to run down.'

I struggled to think. It all seemed very remote and irrelevant. I knew I was being moved sideways so I didn't get in the way and I would have resented it if I'd been able to muster enough energy.

'There were some phone calls I should make,' I said. 'But shouldn't I be at the conference?'

'Better not.' In a flash I realised that he was thinking the same way as Una Burt: I couldn't be trusted. 'This goes double for you. Not a word about Josh's potential involvement, to him or anyone else.'

'I wouldn't,' I said, wounded.

'He's very persuasive. He's manipulated you quite a bit over the course of this investigation, hasn't he? You've even been in his flat and what you were doing there I don't want to know, but I hope it was personal rather than relating to this investigation.'

'I'm not *sleeping* with him, if that's what you're suggesting.'

'It wouldn't be the first time you slept with a colleague.' The words seemed to come out despite his best efforts not to say them.

'I would *never*—'

'It's none of my business.' He sighed. 'I can't pretend

I'm not disappointed in you, Maeve. You've done the exact opposite of what you were told to do, because of Josh.'

'I just wanted to find out the truth,' I whispered. 'I did what had to be done.'

'You did what you wanted. You went against specific orders and the consequences of that have yet to be seen.' Godley looked down at Deena's body. 'If you'd handled things differently, Derwent wouldn't have been with you yesterday to get his face all over the news. Whether he is responsible for this death or not, it seems clear that his sudden elevation to public notice is likely to be the reason Deena is dead.'

'That's not fair.'

'Even so. I can't take the risk of letting you remain involved with this end of the investigation. You might as well follow up the leads on the cold case, but report back to Harry Maitland. Brief him when you get to the office. I'll get him to read your notes. He can take over from you.'

'If you don't trust me, you shouldn't have me on your team,' I said, because I had to.

'If you leave it will be your choice.' He shook his head slowly. 'I don't know why everyone finds it so hard to follow orders, but we're standing beside proof that it's important to do so.'

Una Burt was watching me intently, her expression showing that she agreed with Godley.

The thing was, I couldn't say he was wrong. I had done the opposite of what I'd been told. I had let Derwent order me around. And somehow I'd set off the chain of events that had led to Deena's death.

My vision blurred as I turned away, stumbling to the door. Crying at work for the second time in twenty-four hours. That was really the sort of thing that shouldn't become a habit, I thought, trying to distract myself.

I held myself together while I took off the crime-scene coveralls, even chatting with Pierce about his plans for the weekend. I walked out to a darkening sky as the rain closed in. The wind cut through my clothes, making me shiver. One of the police vans was getting ready to leave and I begged a lift, flipping up my coat collar as I sat in a seat near the back, out of reach of the cameras.

A young female PC leaned across the aisle. 'Aren't you the detective who was shot at yesterday?'

I shook my head and sort of smiled at her to take the sting out of it. It was technically true – Lee Grimes hadn't shot at me. She blushed, knowing that she was right but too polite to persist.

'Leave her be. She doesn't want to talk about it.' I could hear the whisper from where I was sitting, but I affected not to. They were right, I didn't want to talk. I wanted to sleep. I wanted to make sense of the chaotic thoughts that were spiralling around my head. I wanted to work out what was bothering me about what I'd heard in the previous days. I wanted to prove Una Burt wrong and prove Derwent wasn't involved. I wanted to make Godley eat his words.

Most of all, I wanted to stop feeling like I'd blundered, time and time again, because I hadn't the least idea how to make it right.

Chapter 26

By the time I got to the office I was in control of myself. I found Maitland, who looked wary when he saw me. Godley had been in touch, apparently, to tell him to expect me, and to familiarise him with Derwent's background. I was miserably conscious that he would have warned Maitland I might be emotional. He needn't have worried. I was icily calm as I ran through the details of the Angela Poole murder and told him what I was planning to do next. He made absolutely no fuss about letting me make follow-up inquiries before I handed the lot over to him, though I was prepared for a fight. He was a good police officer and I trusted him to do his job well, but this was my case and my investigation and I had questions that I needed to ask, by myself.

'Sure. Of course. That's fine.' Maitland ran a hand up and down his shirt front, fiddling with the buttons. 'Tell me what you find out, obviously, and then maybe we can have a final handover in an hour.' *At which time you will be out of this case for ever and I will be taking your place, but I don't have to tell you that's what's going on because you know.*

'One hour,' I repeated, and headed for my desk. I could work to a deadline, if I had to. And it didn't look as if I was being given any choice. So I had an hour to find someone who was not Derwent but seemed to be pretending to be Derwent.

Or someone who was following Derwent, killing the women he tried to help.

Or Derwent.

Which I was not going to think about because it was impossible. I picked up the phone.

My first calls were to all the care homes I could find in Bromley, working through them in search of a resident named Charles or Charlie Poole. It took five tries before I struck gold at the Tall Pines Care Home. The woman who answered the phone was Eastern European and had a strong accent but her speech was fluent, rapid even.

'Charlie? Yes, he is here. You are a relative?'

I explained who I was and that I wanted to come and see him.'

'Oh dear. This is not a problem, you understand, for us, but for you. Charlie is a long-term sufferer from dementia. He is not capable of conversation. He is not even able to say yes or no.'

'If I showed him some pictures—'

'No. The only thing he responds to is music and only sometimes. We do try, but . . .' The shrug travelled down the telephone line.

'Does he get many visitors?'

'His son, sometimes. He comes to sit with him.'

'Does Charlie still recognise him?'

'Not for a year or more.'

Poor Shane. I thanked her for talking to me and she sighed.

'I have great respect for the residents in our home but I feel sometimes that they are just waiting, waiting, waiting. The ones like Charlie – they are the ones death forgot. It makes me sad.'

I thanked her and said goodbye. She'd been helpful, but if there was a spate of sudden deaths at Tall Pines, I knew where I'd start the investigation.

The next person on my list was Claire Naylor, now back

at work and not pleased to be phoned. She became even frostier when I asked her why she'd given Shane an alibi for his sister's death.

'I don't remember. We must have been together.'

'I don't think so,' I said quietly. 'You told me you found out Angela was dead when Shane rang your house at four in the morning and woke everyone up. You were in bed, asleep.'

She didn't answer and I wished I could see her face.

'Shane told me he was out with some mates smoking weed before he came home and found the police were already there. You wouldn't happen to know who the friends were, would you?'

'No.'

'You told me you liked smoking weed, didn't you? But you weren't there that night.'

No answer. I waited, and as so often, silence did my job for me. She sighed, irritated, and I heard a door close, cutting off the background noise from the shop.

'All right. I said he was with me. What's the big deal?'

'It was a murder case and you lied.'

'Only because he was terrified of the policeman.'

'Lionel Orpen?'

'Him. He'd been giving Vinny a shocking time – he'd got it into his head that Vinny might have killed her. Only he absolutely didn't and there was no evidence. He thought he could get Vinny to confess if he leaned on him hard enough, but there was no way that was going to happen. Vinny had too much spirit.' She sounded proud of her brother, and a little sad.

'So Shane was scared.'

'Yes. Especially since he'd been doing drugs that night. I mean, it was nothing. It was just some weed. In ordinary circumstances the police wouldn't have bothered with it but Orpen was looking for an angle all the time. He was starting to look beyond Vinny and he'd have got to Shane sooner or later. Shane was bricking it.'

'And you weren't suspicious when he asked you to pro-vide him with a fake alibi?'

'Absolutely not. He was a very scary guy, that police officer. None of us trusted him.'

Fine work, Orpen. It was no wonder the case had never been solved.

'And you don't know who Shane was actually with.'

'You'd have to ask him.'

'I will.'

'And don't call me again, please. I don't want to be bothered about Angela's death any more.' Her voice was vibrating with tension.

'I'm sorry. It's just—'

'Just leave me alone.' The phone went dead.

I frowned. It was a bit of an overreaction to a phone call. Again, I had the feeling that I'd missed something. Something Claire was trying, quite desperately, to hide.

Shane was the next person I rang, naturally enough, but his phone went straight to voicemail. I doodled a star next to his name to remind me to call him back and went on to dial Stuart Sinclair's number. The same impersonal voice instructed me to leave a message and I did, hoping he'd get back to me as quickly as he had the previous time. I added another star beside his name as I left a message. He seemed to be the kind of person who never took the risk of answering his phone, preferring to know who was calling him, and why, before he actually engaged with them.

I checked the time. Twenty minutes left. Maitland was unlikely to hold me to a strict sixty minutes but there was no doubt I was up against it. No Shane. No Stuart. I dearly wanted to ring Derwent and ask him if he'd ever prowled the streets of Walthamstow looking for women to rescue, but I knew better than to try to contact him. They would be watching everything he did already. They would be check-ing the calls in and out of his hospital room. It would be useless to say I hadn't told him anything about the case, and it would have been a lie, because Derwent would have known why I was asking straight away. I put out my hand to the phone and took it back again, irresolute.

Better to play it safe. *Sorry, Derwent.*

I filled in the remaining minutes by going through my notes from the various interviews, making sure there was nothing else I'd meant to follow up. I even checked that Claire's son really was at Cambridge, scouting around the Internet for references to him. Whatever else she was lying about, it wasn't that. I found his college, his Twitter account and a Facebook page in seconds. The college was large and prestigious, with extensive grounds and a rowing tradition, and I thought he was lucky. Wondering if Luke had any pictures of Claire, or Vinny, I had a look at Facebook. No privacy settings: perfect. His profile picture was a bottle of beer. I clicked through to his albums and was two pictures in before I'd identified him, and identified a whole new set of problems. I sat and stared at his face, and the sound of things falling into place in my head was deafening.

Oh, *fuck.*

'Your last few words on the subject, then, Kerrigan? Get anywhere with your calls?' Maitland, trying to be amiable and missing by a nervous mile. He started to lean around my computer, looking at what I had in front of me. The only clear thought in my head was that he shouldn't see it until I'd worked out what I was going to do about it. I closed the window and told him I hadn't got very far.

'What about this?' One fat finger descended and pointed at the star beside Shane's name.

'A reminder to try him again. There was no answer from his phone.'

'Who's he again?'

'Angela's brother. He gave a false alibi in the original investigation. The SIO missed it at the time. Apparently he was afraid of getting into trouble for smoking marijuana.'

'Shocking.'

'Well, he was only a teenager. And not outstandingly clever.' Unlike Derwent, apparently. The mind boggled. I made myself think about the case again. 'You know, he was out that night with some people who've never been traced. It would be worth talking to him to find out who they were and whether they might have seen anything.'

'Fine by me,' Maitland said. 'Anything else?'

'Stuart Sinclair. He was the only witness. Except . . .'

'Except what?'

'He lied.'

Maitland shrugged. 'Didn't everybody?'

'Pretty much. But Sinclair lied about what he'd seen. Or maybe he lied about where he was when he saw it. Either way, I think he needs to come clean.'

'You wouldn't think, twenty years on, that they'd even remember to lie, would you?'

'Depends on why they did in the first place, I suppose. If they had a good enough reason – or thought they did – maybe they remember the lie first and the truth second.'

'Well, it's time to jog some memories.' Maitland ran a finger along the desk, looking down. 'Where can I find this Shane Poole?'

'He lives above his bar near Brick Lane.' I wrote down the name and contact details on a loose sheet of paper and handed it to him. 'Go easy with him. He's a bit edgy.'

Instead of going away as I'd expected, Maitland turned my phone around and began to dial. I appreciated the gesture. It meant that I could hear enough of both sides of the conversation to follow it. He was a good DS and he loved Godley but that didn't mean he thought the boss was right to punish me, and I liked him for that.

'Can I speak to Shane Poole, please.'

'. . . not here.'

'Do you know where he is?'

'. . . wish I did. He was supposed to open up, but . . . an hour late . . . *still* hasn't come.'

'Is that unusual for him?'

'First time in six years . . . always reliable.'

'Have you tried ringing his phone?'

'. . . doesn't have it with him.'

'How do you know?' Maitland asked.

'I can hear it ringing upstairs.' The voice had suddenly got a lot louder and more distinct. The fringe benefits of irritating someone.

'Are you sure he's not upstairs too?'

'Well, I haven't seen him.'

Maitland put a hand over the mouthpiece of the receiver. 'Did you get that?'

'Not there but his phone is.'

'That's odd, isn't it?'

'Exceptionally. I'm concerned he may be there and unable to answer his phone. I'm concerned he may be in danger.' I raised my eyebrows. 'Aren't you?'

'Very much so.' It was our passkey to get into the flat without going to the bother and delay of getting a court order. He returned to the call. 'Right. I'll be with you in half an hour. Do you have a key to get into the flat?'

A squawk that I interpreted as a 'yes'.

'Well, don't do it until I get there. And try not to worry.' He hung up. 'Looks as if I'm off to Brick Lane.'

'Good luck.'

He turned around, then turned back. 'You could come. You've met him. You know what to ask him when we find him.'

'I'm not supposed to—'

'It's part of the handover. You'd be helping me.'

'You're being very kind, but I don't want to get you in trouble.'

'What trouble?' Maitland spread his hands wide. 'Who could possibly object?'

I hadn't the heart to list the names but they started with Charles Godley and ended with Una Burt, and I didn't feel like getting shouted at any more that day. I was about to say as much when I checked myself. It was pathetic to ignore the old familiar pull of curiosity that made me a good police officer just because I was scared of getting in trouble. Derwent would have wasted no time even considering saying no, and while his career trajectory was levelling out drastically there were still things he could teach me. And one was being single-minded despite the possible consequences.

'All right. If you insist.'

'I do insist,' Maitland said firmly, hauling his trousers up to rest just under his paunch and setting off. I shut down my computer and followed, shelving all thoughts of Luke Naylor for the moment. *One problem at a time . . .*

Chapter 27

The bar was open already and a few tables were occupied with people having an early lunch. Behind the bar, a woman was serving drinks. She was a bit older than the rest of the staff – mid-forties, I guessed – and something about the set of her shoulders and the droop of her mouth conveyed that she was upset even before she looked up and spotted us. With a mutter to the barman she came out from behind the bar and hurried towards us.

'Are you the man who phoned about Shane?'

Maitland nodded. 'And you are?'

'Ginny Miles. I'm the assistant manager here.'

'No sign of him, I take it?'

'Nothing. I called his phone again, just in case.' Her breathing was shallow and I wondered if she was asthmatic.

'It might be a false alarm,' I said. 'He might have gone out and forgotten it. But we'd still like to check.'

'When was the last time you saw him, again?'

'Yesterday afternoon. He went off for a break before the evening rush. He does lunch and then it goes quiet in the afternoon so he goes upstairs for a lie-down or does some errands then. This place is open until one and he needs to be wide awake.'

'I'm sure.' Maitland scanned the room, then turned back. 'All right, Ginny. Lead the way.'

She took us out through the kitchen where I dodged a rubber-aproned man lifting a huge tray of glasses out of a dishwasher, enveloped in clouds of steam. Two chefs were working, heads down, barely aware of our presence as we passed through to an alley behind the pub where there was a blue door. Her hands were shaking when she produced the key that unlocked it.

'He has a separate entrance to his flat because it's easier when the place is shut up and the alarm is on. And he can come and go as he pleases without getting caught up in work stuff.'

'But you said it was out of character for him not to be there,' Maitland objected.

'It is. He still comes and goes a fair bit. It was strange he didn't come in at all today. I can't remember him doing that before. Ever.'

'Go ahead,' I said, and watched her struggle with the lock. 'Have you been in the flat before?'

'A couple of times.'

'Would you know if anything was missing?'

'I couldn't swear to it.' She held the door open for us, revealing a grey-carpeted flight of stairs rising steeply from just inside the door. It was narrow and claustrophobic and I went up as quickly as I could without stepping on Maitland's heels. In deference to seniority, I let him go first and he checked for signs of life – or death – before coming back to Ginny and me at the top of the stairs.

'Nothing. I found his phone, though, in the kitchen area.' To Ginny, he said, 'I think we should walk through and make sure we're not missing a clue to where he might be.'

She nodded, her arms folded tightly, her expression pure misery. 'It's not to do with those girls, is it? He showed us the pictures. The Gentleman Killer. You don't think it's him, do you?'

'Don't worry about it,' Maitland said easily. 'We're just having a look around.'

I was already getting a feel for the layout. The main room was at the top of the stairs, open plan, with a leather suite of furniture and a table taking up most of the room and the kitchen filling the space on the opposite wall. There was a large bedroom on the left, with a wall of built-in cupboards and an en suite, and a smaller bedroom on the right with a sofa bed and a desk. The furniture was functional but not cheap, and the kitchen looked as if it had been quite expensive to put in, all high-gloss units and granite work surfaces. The overall effect, though, was impersonal and it was cold, as if the heating had been off for a while. I was shivering. It wasn't the kind of place I felt at home. Nor did it tell me a lot about Shane, except that he hadn't stinted on money. There were no personal items on display in the main room, and the smaller bedroom was fitted out as an office. I flicked through the material on the desk, seeing invoices for the bar and accounts. A folder full of bank statements caught my attention but there was nothing particularly exciting about it – bill payments by direct debit, and large sums of cash withdrawn regularly. There were people who preferred to use cash rather than cards to avoid fraud – a lot of police did it, I happened to know – but it was a bugger from an investigative point of view. I circled back to the living room where Ginny was still waiting.

'Was this here? Before?'

'He had it gutted and redesigned,' Ginny said. 'When he had the bar refurbished. He thought this was a good investment but I dunno. Who wants to live above a pub?'

'Handy for last orders,' Maitland said, coming back from the bedroom. 'I've found his passport.'

I held up a card wallet I'd just come across between two stacks of magazines on the coffee table. 'Is this the one he usually carries?'

'Yeah,' Ginny confirmed. I'd thought it was familiar

myself. I opened it and checked, finding bank cards and the picture of Vinny he'd shown me but no cash.

'Who's that?' Maitland asked.

'His friend. He's dead.'

'There's a few pictures of him in the bedroom.'

I went in and looked where Maitland was pointing, at a small collection framed on one wall. His parents on their wedding day, an unposed shot that was a little out of focus. Angela at eight or nine, eating ice cream, her brother's arm around her neck. Claire and Vinny, teenagers, sneering and giving the finger to the camera. And the one Derwent had – all of them together – except that Derwent's face had been coloured in with black marker. I took it down off the wall and stared at it, at the friends together, before the fall, wondering if they had really been as happy as all that, despite the sunshine and the wide smiles.

Behind me, Maitland was getting rid of Ginny, promising to lock up and assuring her he'd call if we found anything that might locate her boss. It took some doing, but she left eventually and he came to find me.

'So he hasn't done a runner. He's just disappeared from one minute to the next. What do you think? Kidnap? Wandered off?'

'No sign of violence if it was a kidnapping. This place is immaculate.' I looked around. 'My hunch is he planned it so carefully he didn't need this stuff. Leave the phone because it acts like a transmitter so we can pinpoint where you are. Leave the bank cards so there are no recorded transactions – he runs a cash business so it's not all that hard to get hold of a lot of money in a hurry. He's probably got a safe full of cash around here somewhere. Leave the passport because you want to come back once you've done what you left to do.'

'And what was that, exactly?'

'I don't know,' I admitted. 'But he disappeared not all that long before Deena Prescott died.'

Maitland gave a sigh that came all the way up from his boots. 'Bloody marvellous. However you cut it, he should be here and he's not, and we've got a big problem.'

My problems were made a lot worse because I wasn't supposed to be anywhere near the Rest Bar. Maitland gave me the option of running away but I turned it down. I wanted to stick around for as long as possible, the urge to know what was going on drowning out the small voice that advocated caution. Godley was taking no chances: a possible lead in the investigation was going to get every resource available. They came in force: SOCOs led by Kev Cox who was as imperturbable and good-tempered as ever, and a spaniel trained as a cadaver dog who might catch a scent of blood or a speck of human remains that we would otherwise miss. Una Burt arrived with Andrew Bradbury and James Peake, fresh from the conference where they'd been discussing Derwent's likely status as a suspect. I didn't doubt that Burt was annoyed I had interrupted it, especially since it was to draw their attention to the fact that there was someone else to consider. Peake was the only one of the three who looked pleased to see me, but in enthusiasm he more than made up for the others. His eyes lit up when he saw me standing outside. He made a beeline for me and I was glad to have him to talk to, if it meant I didn't have to acknowledge the disapproving looks I was getting from his boss and Burt.

'Found a suspect for us, have you?'

'Possibly. We've found a lot of nothing so far.'

'Did you search the place?'

'We gave it the once over, but Maitland wanted to get the SOCOs in before we trampled all over the place.'

'Is this guy really a serious contender? How did you find him?'

I answered the second question first. 'He was involved

in a cold case that had possible relevance to the current inquiry. And I don't know if he's a proper lead or not, but he's the closest thing we've found.'

'You're telling me.' A helicopter hovered overhead and Peake looked up, shading his eyes. 'Not ours. That'll be a news crew.'

'Already?'

'We passed a load of them setting up down the street when we were driving here. There are five or six satellite vans parked up.'

'For God's sake. One of the bar staff must have tipped them off. That's not going to help us if he's on the run. If he knows we're chasing him, it's not going to make him easier to catch.'

Peake shrugged. 'Big news, isn't it. Everyone wants a breakthrough in this case. And speaking of big news, you've had an exciting week of it, haven't you?'

I half-smiled, reluctant to talk about it. Leaning sideways, I saw Burns and Groves making their way up the alley and I went to meet them. We had almost an identical conversation, except that their side of it was full of the double-act banter that came naturally to them.

'Give you a week and you've got a suspect for us. We had months to track him down.' Groves was twinkling at me, obviously delighted.

Burns sniffed. 'Tell you now, I never heard of this bloke before we got the call, but if you're right about him that's all that matters.'

Godley was the last to get there, unusually. Maitland had come to join the group outside in the alley, kicked out by Kev who needed the space.

'Sorry, Harry. I got held up by the press at the cordon.'

'What did you tell them?'

'That I would make a full statement later. But it took a while.' He grinned, then turned to me. 'Maeve. Why am I not surprised to find you here?'

'I asked her to come along,' Maitland said. 'It was my idea.'

'I'm sure it was.' I thought he was going to have a go at me but instead he looked back at Maitland. 'Please tell me you got a search warrant before all this started.'

'We were lawfully on the premises, boss. We were concerned for Mr Poole's safety.'

Godley held up a hand. 'I'm not blaming you, Harry. You have to take the opportunities when they come. But I want the rest of this search to be completely unquestionable in court. If he is our killer, we want to throw everything we can at it.'

'Right you are.'

'What stage are we at?'

'Kev is going through the place at the moment. We gave it a quick look before he started, but we didn't find anything suspicious except his phone and his wallet.' Maitland glanced at me. 'We thought that was potentially his choice, to avoid being tracked.'

'It's possible.' Godley looked up at the building. 'How big is the flat?'

'Not very.' I described it for him and he nodded. 'I don't want everyone tramping around in there when Kev lets us back in. I want a thorough, proper search done. Harry, you can do it, and Colin Vale. I'd like him to do the office to go through the paperwork.'

'Who else?' Maitland asked. 'Just us two? Might take a while.'

Godley turned. 'What about you, Maeve? Searching is your speciality, isn't it?'

I blushed to the roots of my hair. It was a reference to the first time I'd come to his attention a few years before, and I had assumed he would have forgotten it long ago. I hadn't but that was because it was a decisive event in my life. I hadn't expected him to recall a two-minute chat with a uniformed officer on a case that had just blown wide open, even if it was the reason I was working for him now.

Behind him, Una Burt's eyebrows drew together. From his tone, and the fact he was offering me a chance to get involved, it was clear that I was back in his good books. It would burn her, too, if she didn't know the background to his comment.

'I'll do it.'

'Good.' Godley turned around to address the rest of the officers gathered in the alley. 'The rest of us had better find somewhere to wait, I'm afraid. Once we know all we can about Shane Poole, we can start making some plans. Until then—'

'The pub's closed,' Groves observed. 'That might make a good place to wait.'

'Trust you,' Burns said affectionately, then added, 'Not a bad idea, mind.'

'Indeed not.' Godley nodded to Maitland. 'Keep me informed, Harry. We'll wait down here.'

Knowing that the pub below us was full of police officers who would have traded places with us in a heartbeat made me a little bit edgy as I searched Shane Poole's home. Maitland allocated me his bedroom and I spent a long time going through the pockets of everything in his wardrobe. I searched inside shoes and drawers, turning them upside down to make sure there was nothing taped to the underside. I looked inside the cistern of the lavatory in the en suite, and checked that the panelling on the side of the bath didn't come off. I cleared shelves, unfolded jumpers and socks, shook out bedclothes and lay on the floor to check under the bed.

'Anything?'

I looked up at Maitland and shook my head. 'You?'

'We found the safe.'

I'd heard the drilling. 'And?'

'Should have had the week's cash takings in there, but

the notes were gone. He hasn't been to the bank with them, either.'

Unmarked, untraceable, non-consecutive notes. I swore quietly. 'Whatever he needs money for, he's got it.'

'Yeah. Are you almost done?'

'Almost. Give me a hand to lift the mattress, would you?'

He went to the other end of the bed and helped me lever it off the base. There was nothing shoved underneath it, and the mattress itself was as it had come from the manufacturers. The divan, on the other hand, had a hole in it, as we both spotted immediately. Maitland adjusted his gloves and stuck a hand in, retrieving a small envelope.

'Kev,' he yelled. 'You probably want to have a look at this.'

Kev arrived and spread paper on the divan so he could tip out what was in the envelope. A pair of earrings came out first, little silver bows tarnished black. Then came two rings that looked like they had been much worn.

'A wedding band and engagement ring.' I leaned over. 'Quite old-fashioned. His mother's, maybe?'

'Maybe. But the earrings?'

'Angela Poole was wearing them when she died,' I said. 'I recognise them from the crime-scene pictures.'

'What about this?' Kev shook the envelope again, coaxing out the last items. A curl of honey-blonde hair, dry and slightly faded, tied with a scrap of black ribbon. A photograph, passport-picture size, cut from a strip of them – Angela Poole laughing as she sat on the young Derwent's lap. He had his face in her hair, nuzzling her neck. Someone had scraped Derwent's face away with short, angry jabs. And the last thing: a cutting from a newspaper that was some years old, covering the sentencing at the end of a murder trial. An elderly woman, mugged for her handbag, had died of head injuries sustained in the attack and two seventeen-year-olds had been convicted. Highlighted in yellow, near the bottom, a quote from DS Josh Derwent:

'For Beryl's family, this conviction doesn't make up for her loss. She was in good health before the attack and might have had many years ahead of her. Although the people who committed this despicable act are young, they must take responsibility for their actions and I'm glad the court has recognised the serious nature of their crime.'

In the margin beside it, someone – Shane, presumably – had inked an exclamation mark.

I looked at the little pile of things and felt a creeping sense of unease about Shane Poole, and where he might be, and what he might be planning to do.

Chapter 28

It was probably inevitable that I'd be the focus of attention at the conference in the pub. Out of all the police officers in the room, I was the only one who had actually met Shane Poole. I wasn't altogether comfortable with being the main attraction but there was nothing I could do about it. I got a coffee from the bar before the last member of staff was asked to leave, and took a seat near the back, which just meant that everyone turned around to look at me every time my name was mentioned. Godley had got hold of Dr Chen. She was sitting at the front, arms folded, slight but formidable in a navy suit.

The bar staff had drawn the blinds to give us some privacy and the place had the feel of a lock-in, albeit with no booze on offer. The big television in one corner was on with the sound muted, showing a rolling news programme that intermittently displayed live footage of nothing happening outside the pub. Groves was near a window. Now and then he twitched one of the blinds, trying to tempt the cameraman to zoom in on it.

Godley stood by the bar with Maitland and filled in the blanks for those who didn't know. He started with who Shane Poole was. What had happened to his sister. How the current crimes resembled the death twenty years before. Why DI Derwent had come up as a suspect, and why he might be a target for Shane.

'Or,' Una Burt said, 'they could still be friends. Shane could have killed Deena on Derwent's instructions.'

'Shane hates Derwent,' I said, unable to stay quiet. 'He blames him for what happened to Angela. He wanted me to arrest him for statutory rape.'

'A smokescreen.'

'No. He meant it.' I told them about the photograph, coloured in to hide Derwent, and the other picture that was scratched.

'Let's leave Josh Derwent to one side for now,' Godley said. 'What about Shane? He was a teenager when his sister died. Was he a suspect?'

'He had an alibi but it was faked.' A murmur ran around the room. I went on: 'It's worth considering one feature of Angela's death that we've seen in the current series of murders. No obvious sexual element.'

'That doesn't mean that there isn't a sexual thrill involved for the perpetrator,' Dr Chen said.

'I know, but if it was Shane who killed her, that could explain it. Instead of him killing her because he wanted to have sex with her, maybe he wanted to punish her for sleeping with her boyfriend. He was obviously disgusted by the thought of her having sex with Derwent when he spoke to me about it.'

'Okay. Let's look at that,' Godley said. 'He kills his sister. Then what?'

'Then he spent some years taking an awful lot of drugs,' I said. 'And then he got clean, got some money together and started this bar, which is doing very nicely according to the paperwork in his study.'

'A success story. He'd left his past behind him. So why would he risk everything by starting to kill women in the last twelve months?'

'There could have been a triggering event,' Dr Chen said. 'Something that reminded him of what happened twenty years ago. Something that brought him back to the state of mind that made him want to kill.'

'His best friend died,' I said. 'In Afghanistan, about two months before Kirsty's death. He was a big influence on Shane, and he knew Derwent too.'

Dr Chen was nodding. 'That sounds like a possible source of trauma.'

'So what?' Bradbury had folded his arms and his face was stony. 'We're supposed to ignore the evidence pointing us towards a police officer so we can chase a missing bar owner? Was there anything upstairs that connected Shane Poole to the current killings, or did I miss something?'

'Nothing so far,' Maitland admitted. 'But all the forensic work might throw something up.'

'That could take months,' Bradbury pointed out. 'We've got a good suspect already, and we know where he is. I say we stick with the original plan – covert surveillance on Derwent and quietly investigate every single thing we can think of that might prove he's our guy. And if that doesn't work, arrest him and sweat it out of him.'

I couldn't help myself: I laughed. 'Do you really think Derwent would confess because *you* put him under pressure? Good luck.'

Bradbury glared. 'We know where you stand.'

Burt leaned across and whispered something in his ear, shielding her mouth so no one else could hear. He nodded in response. I burned to know what it was while being quite sure it was better not to. If Burt was throwing in her lot with Bradbury, I didn't feel quite the same need to impress her.

Godley cleared his throat, drawing everyone's attention back to the front of the room. 'Some of you know Josh Derwent personally and most of you know him by reputation. I will be extremely relieved if we can rule him out of any involvement with these murders, but I am not going to make the mistake of moving on to a new suspect without investigating him properly. So there's no need to worry, Andy.'

'Isn't that him on the news?' Groves said from his position by the window. 'What's he done now?'

As one, every head in the room turned to the television screen, where a Breaking News banner ran along the bottom of the screen. By the time I looked, the video clip they'd been playing had come to an end, and the screen was filled with a newsreader. Her mouth was moving, the studio lights gleaming on her lipgloss.

'Turn it up,' Godley said tightly.

'. . . we're going to stick with the story and speak to our reporter, who was there when this incident actually happened. Tom, are you there?'

'Yes, hello, Carly.' Tom was young, easy on the eye and wryly amused by whatever had taken place. For a journalist, there was nothing better than being in the right place at the right time, and he was looking more than happy to tell the world what he'd seen. He was standing on a street corner that looked faintly familiar and I frowned, trying to place it. He was in front of the sign, so all I could read was the word 'Street'. Not helpful.

'What can you tell us about what happened this afternoon?'

'Well, extraordinary scenes at St Luke's hospital in London, where Detective Inspector Josh Derwent was recuperating after being shot in the leg yesterday in that incident in a playground. Today he was well enough to be able to discharge himself from hospital, so obviously making a good recovery. We were here around three o'clock this afternoon at the invitation of Philip Pace, the leader of the Dads Matter pressure group, who were of course blamed in some quarters for the actions of the playground gunman, Lee Grimes. Philip Pace was hoping to see DI Derwent to thank him for resolving the situation safely.'

And hoping to use Derwent as a means to getting some

much-needed good publicity. I had a feeling of impending doom.

'But things didn't go according to plan,' the newsreader prompted, a tiny smile hovering around her mouth.

'Indeed they did not. DI Derwent was not keen to speak to Mr Pace, and refused to see him inside the hospital. Philip Pace is not someone who likes taking no for an answer, as we know, and he managed to find out which door the policeman was going to use when leaving the hospital. He approached him and I think our footage probably tells the story better than I can.'

The screen flickered and showed a hospital doorway, with Philip Pace standing to one side of it. The door opened and Derwent hobbled through, on crutches, as unshaven and unkempt as he had been that morning. He glared at the assembled press.

'What are you lot doing here?'

Philip Pace reached out and put a hand on Derwent's left arm. 'On behalf of Dads Matter, I wanted to—'

'I told you, I'm not interested.' He shook the restraining hand off.

A quick glance from Pace to the journalists: you could see him calculating the damage to his reputation, the wheels whirring as he tried to come up with a graceful way out of it. 'Oh, ha ha ha, DI Derwent. It's nice that you still have such a good sense of humour.'

'Who's laughing?' Derwent gave him the most intimidating glower in his repertoire.

Pace misjudged things to the extent that he dropped a chummy arm around Derwent's shoulders before he replied. Derwent was injured, but not incapacitated. He dropped his left shoulder and swung with his right hand, pivoting as the crutches fell to the floor. His fist connected with Pace's nose, making an obscene crunching sound that was followed by a shriek from Pace and a murmur from the journalists off-camera. The leader of Dads

Matter slid to the ground, screaming, both hands to his face where blood was seeping through his fingers, and the camera followed him. In the corner of the screen, someone retrieved one fallen crutch, and Derwent was heard to limp off, refusing all questions. The cameraman turned from Pace at the last minute and caught the back of Derwent's head as he disappeared into a police car. Pace was altogether better box-office, writhing in agony and moaning inarticulately.

Someone in the bar – I couldn't see who – began to applaud, and soon the entire room was cheering. Godley was grinning, I was relieved to see. The police officers quietened down as the newsreader appeared again.

'What's going to happen now? Is DI Derwent under arrest?'

Tom looked amused. 'You may have noticed him getting into a police car. That was actually his lift home, but he delayed his return to his house to speak with officers who were on duty nearby and made a statement to them about what had happened. He wasn't arrested. My understanding is that Philip Pace is unlikely to press charges. He seems rather embarrassed by the whole affair and has refused to take any calls from members of the media, or issue a statement.'

'How bad were his injuries, Tom?'

'I believe he had a broken nose and some severe bruising, Carly. He received immediate treatment in St Luke's accident and emergency department.'

'Has DI Derwent had anything to say, Tom?'

'Well, we dared to ask him about it when he returned home, and this happened.'

The screen again switched to the shaky handheld camera, which was now focusing on a police car drawing up on the street outside Derwent's flat.

'Inspector Derwent, sir, hello. Could you come and speak to us about the incident with Philip Pace, please?'

Derwent was extracting himself from the car. He turned, looking exhausted, and shook his head.

'Did you want to say anything at all?' Tom appeared in the frame, microphone extended to Derwent with the sort of timidity I'd associate with someone hand-feeding a tiger.

'Plenty,' Derwent said. 'But not on camera.'

The screen flickered and went back to Tom on his street corner. He laughed. 'That was all we got, I'm afraid, but at least no one got hurt.'

'Oh, Josh,' Godley said, shaking his head. 'You do have a knack for getting into trouble. I imagine I'll be getting some calls about that before long. Mute it again, please.'

I watched the screen as the reporter signed off. There was a buzz of conversation in the room, most of it approving but some of it very disapproving indeed. No prizes for guessing who was complaining about Derwent's behaviour. Godley clapped his hands.

'Okay. That's enough. Does anyone have any suggestions?'

James Peake raised a hand. 'Release Shane Poole's picture to the media and tell them to report that we want to question him as we think he might have useful information for us. He wasn't planning to go too far, I'd say, especially if he left his passport and didn't clear out his bank accounts.'

'Worth a try. Anyone else?' Godley looked around the room. 'Right. I've asked for details of Shane and his car to be added to briefings across the South-East. All ANPR cameras will be looking for his plates, but he's been canny about other things that might draw our attention so I'd expect him to be using fake ones. We'll keep Derwent on our list and keep digging into their backgrounds. Harry is taking over the cold case, by the way, so address any questions to him.'

Maitland looked terrified. I gathered my things together. Forgiveness only went so far, I could see. I had proved myself to be a useful member of the team but Godley was a long way from reinstating me.

'Where are you going?' Peake strolled over, hands in his pockets.

'Home. Bed. Maybe a bath first.' I wound my scarf around my neck. 'I need a rest.'

'Sounds like fun.'

I wasn't in the mood. 'No fun. Just sleep. And plenty of it.'

'I didn't mean—'

'Yeah, you did.'

In spite of myself I smiled: he was looking at me from under worried eyebrows, biting his lip, overselling the anxiety just a tad but damn cute with it. 'Good luck. I'll see you when Shane lands in custody.'

'If not before,' Peake said, and stood back to let me go. I nodded to Godley as I went, and he nodded back, as if to say: *yes, that's the first sensible thing I've seen you do today.*

I wouldn't have admitted it, but I thought the same.

Chapter 29

It was dark outside, and raining hard, and the air was raw. I reeled, feeling as if I'd walked into a wall of pure exhaustion. I took a roundabout route to the tube, dodging news cameras. It was unlikely that I'd do a Derwent but not impossible.

I had to battle delayed and crowded trains and edgy fellow commuters. I took the shortest possible route from the station to the flat, checking behind me in a cursory way, but far more focused on getting some sleep than on my personal safety. My hair was soaking, the rain seeping down between my coat collar and my neck. It had saturated my shoulders already and the cold struck up through the thin soles of my shoes.

Things didn't get a lot better when I got home. The air in the flat chilled me and something definitely smelled off. I squeezed rainwater out of my hair and tied it back, then went through the kitchen while the kettle boiled and the heat came on, finding nothing in the fridge or cupboards or even the bin that might be responsible. I moved on, searching every other room in the flat, winding up in the sitting room. The light was blinking on the answering machine and I pressed play, letting it squawk in the background while I kept looking. There had to be something. A plate with leftover food under a chair. A mug growing exciting mould. God knows, I wasn't the best housekeeper in the

322

world but just forgetting I'd abandoned food somewhere was a new low.

'Maeve, it's your mother. I was just wondering if you'd had a chance to write to your aunt Niamh. I—'

I cut her off. Next message.

'Maeve. You're not back yet. I was just ringing to see if you'd got my earlier mess—'

I stabbed at it irritably. My mother's refusal to come to terms with the modern world meant she hated ringing me on my mobile. It suited me fine – otherwise my voicemail would have been solid with calls about nothing much that I would never, ever return. But on this occasion, it would have been vibrating on its own, wherever it had ended up, lonely in its evidence bag, and I would have been wonderfully out of range.

'Maeve Áine Kerrigan, what have I just seen on the news? Call me when you get this, please. At once.'

She sounded really cross. I winced and let the next message play in full.

'You could have been killed. I don't know what possessed you to go in there with no gun or anything. And they say your nice boss was shot. Well, it's no more than he deserves, dragging you into a dangerous situation like that and you with no more sense than a day-old chick. Call me as soon as you get this message.'

She was less angry, more scared in the next message, and then in the next one said she'd tried my mobile number but had got no answer, and then in the one after that I got the full, cold, 'Of course, we're the last people who matter but it would be nice if you'd acknowledge our existence now and then.'

I put out my hand for the phone and then stopped as the answering machine beeped again. I put my finger on the delete button, but pulled back when I realised it was Rob. He sounded tense. 'Maeve, I got your message. I've been trying to call you on your phone but you're not picking up

– I don't know why. I've left a message for you at work, too, so maybe you'll get that first. Maeve, don't be scared, but get a bag – now – and go somewhere safe.' He was striving for calm but the urgency kept breaking through, and I stopped lifting sofa cushions, looking for the rogue prawn sandwich that had to be the source of the stench. I stared at the machine as if it could tell me in advance where this was going.

'Your message – you thanked me for the flowers, but I didn't send you any and I don't know who did. I know you'll want to find out who it was, but don't waste any time, please. Just go.'

It was all very well for Rob to tell me to leave without further delay, but it was human nature to examine the flowers to see if there were any clues, and I was only human. The smell was far stronger as I bent over them. The roses had opened fully now, and they were packed so tightly together it was hard to see what was going on – until the overhead light struck a gleam of something that was clearly, obviously flesh. Not needing to put on a brave face since I was alone, I screamed and dropped the vase. It shattered, sending little bits of glass everywhere. In among the glass shards and leaves I saw white, squirming things. Maggots. The smell was strong enough to make me gag. With gloves on, the kitchen scissors in hand and a wooden spoon for poking purposes I managed to pull the bouquet apart so I could see what was at the heart of it: a piece of meat wedged in tightly, surrounded by stems. It was chicken, I thought, or pork, but green with decomposition and alive with maggots. I turned my head away, convinced I was going to be sick. It wasn't just that the meat smelled revolting. Someone had pretended to be Rob to send me a message. They knew where I was. They knew I was alone. And they wanted me to know that they knew.

It didn't take a genius to leap to the same conclusion as Rob. Chris Swain, the guy who had seemed so harmless when he was just my neighbour, had an uncanny ability to track me down, no matter how hard I tried to stay hidden. Up to now, he'd been happy to play games with me. He got his kicks from taking me to the edge of terror and letting me see just how powerless I was to stop myself from falling over. He had marked me out as a victim and I couldn't seem to shake off the role, no matter how much I hated it, and him. He was a sneak, a voyeur, a rapist whose style was to drug his victims to avoid the possibility of them fighting back. A coward.

Dangerous.

And the thing that really bothered me about the game he was playing was that I had no idea what constituted a win. Humiliation? Aggravation?

Death?

I went into the bedroom and changed into jeans, boots and a thick sweatshirt, all too aware of the possibility that I was being watched or filmed with the sort of secret camera Swain had used before. I put a change of clothes and some toiletries in a backpack, then got ready for the hard work: two layers of gloves and the dustpan and brush. I got a bag from the kitchen and shovelled the whole pile into it: the oozing meat and broken glass and bent stems and every last one of the maggots. I excavated the cellophane and tissue paper that had been wrapped around the bouquet from the kitchen bin and folded them into a brown-paper parcel. I got an envelope and went through the recycling to find the florists' card, aware that I had missed a collection the previous day. If I had just been a little bit more efficient, the evidence would have been long gone.

'Score one for me,' I said aloud, trying to keep my spirits up. Trying to keep the fear at bay because I had things to do before I could leave and every instinct for self-preservation I possessed was pushing me towards the door.

I needed the evidence, because I was reporting this as a crime. I wanted it on record. Swain was on the Met's wanted list already because of video evidence we'd seized of him sexually assaulting dozens of unconscious women, but when we caught him – and we would – I wanted him charged with the crimes he'd committed against me. He owed me that much, even if I wasn't going to be first on the indictment. Others had suffered more than me, but I had endured quite enough from Swain. I would have my day in court, and he would hopefully have a decade or so in prison when we finally caught up with him.

I put the bag inside another bag and left it in the hall, hoping it wouldn't stink too badly the next day. There was no point in calling it in now. The response team would never consider it a priority at that time of night; I'd be in a queue behind every domestic and suspected burglary and bar fight in east London, and I wasn't inclined to wait around in the flat for hours, wondering when or if I was going to be attacked. Better to wait until early turn started for the local CID and hand it over to a nice, friendly detective who could take a statement and file a report. I wanted to be free to leave as soon as I was ready to go. Just being in the flat was close to unbearable. My jaw ached and I realised I was clenching it, and my fists, as the adrenalin played on my nerves. What else did I need to do?

Oh yes. That was it. Find somewhere to go. Which was where I ground to a halt for the second time. I didn't know anyone nearby: Rob and I had chosen Dalston in part because we never socialised around there so we could keep a low profile. I had no mobile phone so no numbers for anyone I could trust not to panic, which would teach me to learn some off by heart. I only knew Rob's, my parents' and my brother's. I was not going to involve my parents in this particular flap; I couldn't go to my brother either, because someone – a niece or his wife or even Dec himself – would be bound to let it slip to Mum and then I would be in even more trouble for not having told them in the first place. The rain rattled as the wind caught the drops and flung them against the windows. I couldn't stay in the flat; it wasn't safe. I didn't want to leave without knowing where I was going.

I stood in the middle of the living room, shivering, and considered my options, none of which were appealing. Back to the office, where there was nowhere to sleep at all. Stay where I was and hope Swain had sent the flowers because he couldn't get past our security arrangements. But I already felt I was being watched, and I'd never sleep. Trek to Liv's house, though she lived in Guildford, miles outside London, and it would take me an age to get there. I didn't want to risk it without knowing she'd be in. Call the office, get put through to Godley and let him take over – but he was fully occupied and I couldn't divert him from a murder investigation for the sake of a sick prank, even if it had me terrified. Stay in a hotel – somewhere cheap and soulless but with decent locks on the doors. It wasn't an appealing option. I didn't want to be on my own with my fears, even if it was somewhere other than the flat. I would never relax enough to close my eyes, let alone sleep. But it looked as if I was out of luck.

Except that I knew one person who was nearby, and at home, and would be more than pleased to help. In fact, he would be angry if I didn't call on him. And he owed me a favour. It was a terrible idea, but it was a better option than anything else I'd thought of.

I just hoped the surveillance team wouldn't have started yet.

Chapter 30

'Go. Away.'

'Sir, it's me.' I was crouching by the letterbox, trying not to let the skirt of my coat get wet, the wind tugging at my hair and clothes until it felt as if someone was pulling at me, trying to get my attention. I was half-whispering because I really didn't want to attract the interest of passers-by, the media or even Derwent's neighbours. There was only one person I was trying to reach, and he was having none of it.

'Fuck off. I'm not telling you again.'

'It's Maeve. Kerrigan,' I added, then rolled my eyes. He only knew one Maeve, I was fairly sure. I checked over my shoulder – no one – and levered open the letterbox again. I could see his feet, and realised he was sitting at the top of the stairs. Forgetting about speaking softly, I snarled, 'I'm only here because I need help. Now if you're not going to man up and let me in, I'm going, but I want you to know I think you're a— a—'

'A what?' He sounded interested.

'A twat. Sir.'

'That must be you, Kerrigan. Only you would take so long to come up with the word "twat". I was expecting something really good.' He got to his feet slowly, with some difficulty, balancing on one leg as he turned to reach his crutches. 'I'll let you in but it'll be a while before I can get to the door.'

'Take your time,' I said, shuddering with the cold. I couldn't feel my hands any more, or my ears.

Instead of coming down towards the door, Derwent levered himself up, out of sight.

'Where are you going?'

'I was making tea. It'll be stewed if I don't get the bag out of the mug sharpish.'

I fumed on the doorstep for another five minutes while Derwent did whatever he had to do and then came down the stairs with roughly as much fuss and as many dramatic pauses as an elderly diva making her Vegas debut. When he finally opened the door I pushed in past him.

'Wait until you're invited, missy.'

'That's vampires, not house guests.' I turned. 'When are they coming round with your heavyweight belt?'

'Oh, you saw that?'

'I think the world's seen it by now. It was a hell of a shot.'

'You're telling me. I bruised my hand, look.' He showed me his fist, which was red and swollen and had a gash on top of one finger.

'Is that a fight bite?'

'Yeah. If he didn't have such big horse teeth I'd have been fine because it was a direct hit on his nose. Knowing my luck, he'll have rabies.'

'You got a round of applause from the coppers I was with when they saw it.'

'Really?' He looked pleased. 'The guys at the hospital didn't even consider arresting me. They talked Pace into letting it drop. Nice of them.'

'I think a lot of people were hoping something like that might happen to him.'

'You know me. Being a hero comes natural.'

'I'm sure.' It was freezing in the hall and I made for the stairs. 'I'm going up to get warm.'

'You're not going to wait for me?'

'I've done a lot of waiting for you this evening already.'

I ran up and into the living room, which was warm and softly lit. He had drawn the blinds, shutting the world out, and I started to feel I could relax for the first time in hours. I took off my boots and coat, and held my hands over the radiator, wincing as the warmth started to bring them back to life.

Derwent made it up to the top of the stairs eventually and abandoned the crutches with a clatter. He limped in to the sitting room.

'Make yourself at home.'

'I knew you'd want me to be comfortable.'

He ignored that. 'To what do I owe the pleasure? If you've had a fight with your boyfriend, I'm not providing a sympathetic ear.'

'You wouldn't be the first port of call for that,' I agreed. I was still shivering. At this stage I was starting to think it was because I was ill or in shock. The flat was boiling. Derwent was wearing a T-shirt with his tracksuit bottoms. I tried, very hard, to send a message to my nervous system that it could calm down for the time being. 'I couldn't stay in my flat.'

'Why not?'

'Because of a bunch of flowers, would you believe.'

Derwent listened, asking the occasional question, as I faltered through the story. He had dropped the attitude. I was talking to the police officer version of Derwent, focused on the facts and their implications. I wished I had the luxury of a cool-headed assessment of the situation, but I was far too involved for that.

'First thing: who knew Rob was going to be away?'

'No one.' I got a look for that and tried again. 'Okay. I did, obviously. I mentioned it to Liv, who might have told Joanna, I suppose. People Rob works with. I didn't tell you.'

'No, you didn't.'

'I didn't tell my parents or any of our friends.' I chewed my lip. 'That's it, as far as I know.'

'Did you talk to anyone about it over the phone? Could your landline be bugged?'

'I only use the landline to pick up messages, mainly from Mum. I always use my mobile.'

'What about email?'

'No.'

'Facebook?'

'I'm not on Facebook.' Like I wanted to share details of my personal life with the world. Derwent should have known better.

'Any other social websites?'

I shook my head. 'Nothing.'

'Is your place bugged?'

'I don't know. That's what Swain did before.' I was starting to shake again.

'Get that checked out.' Derwent had sat down on the arm of a chair while we were talking and now he jumped up and started to pace. He got two steps before his leg went from under him and he collapsed inelegantly into the chair. 'Oh, fuck-a-doodle-do.'

'Are you okay?'

'Fine.' He righted himself. 'What about Boyband? Does he keep his mouth shut?'

I ignored the jibe. 'As a rule.'

'And you thought the flowers were from him.'

'Yes, but I didn't think the message sounded like him. It was patronising.'

'Could you imagine Chris Swain saying it?'

'I try not to imagine Chris Swain saying anything at all.' I sighed. 'Look, I don't think we're going to get to the bottom of this tonight. It was creepy as hell and I generally assume that means Swain was involved. I hope you can understand why I ended up here.'

'Yeah, I know why you're here. Let Uncle Josh look after everything.'

I tried not to look repelled but it was a struggle.

331

'Drink?' Derwent said.

'I don't need anything.'

'I was telling you to get me one.'

'Oh.' I bit back *get it yourself*. Being on crutches, he couldn't carry a drink easily, and it was the least I could do. 'What do you want?'

'Beer. In the fridge. You know where the kitchen is.'

I did. I was on my way back, bottle in hand, when a thought struck me. I doubled back to make sure, then went and stood in the doorway of the sitting room until Derwent looked up.

'Over here, love. Don't ever quit and become a waitress, will you? You're rubbish.'

'You lied to me.'

He raised his eyebrows.

'You said you were making tea, but the kettle's cold and there are no mugs in the sink or the dishwasher or in here. You have no milk in your fridge and I couldn't find a single tea bag in your kitchen. You don't even drink tea. You told me that before. What were you doing? Tidying up? Hiding the evidence?'

He gave me his widest, whitest smile, the one that reminded me of a hunting dog grinning. 'Give me the beer.'

'Not before I get an explanation.'

'Come on.' He held out his hand. 'If you need me to say it, I'm impressed, Kerrigan. You put it all together.'

'Yay for me. I still want to know what you were doing.'

'Tidying.'

'You never tidy because you never make a mess.'

'What does it matter?'

'It matters because I don't like being lied to.'

He stretched. 'Well, I've never lied to you about any-thing important. You know that, don't you?'

'I thought I did.'

'It's true.' He looked straight at me, his eyes limpid. 'You can trust me. But you can also trust me to be a bit of a lad.

I thought you were coming round to tick me off for punching Pace on camera. I wanted to make you wait.'

'Thanks very much.'

'Any time.' He looked as ashamed of himself as it was possible for Derwent to look, which was not very. 'You should get to bed. Get some rest. You look like death.'

'Where am I going?'

'In there.' He indicated the room next to the living room.

I picked up my bag and went in, flicking the light on. I stopped for a second, then reversed.

'That's your room.'

'So?'

'So you seem to have misunderstood.' My face was flaming.

'No, you have. This is a one-bedroom flat. I am letting you have the bedroom. I do not propose to sleep with you and that phrase includes any possible meaning you like, from sharing a room to shagging. And don't flatter yourself.'

He was amused, not angry, but I was still mortally embarrassed. It put an edge in my voice when I replied. 'And what about you? Where are you going to sleep?'

'The sofa.'

'No. You're injured. I should sleep there.'

'It's not on offer.'

'I am not sleeping in your bed when you were shot a day and a half ago and you should still be in hospital.'

'Who told you that?'

'It's obvious,' I said. 'You look dreadful.'

'Said the woman with bright red eyes and crazy hair. Fuck me, it's like getting a lecture from Coco the Clown.'

I put a hand up, encountered frizz and decided not to fight that particular battle. 'Never mind how I look. You are recuperating and you shouldn't be doing it on a sofa.'

He rubbed both hands over his face. 'Give me strength. Listen, Kerrigan, I'm going to let you in on a little secret.

This leg? Hurts like buggery. I'm not going to be getting much sleep tonight even if I'm in my own bed.'

'Didn't they give you painkillers to take home?'

'Yeah.'

'And?'

'I don't like them. I'm not taking them.'

'You are so stubborn.'

He levered himself to his feet. 'I know. But it's my body. I don't like drugs and I don't mind pain. I just don't think there's any point pretending I'm going to sleep tonight. And you look as if you could sleep for a week.'

'Two.'

'There you go.' He limped past me, holding on to the wall for support. 'I'll get a spare duvet out and nick a pillow and I'll be fine.'

There was no arguing with him, ever. I was too tired for a fight anyway. The thought of sinking into a real bed at long last was enough to make me give in. I brushed my teeth in a bathroom that was antiseptically clean and male from the toiletries to the towels. When I came out, Derwent was leaning against the wall in the hall.

'Need anything else?'

'No. Thanks.' I hesitated. 'And thanks for this. Letting me stay.'

'It's a pleasure,' he said, as if he meant it.

I said goodnight and shut the door firmly behind me, wishing I could lock it. I trusted Derwent but I wanted the security of being behind an unopenable door. He'd stripped the bed while I was in the bathroom and I spent a few minutes making it again, wrestling with the duvet. It was strange to be doing a domestic task in Derwent's home, his private space, a place I had never imagined being. I could only imagine what Godley would make of it if he knew.

'Mind out of the gutter, boss,' I murmured and climbed into Derwent's bed before switching off the light. I pulled the covers up and huddled, relieved. I was glad that

Derwent had trusted me enough to let me stay. I was glad I had stuck by him when Godley and Burt told me to be wary. I was starting to think we might become friends.

Friends with Derwent? Stranger things had happened. But not many.

Despite everything, I went to sleep with a smile on my face.

At ten to four, I woke up, with no idea where I was or what had disturbed me. I didn't know anything, except that I was scared. It took a couple of seconds for me to remember where I was and why, relief sweeping over me as I reminded myself that I was safe and everything was all right.

A couple of seconds after that, something moved in the room, passing in front of the shaded window so I saw a silhouette for a second. A man.

'Derwent?' I said, my voice blurry with sleep. I assumed, I thought that he had forgotten something, or that he'd forgotten I was there. I thought it was an honest mistake.

I thought that until, without warning, he landed on top of me with his full weight, pinned my arms to my sides with his knees, wrapped his hands around my neck and began to squeeze the life out of me. It wasn't fear I felt, or despair, but anger. I was angry with myself. I'd believed Derwent, and I'd been wrong, and whatever happened was my fault. God, I hated being wrong.

White and red lights burst in the blackness and I couldn't fight, or scream, or do anything at all.

Anything, that is, except die.

THURSDAY

Chapter 31

I'd love to pretend that I found superhuman strength from somewhere and kicked my way free. I'd love to say that I saved my own life by being quick and clever and instinctively good at fighting. The reality was that I was in serious trouble, as close to dying as I had ever been. I was aware of almost nothing as my brain became starved of oxygen, nothing but a bright light and the dreadful weight on top of me that was crushing my ribs, and the impossibility of taking a breath when my body was crying out for it. And then, suddenly, the weight was gone and I could breathe again, dragging air into my lungs as my knees came up to my chest. My throat was on fire, my eyes full of tears, and the sound of my own heart thumping filled my ears. I rolled onto my side in a tight little ball and wheezed piteously.

It was probably a minute – not more than that – before I came round enough to start making sense of my surroundings. The bright light was the main bedroom light. A scuffling sound interspersed with dull thuds and grunts of pain was a fight happening somewhere nearby. The thumping sound was someone trying to batter the front door in. The urgency of doing something galvanised me: I sat up and saw Derwent on the floor, on the wrong side of a fight that was the definition of nasty. The man struggling with him, anonymous in dark clothes and a beanie hat, was big and angry, and while I was still trying to get my head around what was going on he hit Derwent with a short, nasty jab in the stomach that made Derwent groan. He retaliated by forcing the man's head back, pressing against his throat, fingers digging for the pressure point that would – in theory – reduce his assailant to a quivering wreck. The guy retaliated by kneeing him in the crotch, missing his target by a matter of inches as Derwent twisted sideways.

It was time to stop watching and start helping, I realised, and looked around for something to use. The bedside light was metal and surprisingly heavy when I hefted it. I unplugged it and struggled off the bed, ready to hit—

I stopped. I had no idea who I should want to win. I couldn't tell who had attacked me and who had come to the rescue. Derwent caught sight of me and glared, for the split second he could spare, and I could translate it easily enough: *what are you doing, standing there? Get stuck in, Kerrigan.*

Instead, I moved around so I could see his opponent's face. Derwent pushed his head back again, the muscles standing out in his arm as he stretched his fingers towards the man's eyes, and I recognised him at last: the Met's most wanted, Shane Poole. I lifted the lamp and brought it down on the back of his neck, and he collapsed over Derwent like a tower block disintegrating in a controlled explosion.

'Thank fuck.' Derwent pushed at Shane's shoulder, trying to lever him off. 'You took your time. Were you waiting for an invitation?'

'Is he still alive?'

'Yeah. Out cold. Nice job.' Derwent wriggled out and sat up, leaning his arms on his knees as he tried to get his breathing back under control. He looked past me. 'This must be my night for unwanted guests.'

Two men were standing in the doorway when I looked round, one small and one big, both in leather bomber jackets, both so obviously policemen that they might as well not have bothered being in plain clothes.

'We saw him break in. We were waiting for backup to come, but then we heard the fight so we opened your door.'

'Do much damage?' Derwent asked.

'Just a bit.' The larger one lifted up the battering ram he'd used. 'You might need to get the hinges fixed.'

'Fucking marvellous.'

The smaller policeman lifted his radio. 'One in custody. We'll need an ambulance, please. Two ambulances,' he said, looking at me, and I put a hand to my neck, suddenly aware that it was throbbing.

His big friend bent over Shane Poole and put him in the recovery position, then cuffed him, hands in front. 'Not to take any chances,' he said to me. 'Amazing how quickly they recover when they want to.'

'What was he doing here?' I asked Derwent.

'What are these two doing here?' he shot back. 'Were you watching me?' He looked at me. 'Did you know about this?'

'I knew there was going to be surveillance on you. I didn't know they were here.'

'Why the fuck didn't you tell me?' He looked utterly incensed.

'Because I still owe some loyalty to my boss and he told me not to. My career is already in tatters. What do you think Godley would have done if I'd warned you about the surveillance?'

'Sacked you.' Derwent shrugged. 'Not my problem. My problem is being lied to.'

'Get over yourself.' I turned to the plain-clothes guys. 'What did you see?'

'We were parked on the corner. We saw matey here having a look at the place a couple of hours ago and then wander off. He didn't look dodgy enough to stop – all he did was look. We didn't know who he was, obviously, or we'd have had him. He went over the wall at the back about ten minutes ago and in through the bathroom window.'

'Damn it,' Derwent said. 'I bet he's broken it.'

'Sounded like it.'

'Ten minutes ago?' I was stuck on the timings. 'Was that all?'

'He was only in here for a minute before I put the light on,' Derwent said. 'I heard him in the hall. Knew it wasn't you because you don't make that much noise, walking around. He came in to the sitting room first but I wasn't in a position to tackle him then.'

'Where were you?'

'Behind the sofa.'

I tried not to laugh, and failed.

'I wasn't *hiding*. I was trying to sleep there.'

'Oh, sure,' I said. 'I believe you. You thought you'd wait until he was distracted and then take him down.'

'I am just out of hospital,' Derwent said, hurt. 'I'm not at my best.'

'You did all right,' the larger of the two policemen said. 'Not a bad effort.'

Derwent's chest expanded a couple of inches. 'My trouble is I don't know when I'm beaten. I keep fighting even when the odds are against me.' He looked at me. 'That's the definition of a winner, Kerrigan.'

'Sounds like the definition of a moron to me.' I was sailing very close to the edge of what Derwent considered acceptable repartee. I rushed to change the subject. 'So why was he trying to kill me?'

'That's what we'll have to find out.' Derwent looked down at the body at his feet. Shane groaned, but kept his eyes closed. Derwent stuck a toe in his ribcage experimentally and got no response. 'If he ever comes round. Bloody hell, Kerrigan, how hard did you hit him?'

'Very. I imagined it was you.'

Although the paramedics tutted over Shane's head and took him to hospital where he was scanned, tested, prodded and poked, he was concussion-free when he woke up, and passed as fit to be interviewed later that afternoon. I sat in the nearest police station to Derwent's house in a room that was too small for comfort, with Derwent, Maitland, Godley and Una Burt. Derwent was in an edgy mood, inclined to bicker, and more than once Godley had to tell him off for being rude.

'Sorry, guv. This is pissing me off, though. I don't understand why you won't let me speak to him.'

'Because you are far too involved. Maitland and I will handle this and you can watch the video link.'

'Don't do me any favours,' Derwent said under his breath.

'If you want, you can give us some idea of how you would handle the interview. We might find it useful.'

'Ask him why he wanted to find me in the first place. Ask him what all of this has to do with Angela. Ask him if he killed her and the other women. Ask him why he started killing last year.'

'This is revelatory,' Burt said, borrowing Derwent's trademark sarcasm and making it work for her. 'No one would have thought of asking such comprehensive questions without your input.'

'Okay, so maybe I'm not coming up with anything you haven't thought of, but you can't ask it the way I can. You walk into the room and he'll be . . . I want to say *appalled*, but it won't be because he's intimidated by you. He'll laugh at you.'

'Josh,' Godley snapped. 'I'm *warning* you.'

Derwent ignored the interruption. 'When it comes to me, on the other hand, he's scared shitless. I go in there and ask him these questions and he'll give up. I can make him angry. Get under his skin. I *know* him.'

'You used to know him,' Godley said, glancing up as Colin Vale came in holding a file. 'You haven't spoken to him for twenty years. You knew him when he was a teenager and now he's a successful businessman.'

'You're talking about Poole?' Colin checked. 'Well, if now's a good time, I can tell you exactly how successful he is.'

'Go on.'

'He's turned the bar from a seedy local to one of the reliable earners in that street. Talking to the neighbouring businesses, it's all his hard work. He works insane hours, lives for the business, spent a long time putting any profit back into the bar rather than living it up. He's meticulous about his records, which is useful for me, and as a business the place is on the up. It's also on the market.'

'Since when?'

'January. Not a good time to sell, unfortunately, with the downturn in the economy. He's got a high price tag on it, but he's right, according to those who know. He's prepared to wait until someone comes along who'll pay him what he deserves and in the meantime he's keeping back more of the profit to divert into savings and investments. Or he was.'

'What do you mean?' Godley asked.

'Well, it's a funny thing. You noticed the cash thing, Maeve, didn't you?'

I nodded. 'He doesn't seem to use his bank card for personal purchases; everything is in cash, in-person transactions that we can't trace.'

'That's a relatively recent development,' Colin said. 'He started that last year too. So something made him start hiding what he was doing then.'

'Getting ready to start killing,' Burt said.

'Or putting the business on the market,' I pointed out, playing devil's advocate. 'If it sold, the due diligence would have involved all of his records. Maybe he wanted to keep a few things to himself.'

'But this is his personal account we're dealing with,' Burt snapped. 'Nothing to do with the business.'

'You don't know he wasn't paying some casual

employees cash in hand to keep down the staff costs and make the place look more appealing to an investor,' Colin said. 'Staff are the curse of catering because even on the minimum wage they cost a lot, and you have to cover their National Insurance contributions. If you're just taking some money out of the till, on the other hand, they don't have to pay income tax and you can make your overheads a lot smaller.'

'That sounds possible,' I said, remembering the Nigerian cleaner who had looked scared of me.

'He's trying to hide something to do with the killings,' Derwent said, sounding bored. 'Do we really have to fanny about providing him with innocent reasons for using cash all the time?'

'I hate to agree but I feel the same way.' Burt turned to Godley. 'You must think he's a credible suspect.'

'Must I?' Godley looked amused. 'He could be. I'm going to wait until I've spoken to him to see.'

'I want to sit in on the interview.' Burt didn't look at Derwent as she said it, but it was her loss because his face was a picture. It was an obvious power play – a reminder that she was senior, and closer to Godley than him as well. To give him his due, Godley saw it a mile off.

'I don't want anyone there who doesn't have to be. I want to speak to him. I want Harry with me because he's a trained interrogator and the best I have on my team.'

Maitland looked pleased. 'Too kind, boss.'

'Please, both of you – all of you – watch the interview. We'll take breaks so you can give us a steer if we miss something. I do value your input but I don't want you in there.'

Burt got up, muttering something about having to make some calls, and stumped out of the room. Godley and Maitland followed, heading for the interview room to set it up as they wanted it. Derwent laughed and stood up, wobbling as he found out the hard way his leg wasn't working well enough to pace about.

'He doesn't want Burt in there because she'd frighten the wits out of Shane. She's mentioned specifically in the UN mandate against torture, you know. Cruel and unusual punishment, just looking at her.'

'She's all right.'

'She doesn't like *you*.'

'What makes you say that?'

'Gave you evils when you were speaking. Shot down your point about the bar records being up for inspection. That wasn't altogether stupid, I thought. Well done you.'

'I live for your praise,' I said drily.

Derwent sat down again, this time beside me. 'Answer me one thing. It's been bothering me.'

'What?'

'Do you always sleep fully clothed?'

'I didn't pack pyjamas.'

'I'd have lent you something.'

'There was no need. I don't mind sleeping in clothes.'

'Seems a bit extreme. Must save on wear and tear on your hangers, I suppose. But I thought it might be because you didn't trust me. I meant what I said. You are flattering yourself if you think you're my type, Kerrigan.'

I was saved from answering by the video link flickering into life. Beside me, Derwent fell silent, thinking his own thoughts as Godley and Maitland got ready for Shane to be brought in.

It took the usual age for the cast to be assembled – the solicitor was taking a call in the corridor and Shane elected not to enter the room without her – but when they were finally seated around the table, Maitland began, and his technique was a joy to behold. Gentle, persistent, friendly, he was a world away from the table-thumping rhetoric that was popularly supposed to be effective. He persuaded Shane to trust him inside the first three minutes just by talking to him like a human being, and I could sense Shane's confidence growing as his brief became more and more uneasy.

It didn't take long to get to the events of the previous night.

'You broke in.'

'Yes, I did.' Shane seemed relieved to agree.

'What were you planning to do when you broke in?'

The solicitor was a large woman with spiky hair and long, red nails. She leaned over and spoke softly to her client, who shrugged and answered in a matter-of-fact way.

'I wanted to find Josh Derwent and kill him.'

Derwent didn't so much as blink.

'Why?' Maitland asked.

'Because he was responsible for murdering my sister and no one would listen to me when I told them. Because there's a fucking conspiracy of silence just because he's a copper.'

Godley sounded infinitely reasonable when he replied. 'If there was evidence of him having committed a crime, we would take that very seriously. More seriously than if it was a civilian, not less.'

'Tell me another fairy tale.' The bitterness on Shane's face was clear even on the smudgy video.

Maitland took over. 'Why did you attack DC Kerrigan?'

'She was in his bed,' he said, as if that explained everything. I really wished I could explain, for the benefit of the transcript, that I'd been alone, and fully dressed, and not expecting him to join me.

'Was that a good enough reason to try to kill her?'

'No.' He swallowed. 'Is she okay?'

'She's very shaken,' Godley said, his voice cold.

Derwent leaned over and patted my hand. 'Poor dear.'

'Save it.' I touched the scarf around my neck that was hiding a technicolour display of bruises. 'This is all your fault.'

On the screen, Shane put his hands over his face. 'I'm sorry. I shouldn't have done it. It was dark in the bedroom and I didn't know it wasn't Josh until I felt that it was a woman. She'd woken up – I thought she'd scream – and I panicked. I was trying to work out what to do even when I knew I was going to kill her. Then I thought, "Well, what does it matter? He'll find out what it's like to lose someone he loves."'

'You decided to kill her.'

'I didn't know what I was doing.'

The solicitor wrote something on her notepad.

'Have you ever killed anyone?'

'No.'

'Did you kill your sister?'

'No! Of course not.' His voice had risen, the veins standing out in his neck. Godley put a hand flat on the table, a signal to Maitland to let him take the lead again.

'Let's come back to that. I want to know why you disappeared the day before yesterday, Shane.'

'I saw him on the news. Josh, I mean. Being shot in the playground. I realised he was in hospital and I could get at him. I stayed in a hotel near the hospital while I was working out what to do, how to get in to his room. But when I saw the footage of him leaving the next day I thought I'd missed my chance, and I would have if it wasn't for him punching that Pace guy.'

'How did that help?'

'The reporter who followed him filmed his house and then I saw a street name and checked it on Google Maps, and it looked right. I couldn't believe my luck.'

'Nor can I,' Derwent said darkly. 'You get on the news a couple of times and you're a sitting duck. How fair is that?'

'Maybe this will teach you to stop punching people on camera,' Burt observed.

'Name one person I hit who didn't deserve it,' Derwent demanded, and was rewarded with silence.

They took a break before they asked Shane about his switch to cash ('to avoid getting ripped off'), about why the business was on the market ('I've had enough of this country. I want to live somewhere warm') and about the timing of both. He denied any knowledge of the murders beyond the conversation he'd had with me about them.

'Were they in your bar? The women?'

'I don't know. I don't think so.'

'DC Kerrigan said you told her you'd show their images to your staff. Did you?'

'Yeah. No one knew them.' He shook his head. 'I don't know what you're trying to pin on me. I'm admitting what I did last night but that's it. I have nothing else to tell you.'

'Do you have alibis for the nights of the murders?' Maitland reeled off the dates.

Shane put one hand up to his face and rubbed his eyes. 'I don't know. I'd have to check my diary.'

'We'll need you to do that.'

'You have trouble with alibis, don't you?' Godley observed. 'You had to invent one for Angela's death.'

'What? How did you know that?' His face darkened. 'Did Claire tell you—?'

'Did you kill Angela?'

'No, I didn't.'

'Angela wasn't sexually assaulted. That always makes us think it could be a family member who did the killing. You. Your father. Someone who wanted to punish her, not rape her.'

'Please. My dad was on the other side of town and I wasn't even there until after the police came.'

'Why did you need to lie?' Godley asked, intent.

'I was terrified of the copper who was investigating – I thought he'd crucify me for smoking dope. And I didn't want my parents to know I'd been doing drugs instead of looking after Angela. They'd have been mortified, and they'd have hated me for it. I hated myself.'

'Very moving,' Una Burt said in a voice that indicated she thought the exact opposite.

Derwent glared at her. 'You don't know him. He means

it.' Shane could hate Derwent all he wanted, but Derwent was still loyal to him, even after so long.

'When did you decide to lie?' Godley asked.

'It was Vinny's idea. The policeman had been giving Vinny a hard time and he knew I wouldn't be able to cope.'

The story matched Claire's version of events, at least. I was starting to think we had got through all the murky lies to the solid truth, or at least an approximation of it.

'Tell us about Vinny,' Godley said. 'He was in the army, I understand. When did you hear about his death?'

It was an easy question but Shane looked wary. He turned to his lawyer. 'Can we take a break?'

'We've just had a break,' Maitland said quickly.

'My head hurts. I want some painkillers. I need to see the doctor.' He squeezed his eyes shut, then opened them. 'I'm getting double vision.'

Godley reached out to the tape recorder. 'Interview suspended at 16.22.'

'He didn't like that,' Derwent said. 'He didn't like that at all.'

'Why not?' Burt asked. 'You're the one who knows him, after all.'

'I don't want to speculate.' Derwent got up, found his crutches and limped out of the room, banging against most of the furniture on the way. He was clearly heading for Godley and Maitland so he could talk it over with them, and I wasn't surprised Una Burt looked put out, or that she made an excuse to go after him a few seconds later.

Colin Vale was still working through the numbers, shuffling paper behind me, as happy as a child in a sandpit. I was silent. It was nice to have some time to think. I thought about the little group, the relationships, the complicated dynamics of it all. And about Vinny, who'd also had no alibi but held up to Orpen's questioning. Vinny, who'd run away, first to travel and then to join the army. Vinny, whose death came before the current run of murders. Shane, and his cash-based lifestyle. The hospitality industry and its hidden workers. A face I had seen and not recognised at the time, because it was out of context and impossible and wrong.

'I've just got to make a phone call,' I said to an oblivious Colin, and left.

It took a long time to get the information I needed – longer than I'd expected. One phone call became two, and then I had a long wait for someone to get back to me, swivelling on a chair at a borrowed desk and fielding questions from the local CID. It was torture but I made myself wait until I knew the story, or as much of it as I was likely to find out from third parties. I hung up the phone for the last time and gave myself a second to process what I'd found out. Then I headed back to our little room, where the atmosphere was pure poison and Colin Vale looked desperate for someone to referee the Burt/Derwent bitch-off that was in progress. On screen, the interview was continuing.

'We need to interrupt them,' I said.

'Absolutely not,' Burt snapped. 'They've only just started again, and it's going really well.'

'There's something they need to know.'

'Give her a chance,' Derwent said. I'd been sure he would take my side once Burt was against me. 'What is it?'

'Vinny didn't die in Afghanistan. He got an honourable discharge in November last year, and came home. He's in London.'

'Motherfucker,' Derwent whispered. Una Burt looked as if she was thinking the same thing.

In case they hadn't worked out where this was going, I wrapped it up for them. 'And six weeks after Vinny got back to the UK, Kirsty Campbell was killed.'

Chapter 32

There was no need to argue with anyone after that. Burt
herself went and knocked on the interview-room door.
Maitland and Godley came down the corridor at a run to
hear what I'd found out, crowding into the little room with
Burt behind them.

'Are you serious?' Maitland demanded.

'Never more so. He's alive and pretending not to be.'

'Why did he leave the army?' Godley asked.

'There are two versions to that. I only know the truth
because I managed to speak to his commanding officer,
who is now based in Essex. The official story was that he
put in his papers because he'd had enough. I leaned on the
guy a bit and he told me, off the record, that Vinny got in
serious trouble in Helmand. He attacked a teenage boy and
almost killed him. They hushed it up – said the guy was
Taliban and Vinny had been acting in self-defence – but
according to his CO, he beat him half to death and left him
with life-changing injuries.'

'What does that mean?' Derwent demanded.

'He ripped his balls off.' Every man in the room looked
sick, Derwent most of all. 'You asked,' I pointed out.

'Any idea of a motive?'

'A row about a local girl.'

'Huh,' Derwent said. 'A crime of passion. He was bloody
lucky they didn't do him for it.'

'Vinny was very popular, very well respected. No one wanted to see him in a court martial. There was a ton of evidence against him – he didn't bother trying to hide what he was doing or why – so he was looking at considerable jail time and a dishonourable discharge. His CO advised him to put in his papers instead and go home.'

'And they let him?' Maitland was incredulous.

'It's not as if he did this in Warrington or somewhere. Afghanistan is a long way from the UK, and an eye for an eye isn't such a big deal there,' Derwent said.

'The CO actually said to me, "What happens in Helmand stays in Helmand",' I added.

Godley folded his arms. 'Let the army sort out its own mess. If the Red Caps were prepared to let him go, I'm not going to make a case against him for that. But given the timings, I want to find out more about Vinny, and I want to know what Shane knows about him.'

'Start off by asking him where Vinny's been living. Not with him, not in that flat.' I was absolutely sure of it, having searched it.

'Find out if he's been giving him money. That could explain the switch to cash,' Colin said.

'If Vinny's folks think he's dead, he must be sending them his pension,' Burt suggested. 'That'd leave him short.'

'Shane has been giving him money, but not as a hand-out. Vinny's been working for him in the bar.' I was getting used to being the one who dropped the bombshells but that got almost as good a reaction as the news that Vinny wasn't dead after all.

'What the actual f—' Derwent started to say and Godley cut him off.

'How do you know that?'

'I saw him.' I turned to Maitland. 'You saw him too. Remember when we cut through the kitchen at the bar? The guy unloading a dishwasher? Tattoos up both arms? Muscles?'

'Vaguely.'

'He was wearing a blue T-shirt,' I said. Maitland shook his head. I gave up and went on. 'I saw his face but I didn't make the connection until just now because I thought Vinny was dead.'

'So you think he got back, got in touch with Shane and got a job,' Godley said.

'And Shane switched to cash as far as he could to hide whatever money he was sending Vinny's way. I bet he was being paid more than your average kitchen hand,' I said.

'We need to get him picked up,' Burt said.

I shook my head. 'Once I found out he was alive, I did some checking. I had time on my hands while I was waiting to hear from the CO. No one at the bar knows where he lives and no one has seen him since we found out Shane was missing. He's gone.'

'Let's get in there and hit Shane with what we know.' Godley was fidgeting, unusually for him. He wanted this case solved, and not just because of the media interest or the pressure from his bosses. He wanted the person who killed those four women to be stopped.

'If you can't find out anything else, try to get him to tell you if anyone else knows Vinny's alive,' I suggested. 'He's going to need help to get out of sight. It's a place for us to start looking.'

You could have heard a pin drop in the little room where we were waiting. Everyone was staring at the screen, where Maitland and Godley were pulling out their chairs and sitting down.

'All right, Shane? How's the head?' Maitland asked.

'Yeah. Fine.'

'All right for water? Do you want a tea or coffee?'

'No thanks.' Shane was looking suspicious but he didn't have the experience to know what Maitland was doing:

closing off the options for him so he had no legitimate excuse to stop the interview.

'Sorry for the interruption,' Godley said easily. 'This is an active inquiry and we're getting more information all the time that helps us to work out what's been going on.'

'Yeah, but the last bit was a shock, wasn't it?' Maitland said to him, grinning. 'Not every day you find out someone's made a full recovery from being dead.'

Shane's eyes went from Maitland to Godley and back again, trying to read their expressions. Godley leaned forward.

'Vinny Naylor. Rumours of his death have been greatly exaggerated.'

'I don't know what you're talking about.'

'Oh, come on. Course you do. Big lad, works in your kitchen in the bar. Not chatty but nice to the others.'

'That's Jimmy. He's got learning disabilities. No education. Nice guy but all I can give him to do is menial stuff.'

Godley tapped the table. 'Jimmy's disappeared. Around the same time your bar filled up with policemen. Where do you think he went?'

'I don't know.'

'By your own account you headed off to punish Josh Derwent. Did Vinny try to stop you? Was Vinny looking for you while you were holed up in your hotel? Or did Vinny have problems of his own?' Godley was hitting him hard, not even giving him time to answer. Shane's expression was pained.

'We know about what happened in Afghanistan. We know he came home and didn't want anyone to know he was back. We know he came home just before Kirsty Campbell was killed. Are you saying that timing is a coincidence?'

'Yes. It has to be.'

Godley pounced. 'So you're admitting that Jimmy is really your friend Vinny.'

He didn't want to say yes. In the end, he gave a tiny, infinitesimal nod, which Godley described for the benefit of the transcript.

Beside me, Derwent sighed. 'Poor old Shane. Never the sharpest knife in the drawer. Almost makes me feel as if we're taking advantage of him.'

With no such pangs of conscience, Godley went on: 'And you've been giving him cash from the business to cover his costs and pay his family.'

'I've been paying him for working.'

'Why in cash?'

'He doesn't have a bank account,' Shane admitted. 'Cash is easier.'

'Where does he live?'

'I don't know.'

Maitland snorted. 'Come off it.'

'I *don't*. Some sort of hostel in the East End. I asked him about it a couple of times and he told me I was better off not knowing, that it wasn't the sort of place you'd have your mates round for curry anyway.'

Vinny, knowing that Shane was unreliable, taking steps to protect himself in the event that someone came looking for him. It rang alarm bells for me in a big way. Burt and Derwent obviously felt the same way because they were busy exchanging meaningful glances when I looked. Maybe what simmered between them wasn't animosity, but sexual tension. I made a note to suggest it the next time I was alone with Derwent and felt the need to be shouted at.

'Where did he go, Shane?' Maitland asked.

'I don't know. I've been a bit tied up.'

'Have you been in touch with him?'

'No.'

'Got a mobile number for him?'

'No.'

Godley was going through the file in front of him,

looking for something. 'Here's a printout showing all the contacts on your phone. Are you sure Vinny isn't on here?'

'Yeah.'

'Who's Jimmy Vincent?'

'A bloke.'

'Not "Jimmy" whose real name is Vincent?'

Shane looked mortified. 'No comment.'

'It's too late for that. You can't give a no comment interview now.' Godley's voice deepened, sounding more authoritative. 'He's gone underground, Shane, and we need to find him. For his sake and for the safety of others. Why do you think he disappeared?'

'Dunno. Probably because he doesn't like coppers.' Shane shrugged. 'I'm beginning to see his point.'

'We can't let him kill again.'

'He's not a killer.'

'Beating up that boy in Afghanistan – what if it reminded him of Angela? It made him want to hurt someone. It set off the chain of events that have left four young women dead. Four. Do you really want to add to the tally?'

'It's not him.' Shane looked close to desperate. 'I don't know how to explain it to you so you'll understand me. He's not a murderer. He's just not.'

'Sometimes it's the people you think you know best who have the darkest secrets,' Godley said. 'Nothing to be ashamed of. Think of all the wives who defended their husbands until they were proved wrong.'

Maitland stirred. 'You're not married, Shane, are you? How would you describe your relationship with Vinny? Friends? Or more than friends?'

'What are you trying to say?' Shane demanded, his face dark.

'He's not going to like that,' Derwent predicted.

'Someone needs to look into possible addresses for Vinny,' Una Burt said abruptly. 'Maeve, you've been doing well today. Do you want to make some calls?'

No, thanks. I'd like to stay and watch us get within touching distance of London's most wanted killer. She wasn't looking for a proper answer. I got up slowly, reluctantly, and headed for the door.

'And when you come back, bring coffee,' Derwent commanded, not even looking away from the screen.

'I might be a while,' I said.

'That's okay. I can wait.'

'You'll have to,' I said through gritted teeth as I shut the door. I might miss out on the interview, but I was absolutely not going to hurry back.

Allocated the same spare desk in the detectives' room I spent the next two hours doing Internet searches, checking phone books and ringing people. I called hostels, working men's clubs, cheap rented accommodation, charities, churches. I rang the places people went when they had nowhere else to go. I rang anyone who offered cheap, medium- to long-term accommodation in the East End and beyond, prioritising places that could be described as hostels. I described Vincent Naylor, AKA Jimmy, until the words ceased to have any meaning for me, until my voice was hoarse and my hand ached from writing notes. I listed the possibles, passing them on to Colin Vale, who contacted the local police stations and asked for neighbourhood officers to make calls in person as a matter of priority to interview our candidates.

It was a pleasant, slightly vague voice on the other end of the phone that put me out of my misery, a voice belonging to Father Gordon from St Philip's Catholic Church in Bethnal Green. He was responsible for running their hostel. ('Which is a grand name for a house left to us by a parishioner. We house the homeless and others who are down on their luck. They each get a room and share the bathroom and kitchen.')

I explained who I was and where I was calling from,

then described Vinny without saying why I was looking for him.

'Oh, yes. Jimmy has been with us for a while. He's very helpful – I don't know how we'd keep the place running without him. He's already fixed a hole in the roof and a bit of loose guttering and mended the gate where someone reversed into it. Worth his weight in gold.'

'Do you know where he is?'

'He's not here now, I'm afraid.'

'When was the last time you saw him, Father?'

'This morning.' He sounded puzzled. 'Is everything all right?'

'We just want to talk to him about the bar where he works.'

'Oh, I see. But it's closed at the moment.'

'Yes, I know,' I said patiently.

'I'll tell him you were looking for him.'

I got in quickly. 'There's no need. Really. It's not urgent and I was just really making sure we knew where to find him.'

'But if you leave me your name and number, I'm sure he'll get back to you.'

'I wouldn't put you to the trouble,' I said, which was a phrase my mother used when she absolutely didn't want to let someone do something. It was surprisingly effective and worked as well as ever on the priest.

Colin had been hanging over my shoulder and as soon as he got the nod he hurried off to let Godley know we had an address. The superintendent would send a team to arrest him, and in the meantime there was a force-wide alert to keep looking for him, just in case he'd heard of Shane's arrest, just in case he was running now for real. I leaned back in my borrowed chair, fuzzy with tiredness. Now that the chase was almost over I felt as if I'd slipped into neutral. I had nothing left to give. I picked up the phone and rang Rob, just to listen to his voicemail message, just to feel that he wasn't all that far away on the other side of the Atlantic. When the bleep came, I told him I was fine and work was exciting and I'd hardly been in the flat since he left so the danger had been minimal. I made myself sound cheerful and carefree and as if I wasn't missing him at all.

There was no chance he'd be taken in by it, but it made me feel better, and that was more or less the point.

Ninety minutes later I was still at the police station, still exhausted and very bored. From being at the centre of the investigation, the Shane Poole line of inquiry had turned into a bit of a sideshow. Godley had left, accompanied by Colin Vale. Harry Maitland and Una Burt were still asking Shane endless questions about his sister, Vinny and the murdered women. I was there to mind Derwent and make sure he behaved himself, on Godley's instructions. How I was supposed to do that, I didn't know. I'd noted the location of the nearest fire extinguisher and I was prepared to use it on him if need be.

The interview with Shane was staggering to a close. It was late and everyone in the room was exhausted, Maitland most of all. He obviously hated having to work with Una Burt, who kept cutting across him to ask random questions. Shane was having trouble working out what she wanted and how he should answer. I presumed that was her intention, but I couldn't be sure, and certainly Derwent was annoyed enough to heckle whenever she spoke.

The door to our room opened and a uniformed PC leaned in. 'Do either of you know where DC Kerrigan is?'

'That's me,' I said, leaping up.

'There's someone in reception for you.'

I barely let him finish; I was halfway down the hall already. To get out of the stuffy room had been my dearest wish. Literally anything would do if it gave me a reason to leave.

I went through the heavy door into reception wondering

who knew I was even there. One of my colleagues, prob-ably. I had an outside bet on Peake.

He was standing with his back to me, reading a road safety notice pinned to a board. He was enormous in his puffa jacket, and the baseball cap that was pulled down over his eyes made him anonymous. I tacked sideways as I approached, trying to work out how I knew him, and I was feet away when he turned. I stopped dead.

'I heard you were looking for me,' he said.

Derwent came out through the reinforced door at that moment, heading for the exit, still fighting his crutches every step of the way. He glanced at me, then beyond me, and his expression changed in a way that was almost comic, going from bored to incredulous as his eyes opened wide.

'I don't believe it.'

Vinny Naylor grinned. 'Hello, Josh. Long time no see.'

Chapter 33

Here's what should have happened next: I should have arrested, cautioned, searched and processed Vinny Naylor, then handed him over to the custody sergeant who should have tucked him up in a cell to await the arrival of a legal representative and some new interviewers since Maitland and Burt would be worn out. Godley should have returned to claim his scalp and do a quick press conference on the steps of the police station, while inside Vinny confessed to all four murders and anything else we could think to throw at him. And then we should all have patted ourselves on the back for a job well done.

What actually happened was that Derwent limped past me at incredible speed, grabbed Vinny by the arm and hissed, 'What do you think you're doing? Do you want to go to prison?'

'No, of course not,' Vinny snapped. 'But I don't want to leave Shane here answering questions that you really need to ask me.'

'Shane's all right.'

'No, he's not. He'll be getting himself in trouble if I know him. And he doesn't deserve to be.' Vinny was the same height as Derwent and the two of them were nose to nose.

'Come with me.' He let go of Vinny and limped back to the door that led to the police station itself. 'Kerrigan, you need to come too.'

I was standing flat-footed in the middle of the reception area, my mouth hanging open. With his bulky coat I couldn't tell if Vinny was carrying a weapon, and neither could Derwent. And Vinny Naylor was a killer, of that I was absolutely sure. I hung back until Vinny went through the door ahead of Derwent, then caught up with him.

'What are you doing? We've got to do this properly. Godley—'

'Will go fucking mental when he finds out. I know.'

'You don't have any credit to use any more. You're already on your way off the team if you don't start acting like a copper again, and I'm not having you take me with you.'

He rounded on me. 'Look, I need to talk to Vinny. I haven't spoken to him for a long time, but I think I can get him to trust me. You don't know what he's like. He's the definition of hard as nails and none of the interviewers we've got will be able to get him to confess to getting dressed this morning, let alone murder.'

'But you think he might talk to you for old times' sake.'

'It's worth a try.'

'No, it's not. He's killed four women. Four.'

'If he killed them, why is he here?'

'Because he's arrogant enough to think he can get away with it, maybe. Because he knows we're after him and he's trying to do this on his own terms.'

'When the others find out he's here, he'll be charged with murder and I won't get near him, do you understand? This is the only chance I'm going to get.'

'Sir—'

But he was gone, pulling the door to slam behind him, leaving me on the wrong side. I waited for the receptionist to unlock it, fuming. I didn't know what to do. Call Godley and tell him what Derwent was doing? Try to persuade Derwent to stop committing career suicide? Go and sit in the same room so I could at least go and get help when Vinny kicked off, as he probably would?

Derwent had been reckless before. He fancied himself as a bit of a maverick and bull-headed wasn't the word for him: he truly believed he knew the right thing to do at all times. He wasn't going to listen to me, or anyone else. And if Vinny had come to finish off the job Shane started, he was offering him a golden opportunity. Pushing through the door I ran down the corridor, almost colliding with a couple of PCs who pressed themselves against the walls to get out of my way.

Derwent had taken Vinny to the little meeting room where we had been waiting. I opened the door quietly, wary of what I might find. The television was still on, though muted, and Vinny was standing there, staring at it with his hands in his pockets and a frown on his face.

'Have you searched him?' I asked Derwent, who shook his head and moved towards him.

'Come on, Vinny. Coat off.'

He obliged without making a fuss, pulling off his cap too and submitting to Derwent's quick but thorough pat down.

'Nothing,' he said to me.

I wasn't actually all that reassured. It was all very well, Vinny not carrying a weapon, but he'd been an infantry soldier and was trained in unarmed combat. I watched his hands, wished Derwent would stay out of range, and took up a position by the door so I could make a quick escape.

'Right,' Derwent said. 'Sit down.'

Vinny sat. Without the coat and hat I could see him properly. He was rugged rather than handsome and heavy-jawed under stubble that was getting towards being a beard. His expression was open and honest and I thought of the four women who had died, and how they had trusted their killer, and I cautioned myself not to fall for it.

'Here's what we're going to do. We're going to talk, the three of us, and you're going to tell us what's been going on since you got yourself in trouble in Afghanistan.'

He nodded.

'As soon as someone realises you're here, you're going to be arrested. So let's make it quick.'

'All right,' Vinny said. 'I'll do what I'm told if it gets Shane off the hook. I've got nothing to fear anyway. I didn't do anything.'

'You and Shane are doing a fine job of looking guilty,' Derwent said. 'There's nothing much I can do to help. I won't be involved in the interviews – they'll keep us apart.' He glanced at the screen. 'I wasn't allowed to talk to Shane at all.'

'Probably just as well,' Vinny said. 'He's got a bit of a bee in his bonnet about you.'

'He broke into my flat and tried to kill me.'

'Yeah, I thought that was the sort of stupid thing he'd do. I tried to stop him.'

'Thanks. Next time, try harder.'

'Fuck you,' Vinny said pleasantly. 'You haven't changed at all, have you?'

'I'm just saying, you didn't do a very good job.' Derwent sat on the edge of a table, propping his injured leg on a chair. 'Right. No bullshit now. Why did you come here?'

'To see her.' He nodded at me. 'Because she rang the priest who runs the place where I live and he told me she'd been asking for me.'

Damn. And he'd had time to get rid of any evidence he liked since Shane went missing. I could see this one going west, and fast.

'What happened in Afghanistan? Why did you decide to play dead?'

Vinny grimaced. 'I fucked up. There was this man I'd got to know, a local, but he was all right. Same age as us but he had three daughters and four sons. The oldest girl was fifteen. The boys were all under ten. Nice family. No money, but no one has any money there. They had some goats, I think. And some land.'

'And the oldest girl was raped.'

'No.' Vinny sighed. 'It was the youngest girl. The eleven-year-old.'

'Shit.'

'She was just a little kid. The guy who did it was a twat – I'd come across him a few times on patrol and he was always trying to annoy us so we'd beat him up and he could claim compensation. He had pretty good English – I don't know how because the only thing he ever heard from us was "piss off". His family were having a boundary dispute with the girl's dad, and he boasted about raping the girl to teach him a lesson. He said he'd made her worthless and he'd do the same for the others. The local police didn't want to know – they had enough to do just trying to keep the place relatively civilised. It's a crazy country, mate, you can't imagine.'

'So you decided to intervene,' I said. I was watching Maitland and Burt who were still plugging away. It was getting late. They'd be finishing soon. All I needed was for them to find us talking to the chief suspect behind closed doors.

'I was only going to talk to him.' Vinny shook his head. 'I can't explain it. I went mental. He just didn't care. He was talking about how much he'd enjoyed it. He said she was *tight*.' His hands spasmed into fists and I could feel the heat of anger radiate off him.

'I heard you ripped him apart.' Derwent's voice was neutral. I actually didn't know if he approved or not.

'I lost it. I just wanted to make him suffer. And I wanted to stop him from ever doing anything like that again.' Vinny put a hand up to his forehead, a tremor visible in his fingers. 'I can't really believe I did that. I was covered in blood, and I was kicking him, and suddenly I heard what he was saying and I stopped.'

'What was he saying?'

'He wanted me to kill him. He was begging me.'

'But you didn't.'

'I carried him to our camp and found a medic. He was airlifted to Kabul. Got the best medical treatment the British Army can offer, not that it did him much good.'

'Why didn't you kill him?' Derwent asked.

'Couldn't. Not like that. It would have been murder, not a fair fight.'

Oh, very virtuous, I thought. 'Why weren't you arrested?'

'It got hushed up. My CO didn't want a trial in case it turned the locals against us. They wanted to handle it their way, anyway – they didn't care if we had a court martial or not. I had a price on my head. It was too dangerous for me to stay in Helmand.' Vinny looked up at Derwent. 'I wasn't scared, Josh. But if I'd been on patrol and we'd come under attack and someone else had got injured or killed, because of what I did, I'd have been responsible.'

'So you quit.'

'I quit.'

'Why didn't you tell anyone? Why did you play dead?'

Vinny shook his head and looked away. 'It was my folks. I didn't want them to know.'

'Why not?'

'Because I didn't want them to know I had fucked up. The only thing I've ever done right was the army. They were so proud of me. They thought I'd turned my life around, found my feet, all that. I couldn't tell them that I was back to nothing.' He pushed up his sleeve and showed off a tattoo across one massive forearm: *Death Before Dishonour.*

'But they must have mourned for you,' I said. 'How could you do that to them?'

'It's a big family. Eight of us, and most of the others are married. Loads of grandkids. They wouldn't miss me.'

'I don't think that's true,' Derwent said quietly. 'I remember your mum. She wouldn't forget about you.'

'Do you see your family?'

Derwent flinched. 'No. Not since.'

'So you know sometimes it's better to walk away.'

'I didn't get a choice.'

'I didn't think I had one either.'

I moved to interrupt the pity party. 'How did you convince them that you were dead?'

'I'd changed my next of kin to my girlfriend before I went back the last time. We split up while I was there but I got her to tell them she'd been notified that I was dead.'

'No body, though. No funeral.'

'The story was I'd been doing something covert and top secret when I died, so for reasons of national security they couldn't admit publicly that I was dead, or the circumstances.'

'And your parents believed it?' Derwent's eyebrows were up around his hairline.

'Yeah. Apparently. I think they liked the idea I was someone important, doing something brave and risky. And they were used to keeping their mouths shut about what I was doing in the army.'

'Why did you come back to London?'

'I didn't have any money. I didn't know what else to do.'

'Is that why you got in touch with Shane?'

'Yeah. We had an agreement, the two of us, that if either of us ever got in trouble, the other one would do whatever it took to help out. Shane was so glad I was alive, he was well on for giving me a job and a bit of extra cash here and there.'

'What was the plan?' I asked. 'You came back and Shane put the bar on the market. Where was he going to go?'

'Thailand. We were going to open a bar or a restaurant there. I got to know it pretty well when I was younger and Shane was up for a change. Or he said he was. But he's turned down a few offers for the business, so I don't know.'

'What do you think he's waiting for?' Derwent asked.

'For his dad to die.'

'Or because he's found out he likes killing?' The two of

them turned to look at me. 'What? He's still a suspect. And so are you, Vinny.'

'I haven't killed anyone.'

'You didn't get a taste for it when you were beating that boy up? Get a reminder of how good it feels to be in control? To make someone scared? To hear them beg you for mercy?'

'It made me sick,' Vinny said, emphasising every word.

'I've been looking into the Angela Poole murder. Someone I consider to be a reliable witness told me you disliked her.'

Derwent looked at me, obviously surprised. 'Don't be stupid.'

Vinny turned to Derwent. 'It's not a big deal, Josh. I just thought she was a bit of a pain.'

'Angela?' Derwent was baffled. 'Why?'

Vinny glanced at me, then back at Derwent. 'If you must know, she was always trying to get me to kiss her. She was a massive flirt. Pinched my arse when you weren't looking. Rubbed up against me when she got the chance.'

'Bollocks. Why didn't you tell me?'

'You'd have gone tonto.'

'That's like lying to me.' Derwent was outraged. 'How could you keep that to yourself?'

Shamefaced, Vinny said, 'I thought you'd blame me.'

'Did you touch her? Did you kiss her?' Derwent demanded.

'No! Not at all.'

'You fucking *liar*.' The last word cracked through the room.

'It's the truth. Nothing ever happened – ever – but she was a prick tease.'

Forgetting his leg, Derwent jumped to his feet and suffered the indignity of pitching forward, almost falling, and having to be supported by the man he was intending to punch. I bit my lip to stop myself from laughing and looked away, towards the screen, just in time to see the solicitor shuffling her pages together. Maitland was yawning, one hand covering his mouth. Burt was talking.

'Looks as if they're winding up.' I snapped my fingers. 'Hey. Break it up. We don't have long.'

Derwent shook his head, bewildered. 'I can't even think what to ask him.'

'Well, I can. You didn't have an alibi for Angela's murder. Why not? Where were you?'

'Wandering round.' Vinny saw the expression on my face. 'It's the truth. I had a row with my girlfriend. I went and found Shane but he was with some guys who were really into pot and I wasn't in the mood. And Josh was with Angela. So I walked.'

'Did you see anyone or anything strange?'

'Nope.'

'Were you anywhere near Angela's house?'

'I went past late that night to see if you'd brought her home, but the light was off in her room so I thought you were still together.'

'She died around midnight.'

'I know. It was later than that. Half twelve or something. I didn't see her. I didn't see anyone.' He started to laugh. 'Oh, except that weird little fat kid from next door. He was looking out the window in the front room.'

'Why are you laughing?' Derwent asked.

'Because of you. You'd have loved it. He was wearing pyjama bottoms and a T-shirt with HOW SOON IS NOW on it, and you know you used to take the piss out of him for listening to the Smiths all the time. I was pissing myself laughing when I saw him. I couldn't wait to tell you about it the next day but I never got the chance.'

'How did he look?' I asked.

'Fat Stu? Fat.' Vinny started to laugh again. 'Stupid. He was just staring at me, like he always did. That was his life. Looking out of windows, watching people.'

'In his statement, he said he saw someone in clothes similar to the ones DI Derwent was wearing that night. Could it have been you?'

'I suppose.'

'He said he saw them leaving the garden. Did you go through the gate?'

'No. Just glanced up at the window.' Vinny's smile faded. 'I didn't even think she might be there.'

'And you didn't see anyone else running away.'

'No.'

I remembered what Derwent had said about the bruising on Angela's neck, and how the killer had had big hands. Vinny's were like shovels.

'Angela flirted with you, trying to provoke you. It worked on him,' I said, pointing at Derwent. 'Don't tell me you didn't find it a turn-on. You were a teenager. It doesn't take much, I seem to recall.'

Vinny looked uncomfortable. 'She was off-limits. And I didn't like her.'

'You don't have to like someone to want to have sex with them. Especially if you want to rape them.'

'I didn't want to rape her.'

'Did you see her that night? Follow her? Did you want to teach her a lesson?'

'No.' Vinny looked at Derwent. 'Really, no.'

'I don't believe you,' I said. 'And I don't believe that you're innocent. You killed Kirsty, and Maxine, and Anna, and Deena.'

'No.'

'You strangled them, just as you strangled Angela.'

'No.'

'You ran away afterwards. You left everything behind, and everyone.'

'We were all affected by it. It wasn't easy.' Vinny looked at Derwent. 'Tell her, Josh.'

'No, you tell us why you didn't mention being on

Angela's road that night when Orpen interviewed you. It's not in the file,' Derwent said.

'I don't know. It was better to lie. He was terrifying. If he'd put me in the right place around the time she died, I'd have been in the dock before I had time to say, "Please, sir, I didn't do anything wrong." He was desperate for someone to prosecute and I wasn't going to offer myself up on a plate.'

'The interview's over,' I observed. They were standing up and Shane was preparing to go back to his cell.

'*Fuck.*' Derwent pointed at Vinny. 'Don't think you're off the hook. I might not get to interview you but I'm going to be watching, and I'll know when you're lying.'

'I'm not lying about anything.' He smiled blandly and I felt a wave of anger. I knew they weren't going to get anywhere with interviewing him, and I knew he'd probably made sure there was no evidence to find at his address. But I was going to prove he was a killer, somehow.

'They'll have to let Shane go once they've got me in custody. Won't they?'

'They don't have to do anything. Is that why you're here? To save Shane?' Derwent asked.

'He's always looked after me,' Vinny said simply. 'This is the least I can do.'

'How moving,' I said, and the door behind me opened. Una Burt strode in and stopped.

'What's going on? Is that—'

'Vincent Naylor.' He stood up and held out his hand. 'Pleased to meet you.'

She didn't answer him, turning instead to Derwent and hissing, 'What have you done now?'

'Nothing at all. He's all yours.' Derwent swung towards the door at speed, so Burt had to jump back to get out of his way. I fell in behind him, leaving Vinny without a backwards glance. Maitland was just outside the door.

'You're going to need some cuffs.'

He looked surprised. 'What? Why?'

I didn't answer, hurrying to catch up with Derwent. He headed out of the main doors, his jaw set, and I knew better than to try to slow him down. We were halfway down the street before he stopped.

'What do you think?'

'Of him?' I shook my head. 'Guilty as sin.'

'Then why would he hand himself in?'

'He's playing games. I don't know why, and I don't know what the rules are, but there's definitely something he's hoping to achieve. He wants to rescue Shane, doesn't he?'

'So he said.' Derwent rubbed a hand over his face. 'Shit. And you really think he's our killer?'

'I have no reason to think anything else.'

'Do you think he killed Angela?'

'Very likely.'

Derwent winced, as if the very idea hurt. 'So how are we going to prove it?'

'I'm going to go back and talk to the witness.'

'Fat Stu?'

'One and the same. He was so sure it was you he saw. What if it was Vinny? You were very alike. You still are.'

'I'm better-looking,' Derwent said automatically. 'I'll come with you to speak to Stu.'

'Absolutely not.'

'I'd like to see him again.'

I shook my head. 'He'll never talk if you're there. Besides, it's too late to go and see him tonight.'

'Come on, Kerrigan. We work well together. We're a team. Let me come with you.'

'Give it a rest. I've got in enough trouble, thanks, because you want to be involved in my interviews.'

'You're not going to get anywhere without me. You need me.'

'I really don't,' I said, and started to walk away. Derwent hobbled after me.

'Kerrigan, wait.'

I picked up speed instead, leaving him behind.

'This isn't fair,' he yelled after me. 'Taking advantage of my disability. I'm not going to forget this.'

I didn't stop. I did slow down, though, but just so I could walk backwards for a couple of paces. I wanted to enjoy the look on his face as I waved goodbye.

FRIDAY

Chapter 34

The following morning I headed off to see Stuart Sinclair. I had gone back to the office to check my desk the night before and got waylaid by a request from the officer investigating my bunch of flowers, asking for a full statement about previous incidences of harassment. When it came to Chris Swain I could have written a book about all that he'd done and threatened to do to me, and the harm he'd promised to those I loved, but I just gave her the edited highlights. Kev Cox had agreed to take charge of the evidence I'd collected. I met him at the flat so he could pick it up. He was, as ever, unfailingly cheerful, even when handed a bag full of suppurating meat. It would have been a low priority for the forensics lab but he promised me he'd get it looked at sooner rather than later.

'I can't go home until I know if it's Swain,' I'd said to Kev, then wondered why I was in such a hurry to get back to the flat. It was cold, lonely and smelled a lot like work now that I'd had my very own bit of decomposing flesh in my home.

I had decided against going back to Derwent's flat to collect the stuff I'd left there; I'd had more than enough of him for one day. I packed a new bag and took a train out to Guildford, where Liv and Joanne were waiting to look after me and no one talked about work. Joanne found some arnica for my bruised neck, which made Liv snort, especially since she'd already slipped me some codeine. They were easy company. I laughed a lot. While the two of them were in the kitchen, squabbling over the recipe for the pasta sauce Joanne was making, I let myself think about Vinny Naylor, wondering if he was still being interviewed or if they would have stopped for the night.

'Whatever you're thinking about, stop.' Liv dropped down on the sofa beside me. 'You look grim.'

'That's just my face.'

'I think not.' She took my wine glass off the coffee table and handed it to me. 'Have a drink and forget about it, whatever it was.'

I clinked glasses with her and sipped the heavyweight Shiraz Joanne had opened, and I almost succeeded in forgetting, as instructed. Almost. At least, once the wine kicked in, I didn't care so much any more.

So it was the next day, in the company of a vile hangover that I retraced my journey to West Norwood and found Stuart Sinclair's house. I rang the doorbell and listened, resigned, to the ear-splitting screech from inside that told me Oliver was up and about, and in fine voice.

It wasn't Stuart who opened the door but his wife. She frowned at me, not quite recognising me, and she looked different too – jeans and a sweatshirt rather than the formal suit she'd worn the last time I'd seen her. Oliver was perched on her hip, wiping his nose on her shoulder. Her day for childcare, I thought, and smiled.

'Sorry to bother you. I came to talk to Stuart a couple of days ago. I don't know if you remember . . .'

As she placed me, it was as if a steel shutter had slid down behind her eyes. The smile disappeared and she started to close the door. 'Not interested, thank you. I said so at the time.'

'Wait.' I held up my ID. 'I'm a police officer.'

She stopped, looking from my warrant card to me. 'Seriously?'

'Detective Constable Maeve Kerrigan. I'm investigating a series of murders and I wanted to talk to Mr Sinclair again. Is he in?'

'*Stuart*?'

'I just need some information from him,' I said quickly. 'I'm not here to arrest him or anything like that. Do you know where he is?'

Her expression was blank. 'No idea. At his flat, probably.'

'His . . .'

'His flat,' she repeated. 'Where he lives.' *You moron*, I heard in her tone.

I was too confused to be suspicious. 'This is going to sound like a really stupid question, but doesn't Stuart live here?'

'Here? No. What gave you that idea?'

Well, actually, he *did*. Or I thought he had. Maybe I'd got it wrong. Maybe they were separated. 'Do you mind me asking what your relationship is with Mr Sinclair?'

'He's a friend.' She blushed. 'A friend of a friend, really.'

'He's not your husband. Or your ex. He's not Oliver's dad.'

'*No*. God, you don't have a clue, do you?'

'I must have misunderstood.' *I must have been meant to misunderstand*. In my mind, the pieces of the puzzle started to rearrange themselves to form a new picture, and I wondered how I could possibly have missed the way he had held the boy who was supposed to be his son. I wondered how I could possibly have thought he cared for him at all. And I wondered why anyone would lie to that extent, unless they had something to hide.

'Do you know him well?'

'Fairly. I don't know. Quite well. He's a friend.' She hefted Oliver, who had started to slip. 'Look, what's this about?'

'If you don't mind, I think it might be better if I came in so we can have a proper talk.'

'I don't really have time. I'm going out in five minutes.'

'Not unless it's urgent.' I put my foot across the threshold to stop her from closing the door. 'I'm sorry, but this is important.'

She had gone pale. 'Is he in trouble? Has he *done* something?'

'I'd just like to ask you a few questions about him.'

'I left him with my baby. Are you saying he's *dangerous*? Could he have *harmed* him?' Her voice was rising as she spoke, raw-edged with hysteria.

'I really doubt it,' I said. I stepped inside the door and closed it. 'Please, try to calm down.' Good advice for me too. My heart was thumping.

She was holding Oliver so tightly her fingernails were digging into him and he started to sob. 'It's all right, shh baby, shh baby,' she crooned, rocking him from side to side, but her eyes were wide and dark with terror.

'There's no suggestion he's ever harmed a child in any way. Please, don't worry.'

She closed her eyes tightly, trying to calm herself. 'Okay. Okay, I want to hear what you have to say. Of course I don't have to go out. Let me just send my friend a message.'

'Not Stuart,' I said sharply.

'No.'

'Don't mention it's about him. Make some other excuse.'

She nodded, still struggling for composure. Oliver wriggled and shouted, trying to break free.

I went into the kitchen and started to make mugs of tea. She sat down at the table and wrote a quick text, staring at me once she'd finished. Oliver wriggled off her knee and pounced on a toy snake that was on the floor.

'I don't know your name, I'm afraid.' *Not Mrs Sinclair, anyway.*

'Jenny Coppard.'

'Jenny, how long have you known Stuart?'

'Um.' She pulled her jumper down over her hands, thinking. 'A few months. Maybe six months.'

'How did you get to know him?'

'Through a friend. She got talking to him one day in a café and they had a lot in common. Too much, she said, because she really fancied him but she's married. She introduced us. I think she thought we might get together.' Jenny rolled her eyes. 'I get a lot of that.'

'Are you a single mum?'

'Yeah. By choice. I split up with my husband just before Oliver was born.'

'That's tough.'

'He was cheating on me. It's tougher to be lied to all the time and taken for granted. What's Stuart done?'

'Maybe nothing.' I poured boiling water over the tea bags and went looking for milk. 'But he definitely gave me the impression he lived here and Oliver was his child. He called you his wife.'

'I don't believe it.' She was red now, blushing. Flattered, in spite of her worries.

'Do you know where he lives? The address, I mean?'

She nodded, grabbed a flier for a pizza delivery place that was on the table and scrawled the address on it from memory. 'Larchfield Mews. It's about five minutes' walk from here. I don't know the postcode.'

'Don't worry.' I took it from her and put it away carefully, as if it was the Holy Grail and not junk mail. 'So you're just friends.'

'Yes.' The blush was back.

'Has he ever said anything to you that made you think he was romantically interested in you?'

'All the time. But he's like that. Flirty.'

'Has it ever gone beyond flirting?'

'He kissed me a week ago. We were playing around – I was trying to eat an ice cream and he said he wanted a bit and I wouldn't let him have any and – well, he kissed me.

And then he apologised. And I said it was all right, and he said that was good because he wasn't really sorry. You know.'

I did know. It was the sort of thing that a lonely woman with a small, demanding child would find charming. 'But nothing else happened.'

'No. I mean, there hasn't been an opportunity. And I didn't know if I should make the next move.' She shrugged.

'When you left Oliver with him, was that Stuart's idea?'

'Yes. Well, I had a job interview. That wasn't anything to do with him. But my mum couldn't look after Oliver because she had a hospital appointment, and there isn't really anyone else.'

'So that was the first time.'

'The only time.' She was back to looking anguished. 'I put him down for a nap and then I went out. I left him.'

'Jenny, I was here for most of the time he was alone with Oliver. Oliver was in bed when I arrived and he got up just before you came back. There's nothing to worry about.'

She put a hand to her head. 'Oh, thank God.'

I wasn't going to tell her what I suspected. If he really was the Gentleman Killer, she'd find out soon enough. 'What else can you tell me about him? Has he been living in West Norwood for long?'

'No. He came back from Japan about a year ago. He was an English teacher there for a long time but he got tired of it. It was somewhere rural and he said the fun of it wore off after the first five years but he stayed because he couldn't think of anything else to do. I think he was there for seven years in all.'

'What does he do now?'

'He teaches English as a foreign language in a college in Croydon.'

And he had the income from renting out the family home, I happened to know. He'd be doing all right for money.

'Does he live alone?'

'Yes.'

'And he doesn't have a girlfriend.'

'No. Not as far as I know,' she added, sounding disillusioned. She didn't have much luck with finding trustworthy men, all things considered.

I pressed her for any more information that she could give me, but there was nothing else useful. As we sipped tea and Oliver played, Jenny unwound enough to give me a fairly good idea of how hard she had fallen for Stuart, and how good he was at making himself indispensable. He'd never been violent to anyone as far as she knew. The idea shocked her. He'd helped people who needed it, buying groceries for frail neighbours, mowing Jenny's lawn when it was overgrown. He was an all-round good guy, or pretended to be one. The more we talked, the more she forgot why I was there, and the more she spoke warmly of him. He was funny, and charming, and good at DIY.

'The perfect man,' she said wistfully. 'I thought, anyway.'

'He's clearly very good at getting people to trust him.' People, or maybe women. He presented himself as someone you could trust. Someone to like. Someone to let in when he knocked on your door.

I had liked him, I remembered, and felt slightly sick.

When I'd finished my tea and when Jenny was starting to repeat the same stories about Stuart I thanked her for her time and help, asked her not to mention that I'd been around, and left. I took a stroll down to Larchfield Mews, a charmless apartment building behind a small parade of shops, not far from the A road that cut through the area. You probably couldn't see it from his flat, but you could definitely hear it. His flat was on the top floor, on the left, and I glanced up at the windows casually. No sign of life. The building had a small car park underneath it. A gate prevented me from getting into the premises to have a closer look, but I was sure one of the cars would belong to Stuart, and I was equally sure it would be worth a once-over.

But I had no idea how I was going to persuade anyone to believe me. *I* was convinced that Stuart Sinclair was the Gentleman Killer, but that was based on the most tenuous of details. He had lied to me about where he lived and pretended to be a married father of one when he was nothing of the sort. That was strange, but not evidence of a murderous mind. He looked pleasant; he sounded plausible. His connection with Angela Poole was obvious, but his movements on the night of her death were a mystery. All I knew was that he had lied to me about what he'd seen and heard, and even then I wasn't sure if it was a lie or a genuine mistake. He couldn't have seen Derwent but he might have seen Vinny. By all accounts he had been a strange, withdrawn, unattractive teenager who'd become a handsome and outgoing adult. Nothing about that was screaming 'killer' and yet everything was. And I knew that everyone thought Vinny was a cold-blooded killer – I had thought that myself – and Shane's behaviour was outwardly a lot more suspicious than Stuart's, but I still knew. I *knew*.

And I'd prove it if it killed me, I thought, not having the least idea that it might actually do just that.

Chapter 35

Back in the office, I got on the phone to the Japanese embassy and pestered them until they put me through to someone who could look up Stuart Sinclair's visa applications. The records showed he had settled in a place called Takayama in Gifu Prefecture and had a steady job teaching in a local high school. Based on what Jenny had said about when he returned to the UK, it looked as if he had left in the middle of the school year, a long time before his visa was due to expire. It was getting on for midday in London and Japan was nine hours ahead, so I didn't even bother trying to get in touch with the school. I put in a request for a Japanese-speaking translator and spent some time hunting around on the Internet for background information on Takayama and, more importantly, the telephone number for the local police. There was a chance that they would speak English, but since my Japanese was non-existent and this was important, I wanted to understand everything they said. I didn't know how long it would take – hours, probably – but I told myself to be patient and it sort of worked.

He had found a beautiful spot, a tourist destination in the mountains with old buildings and pretty countryside nearby. It was snowy in winter and hot in summer and it looked like a picture-perfect place to live. I couldn't imagine spending seven years there, but I was a city girl and I'd never done a lot of travelling. Freezing summer holidays in Donegal were no preparation for the exotic, even if they did make you hardy as a mountain sheep.

Maitland stopped on his way past. 'Booking a trip?'

'Following something up,' I said. 'Any luck with Vinny?'

'Nope.'

'Shane?'

'Nope.'

'Have either of them been charged yet?'

'Nope.'

'Keep me informed, won't you?'

'Yep,' he said, grinning, then relented. 'They've moved them to Charing Cross nick so they're not such a long way off. Godley's determined to persuade one or other of them to talk. He thinks one did it and the other knows about it, so it's just a matter of waiting until the innocent one cracks. And they haven't reached the custody time limit on either of them yet, luckily enough.'

'What do you think?'

'I don't know. I'd have thought we'd have got somewhere by now. And we've still got nothing on the forensics, from either of them.' He shrugged. 'We're a long way from taking anything to the CPS, put it that way.'

I was encouraged by the news that they were failing to make a case. It meant that Godley might be more receptive to a new suspect. Especially if I could find some reason to get a search warrant for Stuart's flat. In the past, I would have assumed I'd get a fair hearing from Godley and Burt, but I knew they would be a hard pair to convince now. I'd blown through a lot of credit in the past week – probably more than I had to spare.

I had been waiting for about two hours and was making my seventh or eighth cup of tea when Ben Dornton put his head into the kitchen. 'There's a nice Japanese lady asking for you.'

'Brilliant. At last.'

'You get all the interesting cases,' he said wistfully. 'I'm going to interview a guy who stabbed someone for his drugs out the back of Euston. He'll probably plead guilty in the end. That's my career.'

I tilted my head back to show him the aurora borealis of bruising around my neck. 'Interesting is overrated.'

'I wouldn't mind some of that. I could be the hero for a change.'

'Trying to impress someone?' I asked slyly, and laughed as he actually blushed. He was utterly smitten with the lovely Christine and I wished him the best of luck.

When I got back to my desk, the translator was standing near it and I could see immediately why Dornton had described her as a lady. She was in her mid-forties and impeccably dressed in a cashmere twinset, tweed skirt and pearls. More English than the Queen, I thought, and introduced myself.

'I am Akiko Larkin. How can I help?' Her voice was soft, her English practically unaccented. I dragged a chair over so she could sit beside me.

'I want to call a police station in Japan to find out about a suspect.' I filled her in as quickly as I could and she listened, taking in everything I said, making an occasional note.

'It might take a little while to speak to the right person. There will be someone there at this time, but maybe not the person we need.'

'Worth a try,' I said firmly, and handed her the phone. I was relying on her to do my job for me and I hoped she was as efficient as she seemed to be.

It took two or three phone calls to track down the right bit of the prefectural police for Takayama, and then a half-hour wait for the relevant inspector, Nakamura Shoichi, to phone us back once Akiko had explained why we were calling.

'Nakamura is his surname,' Akiko explained, having established that I knew more or less nothing about Japan and Japanese customs. 'In Japanese the surname comes first.'

'So you should be Larkin Akiko?'

She laughed politely. 'Before I was married I was Sakamoto Akiko. But I have been married to an Englishman for more than twenty years and I am used to being Mrs Larkin.'

The phone rang and I answered it, passing it to Akiko when the person on the other end tried to talk to me in Japanese. She spoke rapidly and softly into the phone, as I tried to pick out any phrases I recognised. Stuart's name sounded very odd rendered in its Japanese pronunciation. Aside from '*hai*' and '*arigatou*', I didn't manage to understand much, but Akiko made copious notes. She ended on a flurry of thanks, hung up before I could stop her and turned to me.

'I can call him back if you have any more questions, but I thought you would want to hear what he had to say.'

'Go on.' I hated getting everything second-hand, but there was nothing else I could do.

'Inspector Nakamura knew who I meant immediately. Your suspect was a resident in Takayama for a long time and the local community knew him quite well. He had a Japanese girlfriend who lived with him. He was very settled there and happy, but then a tourist was murdered and he came under suspicion.'

'For what reason?'

'He had met her a couple of days before she died and made friends with her. His girlfriend had just left him and the victim's friends thought they had started a sexual relationship.'

'How did she die?'

'She was strangled,' Akiko said calmly.

'But they didn't arrest him.'

'There was no other evidence against him and he left before they could find anything.'

'Left as in left the country?'

'Yes. He abandoned his car and many belongings. The inspector was quite concerned that he was guilty but he wasn't able to pursue it because there was no evidence beyond his suspicion. Mr Sinclair called Inspector Nakamura from London and said that he was depressed because of his relationship breaking up and he wouldn't return to Japan. He said he left in a hurry because he was suicidal, and he made arrangements to have everything sold or given to charity.'

'Did the inspector tell you anything else?'

'He suggested that you speak to Mr Sinclair's girlfriend. Her name is Takahashi Yumi. She was reluctant to speak to Inspector Nakamura but now some time has passed she might have changed her mind.'

Another phone call to Japan. Super. 'Did he give you any way of contacting her?'

'He had anticipated we might want to speak to her and contacted her family before he phoned us. I have her name and address, and her telephone number. She lives in Bayswater.'

'In London?'

'She's a student at St Martins College.' Akiko put her notebook in her bag. 'She will speak English. You don't need me.'

I stopped thinking about the wonderful, glorious news that the girlfriend was in London, which was practically the first bit of luck I'd had so far. 'I might need you to translate something. I might need you to call someone else in Japan.'

She nodded, not smiling but obviously pleased. I rang the number she gave me and managed to get through to Yumi straight away.

'It's regarding Stuart Sinclair.'

There was a gasp at the other end of the line, and then she spoke again, very quietly. 'Is he in trouble?'

'I need to ask you some background information about him, but it's very important that you keep this confidential.'

She considered that in silence and I asked another, very important question.

'Are you in touch with him at the moment?'

'No. I never want to see Stuart again!' I thought she was going to hang up but after a second she sighed. 'When do you want to meet?'

'Now, if possible.' I gave her the address of the office and she promised to come straight away, even though she had a lecture. I hung up and Akiko picked up her bag.

'You have spoken with her. You know she speaks English well enough.'

'Please, stay.' Something made me feel she might be useful, still. 'Just until after the interview.'

'All right.'

'She does speak English well, but not as well as you do.' It was true. Yumi's speech was halting and she hesitated before each new clause, groping for bits of vocabulary. She seemed to understand everything I said but I couldn't be sure. 'Your English is amazing.'

'I've had a lot of time to practise.'

'Have you lived here long?'

'Twenty-four years.'

It was pleasant to have a conversation that wasn't going to end up with someone being arrested; it didn't happen often enough in my life. While we waited for the girl I found out how Akiko had met Mr Larkin (Paris, 1988, studying at the Sorbonne) and whether she missed Japan (yes, but her life was here with her children) and whether she liked her job (some days yes, some days no). I hoped she didn't mind the questions. I couldn't help myself. Curiosity was more than a habit now and I could no longer switch it off than I could stop blinking.

To prepare for the interview with Takahashi Yumi, I told Akiko what we needed: evidence that the man who had been her boyfriend would make a good suspect in the Gentleman Killer case. 'Did the inspector give you the name of the girl who was killed in Japan?'

'Grace Brumberger. She was American.'

'We'll need him to send us the file on the investigation.'

Akiko called him back while I did an Internet search on Grace Brumberger and turned up a treasure trove of information – her Facebook page, updated since she died with messages from grieving friends and acquaintances, a memorial page, a Grace Brumberger scholarship her parents were offering at the school she had attended, and most useful of all, a sixteen-page article from her local newspaper investigating what had happened to her in Japan. She was from Connecticut. She had been a cheerleader. Her parents were well off and she was an only child. She was bright, and diligent, and a good friend to those in need.

And she looked more or less exactly like Angela Poole.

I felt like bouncing up and down in my chair, but the presence of Akiko inhibited me. And anyway, the fact was that I was no closer to proving anything. Stuart had walked away from the investigation into Grace's death – he wasn't even alluded to in the article I'd read, which mainly focused on Grace's high hopes for her trip, the way the Brumbergers had found out the news and their journey from grief to acceptance.

But now I was absolutely sure I was right.

Akiko hung up the phone and immediately it rang again: reception, downstairs, to tell me that there was a Miss Tacky-something waiting to see me. I gathered up Akiko and my notebook and went to find her.

Takahashi Yumi conformed to the absolute template of a St Martins College fashion student, in that she was so deter-mined *not* to conform. She was wearing lace-up red shoes with exaggerated, curved heels and a platform sole: they looked like an illustration from a fairy tale. Her tights were black but they had been embroidered with white thistles and ivy that snaked up from her anklebone to her thigh. She wore tiny black leather shorts and a big white fluffy jumper that was unravelling at the neck and cuffs. No coat, on a day when the temperature wasn't likely to rise above seven degrees, but she did have an umbrella with a duck's head handle. Small and slender, she wasn't quite pretty but she had dramatic eye make-up and had painted her mouth to match her shoes, creating a 1920s-style Cupid's bow. I stared at her for a good couple of seconds, taking it all in, before I remembered what I was supposed to be doing.

'Thank you for coming.'

She nodded. 'How can I help you?'

Time to be direct. 'I think Stuart might have harmed some women, but I can't prove it yet. I need to know if he ever did anything that made you uneasy, or if he hurt you, or if he acted in any way that made you suspicious of him.'

Three or four rapid blinks. Her false eyelashes had tiny hearts glued to the ends, I noticed. I couldn't begin to imagine how long it took her to get dressed in the morning.

'There were some things . . .' She trailed off.

'Can we start at the beginning? How did you meet him?'

'He was my teacher in school.'

'*Really*?'

'Yes, but we did not have a relationship then. We were friends.'

'I see.'

'I taught him Japanese and he helped me learn English. I wanted to come to London to study but I was very bad student.'

'So you helped each other.'

'For a year. And then I finished school and we became more than friends.'

'You moved in with him.'

She nodded, biting her lip gently. 'My parents were sad. I was in love with him.'

'How long did you live together?'

'Two years, almost. I would not go abroad to study or leave Takayama. I wanted to be with him. I stopped doing everything that made me happy. No fashion, no dressing up. No Internet. No friends. He was everything.' Her voice broke and she twisted her hands together, striving to keep the tears back.

'Was he controlling?'

She looked blank. Akiko leaned forward and offered a phrase in Japanese that made her nod. 'Yes.'

'He made you follow his rules.'

'And would not let me speak with my parents.'

'Was he nice to you?'

'Yes.' She looked away. 'No.'

'Was he violent?'

Two tears slid down Yumi's cheeks. 'Yes. No.'

'What do you mean?'

'He was but it was what I liked. I thought I liked it. I didn't know any different.'

Again, Akiko leaned in and said something softly, and Yumi replied to her, the words rapid. When the two of them were in full flow the sound of their voices reminded me of running water or gloved hands clapping. There was no harshness to it at all, no edge despite the subject matter.

Akiko turned to me. 'There was an element of sado-masochism in their relationship. She says that Stuart was unable to have sexual relations with her properly and only became aroused if he was choking her. He liked her to play dead and then he would masturbate on her.' There was something very odd about hearing those words come out of Akiko's mouth but she wasn't embarrassed. She went on: 'She says she had come to enjoy it and look forward to surrendering to him, but then on one occasion he choked her until she passed out. When she came round, he was elated, not sorry. She was terrified that the next time he would kill her. She refused to do it any more.'

'What was his reaction?'

'He started to go to the nearest city and visit prostitutes. He refused to speak to her. She apologised and told him she would do whatever he wanted.'

'And?'

Akiko turned to Yumi, who faltered through a few sentences before dissolving into tears.

'He choked her again and again she fell unconscious, but when she came round her eyes were bruised and swollen. She couldn't see anything for two days. The doctors were concerned that she could lose her sight but she recovered. After that, she knew he was too dangerous to stay with, and she left him.'

Yumi was crying properly now, a handkerchief pressed to her face. She peeled her eyelashes off and laid them on her knee, where they lay like two dead centipedes. 'I did not know anything else. I thought he did those things because he loved me. And I loved him.'

'Are you scared of him?'

She nodded. 'But he hasn't tried to contact me. Not since last October.'

Around the time Grace Brumberger died. I thought of Stuart killing her and realising he could make his fantasies a reality. It made me feel sick, but it also made sense.

'Are you willing to make a statement about Stuart?'

She looked horrified. 'I don't want to tell everyone what he did.'

'You don't have to be embarrassed,' I said gently. 'He was the one who decided to behave that way.'

Yumi muttered something and shook her head.

'May I?' Akiko murmured to me.

'Please.'

I couldn't guess what the older woman was saying to Yumi, but as she spoke the tears welled up in the fashion student's eyes again. Akiko kept talking, persuading, cajoling, and at last Yumi nodded.

'She'll give you a statement. I will help her,' Akiko said.

Yumi stood up, wobbly as a newborn fawn. 'I must go to the bathroom, I think.'

I showed her where to go. Once the door was closed behind her, I turned to Akiko.

'What did you say to her?'

'I told her I have a daughter. I told her my daughter is twenty, and very beautiful. I told her I worry about her. I told her the girls Stuart Sinclair killed had parents who loved them very much.' Akiko smiled, but her eyes were sad. 'I told her she was lucky.'

Chapter 36

I was pretty good at being a copper, which was lucky because I could never have been a burglar. The flat was empty, and I knew it was empty, but my heart rate was towards the upper limit of survivable. Perspiration was making my gloves slip a little on my hands. I pulled them further up my wrists and blew hair out of my face.

'Good to go?'

'Yeah.' Maitland stood behind me, in a heavy overcoat, with a police radio in one hand and a camera in the other. He looked as tense as if he was going on a picnic, and he grinned at me. 'Don't worry. We'll get plenty of warning if he shows up.'

'Are you sure that works in here?' Reception could be patchy. I really didn't want any surprises because the radio was only getting static.

'I've checked.' He folded his arms in front of him and looked at me expectantly. 'But the longer you take, the riskier it gets.'

'Okay, okay. Don't hurry me.'

We were standing by the front door in the narrow hallway that ran down the middle of Stuart Sinclair's flat. It was dark but smelled chemically clean. On my right was a bedroom, with a small bathroom beyond it. On my left, there was a living room and an equally small kitchen.

'At least you don't have many rooms to search.'

'That can be harder.' I could see telltale signs that he was both neat and a pack rat: an overfull bookcase stood at the end of the hall, with boxes stacked on top of it and piles of magazines underneath, all squared off and organised. Chaos would have been easier to rummage through. 'If everything is jammed in together, I'll have to take it all out to see if there's anything useful.'

'Go on, Chuckles. What are you waiting for?'

The truth was, I didn't know. I was waiting for the blinding flash of inspiration that would show me where Sinclair had stashed everything that related to his little hobby. I was also on edge in case he was expecting a visit from the police and had booby-trapped the place accordingly. Under the terms of our search warrant we could go through the place without getting his permission to be there. I had a feeling he wouldn't grant it, if he was offered the option. I didn't want to tip him off that we'd been there if we didn't find anything – we'd need to set up surveillance on him and try to catch him doing something incriminating, which would only work if he was confident our attention was elsewhere. So I was keeping my eyes peeled for stray hairs, black threads or artlessly arranged piles of paper that would give the game away. It was a lot easier to set a trap than to avoid springing it. That was why I'd been sent in on my own, with Maitland for muscle, just in case. The fewer people there were in Stuart Sinclair's flat, the less chance there was we'd leave a trace.

'Where are you going to start?'

'Bedroom.'

'Not the living room?'

'It doesn't look as if he has many visitors, but if he did, that's where they would go. I'm betting anything dodgy is in here.'

'On you go.'

I pushed open the bedroom door slowly and slipped inside, straining to see in the dim light. He had dark blue curtains that were still drawn even though it was daylight. I made sure there wasn't a gap in the middle, then took out my torch and started looking.

The bed was made, the duvet smooth. His shoes were lined up underneath it: many pairs of trainers, two pairs of smart shoes, one pair of desert boots. I checked the soles, quickly, and shook every shoe to check there was nothing inside it. The floor was carpeted and looked clean. I recalled that the killer had been scrupulous about leaving the crime scenes neat and tidy. It really would have been a lot more helpful if he'd been a slob.

I nudged the wardrobe doors open and bit back a gasp.

'You okay?' Maitland suddenly loomed in the doorway.

'Got a shock.' I swung the doors back so he could see the full-length mirror on one side and the full-length poster Stuart Sinclair had stuck on the other.

'Is that him?'

'It certainly is.' In the picture he was wearing a small pair of shorts and had a deep tan. His muscles were sharply defined, gleaming with oil, and he was posing with his hands on his waist in the best bodybuilder style, biceps bulging. 'Mr Fitness. I think this is his motivational material.'

'Twat,' Maitland said, and snapped a couple of pictures before he retreated. We needed to record anything remotely suspicious where we found it because Sinclair could remove it before we got a chance to come back.

I carried on searching, finding three smart suits with ties and shirts among the more casual clothes. To myself, I murmured, 'What do you need suits for? You're a teacher. Go to a lot of funerals?'

Nothing in the bottom of the wardrobe. Nothing on top. The bedside tables were empty. The chest of drawers contained neat piles of folded clothes. The drawers didn't pull out all the way but I checked the undersides anyway, lying on the floor, and even ran a hand along the back panel of the drawer to make sure there was nothing dangling down behind. I checked under the mattress and found nothing except slats. I checked under the pillow. Inside the pillowcases. Inside the duvet cover.

'Anything?'

I took the torch out of my mouth, where I'd held it while I was replacing the bedclothes. 'You'll be the first to know.'

'Five minutes.'

'Got it.'

I did the bathroom in two minutes: whitening toothpaste, hair dye and moisturiser. Expensive shampoo and conditioner. Eye cream. The guy used more products than I did.

The kitchen was tiny and so clean I wondered if he ever used it. The cupboards were full of protein powder and energy bars. The fridge contained egg whites, rice milk, turkey, chicken and cod, and a couple of bags of spinach.

'Fun,' I said.

Maitland was pacing up and down the hall like a bear in a zoo. 'Wish he'd invite me round for dinner.'

I kept searching. No wine or beer. A box of green tea, loose, with a Japanese tea set and little cups without handles. Some rice cakes and noodles.

There was a small freezer in the corner, with three drawers, and I ripped through it. Top drawer: more fish and lean meat. No ice cream. Middle drawer: frozen vegetables. No chips. Bottom drawer: plastic storage boxes opaque with frost. The top two seemed to be mince. A larger, flat one underneath them was far too light when I picked it up. I peeled the lid back and jumped.

'Whoa.'

'What've you got?'

'It's okay.' I lifted it up very carefully and draped it over my fingertips so it could hang properly. 'It's just a wig.'

'In the *freezer*?'

'Yep.' I couldn't stop smiling. 'Nice hiding place. The

colour matches Angela Poole's hair. The length and style is the same as hers was. And I bet we'll be able to match the hair we found on Anna Melville's body.'

Maitland took some pictures while I detached a couple of hairs and folded them into an evidence envelope. Then I replaced the wig in the box and the box in the freezer.

'Can I tell them?' He lifted the radio.

'Be my guest. I'm going to keep looking, though.'

In the living room I found weights and exercise DVDs, along with four stainless steel knives in a flat holder taped to the underside of the dining table. They were a Japanese make and exceedingly sharp. There was a gap in the middle.

'He could be carrying a knife.'

'I'll let them know.'

More bookcases, more books. I liked a room full of books, but not when I was in a hurry and trying to search with a light touch, because Godley had said to stay wary in case the wig wasn't a match. There was no way I could go through every book and check there was nothing hidden inside and I chewed my lip, knowing I was missing something.

Nothing hidden under a sofa cushion. Nothing inside the loose covers. Nothing under the rug.

A big rubber plant in the corner caught my attention. It was in a pot with wheels so you could move it around easily. I pulled it away from where it had been standing and saw that the fitted carpet wasn't quite level. It rose up in the corner, where the carpet tacks had been removed.

'Gotcha.'

It was easy to peel back the carpet, though I panicked a little when I saw nothing but floorboards. I stuck my hand in under the carpet as far as it would go and swept it back and forth in an arc, swearing as my muscles complained about the awkward angle. I forgot all discomfort when my fingertips brushed against something. I stretched even further and managed to get a grip on the corner of what proved to be an A4 envelope. I checked there wasn't anything else to find, and came up with two more.

'Harry? I've got something.'

He came and stood in the doorway, watching as I shook out the contents of the first envelope on the table. Pictures and medical notes. It was a history of remaking Stuart Sinclair from the tubby buck-toothed boy Derwent had tormented into, well—

'Is that Josh Derwent?' Maitland asked.

It was a picture I hadn't seen before, a close-up of Derwent smirking at the camera, wearing school uniform. Two smaller pictures were clipped to the back. The first proved to be a candid shot of him talking, in profile, while the second was him smiling at someone. He must have just been in the shower. His hair was wet and slicked back instead of hanging around his face, so you could see the details – the planes of his face, the line his hair followed, the shape of his ears.

'I think Derwent was his ideal. Like the world needed two of them.'

Maitland snorted. I skimmed through the paperwork.

He'd had dental work on the NHS but the major stuff – a jaw realignment and a set of crowns – had been done in Hungary. He'd gone to Los Angeles for a nose job and chin implant, at a cost that made my eyes wide. Over four visits to South Africa he'd had extensive liposuction and an eyelift, and had his ears pinned back. The pictures told the full story: a transformation from an unhappy, sagging young man to the toned, even-featured man I had met. He had removed body hair, tanned, reshaped his hairline, lightened his hair, exercised obsessively and it all *worked*. I tried to remember if I'd noticed anything strange about his face and how it moved, which was the usual giveaway with plastic surgery. The only thing I'd noticed was a resemblance to Derwent, which I'd put down to coincidence. And I'd noticed he was surprisingly hot.

'Creepy,' Maitland said. 'What else?'

The next envelope was a gut punch: a full set of crime-scene and autopsy pictures from the Angela Poole case.

'How did he get those?'

'Stole them. They went missing during the investigation. The SIO left them lying around. Stuart was the main witness – I bet he was in and out of the police station all the time.' I tapped one. 'He must have uploaded them to the website he showed me. These pictures were his reference material for the murders he committed and he had to make sure anyone could have seen them and done the same.'

'Clever.'

'No one is saying he's not clever.' I was really starting to hate Stuart Sinclair. I could taste it like bile at the back of my throat. He'd come so close to being discounted as a suspect. I'd come so close to overlooking him.

I'd met him and interviewed him before Deena died, and I hadn't suspected him for one second.

The third envelope was in some ways the most interesting. It contained maybe fifty file cards with names, addresses, personal details and physical descriptions of women, and a card wallet. I flipped it open. 'Bingo.'

'What've you got?'

'Fake police ID in the name of DI Josh Derwent, but that's Sinclair in the picture.'

Maitland leaned in to see. 'It looks rubbish. Nothing like the real thing.'

'Good enough to pass on the street, in the dark, especially if he just waves it at them.' I sat back on my heels. 'Got him.'

'I'd have thought so. What else is in there? What are all the cards?'

'Research.' I flipped through them, finding Jenny Coppard. Her card had a red asterisk on it, and the information that she was a mother was circled in the same pen.

He liked virginal women, I thought, not mothers. But Jenny had been useful all the same.

'I haven't found cards for any of our victims,' I said, shuffling through.

'Maybe he hides them somewhere else.'

'Maybe he doesn't keep them once they're dead.' They were no longer targets then. No longer a challenge. Not interesting.

I sped through the last cards and froze. 'You're fucking kidding me.'

'What?' Maitland leaned in. 'Oh, lucky you.'

Stuart had filled out a card for me, with my phone number and a physical description and – in capitals – KNOWS JD!!! There was a red asterisk on the top, though.

'I wonder why I failed.'

'Too tall,' Maitland suggested, and grinned when I glared. 'Too risky.'

'He doesn't like taking risks,' I agreed. 'He likes to feel safe.'

'Well, let's hope he's yearning for the comfort of home.' Maitland pointed with the radio. 'Collect all the paperwork. We'll take it with us. Let's put the plant back where it was, just in case he gets back here without us spotting him. But I'd say we've got more than enough to arrest him. And once we've done that, we can tear this place apart to make sure we've found everything.'

I rearranged the carpet and plant, then had a last walk through the flat, checking that everything was as I had found it.

'Happy?' Maitland asked.

'Ecstatic,' I said, and meant it. All we had to do now was catch him.

Chapter 37

Catching Stuart Sinclair, of course, was easier said than done, because all we could do was wait. Godley had a team of about twenty officers deployed in cars and vans around the area, all watching, all ready to go at any moment. The tension was a killer. The atmosphere was so highly charged I couldn't see how Sinclair would miss it when he came home. Or maybe he'd seen us already and was on the run. Maybe he'd had a silent alarm in his flat and he was never coming back.

For two hours and through four suspects who turned out not to be him I tortured myself with worrying about whether I'd done something wrong and scared him off. Eventually I put my head down on the steering wheel of the car and moaned.

'He's never coming back. We're never going to catch him. He's going to go abroad again and get more plastic surgery and a fake passport.'

'He's not a criminal mastermind,' Liv said. 'He's not any kind of mastermind. He spent hundreds of thousands of pounds to look like Derwent. What does that tell you?'

'Obsessive personality. Bad judgement. Serial killer. You're right. I'm not taking him home to meet my parents.' I stayed where I was, though, my hands gripping the wheel so hard my knuckles bleached.

'I don't think I've ever seen you so edgy. Are you okay?'

'This has been the week from hell. Of course I'm not okay.'

'Are you missing Rob?'

'Yes.'

Her eyes went round. 'Wow. No prevarication. No excuses. It must be love.'

'So what?' I was grinning, though.

'So I didn't think you'd ever admit it.'

'Yeah. I should really tell him.'

'Maeve Kerrigan, are you actually telling me you haven't said "I love you" yet to the perfect man? Your soulmate? The guy who makes you smile every time I even mention his name?'

'He knows,' I protested.

'That doesn't mean he shouldn't hear it occasionally.' The radio in the footwell by Liv's feet crackled and she picked it up.

'We've got an IC-1 male on foot towards the address. Just turned off Argyle Road onto Larchfield Avenue.' It was James Peake's voice, and he sounded calm and matter-of-fact. Good radio voice, I thought irrelevantly, trying to stop my heart from racing.

'He's coming from over there,' Liv said, having checked the map. She was pointing to the other side of the area we were watching. I sat back in my seat, the tension still knotting my stomach even though we were on the wrong side and too far away to be involved.

'Blue jeans, black jacket with a Superdry logo on the shoulder, grey trainers,' Peake added.

'Stand by,' Godley said. 'Let's confirm the ID before we move.'

I felt the tension in my arms as I put one hand on the door handle. Our car was parked near the main road, a short distance from the flat. I calculated there were ten or twelve officers closer than us or in a better position to bring him down, but I was still going to be in the game, and from Liv's face she felt the same way.

And I could see him now, in the distance. He was maybe thirty metres away from the gate to the flats. He was walking easily, looking relaxed, a gym bag slung over his shoulder. 'It's him.'

'Definitely our man,' Maitland said over the radio at more or less the same time.

It was all that Godley had been waiting for. 'Strike, strike, strike.'

The street came alive with people as everyone bundled out of their cars, converging on Sinclair. The strategy was to move fast, confuse and disorientate the target and control them by getting them down on the ground before they could think about fighting back. He had the reactions of a cat, though. He'd had no warning but in less time than it took to blink he was running, sprinting up the pavement towards our position.

'Coming this way,' I said to Liv in a rush.

Before Sinclair got close to us DI Bradbury got in front of him. Without hesitating, Sinclair threw the gym bag at his head, scoring a direct hit. Bradbury went down like a felled tree and the next officer, who happened to be Harry Maitland, tripped over him. Together they made quite a formidable obstacle for the pursuers behind, who crashed into each other and slowed themselves down. Sinclair didn't look back as he raced away, taking advantage of the mayhem. The smooth, organised arrest had disintegrated into chaos in seconds and I couldn't quite understand how, except that we'd had all the time in the world to prepare but Sinclair had had all the luck. James Peake kicked himself clear and put on an extra turn of speed but Sinclair had gained five or six metres on him.

Which left me and Liv to block Sinclair before he got to the open road. Seeing us in front of him he swerved, diving across the street to the opposite pavement. I bolted to do the same and cut him off, careless of traffic, my Asp racked and ready to use. Liv was right beside me, shouting to him to stop.

He didn't stop. He put his head down and ran straight at us. He hit Liv, hard, and I heard her stumble and go down with a cry as he straight-armed me out of his path, grabbing the Asp and using it to pull me off balance. I let go, twisted and stayed on my feet by a miracle, and the one thought in my mind was that I was not going to be the scapegoat for this going wrong, just because he had been more powerful than two female officers. I pelted after him, angry as hell, matching him stride for stride but with a height advantage that got me further than him with every step. He risked a glance back as we got near the end of the street: I was gaining on him, and he knew it.

My only focus was Sinclair. I was flying, close enough to touch him with the very tips of my fingers, almost close enough to grab him and bring him down . . .

I honestly don't know what he meant to do when he reached the metal barrier at the end of the street. It was designed to stop pedestrians from crossing the very busy A road that was four lanes of constantly thundering traffic, and it was roughly hip-height. I thought at the time, and I still think, he intended to jump over it and dodge through the cars, taking his chances. He was arrogant. He might have thought he'd be quick enough to avoid getting knocked down.

Whatever he'd intended, he clipped the top of the barrier as he jumped, and fell. He sprawled on the tarmac, arms and legs outstretched, and his head turned to see what was coming. That was all he had time to do before a fully loaded articulated lorry went straight over him, at speed. I felt the rush of wind as it passed me. I had been a split second behind Sinclair, and a lifetime. The wind dragged at my hair, my clothes, as I crashed into the barrier, going too fast to stop, and pitched forward over the top of it. I grabbed hold of it but I could do nothing about the momentum that had my feet off the ground as I pivoted, unable to prevent myself from following Sinclair into traffic that was nowhere near stopping, that hadn't even started to notice a man had just died there.

I was well past the point of no return when someone behind me grabbed a handful of my jacket and hauled me back, out of danger, to stand on solid ground. I stared into the road, at the red smear that was what remained of Stuart Sinclair. The cars and vans and trucks slammed on their brakes, just that little bit too late for me if I'd gone all the way over. I looked up into James Peake's face, then collapsed against his chest, too weak to stand. I was too shocked to think about what could have happened, or what had happened to Sinclair. I could barely form a coherent thought, let alone words.

It felt like for ever, but I finally managed to speak. 'You saved my life.'

'More than likely. It was no trouble.' He put his head down on top of mine for a second. 'Bloody hell, though.'

'I lost him. Another second, and I'd have had him.'

'Never mind about that. The important thing is that you're okay.'

I peeled myself off him and stood on my own two feet as the rest of the chasing police officers finally caught up with us. Godley's face was grim.

'Are you all right?'

'Fine.' I glanced into the road again. Dave Kemp and Ben Dornton were standing guard over the body, moving the traffic out of the lane where the various parts of Stuart were all too vividly displayed. It involved a lot of irritable shouting and furious gesturing as the drivers slowed to a crawl the better to get a good look, and it was as dangerous as anything I'd done that day even though they'd get little enough credit for it. Standing around on a fast-moving road without a high-vis jacket, without so much as a traffic cone, was one way to look death in the face. Neither of them appeared to be enjoying it much.

Further down the road, the truck had stopped, hazard lights flashing, and the driver climbed down from his cab. A couple of officers had gone down to speak him. He looked agitated, one hand to his head, one to his mouth.

'Better tell the driver not to worry about it,' I said. 'No one's going to miss this one.'

'I'd have liked the chance to arrest him,' Godley said softly. 'I'd have liked to hear what he had to say.'

'He'd just have lied.' I was starting to shiver as the shock kicked in. 'They all lie. You never really get near the truth.'

'That's truer than you know,' he said, so quietly only I could hear it, and I looked up at him, wondering what he meant. He didn't add anything else, striding off to speak to the lorry driver as a couple of response cars arrived, lights and siren on, to take over the traffic duties. An ambulance was right behind them, also on blues, and I wondered why they were bothering to hurry. Sinclair was far beyond anyone's help now.

Maitland finally made it to my side. He was looking anguished. 'Are you all right?'

'Never better.' I tried to stop my teeth from chattering. 'I'm fine.'

'Good.' He still looked upset.

'Really, I'm okay.'

'I believe you. But you need to come with me.'

'What's wrong?'

'You were right. He did have a knife.'

I stared at him, waiting, and I could see him decide there was no good way to break the news, given what it was. Two words were enough.

'It's Liv.'

MONDAY

Chapter 38

'Knock knock.'

I looked up from my work and gasped. 'No way.'

'Oh, there was a way. It just involved buying a new ticket.' Rob slung his bag on the floor and came across the deserted waiting room as I jumped up and ran into his arms. 'How are you doing?'

'I'm okay,' I said, my mouth muffled against his chest. 'I can't believe you came.'

'As soon as I could. I was away for a week and you almost got shot. And strangled.'

'Don't forget I almost got run over too.'

'I was getting to that.' He held me even closer. 'Then there was Swain. He's enough to get me on a plane on his own. Who knows what would have happened if I'd stayed the full two weeks?'

'Nothing good,' I said, shivering. 'But I'm not hurt. And I'm not scared of Chris Swain.'

'This again.' He shook me gently. 'You should be.'

'But then he wins.'

'So he wins. Be a good loser and live a long life. For me.'

'For you,' I said. I hadn't let go of him. It was still sinking in that he was really there. 'How come you were able to leave early? Did Debbie agree?'

'Not really.'

'Rob!'

'Look, I told her it was important. She'll get over it.'

'She doesn't even like me,' I said. 'She'll be furious.'

'Don't worry about it.'

'You can't destroy your career for me.' I was really worried now.

'I didn't destroy anything. I promise, she'll be fine.' He ran his thumb down my cheek, then bent his head and kissed me. I shivered in sheer pleasure this time and pressed against him, my arms around his neck. When we came up for air, he looked into my eyes. 'Let's be clear. If I have a choice to make between work and you, I'll always pick you. You come first for me.'

'I love you.'

His face went blank. Shock. 'What did you say?'

'You heard.'

'I don't know that I did.'

'I love you,' I said slowly and clearly.

He grinned, delighted. 'A hospital waiting room. Not the most romantic setting you could have chosen but I'll take it. I love you too.'

'I know.' I leaned my head on his shoulder, my cheek against his neck. I'd missed him more than I could have thought possible.

'Are you really okay? How's Liv?'

Tears caught at the back of my throat. 'Not great.'

For three agonising days we had been waiting to hear if Liv was going to pull through after emergency surgery to repair the damage Stuart Sinclair had done to her with the knife he had been carrying, the knife no one had seen, the knife I'd warned them about. He'd stabbed her in the stomach, almost casually, as he passed, leaving the knife in her as he ran on. She'd been wearing her protective stab vest but it had ridden up, as they tended to, and Sinclair had got lucky. Although the surgeons had been able to stitch her back together, she'd developed a post-operative infection that was causing a lot of headshaking and concern.

I felt paralysed, desperate to help but with no way of doing anything useful.

'Have you been here since it happened?'

'Most of the time,' I admitted. 'How did you guess?'

'You look as if you've just come off a long-haul flight.'

'Whereas you look just fine. How do you do it?'

'I make these things look good,' he said. 'But I am starving. I slept through the meal on the plane and I didn't stop for anything on my way here.'

'The café on the third floor is all right.'

'Not a rave review, but okay. I'll go and find it in a bit.' He pulled me a little bit closer. 'All this excitement. Your mum must be a wreck.'

'I think she's quite proud of me, for once. But she made me promise not to do it again.'

'Sensible woman. That was my next move.'

I leaned my head against him. 'Oh, Rob.'

'Very touching.' Derwent let the door slam behind him and limped towards us. 'Welcome home, lover.'

'Thanks,' Rob said drily, letting go of me. 'Good to see you too.'

Derwent was looking around. 'This place is like a morgue.'

'That remark is in poor taste,' I snapped.

'Sorry.' He didn't look it.

'I know you don't like Liv much but she's in intensive care. She's fighting for her life. The least you could do is show some respect.'

'I'm showing plenty of respect,' he protested. 'I'm here, for one thing. And I've just been along to see how she's doing.'

My heart jumped. 'Any news?'

Godley had come in behind him and answered for him. 'She's the same.' He nodded to Rob. 'Good to see you. How's the Flying Squad?'

'Fun and games.'

Godley grinned. 'Do you mind if we borrow Maeve for a minute? Just to catch up?'

'No problem. I was going to find something to eat anyway. I'll stay out of your way. Does anyone want anything from the café?'

'I need a coffee,' Derwent announced. 'I'll come with you.'

Rob looked at me. 'Coffee?'

I shook my head, and the two of them headed off together. I missed one of them before the door had even closed behind them. The other was welcome to stay away as long as he liked.

'You need to go home. Get some rest,' Godley said, sitting down.

'I'm fine.' I could work well enough in the hospital with my phone, which had at long last been returned, and my paperwork, and I wasn't going anywhere until I knew what was happening with Liv.

'You look tired.'

'I am. But I'll be okay.'

'I know the two of you are close.' He reached out and put his hand on my shoulder. I was surprised that he did it, but comforted by it too. 'You know, you've put us through this in the past.'

'It's easier to be the one who's out cold.'

'Very true.' He sat back.

'Do I have to talk to Derwent? Does he have to be here?'

Godley looked surprised. 'What's the problem?'

'I can't deal with him at the moment. Not with Liv the way she is. He doesn't even care.'

'He's been here every day, even if you haven't seen him. He's got the nurses eating out of his hand.'

'Am I supposed to be impressed just because he's flirting with the nurses?'

'They've been extra-nice to Joanne and Liv's family. It all helps.'

'He's totally motivated by self-interest.'

'He got here an hour ago. He's been sitting with Joanne, letting her talk about Liv. When I got there, he was making her laugh.'

'Seriously?'

'Absolutely.'

I swallowed. 'How did I not know this?'

'He keeps his good side well hidden, but it's there.'

'If you say so.'

Godley shifted in his seat. 'While Josh isn't here, I want to apologise.'

'For what?'

'For giving you a hard time. I don't want you to leave the team, Maeve. You're an asset I don't want to lose.' Godley looked at me. 'I don't know why you still want to work for me, given what you know about me, but for as long as you do, you have a job on my team.'

I could have wept. 'Sir—'

'It's not money. I want you to know that.'

I stared at him. 'I don't—'

'He didn't give me a choice. I try not to tell him anything he'll find useful. I take the view that if I wasn't doing it, someone else would be. At least this way I know what he knows.'

'You don't have to explain.'

'I want to.' He looked down at his hands, his expression rueful. 'You know, you're the last person I would have wanted to find out about it.'

'Why? I haven't told anyone.'

He looked back at me. 'Because you'd have said no and taken the consequences.'

Before I could put together a cogent reply, the door swung open as Derwent returned alone, except for a hospital orderly carrying two coffees on a tray, since the crutches meant he couldn't manage one. He had a genius for getting people to do things for him for nothing more than a smile.

'Thanks, darling,' he said, and winked at her as he lowered himself into a seat. The smile turned into a wince.

'How's your leg?' I asked.

'Agony. How's your neck?'

'Better.'

'For the record,' Derwent said, stirring his coffee, 'I'm glad you didn't fall under a truck the other day. But I wish you'd run a bit faster.'

'I did my best.'

'And it wasn't good enough.'

'I'm aware of that,' I snapped.

Godley cleared his throat. 'No one blames you, Maeve. You did a good job.'

'It pisses me off, though,' Derwent said. 'Twenty years I've been waiting to find out what really happened to Ange. Twenty years. And you're just a couple of seconds too slow, so now I'll never know.'

I took a deep breath before I replied. I needed some sort of mantra to cope with Derwent, something soothing and centring so that he didn't get to me any more, but the only things I could think of were swear words. 'Well, actually, I've been doing some digging while I've been sitting around here and I think I've worked out what happened. And almost all of this information was openly available, so you could have found it out for yourself at any point in the last twenty years. It's not my fault that you couldn't see the wood for the trees.'

'Hey,' Derwent said, hurt, and Godley shut him up with a look.

'Go on, Maeve.'

'Okay. Well, during the original investigation, the only people who told the truth were you and Angela's dad, and the two of you cancelled each other out as suspects. Orpen was a disaster. He kept really bad records of the interviews he did, and he had everyone running scared so they didn't tell him what he actually needed to know.' The next bit was mildly tricky. I hoped Derwent was concentrating on what I'd found out rather than how I'd done it. 'One of the witnesses I traced mentioned a guy named Craig – first name or last name, she didn't know – who'd been hanging around a couple of weeks before Angela died. He was a drifter, passing through on his way from somewhere in the north of England to France. He was a good source of quality dope and he liked to hang around with teenage girls although he was probably in his late twenties or thirties.'

'I don't remember him,' Derwent said, frowning.

'He might have only spoken to Angela once before she died, according to the witness. He seemed to disappear. He never came up in the original inquiry because no one ever told Orpen about him.'

'What makes you think he's relevant?' Godley asked.

'Because the night Angela died, Shane was smoking dope with people he described as friends, but they were really people he barely knew. I got in touch with him yesterday to see if he remembered anyone matching the description of Craig and he said he did, that the guy had given them the drugs and chatted to them for a bit. He'd never seen him before and he never saw him again. The guy wandered off halfway through the evening and I pressed Shane for the details but he really doesn't remember.'

'Drugs will do that to you.' Derwent sounded like his usual sanctimonious self but his eyes were fixed on me and he was very still, paying close attention.

'I think Craig was on the lookout for a girl to kill that night. I think he was hoping to get someone stoned and then take her somewhere private to kill her, but it didn't work out. He gave up on the teenagers in the park when no one suitable showed up, and went for a wander. He must have seen Angela walking home alone and followed her.' I laid a couple of sheets of paper out on the table in front of me so Godley and Derwent could see. 'He said he'd been up north before so I had a look through the records. Here's an unsolved murder in Bradford two months before Angela died – Laurie Morrows, aged sixteen. She was a drug addict and worked as a prostitute from time to time. She was raped and strangled and her face was mutilated. That case has just been sitting in West Yorkshire Police's files and no one ever thought it could be relevant until I went looking for cases that might be connected. Laurie's job confused the issue – they were looking for a client. Angela wasn't a prostitute, obviously, so that didn't ring any bells for West Yorkshire, and no one down here knew about Laurie's death in the first place. And this case: Coventry, the month before Angela's death. A teenage girl walking her dog was choked but managed to get away from her attacker. The description is patchy but it could be Craig.'

'Bit different from Angela.'

'Yes, it is. But after Angela, there are three murders in France.' I'd marked them on a map, in a curve that ran from the Pas de Calais to the Pyrenees. 'One, two, three. All teenage girls. All strangled. All sexually assaulted. All mutilated facially in various horrible ways – teeth knocked out, eyes removed. One had her nose and ears cut off. No one was ever caught for them though the French did make the connection between the three killings. They got DNA but they've never matched it to anyone.'

'And then what? He disappeared?'

'I'm still waiting to hear from the Spanish authorities but I bet there'll be more. They don't have any record of anyone with the name Craig being arrested for murder or anything else around that time, but that's where he was heading. From there—' I shrugged. 'Portugal? North Africa? Plenty of places he could disappear. I can't go any further at the moment. The trail is not what you'd call hot. I'm not giving up, though. Twenty years is a long time but people remember strangers, and Craig sounds pretty distinctive.'

'Why didn't he rape Angela?' Derwent touched one of the pieces of paper for no real reason, moving it around, rearranging the layout. The old OCD kicking in again, I thought.

'That's where Stuart comes in. He was in his bedroom, where he couldn't have seen what was going on in the garden next door but by his own account he *heard* it. That was why he woke up. That was what attracted his attention.'

'And?'

'And he thought it was you and Angela. I've spoken to Stuart's Japanese girlfriend a few times on the phone and she's been very helpful in filling in the background details for me. Stuart liked to get drunk about once every six weeks – his way of letting off steam because he was so disciplined about his diet and exercise usually. I told her about Angela and what we knew, as opposed to what Stuart had told us. She said he had talked about it a couple of times. That night, Stuart heard Angela moaning, thought he was listening to the two of you and his first thought was to disturb you and Angela if you were having sex. Then he decided it would be better to watch you. He was obsessed with you, wasn't he? And Angela was a flirt. Vinny said she was a tease. She loved the attention and you have to wonder if she'd been leading him on as well. He was a sexually frustrated teenage boy with absolutely no chance of finding a girlfriend, and he was never going to get closer to actual sex.'

'So he saw them?' Godley asked.

'He couldn't see anything out of the window. He had to go downstairs and out the front door. He found Angela lying in the grass, dead. It's just conjecture but if it was Craig who attacked the girl in Coventry, he might have been angry and frustrated. He seems to have started the attack by gouging Angela's eyes, to control her and subdue her. He was in a high-risk area, surrounded by people in their houses, so he would have wanted to keep her quiet too, and he strangled her. Maybe it didn't matter to him if she was alive or dead before he raped her. As it turned out, he didn't get the chance. Stuart's arrival on the scene disturbed Craig in the act, which meant that he had to run away before he could sexually assault her.'

'But all of this had a lasting effect on Stuart,' Godley said.

I nodded. 'I think he stole Angela's autopsy photographs because he found the sight of her arousing. He was troubled, unhappy and traumatised by his parents' divorce, and this was his first real sexual experience, according to his Japanese girlfriend. It was a shattering, exciting event and he never got over it. Afterwards he was, briefly, very important. He was able to get his revenge on the bully who'd tormented him.' I looked at Derwent. 'That's you, by the way.'

'Noted.'

'It was a turning point. He grew in confidence. He decided to remake himself in a different image. He became his ideal and then he was able to live out his fantasies. It just took him a long time to get up the nerve. And as it turned out, he had a gift for it. Killing came easy. Kirsty, Maxine and Anna didn't matter to him as people – that's why we had so much trouble making a connection between them. They looked right and that was all he wanted.'

'How did he get them to trust him?' Godley asked.

'He pretended to be me.' Derwent sounded weirdly detached, but he had to be upset about it.

I nodded. 'I've been going through the file cards we found in his flat, talking to the women who interested him. He was working on two or three at a time, I think, and sometimes he didn't pursue them – maybe if they asked too many questions or if they were too risky. From what I can work out, his technique was to stalk women who reminded him of Angela. He'd find out if they lived alone, then get talking to them. He told them he was a police officer named Josh and gave DI Derwent's surname and rank if they asked for more details. He gave them advice on their home security, probably culled from the Met website if you go by Kirsty Campbell's wish list. He promised to come round and check their locks, and he sent them flowers. White ones. So the flowers were there waiting for him, and the women trusted him when he went round to kill them.'

Derwent winced. 'Calculating bastard. What a creep.'

I narrowed my eyes. 'Let's not forget that you do actually follow women around for their own safety.'

'Leaving that aside.'

'Josh . . .' Godley looked appalled.

'Irrelevant,' Derwent said. 'It just sounds bad.'

'Angela's death had a big impact on both of you. Sinclair wanted to kill women because of it. You want to save them. You weren't all that different, really.'

Derwent glowered at me and Godley asked hastily, 'Why was it that he didn't have sex with them?'

'I don't think he could, from what his girlfriend says. Dr Chen would probably be able to explain it in technical terms, but my take on it is that he was squeamish. His flat was sterile. He didn't like mess. He didn't like getting dirty and that included having sex. The way he took out the eyes – it wasn't something he enjoyed, particularly, but it was part of the ritual. Killing Angela over and over again. Staring at her dead body for as long as he liked this time. Revelling in the moment. Being aroused but in control. I imagine that killing Deena was a very different experience for him because he was angry, not enjoying himself. He wouldn't have counted her murder because it was just practical, not for pleasure.'

'And now he's dead.' Derwent leaned back, his hands clasped behind his head. 'It seems like justice, somehow. Better than him getting fat and living a long life behind bars at the taxpayer's expense.'

'Happy to help,' I said, grinning.

Godley's phone rang and he glanced at the screen, then pulled a face. 'My wife. I'd better take this.'

He left the room and Derwent looked at me. 'You know, no matter what I say, you're a good copper.'

Before I could respond, the door opened again and Kev Cox poked his head in. 'All right? No news on the patient, I hear.'

'She's hanging on,' I said, coming down to earth with a thud. Oh, *Liv*.

'I just wanted to see you in person.' Kev advanced across the room, looking from Derwent to me. 'Is it all right to speak about that other matter?' he asked me.

'The flowers? DI Derwent knows all about it.'

Kev looked relieved. 'Well. This is unofficial, you understand, but we've got the results back on tests we did on the evidence you collected.'

'And?'

'We found a partial fingerprint on the tape that held the cellophane wrapper around the bunch originally, and we matched it to someone we have on file.'

'Chris Swain,' I said.

'Try DI Deborah Ormond.'

I stared at him, stupefied, as Derwent roared with laughter. 'Naughty Debbie.'

'Why would she do that?'

'Dunno. But she wanted you to know she'd done it,' Derwent said. 'Debbie knows enough to keep her fingerprints to herself. You can't tell me she'd make a mistake like that.'

'It was more than a smudge, if that helps. Pin-sharp. No mistaking it. Anyway, here's the report. I'll leave it with you. It's confidential at the moment but let me know what you want to do. I can always lose it.' Kev laid two pages down on the table and hurried out before I could so much as thank him.

Derwent picked them up, glanced at them and ripped them into pieces.

'What are you doing?'

'This never happened.'

'Yes, it fucking well did.' I was livid. 'That *bitch*.'

'Forget it.'

'No way.'

'Listen, Kerrigan. I'm going to help you out.' He jabbed a finger at me. 'You don't want to do this. You don't want the publicity. You're already front-page news and the tabloids will be all over this. Your boyfriend works for Debbie. He likes the Flying Squad and he's not going to want to leave it. If you try to bring her down, you will suffer, and what's more you'll fuck up your boyfriend's career. Let it go. Be glad it wasn't Swain after all and move on.'

'I have to tell him. How can he work with her if she's done something so unprofessional? So *horrible*?'

'In blissful ignorance,' Derwent said. 'He doesn't need to know the truth.'

'I would.'

'You don't know what's good for you. You can't tell him because it's not fair. He can't work with her if he knows, and you've already done him out of one decent job by shagging him.'

I couldn't argue with that. Saying nothing made sense even though I was beyond outraged – too angry to see straight, let alone think straight. But I had the horrible and unfamiliar feeling that Derwent was right.

He picked up his crutches. 'Come on. You need to get out of here. Find your bloke. I'll even buy you lunch.'

'Wow.' I gathered up my pages of research and stuffed them into my bag. 'This is a red-letter day.'

'Don't get used to it.'

We had just come out into the corridor when someone called my name and I turned to see James Peake jogging towards me. 'Maeve. How are you?'

'I'm fine.'

'No ill effects? I'm glad. I still can't believe what happened the other day.'

'I was lucky.' To Derwent, I said, 'James saved my life.'

'I heard.' Derwent was glowering.

'I'm sorry about Liv. How's she doing?'

'Holding on.'

'Tough on you,' Peake said, full of sympathy, and I felt the tears start into my eyes. He reached out and folded me into his arms. 'Come here.'

I had enough time to register the situation as awkward before Derwent intervened.

'Hey, hey, hey. That's enough.'

Peake let go of me because he had to. The rubber ferrule on the end of Derwent's right crutch was pressing against his windpipe. He grabbed it but by now Derwent had him pinned against the wall.

'What are you doing?' I hissed.

'Letting him know to keep his hands to himself.' To Peake, who was turning purple, Derwent said, 'Back off, mate. She's taken.'

Peake knocked the crutch away and coughed. When he could speak, he said, 'Sorry. I didn't know. Are the two of you—'

'No,' we said in unison.

'She's got a boyfriend, though. And he's a big lad. Big muscles. Short temper. Two floors down as we speak.' Derwent made a shooing motion. 'Go on. Jog on, Ginger. She's not for you.'

I think if Derwent hadn't been on crutches, Peake might have punched him. As it was he glared, then nodded to me, all ice and wounded pride. I watched him go down the corridor and when he was out of sight I turned on Derwent.

'"She's taken." Thank you very much.'

'Sorry. I didn't think you'd be interested. Go on, go after him.'

'No, of course not. I'm not interested. At all. I'm glad he knows.'

'Why didn't you tell him?'

I tried to think how I'd explain to Derwent that you couldn't assume someone was interested in you in that way, and it was presumptuous to warn them off before there was even an issue, and anyway I was my own person and not Rob's chattel, but I gave up. 'It was never the right moment.'

'Not difficult, is it? "I have a boyfriend." There you go.'

'Whatever,' I said irritably.

'Poor guy.' I thought he was talking about Peake until he went on. 'He's never going to get a ring on it, is he? Never going to pin you down. You like your freedom too much.'

'That's not it, actually.'

He raised his eyebrows and waited.

'He's too good for me. He's better than I deserve.'

'Horseshit.' Derwent leaned one crutch against the wall and dropped an arm around my shoulders. 'Your trouble is low self-esteem. You need to start thinking more of yourself. Build up your confidence.'

'And you're going to help?'

'Probably not. I like you meek.'

'*Meek*?'

'Biddable.' He snapped his fingers. 'Oh, I've been meaning to tell you. You couldn't have seen the Philip Pace briefings. They were from anti-terrorism and you don't get them.'

It took me a second but when I worked out what he was telling me, I was outraged all over again. 'Did you know that when you were giving me a hard time about them?'

'Of course.' He retrieved his crutches and set off down the corridor. 'I felt a bit bad about it afterwards. Especially since you helped me.'

'I went above and beyond the call of duty, or even friendship. And we're not friends.'

'No, we are not. But hey, now we're even.'

'Because you told me you were just being an arsehole, deliberately, and I'm not actually incompetent, and that cancels out me solving a twenty-year-old crime and clearing you as a murder suspect.'

'Exactly.'

We had reached the lift. I pressed the button and turned to look at him. He was the same as ever, despite everything that had happened. His confidence was undented.

'Has it occurred to you that all of this happened the way it did because Stuart Sinclair wanted to be like you?'

'Yep.'

The lift arrived and I stood aside while a motley collection of patients, visitors and medical staff trooped out. I waited until the lift was empty, then held the door for Derwent. When he was in and the doors had closed, I tried again. 'All of this was because of you. Don't you think that's strange?'

'Not really.'

'But you were his ideal. You were what he aspired to be.'

'So? Makes perfect sense, if you ask me.'

And Derwent gave me his widest smile.

ONE WEEK LATER

Chapter 39

I almost didn't go. I almost convinced myself that it was none of my business.

It just wasn't in my character not to interfere.

This time, I didn't call ahead. I rang the doorbell and waited. When she answered the door, Claire looked a lot better – younger, prettier, with more colour in her cheeks. She was just as hostile, though. 'What do you want?'

'Can I come in?'

She hesitated. 'It's not a good time.'

'I won't be long.'

'Can I tidy up first?'

'There's no need,' I said. 'I know.'

She got it straight away and her face crumpled. 'How did you find out?'

'I just worked it out. Can I come in?'

She went ahead of me into the sitting room and sat down on the edge of an armchair, shivering. I wandered up and down looking at the photographs of Luke that she had hidden before, seeing exactly why she had wanted to keep them out of sight. The pictures, on walls and shelves and every available surface, recorded his progress from adorable baby to toddler to small boy to teenager to university student, formal in an academic gown, and in each and every image he looked exactly, precisely like his father.

I sat down opposite her. 'You know what I'm going to say, don't you? You should tell him.'

'No.'

'He deserves to know.'

'We didn't need him. We did fine without him.'

'Yeah, you don't need him. But maybe he needs Luke.'

'Don't be stupid. He wouldn't be interested.'

'I don't think that's true, but even if it is, what do you have to lose? You don't have to tell Luke until you know either way. You don't have to tell Luke at all, if it comes to that. But you should tell his father.'

'I don't want to have to share him,' she said through gritted teeth. 'Luke is mine. Just mine. Nothing to do with Josh.'

I hadn't wanted to say his name until she did, even though I'd been absolutely sure Luke was Derwent's son. 'He's so like him, Claire. At least in looks.'

She stared away from me, her eyes streaming, and nodded. 'Personality too.'

'Really?'

'Josh all over again.'

I hoped for Luke's sake that wasn't completely true. 'What does Luke think? Doesn't he want to see his father?'

'He doesn't know who he is. I've never told him what happened. He thinks it was a random guy in Birmingham, just like everybody else did.'

'Didn't anyone else notice?' I asked, incredulous. 'They are identical.'

'People see what they want to see. My mother thought he looked just like Vinny did when he was a baby.' She rolled her eyes. 'I didn't argue, but really, no.'

'I didn't know that you and Josh had a relationship.'

She blew her nose. 'We didn't. It was just an accident. One of those things. You know Josh came and lived with us for a while after his parents kicked him out. He was so sad, and so hurt by his parents, and just heart-breaking, really.'

She shook her head. 'Such bad luck. It was pure chance that one Saturday evening, everyone was out. My parents and the younger kids were at Mass. I had homework. Vinny was with his girlfriend. Josh had been out for a walk but he came back, and I went in to see if he was all right. He was lying on the bed and I lay down beside him and just put my arms around him, just to let him know I cared. And one thing led to another.'

I could imagine it, very easily: the young Derwent, handsome and aching with sadness, in need of comfort. Claire trying to make him feel better. Being kind. Trying to take his pain away. The memory of the awkward, embarrassing, tragic sex with Angela was overwritten with a new experience – something tender and surprising that gave Derwent his confidence back and changed Claire's life for ever.

'Why didn't you tell anyone?'

'Vinny would have killed Josh. *Killed* him. And Josh wasn't exactly popular. I was scared to tell anyone about the baby. He was gone before I finally admitted it to my mother, and she just arranged for me to go and stay in Birmingham with my aunt and uncle. She believed me when I told her the father was a boy I'd been seeing. She never dreamed Josh was the one.'

'Did you get in trouble?'

'Oh my God, yes. And it got worse. I wasn't supposed to keep Luke, you know. He was supposed to be adopted, but I couldn't do it. So all the secrecy and running away was pointless.'

'Did your parents support you?'

'In the end.' Her face softened. 'Once they saw Luke, they loved him too.'

'Don't you think Josh would have felt the same way?' I asked carefully.

'Yes, I do. But he was just a kid. We were both kids.' She sighed. 'If I'd known I was going to bring Luke up I might have told the truth, but by the time I knew what I wanted to do it was too late. And then I'd lost touch with Josh anyway.'

I put a business card on the table, face down. 'It's up to you, but if you want to get in touch with him, here are his details.'

She looked at the card as if it was seeping poison. 'I don't want to. And you can't tell him. Or Luke. You mustn't go near him.'

'I won't,' I promised. 'But think about it. You're so proud of Luke. You've done such a good job of bringing him up. You should give Derwent the chance to get to know him too.'

She didn't reply, but she didn't say she wouldn't, at least. I had no idea what she would do, but I meant what I said – I wasn't going to tell him. Although I would have dearly loved to see his face when he realised he had something in common with Philip Pace after all. I left the card where it was and said goodbye. Claire was lost in her own thoughts and didn't answer. I let myself out, hoping I'd done the right thing.

I couldn't help feeling sad as I walked down the path back to the car. I wondered what the specific weight of secrets was – if that was why I felt I was shouldering an extra burden. But I could do it, and I would do it.

It was just one more secret to keep.

Acknowledgements

In some ways, this is the best bit: getting to say thank you to the many people who made this book become a reality. Firstly, the fiction team at Ebury – Gillian Green, Emily Yau, Hannah Robinson, Louise Jones, Helen Arnold, Jake Lingwood, Fiona MacIntyre, Martin Higgins and everyone in the sales department, as well as Beccy Jones in production and Jeanette Slinger. The world is divided into those who like Derwent and those who don't. My lovely editor, Gillian, thinks he can do no wrong. (Otherwise, however, she shows impeccable judgement.)

Secondly, I'm immensely grateful to all at United Agents for their support and guidance. My agent, Ariella Feiner, is as wise as she is lovely, and as glamorous as she is encouraging, which is saying a lot. They are all a pleasure to work with.

Thirdly, my thanks to all of the people who gave me the benefit of their knowledge. Without Gemma Golder and her wonderful friend Jon Morrell, who advised on Japanese geography, customs and names, I would have had a breakdown somewhere around Chapter 35. I learned a lot about Afghanistan from Rory Stewart's amazing book *The Places in Between*, and about soldiering there from *Dead Men Risen* by Toby Harnden.

Fourthly, my friends and family deserve at least a

round of applause for putting up with me while I fail to respond to phone calls, texts, emails and more. If I was inventing a husband for a crime writer, I would come up with something very like my own. In addition to being an encyclopedia of all things criminal, James has a great gift for remaining calm in the face of my impossible deadlines. Edward, Patrick and Fred are infinitely forgiving about my work and how little they see of me sometimes.

Fifthly, I must thank Frank Burns, Jonty Johnson and Caitriona Bennett for lending me their names for characters. The fictional Caitriona first appeared in *The Last Girl* and I liked her too much to leave her out of this book.

Finally, a note on places. London is a great backdrop for a crime novelist, with plenty of suitable locations for killings. This book ranges widely across London, but it's far from a guide to the city. I am reluctant to litter people's neighbourhoods with fictional corpses, so like the murderer, his victims and all the other characters, these specific locations exist only in my imagination.